Lost in Chaos

Lost in Chaos

Tate Connors

authorHOUSE®

AuthorHouse™
1663 Liberty Drive
Bloomington, IN 47403
www.authorhouse.com
Phone: 1 (800) 839-8640

Published by AuthorHouse   08/03/2015

ISBN: 978-1-5049-1331-7 (sc)
ISBN: 978-1-5049-1330-0 (e)

Print information available on the last page.

Any people depicted in stock imagery provided by Thinkstock are models,
and such images are being used for illustrative purposes only.
Certain stock imagery © Thinkstock.

This book is printed on acid-free paper.

Because of the dynamic nature of the Internet, any web addresses or links contained in
this book may have changed since publication and may no longer be valid. The views
expressed in this work are solely those of the author and do not necessarily reflect the
views of the publisher, and the publisher hereby disclaims any responsibility for them.

Contents

Prologue

Hello there I am a 30 something year old New York transplant, living in Los Angeles and these are my Pet Peeves:

Latino stereotypes, bad breath, fat trainers, people who drive like idiots while talking on their cell phones, allergies, student drivers, "stupid and tired scripted "reality" shows, my tattoo fading, when gay guys call me girl, body glitter on guys, cell phones on dates, screaming kids in department stores, screaming kids, forgetting not to spit against the wind, 10 minute quickies, people who do not use their turn signals, the plastic around new CD's, drama queens, label queens, rude queens, men who talk like women, horror movies that aren't really horror movies(example: "Freddie Vs. Jason"), crashing PC's, Asian women driving, sunglasses, pop up screens, people who blame cheating on alcohol, women who think they can make a gay man straight after consuming 3 plus cocktails, restaurants that wont seat you until your whole party arrives, paper cuts, the dentist, school teachers being underpaid, uncomfortable silence in elevators, *69, people who clip their finger nails within 500 feet of me, anything that says "Abercrombie" on it, police cars with screaming sirens, baby wails, stray dog howling, people who say they never fart or pick their nose, the sound of popcorn crunching in someone's mouth, people who brag about getting drunk, people who say "OMG me and my friends are like Will and Grace, people who walk and text, or drive and text, socializing at the gym, when you call someone and leave a message AND then they text you back, Don't you know WHO I am, sorority girls who can't hold their liquor, smeared ink on the side of my hand when I write(I'm a righty), stupid Carl's Jr. commercials, people who wear sunglasses in the club.........................more to be added soon, as more people, places and things piss me off as time drags forward.

Guilty Pleasures: Watching Real Housewives of any Cityl, Anything Bravo! Sleeping the day away, Krispy Kreme doughnuts, cracking my knuckles, smacking my gum, hot Latin boys(actually more of a weakness), leaving my bed undone, having a wandering eye at the urinal, day dreaming, guys who free ball at the gym, eating cheetos and sucking my fingers afterwards, always wanting to be the passenger instead of the driver, Golden Girls, closing the elevator while someone is running to catch it, watching porn, drinking milk from the carton, burping out loud, tailgating, people watching, guys in Speedos, making people laugh. Stupid pet tricks, picking my nose hairs and then sneezing, The ladies of The View, Politically incorrect jokes, Sex and the City reruns, eating pickles out of the jar. And many more to cum. I like that tooooooooooo!!!!

I dedicate this book to Carlos…. Thank you for all of your love and support. I needed it!!!

Instant Gratification and Long Term Procrastination!!

As I get older I realized that I tend to procrastinate and then cram to get things done at the last minute. I am not proud of this or is it my defining moment but it has become a reality. By saying that you will come to an assumption as to why it took 4 years for me to complete this book. I never had any deadlines or a due date so why finish? I never felt like there was a test coming up or a quiz looming so I just kept finding excuses as to why I had not finished the book. Damn college degree!! College made me learn that the only time I had to finish something was for a test or a good grade. Work is work and I have had a boss tell me what to do…... Well um…...I at least make them think that they are telling me what to do. Anyway but I basically beat to my own drum. I am a competitive person but I had no one up against me to finish this book. So the bottom line was no deadline = no completed book. That is up until now and my 2015 resolution is change! My intentions in years past were always good but DAMN I am an expert on procrastination. Do you know how long it took me to write this paragraph? I cannot even remember when I came up with the title for this chapter – that's how long it has been since I have delved into my creative side. I could blame work or friends about my distractions but ultimately it was my lazy ass that didn't want to do the work. It's the same as having lipo verses exercising and for the record I have not done liposuction but I have thought about it many times. Especially when I am at that damn treadmill listening to some whiney bitch on the next treadmill bitching on her cell phone that there are no "good men" in LA. I am not fat "God forbid" but my 6 pack abs went into hibernation the winter of 2012 and the alarm clock must have broken that winter. I can see them but even with my glasses on they are under a warm blanket of skin. I need to stop spilling wine, cheese, pizza and carbs on the blanket as well because it doesn't help the visual for my abs. What was I talking about again?? See what I mean? My brain tends to go in any and all directions except writing. I can write small articles or blurbs on facebook but completing a whole book has been daunting. I have never failed at anything I have set out to do but enough is enough you people need to read my words. I am fucking brilliant, funny, obnoxious, crude, caring, good willed, evil, manipulative, sweet and uniquely qualified to give you either a good or bad time. People either love me or hate me and I am fine with that. I would rather you tell me to fuck off than smile in my face and talk shit behind my back. I am an equal opportunity offender as I told you and I am proud of that. I am not a racist or prejudice because I make fun of all. So whether you are Asian, African American, Gay, Straight, Single, Married or just plain stupid I make fun of all but I especially make fun of myself. I am a walking disaster people! Seriously I am an accident waiting for a place to happen; I trip over my own two feet if not yours too. I am constantly trying to grab the words out of my mouth after they have been sent like" Don't you have any mirrors in your house? Or just because they make it in your size doesn't mean you should wear it. I can be a dickhead but I am also the person who would sacrifice his own life to save a friend from a burning building. I am very politically incorrect, an equal opportunity offender but yet a loyal friend who will give you the shirt off my back. Wait didn't I say that hmm maybe I am trying to convince myself that I would actually give you the shirt off my back,,,,, hmm – I guess it really depend how much I liked you and how much I liked the shirt. I mean if I was wearing a ratty old T shirt and you were a friend in need than sure! I can dish it out and I can take it…..in more than one way too!!!HA!

There are no boundaries with me unless we have discussed or achieved them prior. I have girlfriends that love saying the word cunt and I have others that despise it. Then again I have girlfriends that hate the word moist and cringe when it is said which I will never fully get or understand no matter how many reasons they tell me why. I think life is all about boundaries and how you set them up with each individual. A complete stranger would have different boundaries than say my best friend. I wouldn't treat someone's mom the way I treat my best friend but I also wouldn't treat someone's mom like I treat my best friend. Get it? No? OK this should help – I am kind of a dick towards my sister but I wouldn't treat your sister like a dick...To be honest with you I really cannot stand my sister but you will learn that as you read on in the book. I am not one of those people who think because we are blood related I have to love them. I have plenty of people I love that are not blood related but then again I have plenty of people that I am blood related to that let's just say....I wish I wasn't.

I think gossip is bullshit when you are talking about me but if it is about someone else. Err maybe a little! I have flaws and I like people who have flaws. Flaws make people unique and man do I have flaws which anybody who knows me makes me extremely unique. I am proud of that. I keep my fingers on the pulse but do it my way. I own myself and make no excuses or apologize for who I am or what I do. I am proud of my sexuality and who I choose to love. I will apologize if I unintentionally hurt someone or something. I can at times hurt someone on purpose. I am not self-righteous and I do make mistakes. I learn something from every hello and definitely from every goodbye. For example I will never cosign a car loan no matter how good in bed you are. I am as loyal as a golden retriever as long as you feed me my treats. Treats for me are fun, laughter, loyalty, honesty and enjoying spending life together. There are various definitions of each of these words but they tend to mean different things to different people. Some people don't get my humor and some get it way to much! Other people just tolerate me usually because they have to --for various reasons. We all have to tolerate certain people at certain times right? For instance my Father's wife....I can't stand the bitch but if I want to spend Christmas with dear ole dad I have to tolerate her... well I do try...sometimes.....I think too much but then again I don't think things through. I honestly love my life and the good ol days are the present for me. Do I reminisce with old friends? Of course I do but would I want to go back in time? No fucking way!! I love my life with its wayward balancing act, hap hazard nightly adventures or boring quiet evenings at home and I wouldn't want it any other way. So....if anything I said so far has offended you, you find morally wrong/challenging or feel that I am wrong in saying what I have then.... Stop reading, close the fucking book, and give it to a really cool open minded person because obviously you are not cool and by my definition probably an asshole who doesn't deserve or have the right to judge me. Judging people leave no room left for loving them.........and I SOOO want to be loved! Yeah right! Besos for all. BTW I am an extremely insecure guy if you haven't figured that out yet...who am I kidding...everybody figures that out...really fucking quickly...Besos for all...

I kept telling everyone I had a book coming out, promised editors a revised edition but I would always have an excuse that is till now.... It is 2015 and this book needs to see the light this year. I am no longer going to worry about money, job security or scheduling conflicts. I am not just dipping my body and soul into shallow waters but I am diving off a cliff into shark infested waters and I will come out, not only without a scratch but with a new found achievement as a published author. My publishers always felt like people wouldn't get the book unless they knew me so I hope this helps! If not...fuck off....

With love,

Tate

Chapter 1

The Move

I moved to Los Angeles in June, the 29th to be exact. Being that I was born and raised in Brooklyn and I have tried to escape several times before I will always be a New Yorker. I have always wanted to move to California ever since I visited with my Mother when I was 12 years old. I am kinda obsessed with California and watched every single episode of Beverly Hill 90210 and Melrose Place. I want to live in a place like Melrose Place. Moving out west, especially to Hollywood California, I must say I definitely had delusions of (Whatever the hell that word is) granger. I want the amazing apartment, the intense friends/relationships and where could you beat the amazing weather. LA is perfect for me and I was born to live there…It is the most amazing and perfect place in the world for me. I just know it regardless of what my Mother says…Oh well, as you read on you will come to realize is that not everything is perfect and amazing in good ole sunny California. It can be glamorous but it can also punch you right in the gut. There are ups and downs in every person's journeys throughout their lives but for some magical reason in Los Angeles they are magnified times ten. I have had some amazing peaks here in LA but I have also hit many valleys and I am not talking about San Fernando Valley either. Enjoy the mishaps and mayhem of my life; the reckless passages of an insecure, know it all and the genuine chaos I get lost in on a daily basis. I promise you I am not an idiot. I promise……….. Or I can hope………………. right? You be the judge, so ready, set, go!

It all started at 6AM New York time. I woke up late to a brutal rainstorm from hell. I was so nervous as it was with my impending move but now I am late…damn it!!! I jumped out of bed in a panic and I just looked around at all of my packed suitcases…. Thank God I was smart enough to ship a bunch of boxes last week. More knots in my stomach were growing by the second but I just took a deep breath and sprinted to the bathroom. Upon skidding into the bathroom I glanced at my pre-arranged clothes….Yes…I prearranged clothes…Wow how grown up of me huh? I feel like I am going to throw up now. I jumped into the shower and took one of the fastest showers I ever had in my life. I am so not going to miss this shitty water pressure that's for sure! I got my soon to be ex roommate up, (he is definitely not a morning person) it's 630 in the God damn morning why are you yelling at me he yells and I explain to him that we are late…Ahh one of the last snarls I will ever get for waking him up before fucking noon. What a great going away present, I must exclaim! …just knowing that I will never be snarled at by this little bitch again was enough to keep my spirits up. I scooped up the cat, Spencer is his name and he was not that thrilled to be woken up either. Can't really figure out who was more pissed at me this morning, Danny or Spencer. I actually do not even have a second to think about that! Shit the time is flying. I was just grabbing things and just spinning around and around and getting nowhere really. Thank goodness I packed yesterday because I think I am still drunk from last night. My friends threw me a going away party last night and we partied way too long. To be honest I will not miss many of them, but some…. maybe one….maybe… we shall see. I am sure they will all miss me though… Ha! You know what? It is not nerves it's this fucking hangover! No time to find aspirin right now. So I am racing around the house like a husband that just got caught by his wife in bed with a hooker. Nobody is actually chasing me but it is just one of my gazillion analogies so you get the grand picture. I know I am forgetting things but shit I don't want to miss that plane. Time is up and we have got to go! Ok I think I have everything!

You ready Danny? I yell frantically.

Coming…stop screaming at me bitch, Danny snaps.

I am not screaming Danny. I'm … I'm just excited and really nervous! I explain to Danny.

Don't forget that damn cat Tate, Danny states.

I am thinking to myself –Listen you little fucking obnoxious elf he is not the one I am planning on forgetting. I cannot wait to get away from this gnome. How did I end up living with this guy for over a year??

I would never forget Spenny boy as I pick up Spencer's Sherpa bag that I battled to get him into for over 15 minutes. I love my Spenny more than almost anyone else in the entire world you included Danny. Cats really know how to use those damn claws and Spencer is no exception. I can tell he could definitely win the cat revolution, if there was one, just by the way he battled me to get into his traveling cage this morning. I knew I should have put him in there last night but I am too nice. Seriously some people do tell me I am too nice….they really do. I swear I am not lying. I opened up the front door, took a deep breath and turned to Danny and say. Let's go please? As Danny exits in front of me I turn back to look at the apartment, I sigh and say to myself….I won't miss an inch of this dump. So let's see I woke up late; with a hangover: to a monsoon rain storm in June; shitty water pressure; a snarl from my nasty, little soon to be ex roommate and 2 hisses and 3 scratches from Spencer! I am so excited…what a **great day this is turning out to be and it is only 645am!** Woo hoo!!!

Out we go in the pouring rain to catch a cab (have you **ever** tried catching a cab in New York City in the rain? At 630am? Not going to happen. You have a better chance of not hitting traffic on any God forsaken highway during rush hour than catching a cab in the rain especially in this **rain**. I start thinking about the 405 in California which is one of the main highways there. Oh wait they call them freeways out there Ya see? I am already there mentally.

Taxi? Cab flies by…..Splash!

Taxi? Cab flies by……Splash!

Taxi? Guess what? Cab flies by…I am fucking soaked!!!

I cannot believe that I am freezing in June…this would never happen in LA. They say it never rains in Southern California. I think there is actually a song about that so it **has** to be true! Finally after my second complete shower of the day a cab stops. Hooray!! We load up the cab as quickly as we can, throw the cat inside, jump in and off we go. JFK…American Airlines please!!! Once we settle in I start to smell something really bad and I turn to Danny and ask what is that **smell**? He whispers curry…what? Curry he whispers again… Curry I ask? I then realize phew the cab drivers wife must have cooked a whole mess of curry the night before. Whew weeeeee it fuckin stank in that damn cab. As we are gasping for air I ask the cab driver if I can open a window. He gave me a look like are you fucking crazy, its pouring out there! It was so bad that even the cat stopped meowing to hold its breath!! It felt like someone was holding his or her armpit up to my nose after a rather intense game of racquetball. Every New Yorker knows that curry smells a whole lot like body odor, especially on certain Pakistani gentlemen that drive taxi cabs. I know I had to be told by Danny but I would have gotten it eventually…well at least I think I would have….plus we eventually got used to it.

I cannot believe you are moving to LA girl? Danny sings it to me.

Believe it and stop calling me girl I snap. I can prove to you in 10 seconds that I am not a girl Danny (I start to unzip my zipper) so stop! Could you be any gayer? Really it's like there is a gay pride float coming out of your mouth.

Danny looks at me and in his genuinely queeny, obnoxious voice say's to me "I wear glasses not magnifying glasses **girl!!**

So I drop my pants....right in the back of the taxi as we head to the airport.

OK OK OK Danny screams! Pull your pants up Tate.....You know you are sick in the head Tate? Ugh that is a visual I didn't need to see. Gross....

I warned you…next time you call me girl I am going to slap you with it. (Again I am pointing to my penis) Would I have actually done it? Probably not but I do talk a lot of shit BTW.

You are going to miss me, when you are in LA, Danny tells me.

No I'm not Danny....sorry but what's to miss? You are an irritable little queen who doesn't rise before noon, you never pick up after yourself, never buy any food for the house, you stay up all night watching stupid TV and shall I go on?

You are an asshole but who else are you going to have to taunt and abuse in LA? Who is going to be your whipping boy when you are in a mood huh? I am one of a kind. An original and unique guy who is fun to be around, Danny boasts. You soo are going to miss me girl.. Um I mean Tate. I hear LA is a very lonely city.

Don't worry Danny I will find someone....trust me....don't lose any sleep over it. Then again all you do is sleep and you are not as original as you think.

Fuck you bitch. I got up at 630 in the fucking morning to swim through the streets of Queens with you, in **this** storm, to accompany **you** to the airport. Did anyone else volunteer? No I don't think so, Danny snaps.

Sorry Danny I am just nervous, I sigh.

Well it's no reason to be an asshole. Tell me you will miss me, Danny hissed.

I will miss you drama queen….at least I will let you think I will I say to myself with a laugh.

Here we are………. the Mr. Curry Cab Driver announces.

Thank God no traffic! I cannot believe we made it all the way to JFK already! In this pouring rain.

I learned as a kid to hold my breath under water but not under, rain soaked, curry air freshener. When I finally see the American Airlines sign I actually don't care it is still raining out. I just hope this doesn't delay my flight. I hop out, pay the driver and grab my luggage and the cat. The cat is hissing again and all I want to do is get the luggage checked and settle in with this damn cat ASAP! If I heard one more freaking meow or hiss…I…I…I nothing. Let me just try and convince myself that they are hisses of love….right? Enough already Spencer…enough please! I am up for almost any challenge but come on enough already….Can you tell I am frustrated with my beloved cat?

I am now running to the ticket counter but the cat has quieted down for now. Maybe he genuinely knows what enough means…HA… I think out of fear he has stopped meowing because he is now thinking where the hell am I? Where am I going? This doesn't look like that jack asses office who puts needles up my ass. Doesn't look like Grandma's house either….hmm.. Don't you love it when people or pet owners think we know what are pet is thinking? So ridiculous but we all do it…don't lie. I bet you think that your Fluffy talks to you as well.

I get to the ticket counter rather quickly and there is no line. See Tate your luck is changing already I say to myself. I get up to the counter and check in my luggage lickity split. I am about to say I need a pet ticket, when the ticket agent points to the cat carrier and says you have to check that.

Check what I say?

The pet carrier, it is way too big for under the seat, she informs me.

Really? But I called the 800 number and they gave me the dimensions for the carrier. I plead with the American airlines ticket agent.

It is not going to fit I am sorry dear, but you will have to check the cat.

No…I cannot do that. Can I buy a pet carrier that will fit here at the airport?

No…the ticket agents says getting annoyed.

No?

Nope….even more annoyed by now

What am I going to do Danny? I ask as I turn to Danny.

Well he is **not** coming home with me. That **cat** is pure evil. Just check him in. He will be fine. Tate he is a cat. I know you think he is a human being but in fact…he is a cat. **Check him in!**

I am standing there just stunned. What do I do? I don't want to miss the flight but I don't want the cat in cargo either.

Sir? Sir? SIR? I hear the voice saying as I am in shock of what is happening. The ticket agent in now clearly perturbed. You need to either check the cat or not. It is clearly up to you but there is a line forming and I have other passengers to attend to.

Check the fucking cat Tate!!! Danny screams.

OK OK but he will be alright? I ask the ticket Agent sincerely.

He will be fine sir. People check their animals in all the time.

I stammer and reluctantly say OK, As I hand over Spencer to the ticket lady I say to him "I will see you in about 6 hours Spenny, be a good boy, I love you and we are going to have so much fun in California, A brand new fresh start!"

God really? You said fewer words to your **Mother** before she left the restaurant last night Tate. And….you probably won't see her for months and **she** is actually human!

Give me a definition of human? I snap at Danny.

Ha Ha Danny snarls.

So I finish up with getting Spencer all onboard, I thank the "kind" ticket agent and start to head for the security gate. As I walk through the airport I notice that there are not that many people traveling this time in the morning. Stores are just opening up and it is very ghost like, I find that very strange and almost eerie. Even inside the airport it smells like rain or maybe it's that I am still soaked to the bone. Even my underwear is soaked like I peed in my pants…wait no at least my pee would be warm in my underwear…but my junk is shivering as well. My sneakers are squashing through the airport proving to people throughout the airport that I buy cheap shoes. I must say that my stomach has calmed down some and the excitement of moving to California is really starting to build again…..

Well this is it I say as I turn to Danny. He has this weird frown on his face. Strange that in almost a year I haven't seen this face but it was now time to say goodbye, to this chain-smoking little queen known as my roommate Danny.

We get to the security gate and I turn to Danny and say:

I will talk to you soon. Give me a hug goodbye. Danny seriously thank you for coming to the airport with me I really do appreciate the help. Do you need cab fare back home?

All of a sudden the Hover damn has just broken loose all over his face, Danny starts sobbing, I gonna miss you **Sniff Sniff** I love you, you're my best friend!!!! It is not going to be the same New York City without you. We have had so many amazing and fun times together!

Amazing and fun times...together with me..is he sure, it was me? Where was I? Did I forget about these amazing and fun times? Maybe it is true, my Mother says and I do drink way too much and forget some of the things I do. Hmmm...All I keep thinking is **get me away from this little leprechaun already!** Does he need an **enough already** speech as well? Is he seriously crying? For me no less? He should be thrilled and happy to get rid of me. I am no **prize** to live with either. I know for a fact that he has a Hot Brazilian roommate moving into my bedroom this afternoon. I am looking at him thinking to myself I didn't even think you **liked** me but now I am your best friend? I thought he came to the airport with me because he was worried I wasn't going to get on that plane and actually go to LA. I thought maybe he didn't want me to screw up his plans with the Brazilian so he was making sure I got on the plane. Yeah that has to be it right? I mean the way he was yelling at me about the cat and checking him in. I assumed he was just...oh screw it... I am getting the hell away from him one way or another! Just be nice to him for a couple more minutes. Tell him that you will miss him after all you are a really good liar anyway. So I have a Sally Field moment of clarity—you like me, you really like me? So what do I do? Yup I lie and say:

Me too Danny, me too!

We hug and say we will keep in touch but I don't have any intentions to ever talk to him again. I mean I haven't even told you how much of a fucking pig he is. Dirty dishes in the sink that he will never wash, pit stains on his T shirts or the dirty underwear with skid marks he leaves on the bathroom floor for me. He is a smoker but he is one of those guys that smell like an ashtray after just one cigarette. Danny was my roommate and for a small time he was my friend. He would always compete with me regardless of what the situation was. Men, board games, work and even with mutual friends of ours. It was my friend this or your friend that. I still cannot get over that he thinks of me as his best friend. I wonder what his true definition of a best friend really is. I know you probably think I am a dick for saying these things. I mean after all he did come to the airport with me, in the pouring rain, to say goodbye. Sorry but he just bugs the shit out of me. I am not one of those people that wonder why Danny has never had a boyfriend. I know why......

Take care I say, as Danny starts to walk away (I am human after all) Enjoy your new roommate I yell as he turns back around and smiles at me.

I love you Tate Connors. You are an amazing person and do not let anyone tell you anything different. Have a safe flight and now go become a movie star in LA, like you were destined to become. (As Danny is blowing kisses at me)

I think to myself who is this guy? Why couldn't he be like this before? You know... be human...Ahh the puzzle of life. I am done with puzzle Danny and his twisted emotions and I will never find his end piece after all...so I am done! Next puzzle please!

Well finally "Peace" for the next 6 hours that is. No cat, no annoying little leprechaun and no rain. I am actually starting to dry! God I love the airport. Is it too early for a glass of wine? I love to people watch and imagine what people do and where they are coming or going to. I don't have much time to do this because by the time I got through security they were boarding the plane. I know that after 9-11 security is tight but I was about to ask the TSA security woman if I ever pissed her off in a previously life. I mean the things she had me do. Open my mouth, spread my legs, show the bottom of my feet etc etc. Was she doing her job? Probably but I think she was either bored or hated men. Come to think of it she did look like a lesbian. A really hard core lesbian type and not like the ones who look like Ellen and Portia. They are actually more of exceptions come to think of it, Ellen and Portia that is. Portia is **hot**, good job Ellen. Lesbians generally don't like me but for the life of me I cannot figure out why. Can you?

I go straight to the gate to board the plane because they are already announcing boarding. I hand over my ticket to the American Airlines agent and I continue to board the plane. I look back at the ticket agent and think, wow she was pretty, and she must be from LA. As I head down the ramp and enter the plane I hope there is a good movie on the flight. I love watching movies on a plane it comforts me immensely. Actually I am still hung over from the night before so I am going to try and sleep though. We shall see what the movie is first. The plane is pretty empty right now and that excites and worries me at the same time. I do not have a fear of flying but I do have a fear of terrorists. Let me look around and see if I see any. I look around and I do not see any so I decide to pray. Please God get us to LA safely and I beg you not to have any screaming kids sit next to me. The plane is filling up but still no terrorists and still no kids.

Just my luck…right as I said it… here is Suzy Sunshine and her obnoxious crying baby inching closer and closer to my aisle. The worst part is the louder the baby wails, the more this woman smiles. She is smiling so big that she actually could play the Jokers wife in the next Batman sequel. Please don't sit next to me…Please don't sit next to me …Come on God I prayed to you!!! I know God is like screw you…now you want to pray to me? When is the last time you went to church? Funerals and wedding don't count either. I will fix you Tate Connors. Just as I feared and predicted, Suzy Sunshine and her wailing child stops right in my aisle.

Is this 22 B?

No it's 20 B you are two rows behind me. (Phew in my head I think I dodged a kid bullet)

Thank you sir it is hard maneuvering down these rows with a baby and carry-on luggage she laughs

I am sure it is I say with a smile.

Well not even 2 seconds behind her comes Ms. Cherry Jubilee and she is wearing what looks like every swatch color from the Home Depot paint aisle. Her hair is bleached blonde, face painted like a drunken clown; her dress looks like what a painter would dip his brush in and the skirt, what there was of it had to be purchased at Sluts R Us.

Is this 22 B?

I think so I muster

Well I am your co passengers on this flight. I am so excited to be going home to Pasadena today. New York City is not for me but my shithead husband is working in the Big Apple and he implied that he missed his girl so much, that I decided to surprised him with a visit.

Was he surprised I asked?

More like I was surprised she exclaims!

How come?

Do you really want to hear Ms. Cherry Jubilee asks?

I say to myself not really but out loud I say **Sure!**

Ms. Cherry Jubilee is not so full of jubilee anymore. Well I flew all the way to New York City to surprise my husband. I have gone to the gym every day for 3 weeks; got my hair done, spray tanned and even bought a bunch of new sexy clothes, all for him! I traveled all the way to New York City to surprise him. I had never been here before. I had no idea where I was going and had to rely on strangers to figure out how to get to the Marriot Marquis in Times Square where my husband was staying. I took a shuttle, a train ride and finally a cab but I found it.

Did you know there are so many beggars on the trains here in New York?

Yes I am aware I said kind of mockingly but she just continued with the story...

Once I arrived I couldn't **believe** how enormous it was. I needed a map just to find the front desk but I did. I waited on line and finally I was next. I explained to the front desk staff that I wanted to surprise my husband and I showed ID to the front desk captain so they would give me a room key. They were very nice and very accommodating to me. It is a beautiful hotel, have you been?

Yes!

Oh OK, Do you know what that bastard did?

What bastard?

My **Husband** Ms. Cherry Jubilee snaps.

No idea I say...(This bitch better not catch a tude with me she has no idea who she is talking to)

He cheated on me!

Oh...

With his assistant! She shrieks louder than the crying baby 2 rows behind!

Typical guy I say. When the cat is away the mice will play.

Really? Typical? Ask me the assistant's name then?

What?

Ask me the assistant's name? (she says extremely agitated)

What is the assistant's name I ask?

Benjamin she sobs!

Benjamin I repeat.

Yes Benjamin, as in a man! After I got the room key I went to the elevators. They are very confusing by the way but I finally found the 17th floor. It took a while but I found it. I stopped by a mirror to fix my hair and then I hunted down Room 1756. I was so excited to surprise my husband and couldn't wait to see the expression on his face when I walk in. As I opened the door I start to hear noises that sound like fuck me, fuck me, **fuck me.** I am just mortified because I think the hotel has gone and gave me the wrong room key but then I look up.

(Ms. Cherry – Not – So-Jubilee -no-more has drawn a crowd on the plane by now)

It's my husband squealing like a little pig. Benjamin has his tally wacker up my husband's shit hole she exclaims. Things are supposed to come out of that hole. Not put things in she says very sternly.

So he is a bottom I ask?

What's a bottom she asks?

Never mind go on, what did you do?

I screamed Get your pecker out of my husband's shit hole Benjamin!

Then?

The bell boy showed up with our luggage she sighs….

Then?

Well I just turned and ran and ran and ran. I almost dropped my purse twice. I ran to the elevator and I ran on to the streets. I just kept moving through the crowds. Did you know Time Square has a lot of people?

Yes I do, so what did you do next I inquire.

Well I um…well I went and saw Wicked.

Wicked as in the Broadway musical I ask?

Yes!

So how was it? (What else would **you** say?)

It was wonderful. The music was amazing. The dancing, the lights were incredible but the singing was out of this world. It was my first Broadway musical and I just loved it. I was mesmerized by the music. I even bought a T shirt and a cast book! Do you want to see?

(I am thinking to myself. This woman is a fucking lunatic. She just found out her husband takes cock up his ass and she goes to see Wicked?)

No I have seen it. I have a T- shirt as well! (Again what the hell else could I say to her?)

So what did you do after the show?

I went to dinner.

You went to dinner after and you didn't speak to your husband?

Yes and Hell no. He up rooted my life from Nashville Kentucky and moved us to Pasadena California for his job; right after we got married. I left my family, my friends and even my little dog Dolly Parton back in Nashville! I was going to be a country star. I was singing on Painters Alley, every Tuesday night, when I first met my husband. We had a whirlwind romance and an elegant wedding. There were flowers for days. He promised me that once we got settled in California that I could go back to singing. But here we are a year later and all I am doing is playing Real Housewife of Pasadena and now apparently playing a beard!

(Wow she knows what beard means… but not bottom….interesting)

So what did you do after dinner?

I checked into the Plaza Hotel.

The Plaza?

Yup I may be Southern but I am not stupid. My husband and his family have money and he is going to pay for squealing like a little pig on me. I checked in, took a long shower, ordered some porn, yup woman like porn too, did my business, then passed out and had a full good night sleep. I didn't even cry at all.

Did your husband try and call you?

Maybe…probably I turned my phone off when I went to see Wicked. Did you know you have to turn your cell phones off in the theater?

Yes….um I have a question…when did this happen?

Last Thursday she states.

Last Thursday what have you been doing since?

Shopping and sightseeing. I went to Central Park, the zoo, Bloomingdales, Macy's, had frozen hot chocolates at Serendipity and we went to the Empire State Building, Ground Zero and the Statue of Liberty. Have you been?

I have climbed that bitches skirt twice and I have no desire to do it again.

Whose skirt?

Nothing, nothing I was trying to be funny. So you haven't spoken to anyone?

Nope.

So you made no phone calls to your Mother, father, sister, cousin or even possibly a friend?

No.

Why not?

Why? To what…. tell them that my husband is taking his assistant **Benjamin's** tallywacker up his shit hole. From what I keep envisioning from the first look preview he was rather enjoying himself as well.

(I wish she could just say ass instead of **shit hole**)

Do you think he called anyone?

Who?

Your husband I state.

Why would he go and do a dang thing like that? What is he going to tell them? Darlene surprised me at my hotel last Thursday while I had Benjamin's tally Wacker up in my shit hole and I was squealing like a pig in heat. No I don't think so. His Papa would shoot him like an old barn dog and then hang his head over the fireplace. No I have a better plan. I am going to torture that man for the rest of his life. He is going to give me that singer career now. I will bet the milk money on it. I know in California and New York they are liberal bout the homosexuals but in Kentucky they would roast him like a pig for Sunday dinner.

(So Ms. Cherry Jubilees name is Darlene huh? I also realized the baby has stopped crying 2 rows back so everybody on the plane must be listening now. I wonder when that happened, the baby not crying anymore that is. I look at this poor woman and I don't know what else to do or say. I don't know if this woman is in shock, is cra, cra or is on the verge of a nervous breakdown but I actually like her and feel sorry for her. I might be a lot of things but I am not a cheater. My Father cheated on my Mother and it devastated her but at least it was with another woman. My Mother would have pulled the heart out of my Fathers chest instead of pulling his wallet out of his bank account)

My name is Tate by the way as I reach out my hand to her.

She maneuvers the tissue and accepts my hand.

I am Darlene nice to meet you. I wish it was on more joyous circumstances.

Me too Darlene that is some story! Do you have someone picking you up at the airport? (Hey I am worried about her)

I called car service but I used my maiden name so I won't have to see a sign with **that cheating bastards'** name on it.

Oh OK…..I get it.

So why are you going to California Darlene asks? I feel like all we have been doing is talking about me for the past hour.

(Now while I do like her but do I **want** to tell a questionable crazy person my life story? I pause for a moment to think…Ah so what…what could she possibly do?)

I am moving to California I proclaim.

Is it for work or to just to escape and start a new life?

A little bit of both actually. I am an actor and there is a lot more work and opportunities in Los Angeles than New York, plus I need some space from my crazy Mother. I didn't live with her but my mandatory Sunday dinners will be much less often now. Bonus Ding-Ding!

I miss my Momma Darlene sighs.

Is she back in Nashville?

No she is dead. My neighbor shot her by accident while he was cleaning his gun. Momma was in the garden planting…oh how she loved that garden. The gun accidently went over and pretty much blew her head off.

(I look at this woman with horror)

You are one open book huh? I am so sorry…um wow so sorry.

Why you didn't kill her?

No but that's horrible.

No what was horrible was my Daddy marrying my neighbor's wife after he went to prison for killing my Momma…it's true, that's what was so terrible.

I have a step Mother that I cannot stand as well.

Selma's alright, that's her name and she makes my Daddy happy. I just worry in about 2 years when Jimmy, that's my neighbors name that shot my Momma gets out of prison. He still declared he loves her. You know what they say; once you kill someone the next one is like getting a coupon on a new shot gun. You see, I am the girl from the wrong side of the tracks who marries the rich boy. Total fairytale courtship and all. Parents were hating me and all too. I wish my Momma could have been there….at the wedding that is. Chads Momma told him not to marry me right up to the very end. Chad could never get his mouth off his Momma's titty and that is just the way she liked it. It was a very hard time for me. You are lucky you still have a Momma.

Yes I am (I feel like a total shit now)

I was 16 when my Momma died. I was so boy crazy that I didn't miss her so much back then. I was too busy chasing boys and getting them too. When I met Chad I felt my life was perfect. Chad was a **Gorgeous** Boy, athletic, charming as well, wealthy, funny, fashionable and witty. All the girls wanted Chad but he was mine. Maybe I should have let them have Chad, come to think of it. Days like these are when I wish I still had my Mother.

I am sorry. (What else should I say?)

Stop saying sorry, you didn't kill her.

I am going to have an affair. I have just decided Darlene states. Can I ask you a question?

(please, please do not ask me to have an affair with you?)

UM….I am scared what you are going to ask but OK what?

Would you ever cheat on your wife? I know you don't have a ring on and are probably still too young but do you have a wife? Would you cheat on her?

I can honestly tell you I would not cheat on my wife I say as I look directly into her eyes. (What I am **not** telling her a lie, but the question remains, do

I tell this crazy Ms. Cherry Jubilee Darlene that I like to put my pecker in another guys um shit holes too?)

Can I ask you **another** question?

Sure what the hell!

Have you ever heard of the mile high club?

(OK **now** she is flirting. It is such a curse to be so damn cute!)

Sure I have heard of it.

Are you a member?

Um…no I stammer and this is getting a little uncomfortable I tell her.

Darlene whispers…do you want to become a member?

With who? (as I am trying to prolong the inevitable)

With me silly she leans in and whispers in my ear. I still have it and can rock your world.

Um…um…(I am sweating now and my mouth is racing like it is running a triathlon) No thanks we just met and you are technically still married and besides that, every person on this plane knows what happened. You were not that discrete when you were telling me the story. Plus I am claustrophobic and airline bathrooms are small. (I am grasping for anything here people)

What about after we land? We could get a hotel room. I would pay and you can just call me Sugar Momma. I can get rather kinky in bed boy. How old are you?

26 I say….How do you know I don't have a girlfriend I ask?

Do you have a girlfriend she asks softly and she is now stroking my leg.

No I do not have a girlfriend.

So?

So what?

Do you want to have sex with me? Darlene asks and rather loudly I might add.

No thanks I try and say as politely as possible.

Why not? Am I not pretty enough for you Tate?

No you are very pretty(Remember I told you I was a liar)

Oh I know, you are a **Virgin?**

(Ok now I am getting annoyed)

Darlene would you please do me a favor and look at this face. Do you see how cute I am? Do you think a 26 year old guy, who looks as good as me would still be a virgin?

That's true she exclaims. Are you Irish?

Half Irish and half Croatian, I tell her

(Why am I feeding this crazy bitch with even more information about me? Am I that sick in the head that I need attention from this loon? Am I enjoying this? What is wrong with me…just shut up Tate. Do not tell her another fucking thing you, you insecure dumb ass. I wonder who screwed me up so bad. Was it my Mom, Dad or siblings? Nah they all turned out well so what is it with my fascination with people wanting to have sex with me regardless if I am attracted to them or not? Tate Connors you have some seriously issues and probably shouldn't be going to LA but to a Psychiatric facility.)

That's Hot. I like Irish guys and the Croatian thing just make you even more exotic. I am so turned on. Come on, come with me to the bathroom sexy Tate.

(Now she thinks I am sexy too…I am as giddy as a school girl)

(she is grabbing for my junk now)

No thanks and now you are making me really uncomfortable as I start to look for a flight attendant for help. Get your fucking hands off my dick!!!

No…I know you want it. I will give you a hand job right here.

No stop it this is so uncomfortable and rude of you, as I am trying desperately to keep her hands out of my crotch.

(Darlene starts to shout)

You're uncomfortable Tate. I flew to New York City to find out that my husband and his assistant **Benjamin are drilling each other's shit holes** probably on a daily basis. You're uncomfortable???I have no family, no friends to turn to and I live in fucking Pasadena! I exercise every God damn day, stay in shape, buy the latest fashions and I am the complete package. I have needs as well Tate. I could have had any guy I wanted in high school. Guys throughout New York City would whistle at me all day long, while I was visiting.

Yeah I say and now I am pissed.

Yeah she says and she is completely in my face.

Well than why don't you **go** get one of them to fuck you in the bathroom!!!!!

Is there a problem? I hear it before I look up and see it is one of the American Airlines flight attendants.

Yes…this bitch is crazy. Please you have to get me away from her.

Darlene is sobbing. I am sorry…I am sorry…I just want someone to fuck me. Anyone Tate so don't flatter yourself. Typical man and his ego. Why did I have to be sitting next to probably the only guy who doesn't think with his dick? Why me? Some guys would give their left nut to sleep with me. Not Mr. Self-Righteous Tate…

You turn faster than a lesbian pancake I say to myself.

I turn to Darlene and say: I actually felt sorry for you, I really did. What your husband did was unconscionable and I was trying to be a friend. It seems like you had it rough and I am sorry for you. I was trying to be a nice guy something I don't always do. You took that and made it sexual. I don't have sex in bathrooms with strangers. (Remember I am a liar) You completely violated me. If I guy did what you did to me they would be arrested for assault.

The flight attendant looks around and says there is a seat two rows back we can move you to.

I will take it as I spring up. I would sit in cargo if it would get me away from this lady.

Darlene looks at me with the means eyes again and starts to scream, ….hey Tate…All I wanted to do was surprise my husband and he cheated on me. You seemed like a nice guy and I am horny. Internet porn only goes so far asshole. I haven't eaten in a fucking month and you could have at least fucked me in the bathroom? Was that too much to ask?

(This chick is bat shit crazy) Get some help I say as I walk away.….I turn to the flight attendant and I say can I tell you what happened?

The flight attendant looks at me, smiles and says Mr. Connors the **whole p**lane knows what happened to you. We were taking bets to see how long you were going to last sitting next to her.

Who won the bet I ask?

No one, you far out lasted any of us she says and she motions to my new seat.

Guess where my new seat is? Yup right next to Suzy Sunshine and her wailing child. I get settled in my new seat and buckle in. Suzy Sunshine looks at me and says:

I don't want any drama….I have a fucking screaming kid to deal with and I don't need two! Ya got it?

I got it I say to her. What the hell did I do?

You baited that poor sweet girl like a worm on a fishing pole and you make me sick. That poor woman and what she has gone through. Men!!!!

I was trying to help I say meekly.....

Well you didn't help so just sit there and shut up.

(I look at her and say to myself I am renaming your nickname, you are not Suzy Sunshine, you are a bitch)

OK I muster......

Will she cry the whole flight? As I point to the baby.

I don't know but probably...I bet you wish you had a different seat huh?

Yup I do.....

Well if you didn't torment the nut case you were sitting with prior to this, you would have been in a different seat she snaps.

Well 10 minutes later I am emotionally drained and I am going to sleep. I hope I snore louder than the wailing baby.

Well after a rather "smooth" flight I arrive in Los Angeles cocky and confident and ready to take over this town like a tornado hitting a Midwest farm. I got almost 2 hours of sleep. The first thing I think of is, please let me get off this damn plane without seeing bat shit crazy Darlene. I plan on waiting till everyone is off the plane before I disembark. As row by row walk past me I am getting varying looks from people. Some smile, some shoot dirty looks but most just look down and refuse to make eye contact with me. It's cool I get. It is like when you are at the zoo and it says "Don't feed the animals" and I throw a cheeseburger to the monkeys. The monkey than goes crazy and jumps the fence and starts humping a grandma....Wait...Darlene is the monkey but am I the cheeseburger or the grandma?

(Shut up Tate)

OK the plane is empty now and it is safe to leave. I grab my carry on and head to the front of the plane to disembark. The nice flight attendant that moved me to a different seat is standing at the doorway as I start to exit the plane.

Enjoy your stay here in Los Angeles she says with a smile You luggage will be at baggage Claim # 4.

Thank you again and I am sorry for the interruptions. I will try really hard not to feed the crazies anymore.

She laughs and says Enjoy your day!

(See??? I am funny)

As I walk off the plane I start to replay in my head what happened on the plane. It started off genuine right? Did I mislead Darlene? Did I bait her too much? At the end was I trying to feed my ego? Whatever....this is giving me a headache and I need to move on. I am sure by now Darlene has and is not plotting revenge on her dick loving husband....Lesson learned...when a woman tells you her husband likes dick up his ass....run!

It is a long walk to the baggage claims here at LAX. As I am walking I start to think about Spencer and how he is doing. I am sure he had an easier flight than me. Maybe I should have been caged and put in cargo as well. Finally I am at the baggage claim. I nervously look around and viola that **she** is.... Darlene and she is talking to Ms. Suzy Sun-bitch. My mind starts to race:

what are they saying about me, what are they plotting for me or maybe how can they sleep with me? Ha probably not on that last one. I think I will stand on the opposite side of the conveyer belt. Just as the conveyer belt starts Darlene spots me and starts to stare me down. I do my best to try and ignore her but after a few minutes she begins to walk over.

(Luggage please come, luggage please come…I beg of you luggage please come. My mind starts to race. Do I **really** need what's in my luggage? If I could just grab Spenny and split it would be OK…I hear a voice.

You humiliated me!

I whirl around and I say with my full on Brooklyn accent…You humiliated yourself lady!

I was in a fragile state and you baited me Darlene informs me.

Baited you? I wonder where you heard that from. Possibly you learned the new vocabulary word from the bitch with the baby over there, as I point across the conveyer belt. Are you drunk?

Yes…

Yes what?

I am drunk.

Well goody, goody for you.

Yup I am drunk, fragile and still horny. You don't turn me on anymore though. The other women and me discussed it and we think you are probably gay anyway. I am going to find myself a real man anyway Tate.

Would you like me to Google the closest truck stop from LAX?

Sir here is your cat as the American Airlines attendant hands me Spencer's cage. Darlene starts making these laughing sounds.

Spenny boy! How are you? I missed you!

Hiss, hiss, hiss...

I hear Darlene's voice again: Yup I knew it. You are so gay! Just like my husband. Straight men do not have cats...No straight man owns a cat, never the less travel with one. You aren't right...just like my husband. Meow....

(Ok I have had it)

Darlene the difference is I am a top.

Top of what jack ass?

Let me explain this to you in idiot terms Darlene. Let me introduce myself.... my name in Benjamin!

She looks at me in horror and turns and runs. I cannot resist as I yell out, I hear The Book of Mormon is playing at The Pantages....

(Not sure she got that but I did. I should have known she was bat shit crazy when she told me that after witnessing her husband getting plowed by a guy she goes off and sees a fucking musical....should've known....should've known...Ahh here comes my luggage **Yea!**

Luggage arrived on time, the cat arrived with a look of like wait till I get out of this damn box but I could tell under the hissing and spitting that he truly did love me. OK I am off to pick up the rental car. The rental car shuttle came right away. I didn't even get a moment to bask in the California sunshine. I hoped on board the crowded shuttle, with my luggage and Spencer and off he went. I was starting to get embarrassed because Spencer wouldn't stop crying and meowing. Slowly other passengers began to notice Spencer and start cooing at him. Yup Spencer is just like his Dad (that's me) and has to be the center of attention in all crowds…I think I hear him purring now. Avis rental car I hear on the loud speaker and I jump up. I turn to Spencer and say this is us boy. Let's hope this goes smoothly…nothing else has so here is to hope. The driver unloaded my bags and I tipped him very kindly. As I got off the shuttle I took a deep breath, gazed into the sun and I walked into the rental office.

Waiting for some drama? Well guess what it didn't happen. Went in, gave them my reservation number, driver's license and credit card. They gave me a compact car with unlimited mileage. Who could beat that? I haven't driven in a long ass time so I took the additional insurance. It is better to be safe right? I wasn't that good of a driver when I actually did own a car. This is the first thing that has gone well for me today. Hmm well second we didn't crash. Hmm well third Spenny and my luggage arrived safely as well. Shut up already Tate. I wish there was a pause button in my brain sometimes.….Off I go on a brand new set of adventures. LA here I come baby.

As I am driving in the rental car I start to wonder what do I want out of LA? What am I gonna do with my life? Will I make friends with a celebrity? Will I become famous? What about a hot Latino boyfriend to top it off? Or what about a Brazilian or Argentina guys? I heard there are A LOT of them out here. How am I going to map out my success here in LA? You never get a second chance to make a first impression. I am so going to love being fresh meat out here. Fresh meat is the New Guy! The new guy is somebody nobody has slept with yet. I really don't mind being anonymous but I am sure I will not be for very long. I have a tendency to cause a commotion pretty much everywhere I go. I don't do it on purpose…I swear…seriously I swear!

My mind just won't stop racing so keep up with me here folks!

All of a sudden here comes a Range Rover swerving from lane to lane. Please do not tell me it is Darlene. Shit it can't be! Wait I think she told me she was getting a car to pick her up. Phew…that is the last thing I need. I am trying to see the driver, who is swerving all over the place but she is tiny. From what I can tell she is Asian but I am not 100% sure at this exact moment. All I do know is this Asian "looking" woman is erratically driving an SUV all over the freeway. I cannot believe that she is moving from lane to lane like a drunk fraternity boy after a keg party or Darlene. Where are the police? What the hell is wrong with this driver? **Now** she is merging right into my lane heading straight in front of me. She has got to see me right?

Boom – Crash- I am spinning out of control. Holy Shit She is not Fucking stopping!!!!!!!!!!

Bam Poof…Ugh.

So that is how an actual airbag feels when it pummels your chest. Watched a million commercials about them never thought. Great I am here an hour and I have already wrecked the rental car. You think the cat was pissed before huh? Spenny boy are you OK?

Hiss, growl, meow, hiss, hiss, meow.

I manage to get the spitting and sneezing rental car to the side of the 405 freeway praying that this "compact" car does not blow up and fry me and my pissed off furry feline. About 200 feet in front stops the smashed SUV and out comes this Asian munchkin. I **was right** she was **Asian!!!** She starts to walk towards me and all I can think is how the fuck did they let this little Asian dwarf get behind the wheel of that damn monstrous truck? Did she have her husband buy it? Did she forget to get in her booster chair? Before I could even analyze any further here she is screaming:

I no see you. Where you come from?

Why I hit you?

All I am thinking is this stupid, short and Asian woman has a very limited English vocabulary, so I say

What?

I no see you. Where you come from?

Why I hit you?

This cannot be happening....This cannot be happening....Do you speak English?

I no see you. Where you come from? I no see you....I **no** see you.

Why I hit you?

Now I am starting to lose my cool between this yammering idiot, the hissing coming out of the rental car, the cat growling and the actual noise you hear when you are indeed on the side of a very busy highway. So I say:

Lady, you went all of the way from the left hand lane to the far right hand lane, with no regards to looking to see if there were any cars actually in the lanes in between. You didn't use any turning signal either. I thought maybe you were having a seizure or something.

She looks at me with utter bewilderment and says:

I no see you. Where you come from?

Why I hit you?

Are you fucking kidding me you stupid idiot? Do you understand **any** English? Do you? While I am yelling I hear a voice within saying" Calm down Tate your scaring her." To which I in turn choose to ignore that voice. Yes it is the same voice of sanity that I have chosen to ignore all damn day long. What is wrong with you? Do you understand any English? Say something….say anything…I am pleading with you….

Chong, Ching Chang. Ching, Chang Woo..(Hey I don't speak Chinese but that is how it sounded to me)

What happened? Are you OK? What the hell happened?

I no see you? Where you come from?

Why I hit you? Why I hit you?

OK this is getting nowhere so I try a different approach.

You didn't see me?

I no see you?

Where you come from?

Where did I come from as in lanes, highways, cities, states or are we talking planets…?

Why did you hit me ----as in maybe you didn't like the color of my car, maybe there were too many people on the road and you wanted to get rid of some, maybe my cat was pissing you off too. I **have** no **single fucking** idea Why **you** hit me!!!!

………………Why I hit you??? She shrieked flailing her stubby tiny hands in the air.

I turn to her and I say Let's just call the police. I give up. I start to walk back towards my car to get my cell phone and she is chasing after me screaming in Chinese. I don't know for a fact it was Chinese either. I mean she wasn't yelling egg rolls or fried rice but I am guessing it is Chinese. (**Don't hate we all think it but I just said it**)So I then call 911 and explain what had just occurred. I give the police a much more "abridged version" of what has occurred in the last 30 minutes of my new life here in sunny California. The woman from the police department goes:

Was anybody hurt?

(And I am thinking "Not Yet.")

No, no one is hurt.

Sir, we only will send an officer if someone has been injured or hurt.

(Again thinking "Do you want me to injure or hurt someone??")

I calmly inform the police officer what is going down. She doesn't understand English I have asked her several times and I get the same thing over and over again. Trust me **Repeatedly**! She is screaming at me in Chinese…I think and I can barely understand a word that she is saying to me.

The officer on the phone had no interest in talking to me anymore. She tried to be nice and gave me the following information. Well just get her license plate, make and model and any information that she can give you. So I say OK with truly well intentioned belief that everything would work out and hang up the cell phone. I walk over to the SUV and the license plate says Hornburg. So I shrug and write down Hornburg. I later will come to find out that Hornburg is the name of the car dealership where she bought the car. I finally get some information out of her, not much but her name is Mei Lee sounds Chinese right? See I told you....

Is this a sign? Are the higher powers that be telling me to run as fast as I can out of California? Or is this a test? I am going to go with Ahhhhhhh things happen. Everyone gets into accidents. I got mine over with right away. It's just a little snafu.

Eventually with much more time and patience we were able to exchange information and the rental car company came with its next victim.....um I mean car for me to destroy. I explain everything to the Avis guy and he just smiles and says it is just great no one was hurt or injured.

Do you want the extended insurance again? The Avis guy asks me.

Yes please I say.

Packed up the new car and as I look at it I kinda like this one better anyway. I just wish I could get the cat to calm down but that is not going to happen. Nope I don't think a tranquillizer gun could calm him down **now!** Off I go again. Man is it hard to pull off the shoulder on this highway! Well after patiently waiting I see an opening and take off so my journey to the next level of my life has begun. Yeah right -----more like next disaster. This car is newer and nicer than the last one. What is this as I pick up this big atlas?

What the hell is a Tommy guide???? And who the hell is this Tommy guy? Did the last person forget their maps in the car?

Who knows but I am not going back….Only going forward from now on….. unless another Asian lady has the urge to hit me again. Lots of People have had urges to hit me today. Mostly women especially if you lump Danny in as a woman. I don't understand why I have had such a hard day…it is not me… It can't **all** be my fault right? Impossible right? Just a string of bad luck right? I fucking hope so….gulp….

Chapter 2

The Apartment

I arrived at my new apartment building 3 hours late but I am still so excited. Even after all the drama of getting here I am very excited. I look at my new home like a fat lady on Jenny Craig on her cheat day. It is so awesome! Alta Vista Gardens is so big and it looks so glamorous. It looks nothing like Melrose Place but I don't care. It is 4 stories high with huge balconies and the pool is awesome. I am finally at a really happy place. That is until the bitchy landlady who is about 35 years old, wearing the most unattractive brown business suit (looks kinda like a talking fudge pop) say's to me:

"You're late!"

Thinking to myself "Really lady… No fuckin kidding!!"

So as nice as I can possibly say to the bitchy landlady: Sorry I was in a car accident on the 405 with an Asian woman who didn't speak a word of English ……..or matter of fact knows how to drive either. I start to tell her what happened…..

I don't have time for this.(she cuts me off) **Here** are your keys.(as she slaps them in my hand) Your boxes were delivered this morning and are in front of your door. You remember it is Unit #406 right? I nervously nod as she continues; I have to go, **somebody** has made me **late** for an appointment. I hope you don't pay your rent, the way you show up for appointments she snaps.

I will always pay my rent on time I say as factual as I can.

Good… she snarls and storms away.

Again, thinking to myself "W**hat a Bitch**!" She was much nicer when she wanted me to rent the apartment and sign the damn lease. Ahh she is probably just riding the cotton pony because she couldn't possibly have had a boyfriend to be dumped by but…………. maybe a girlfriend? She looks like the type that would have her **lick-her license….Ha** I am starting already as I have a flashback to mean Suzy Sunshine as she says I baited Darlene…just shut up already do you want another plane situation? You are here…just enjoy the moment. I look around at the lobby, take a deep breath and I take it all in. The small gym to the left, the beautiful floral arrangements in the middle of the lobby, the beveled mirrors on the wall and the really cool furniture sprawled throughout the entire lobby. I say to myself….I am home!

As I make my way up the elevator with my suitcases and my freaked out feline. I look out the elevator window and see the amazing pool. It is a very large pool and you can tell it has been renovated recently. It is a quick trip on the elevator to the second floor but what I did notice by the pool was that there weren't many people there. I saw some old people though. I hope I didn't move into an old persons building…the **horror** but then I realize most people my age would be working, auditioning or probably filming. As I exit the elevator I see all my boxes, down the hall that I had shipped in front of my door. Well at least that worked out and think finally things are going my way. As I arrive in front of my door, I feel butterflies in my stomach again but these are happy butterflies. I am here! I did it! I have moved to LA! I live in Hollywood California now….Wow I can't believe I really did it! I start to push some of the boxes around, climb over others, get the key in the door and hop on in. Finally my new home is a reality. I look around at the apartment and it is even bigger than I remembered. It has wall to wall beige carpet which I wasn't thrilled about but it was brand new. Being a New Yorker I am used to hard wood floors but I am in California now! The kitchen is a little smaller than I remember but everything else is enormous. It might look enormous because there is very little furniture besides what we bought from the tenants that lived here before us. I start to bring in the boxes I had shipped and drag them to my room. I did get the smaller room in the coin flip but I didn't care because it was still bigger than any room I have ever had, in my entire life! The closet is half the size of my last bedroom or almost! I start to unpack and settle in. I let the cat out of his cage and he begins to wander around the empty apartment angrily meowing over and over. As I am beginning to unpack and the cat is still meowing I realize that Spencer has not pissed or shit in 10 hours. I need to go buy a litter box and kitty litter. Just when I thought I had thought of everything…shit! Let me put him back in his travel bag until I can buy kitty litter. Hey he has made it this far what is another half hour right? Before I could turn the corner of the bedroom to scoop Spencer back up, I hear the sound of what seems like cat pissing on the floor. I look straight towards the kitchen and it has become one hell of a yellow river. I yell "Spencer **No!!!**" He looks me dead in the eyes and with a look that say's "**Fuck You Ass**! you lock me in that box for hours and hours, you don't feed me, you bring me to this strange place, well now it's payback time master! Yes I do believe he said all that to me…I really do. Don't all cats talk to their owners?

Of course I didn't think to pack a mop either.

Well I remember there is a grocery store somewhere around here. I know it is walking distance as well. So I decide to venture out to the grocery store on foot to get some things, I need for the apartment especially cleaning products and kitty litter plus I don't want to forget the damn mop. I ask this woman sitting in the lobby:

Where is the closest grocery store I ask politely?

She rises up off the chair, goes to the door and points. With her broken English she says: That way and left. I figure she is pointing to Fountain Ave and once I get there I should make a left. So I politely say thank you and off I go.

I walk about 2 blocks to the local supermarket and it is named "Ralph's. "What an unattractive name for a grocery store I say to myself. So I say it again **Ralphs**..... Yuck, how stupid! It sounds like what you say to describe someone throwing up. I remember in college someone asking me if I was raulphing in the bathroom. Odd but Ok let's venture inside.

The store itself is actually kind of nice and much, much bigger than the ones in New York City. The supermarket is very modern and Wow!!! It has everything. It is like being in a mini food mall. Deli section, sushi bar, bakery and even a bank! I keep walking from aisle to aisle I am astonished by everything this store has and wondering what it will have next…possibly a Gap? Then all of a sudden….. Holy Shit!! The angels have brought upon me a miracle. I look in aisle 10 and I freeze in my tracks.

You can buy liquor in the grocery store! Oh happy day!! California is grrrreat!! Look at all the **brands** of vodka on the shelves. I must be dreaming. Grey Goose, Kettle One, Oh My God!!!!!!!!! B-e-l-v-e-d-e-r-e!! I can't breathe. I love California! Who cares about Asian midgets behind the wheel of SUV's when you can buy **liquor i**n the supermarket!!! I must start marinating in vodka Pronto!! Well I was going to have a little celebration for my first night in California so I might as well start now! Hey I deserve it after the day I have had. And besides, as I look down at my watch it is 830pm in New York so why not?

I run around the store like a crazy person who just escaped the asylum to get everything I need. I just grabbed the necessities for now. After I have gathered everything I need I go to the checkout and pay for my groceries, my mop and my **Vodka** bottles. Notice the way I said bottles? I say to the cashier:

You better double bag that one sweetie, as I point to the bag with the vodka in it. She smiles at me as I fondly stare into my vodka bottles. I feel like I am on a first date. I pay for my groceries and I quickly jet out of the store. I cannot wait to have a drink!

As I begin to trudge down Fountain towards home with my groceries, mop and Vodka bottles; I begin to think that maybe 3 bottles of vodka was to say a bit excessive. Well I had to buy mixers as well. Can't drink vodka straight ya know? I am thinking about this now because man does my arms hurt now. Damn mop, stupid cat, you alcoholic idiot, you know they do have take-out and delivery here in LA too ya dumb fuck. Why do you never think things through Tate? Why do you always make things so hard on yourself? I need to take a rest. Let me just lay the bags down here for a second. As I am placing the grocery bags down I lose my balance between the grass and the sidewalk. Oh Shit! **Crash!**

Oh no **not** the vodka, please not the vodka.

No. No. No. Crap…..

As I look into the grocery bag, my gummy bears are being marinated in vodka. For a quick second I was jealous of the gummy bears. Hey that shoulda been me gummies! As I am trying to salvage what is in the grocery bags, vodka is pouring onto my arms, my shirt, and shorts but alas I have saved the Kettle One bottle and the Shrimp Cup of Noodles. Belvedere is not that great anyway, I say to myself just really expensive. I wonder if there really is a difference in vodkas **anyway. OK** this minor setback I say as I precede to pick up the remaining grocery bags," the mop," my one salvaged bottle of vodka and continue on my journey back home from the supermarket. All this time I'm asking myself "What did you rent a car for Stupid?" It's parked in your parking garage, you paid for it. Do you see anyone else walking? Tate you have got to start thinking things through or LA is going to kill you. Man am I an ass or what?

As I turn the corner onto my block and about 500 feet from the apartment complex, I have this sudden panic attack. I just realized that I now smell like a vodka brewery. There is vodka literally all over me and it is starting to dry into my clothes. What am I going to do? I have to walk through the apartment lobby and it is 6 o clock in the evening, right when everyone is getting home from work. OK dumbass how are going to get out of this one? I pull my shirt up to my nose and smell it. **Woa** it is soaked to the bone in pure vodka. Should I dilute it with some club soda I just purchased? Add some cranberry? I didn't see a clothing store around here plus I cannot lug these grocery bags much longer. So what do I do? So I decide to just ditch the T shirt. I will just squeeze it dry and put it in one of the grocery bags. I am a genius! It is 85 degrees after all. Less clothes, less vodka. I squeeze dry the shirt which in turn puts **more** vodka on my hands but I still feel a little victorious. I arrive across the street from my building and wait. I wait for the coast to be clear, so that hopefully nobody will see or smell me. Finally all clear and I race into the building, just as my roommate Tommy, who moved here a week before I did is coming through the side door from the parking lot.

Hey you made it buddy he says with all smiles!

Yup I did(as I am pressing the elevator button 50 times like somehow thinking it will show up faster than if you just pressed it once).

As Tommy gets closer to me he looks at me up and down. He puts this scowl on his face and says **Dude** what happened to you? You smell like you showered in booze! Partying already? You just got here man.

I turn to Tommy and say **No Dude** I have not been drinking…yet!(sarcasm at its finest)…Wait till you hear about my day!

As we both wait for the elevator I start to explain my shitty day, the car accident, bitchy landlady and then the pure excitement of finding liquor in the super market. I then explain what progressed on my journey home and all without taking a breath of air to breathe. Wow this elevator takes a long time to come with only four floors to go up and down huh. I'm lightheaded from the vodka fumes and just then the elevator door flings opens and **gues**s who?? That's right-- the bitchy landlady. The only difference now is that she doesn't look like a fudge cycle anymore. Now instead she likes a Bomb Pop with a red face, blue top and white shorts. I wonder who dresses her. People in LA do not dress like this; I mean seriously does she not have a mirror in her house. Maybe she can borrow one from the lobby. She scowls at me:

You **must** always be wearing a shirt in this lobby young man. Do you hear me?

Yes, sorry with not a drop of energy left in me to explain as I sink my head down

What is **Thaat** smell?

Vodka. I say as sullen as possible.

Vodka she scowls?

Yes Vodka as I look at her in her mean ass eyes.

Why do you smell like Vodka?

(I was going to try and say this to her as intelligently as I could and plus I have incurred a rather large crowd of spectators now)

I was walking home from that ridiculously named supermarket "Ralphs" and I was a little overzealous (S.A.T word) with my purchases. The bags were hurting my arms and I wanted to take a quick rest before walking the rest of the way back. As I was resting the bags on the sidewalk I heard a crash and it was 2 of the vodka bottles I purchased.(as I was saying this, I knew I should not have divulged the that particular piece of information to my landlady. Especially not the amount of vodka I bought)

Are you planning a party?

No. (As I say in my head how am I going to get out of this? She looks Hispanic and maybe I can charm her with my broken Spanglish.

Lo ciento, lo ciento, Tiene muchos problemas hoy!

Te gusta beber alcohol?

(Ok Tate turn on the charm) Si. No hay fiesta en mi apartemento. Mi primer dia en California. Yo quiero celeblar con mi amigo Tommy.

(All of a sudden the scour on her face turned a lot less red)Tu hablas español muy bien.

Gracias!! (It worked Tate you are brilliant!)

Now go and take a fucking shower and put a shirt on ass!!

OK OK I say as thankful as I possibly can say it.

So Tommy drags me I into the elevator with my groceries, the mop and my one salvaged bottle of vodka. Once the elevator door closes he turns to me and says "What a way to make a first impression on the neighbor's dude." You are not even here a day and already you are causing drama. People back in New York warned me that I shouldn't live with you. I just told them that you gotta get to know him. He is a cool guy and not a head case.

I know Tommy. I am sorry man. It didn't even take a day for the entire apartment complex to find out that I am an idiot. It usually takes **at least** a week....

Nah but usually 2 or 3 days max...Tommy teases.

(We laughed as walk down the hall to our apartment. We are laughing and joking all the way down the hall.

What happened to **you** today could only **happen** to you Tate. If you tried telling these stories to anyone else they would never believe you man and call you a liar! You are a disaster and chaos follows you everywhere you go man. It is funny um **most of the time** but not always douchebag Tommy says laughing. I only wish that laughter could have lasted a BIT longer I say to myself)

As Tommy puts the key in and opens the door, we walk in and we both smell what has to be one of the worst smells in the history of mankind. This is worse than the curry cab driver and then Tommy screams:

What the **fuck** is that smell??????

Oh I forgot to mention what the mop was for............trying to keep the "funny" going

I start yammering...You see the cat was in his travel bag for 10 hours and I forget to buy kitty litter. Just as I was remembering that I needed cat litter, Spencer decided he couldn't wait any longer and he went on the kitchen floor.

And my bedroom!!! Tommy rants

Right in the middle of his bedroom floor is a hefty size cat terd...Oh shit...

Well that gift wasn't there before I left...

Why did you take him out of the bag without having kitty litter asshole? Tommy is pissed.

I forgot Tommy Sorry man I will take care of it. Bad Spencer...Bad! Where is that fucking cat anyway? I have had it.

I am now praying to God to please stop the madness!! Will this day ever end? I am running around trying to calm Tommy down and explain this will never happen again. I am scrubbing the carpet and just apologizing to Tommy over and over. Just when I think I have him, the apartment, the cat and my life in control.

Just fucking get this place and **that smell** out of this apartment now. I am going to KILL that cat Tommy roars.

OK. OK. I say everything will be fine.

All of a sudden Knock, Knock! It's the door.....damn it... what the fuck now?

I walk towards the closed door and I say Hello.

(2 valley girl sounding voices come from the other side of the door) We are your new neighbor's and we wanted to welcome you to the building.

Umm. Can you come back a little later? I am kinda in the middle with something...

The girls go: Well OOOO-KEE but there is this horrendous smell wafting from under your door and it is making us nauseous.

OK how can I handle this without becoming unglued? So I try and appease the situation by saying. I am attending to the odor as we speak and the problem should be rectified momentarily. If the problem persists please make us aware of it. I am sounding like the annoying bitch on the customer service bank phone line. For Balance Press 1, Activity Press 2.

OK Thanks bye as the girls walk back to their units and hopefully NOT to the landlady to complain.

So here I am standing in the middle of cat piss, soaked in vodka and ready to start cleaning the cat piss when guess what? I turn on the kitchen sink and yup...no water....I run to the bathroom and again no water.

That's fucking it. Tommy please can you go find out why we have no water?

There is a sign in the elevator that they were turning off the water from 6pm to 9pm for some plumbing work. What did you forget how to read also?

I didn't see it Tommy! I honestly didn't see it...

Your day keeps getting better and better Tommy snide from his bedroom. I can barely hear it over his X Box playing…but I got it.

I have to do something but I am just running in circles. Do I jump in the pool? Yes. Fuck it I can't stand the smell of dry vodka on me. Let the landlady bitch or yell at me for jumping in the pool. Again, I don't care!!! I run down the stairs, take off all my clothes, except my underwear (of course) and I jump directly into to the pool.

Jump. Splash Ahhhhhhhhhhhh this feels good. It is kind of warm but it will do. Chlorine smells better than dried vodka any day! I put my finger on my nose and submerge under the water. I spend about 5 seconds under water. I don't spend much time in the pool and I race out in fear of being yelled at… **Again**!. As usual I didn't think to bring a towel, so I am standing outside the pool in my wet underwear for all to see. The sun has already gone down too so I am freezing. I am not supposed to be shivering in sunny California. What the hell? So I eventually air dry while shivering in the dark and I race back to my apartment praying that no one will see me. Hey I am wearing boxer briefs so they can pass as a bathing suit after all. I pick up my vodka soaked clothes and I head for the elevator. Please let no one be in the elevator please God. Do you hear me now?

Well as any disaster would play out, the elevator comes and it is full of people. I can't handle anymore grief so I just run away. I run down the hall. Where the fuck are the stairs in this freakin building! My evening would have turned out so much better if I knew where the God forsaken stairs were! Wait that sign says Exit…it has to be the stairs right? I fling open the door and jump through…wait this isn't stairs I am outside again….

Click….yup that is the noise you hear when a door closes behind you. I turn around and pull and pull on the door. Shit I didn't bring any keys…what am I going to do? All these different scenarios are playing out in my head. I would rather slice my nuts off than go back through **that** lobby again… You didn't see how many people were in that elevator! I frantically bang on the door and I am begging someone to open it. As I am begging with the door, the world, God, the universe and anything else I can plead to, one of the plumbers opens the door.

Can I help you papi?

I got locked out I frantically chant

You live here?

In my head I feel like saying no dumbass I live 3 blocks away but I compose myself and say:

Yes I thought this door was the door to the stairs.

No it isn't the plumber informs me (thank you Mr. Plumber)

Can you tell me where the stairs are?

He points and says there… where it says stairs…

I say thank you and I start running to the stairs. Tommy is right. I can't fucking read. Can I be any more of a moron? I so need a drink.

I find the stairs and my apartment quickly. Thank God there was no one in the hallway. I reach for the door and it is locked. I drop my vodka soaked clothes on the floor and just start banging on the door. Tommy I am going to kill you, open the door…open the door…open the fucking door! I hear Tommy laughing and he opens the door.

Just messing with you man but if you don't get that cat pissed cleaned up in the next 2 minutes I am going to throw **that cat off the balcony!** I look down and Spenny cat has reappeared!

I will…I will….

I run to my room, rummage through my suitcase and put new clothes on. Finally I feel somewhat human with new clothes on back in the apartment. On my way up to the apartment I did get a brilliant idea…I grab a bucket from under the sink, run back down to the pool and fill it up with pool water. Hey chlorine water still smells a lot better than cat piss that is for sure! To be expected on my way down to the pool, at the pool and on my way up I did not see a single person. You know why? Because I was fully clothed and I didn't smell like vodka…that's why there was no one in the halls… I get upstairs I dump some soft scrub into the bucket and I start to clean the cat piss up.

As I am scrubbing urine off the kitchen floor, I start to think about my day. What a day it has been huh! It has just been one disaster after another, after another today. I am exhausted. I think today has been one of the hardest days of my life. It has been like a self-inflicted gunshot to my leg and my ego. This would never happen to a "normal' person. Just as I start to throw myself a pity party Tommy comes out from his bedroom:

It is cocktail hour buddy! Where is the booze dude?

I point to the bag, which is still on the floor next to kitchen.

Tommy grabs the Kettle One bottle, picks it up and starts talking to the vodka bottle: All this trouble for you, you better be worth it.

Shut up Tommy and make me a healthy vodka and soda already.

Tommy steps over me as I wrap up cleaning the kitchen floor and goes to the sink. I hear the water running before he can even open his mouth.

Water is back on, Tommy sings

Of course it is, as I stand up and throw my hands in the air…of course it is…

I head to my bathroom to wash my hands and splash some non-chlorine water on my face. Take a deep breath Tate…it has to get better. This has all been a test. You have had more challenges today that some people have in a life time. It's over and you lived through it. As I stare at my rather handsome face in the mirror and I think back at the entire day. The rain, Danny, overzealous TSA security, Darlene, Ms. Suzy Bitchshine, Darlene, non-speaking Asian lady driving an SUV, my new landlady and vodka…Wait speaking of vodka…. Tommy where is my drink?

In the kitchen Tate…I am not your fucking maid dude Tommy yells but if I little sarcasm in his inflection. Get out of the mirror and come drink with me.

Coming…..

I grab my drink from the kitchen and head to his room. I plop into a chair that we bought together, but Tommy has decided to move into his room.

Nice chair I say as dick headish as possible.

Don't start Tate it is just here till we get more furniture for the living room. Cheers (As Tommy lifts up his glass)

Cheers! (clink, clink)

What a day Tommy says as we clink.

I don't want to even talk about it anymore but I guess it is a story I will be able to tell for the rest of my life huh?

I guess so Tate but that landlady seriously will hate you for the rest of her life, you know that right?

Nah…I spoke Spanish to her she will love me. It might take me a little time but I will get her to fall in love with me….

Are you sure about that Tate?

Yup I will turn on the Tate charm and she will be eating out of my hands in a week. Like a kitten drinking warm milk.

Are you sure about that?

Sure as I can be I boast with utter confidence.

Well good luck with that Tommy growls as he takes another gulp out of this extremely healthy vodka and soda.

Why did you say it like that Tommy?

He looks up at me and stares at me for about 20 seconds. He looks at me like I couldn't possibly be any more of an idiot than I was. You really do not know why I said good luck to that. You seriously do not know?

No I say as I look down…..

Because she is a **dike** dude!

I knew it I exclaim!!!

Yeah you knew it Tate. Get out of my room. You haven't even been here 4 hours yet and I already have a headache from you. Go unpack, take a real shower and remember I don't want that fucking cat in my bedroom.

We both look down and Spencer is sitting there staring at us. I pick up the cat, my drink and off I go into my bedroom. Once I put the cat in my room I head back to the kitchen. I refresh my drink and I start to head back into my room. Wait a minute….I turn around go back to the kitchen and grab the half full vodka bottle….Fuck Tommy go get your own vodka you prick. What an asshole. As soon as I become a series regular on a sitcom I am so outta here. Hopefully within a few months, cause I am fucking hysterical.

Well I think I fully unpacked. I think I made a make shift bed on the floor. I think I took a shower but the one thing I do know is….I finished the vodka bottle…all by myself.

Fuck…why didn't I buy aspirin?

Chapter 3

Getting around LA

So coming from New York City where you don't need a car to then moving to Los Angeles where you must have a car was definitely an adjustment. I kept my rental car for about a week but I was very timid driving after my collision on the 405 with the Asian aggravation. I barely used it and when I did I would get so lost. I memorized a grid in my head that started with Hollywood Blvd and ended with Melrose. I tried to use the cross streets of La Cienega and La Brea but I would get thrown off by Crescent heights and Fairfax. I realized that the Thomas Guide that was in the car was actually a map. Every confusing one at that but I realized my biggest problem was the ocean was on the wrong side. For 26 years the ocean was always on the east but here in California it is on the west. I would think I was driving to the beach and I would end up downtown Los Angeles. I decided that for the time being I would return the rental car just take cabs. If I didn't have to worry about crashing into people and just read the signs I would learn my way around much quicker. There are also bunches of buses that go right by my house all day and night. I had never taken a bus before but it couldn't be that bad could it? I was kind of proud of myself upon returning my rental car to the airport. Only slammed on my brakes 6 times, just 4 illegal U-turns and my road rage was at a bare minimum. I returned the rental car to the airport rental office without incident. I asked the receptionist at Avis where the bus stops was. She gave me very thorough yet confusing directions. I thanked her and I actually figured out where the bus stop was. I waited at the bus stop for the bus for about 10 minutes but I didn't mind because it was a beautiful sunny afternoon in California!

The bus arrived and I got on the bus. As I stepped on there was this vending like machine next to the bus driver. After reading the machine I figured it was a way to pay for your bus ticket. I am not going to lie; I did think it was a vending machine because the bus driver was really fat. My observations are not always up to par but I still do it anyway. I didn't know that you had to have exact change for the bus. The bus driver does not make change. It made sense, he was there to drive the bus, not eat out of a vending machine and not be a cashier either. I actually had the exact change, so I proceeded to put it in the slot and then went to find a seat in the middle of the bus.

Every walk of life was on this bus. People listening to iPods, kids wailing (always a favorite noise of mine...not,) people reading, various arguments about everything from who is wearing the better "kicks," to who knows more about politics. This bus is a zoo. It is worse than the playground at a mental health facility. It is seriously an after school special gone terribly wrong. Please get me home in one piece...please....pretty please?

Well I hoped way too soon because a fight has just broken out and it is getting uglier by the second. Out comes a knife and the other one has an umbrella. I am thinking...umbrella? What the hell is he going to do with a damn umbrella? Well one of the guys is hitting the other over the head with an umbrella while the other is thrashing the knife towards the umbrella guy. All I am thinking about is please don't stab me. I don't want to die....especially on a bus!!! If I do get stabbed, please not the face, I want an open casket. What would people back home think? Tate went all the way to LA and got stabbed on a bus. He just should have stayed in New York City, got drunk and passed out on the subway. At least it would have been more economical. Now his poor Mother has to pay for a plane ticket to ship his dead ass back to New

York, for a proper funeral. What a shame and what a waste of money. What was he living in Los Angeles for like a minute? I finally get out of my "what if" self-pity haze in time to witness what just happened. The knife has made contact into umbrella man's stomach. Everyone gasps and starts screaming and yelling. We were all waiting for the guy to start screaming but nothing… it looked like he didn't even feel it!

The guy was higher than a jumper on a plane. He was flying solo on American Crack Airline. No turbulence for him, just a smooth flight, with high as a kite altitude. I thought for a minute that he was a junkie who wanted and needed some attention. A young dumb ass junkie…He just looked like a lost soul and I started to feel sorry for him. His only defense was an umbrella. The guy with the knife jumped off the bus and took off. I wonder if this was a drug deal gone wrong….growing up in New York City you would think I would know these things but at this very moment I am fucking clueless! I was kind of relieved because an umbrella couldn't hurt me that much…could it? Next thing I hear is:

This is gonna be some shit now…gonna be some shit now. Dag gone it my shift was almost fucking over. The bus driver is yelling now…

I look out the window of the bus. No knife wielding psycho in sight. Now I am in a panic, my heart is racing a mile a minute but I am feeling kind of bold. I see a sign on the street that says Inglewood and I know that in New Jersey, Inglewood is a beautiful neighborhood. So I yell:

Can we just get off the bus? As macho and confident as I possibly can in this current situation.

This short Mexican guy leans over and whispers: "Papi, you don't want to get off the bus in this neighborhood; you're safer on the bus."

So I meekly say OK and thanks.

About 15 minutes go by and the police finally show up. Passengers on the bus now are getting very vocal and agitated. People are talking to each other, on cell phones and yelling at the bus driver. The police enter the bus and talk to the bus driver. After the bus driver gives him blows by blow of the incident they make us all get off the bus because they have to inspect the scene. The ambulance comes and takes the Crack head junkie "umbrella man" to the hospital. Thank God the ambulance came when it did because the "umbrella man" was bleeding more and more and if he woke up, he would probably try and kill all of us with his umbrella.

The two officers depart the bus and start asking people questions. I am trying to avoid the police but I am desperately looking for the news vans. Eye Witness news has to be here any second and I want to be on camera. You never know who is watching….especially in LA. Hey I do what I gotta do.

Well to my shock and dismay the news vans never showed up and they also have to take the bus out of commission for evidence. The police tell us that a replacement bus will be here shortly.

An hour and a half shortly later…. a bus does finally arrive. Many drove past us while we waited but none of the buses would stop. It was like we were contaminated with some deadly virus or something. Once the bus finally stops and opens the doors we all get on the bus one by one. After what feels like an eternity of time, we begin to move. Ahh finally I say out loud. I got a few smiles from my fellow passengers who I am sure are also relieved that we are moving again. Once we get to La Cienega Blvd, the bus starts to turn right but guess what? Hollywood is left. I sit there in disbelief for a second. Wait where is the beach? North, South, East, West….shit I should have paid more attention in school. Maybe I am wrong….No, no, no….shit!

My mind is racing: OK Tate get a grip, keep it together and go ask the bus driver how to get home. So I go up to him weaving from bus rail to bus rail. I get to the bus driver and I say I need to get to Hollywood.

Well you're on the wrong bus!! The bus driver says

I'm thinking in my head, really fuckwad you must have been valedictorian of your high school class.

I realize that and say. What can I do to get to Hollywood? The bus driver snaps this ticket off a pad and hands it to me. He tells me: take this transfer and wait on the other side of the street over there.

Thank you sir I say as politely as I can.

Be careful son. You're not in Hollywood anymore. Stay at the bus stop. The next bus will be here in less than 5 minutes.

I exited the bus and smile to him and I can see he has a worried face. Yet I am clueless at this point as to why he does.

So now it's like 845 at night and pitch black out. I walk across the street and I am on the corner of Century Blvd and La Cienega. I am waiting patiently for a bus to take me to Hollywood. I know I am not in a very nice area when low riders keep slowing down at the bus stop, to see who this fucking crazy white boy is waiting for the bus. I know I am in even more trouble when I look into their cars and all I can see are eyeballs looking at me through tinted windows. When I was growing up in Brooklyn you would know where to go and not to go at certain times. This definitely was a place I would not go. Please nobody shoot me. I probably deserve to be though. I never think things through. Who else would ever get themselves in a situation like this? I feel so dumb, like I am the red circle on an archery board right about now. Just as I am about to take a crap in my pants I see a bus

Oh my God here comes a bus. Please by my bus…..please! The bus stops and just as the door opens the bus driver Yells; Are you crazy! What in hells earth are you doing out here after dark? They will rob you, hurt you really bad and someone would put a shank in your heart, just because of the color of your skin. Come on now get in here.

I handed the bus driver my transfer ticket and I mumbled that I got on the wrong bus.

The bus was rather empty so I sat in the seat right behind the bus driver. Come to think of it I am in the same seat as the knife wielding crazy man that stabbed cracked out umbrella man. The only difference was it was a different bus and a different driver but this one was just as slow as the last bus. I looked around the bus and the few people that were on this bus, looked like they were also escaping from a mental hospital.

I am sitting there thinking about what went down today. I hate the bus, I really do. It doesn't seem like any form of transportation is going to be easier here. 45 minutes later I realize the bus is on the corner of Santa Monica Blvd and La Cienega. I know how to get home from here! I ring the bell as I standup and take a few steps to the front door of the bus.

The bus driver lady says to me:

Next time you need to score drugs do it during the day ya dumbass, someone could have killed you out there tonight.

I don't even try and explain, I just say thanks as meekly as I can and I exit the bus.

As I am walking back to my apartment I start to reflect on my time here in Los Angeles so far. I have only been here for a week and I am over LA. I am starting to miss New York. These things never happened to me in New York, or Washington DC or even Miami for that matter! Did I make a mistake moving here? Test after test and trial after tribulation since I have moved here. It has only been a week but I am exhausted. Things have to turn around for me here right? They just have to! I have waited my whole life to live in Los Angeles and I am not about to give up now. Why so many tests? I take a deep breath and I say out loud "They will have to shoot me dead before I give up on you LA." That doesn't kill me will only make me stronger. I should feel like the incredible hulk by now then…Yup you heard me, just a week here. What is next? Good things…positive things…No more negativity….I wonder if my Mother has put a curse on me. I think for a second and then I say….nah

I walk about 20 blocks to my apartment replaying all the events of the day. Everything from the umbrella man getting stabbed, to could I really have been killed waiting for the bus? Every day seems to be a new challenge for me here in LA. I am not going to call them challenges anymore….they are now just new adventures. Yes new exciting adventures. I like that. Wow is that my block already? It is!

I walk up to my apartment. I smile and proceed to put the key in the door. I walk directly to the elevator and it is waiting for me. I get in and push my floor. I take a deep sigh. The day is over and lessons have been learned. Usually I have to smash my head into a brick wall to learn a lesson. I would call today a brick wall huh.

As I open the door to my apartment my roommate Thomas is watching TV. He turns to me from his nose in the remote:

Where have you been all day Tate?

Long story but I am glad to be alive, I cheer.

Alive? What now drama queen…what now? Thomas sighs.

Don't ask…don't ask… but tomorrow you are taking me to buy a fucking car!!!"

I can't

You can't what? I look at him with an angrily stare.

I am kidding bud…kidding. Relax man; don't get your knickers all up in a knot. The first week I was here was an utter mess too.

I get it Thomas but I am starting to feel that I walk from one round of chaos right into the next awaiting round of chaos. Like a taxi line….When one chaos cannot get you to a certain destination, don't worry because the next chaos definitely can. Unfortunately the destination always seems to be the same, Big fat Mess-ville!

I bought some vodka, go make yourself a drink Tate.

My eyes just lit up…ahh vodka can always make any day better!

Chapter 4

The Gym

One of the social rules of LA is that you must belong to a gym. I was in relatively good shape but the exercise and physical fitness in LA is almost at the need for perfection. Just walk down Robertson Blvd and you feel like all these people just came from the plastic surgeon's office. Ripped and fit, looking amazing and flawless. They don't always look human but they have less than 3% body fat....who could ask for anything more!

I know I needed to get myself in better shape. You see in New York you can hide your weight for almost 9 months behind sweaters, coats and baggy clothes, but here in LA maybe you can hide it for 3 months. I needed to get myself on a great exercise regime...especially if I wanted to get laid.

I was trying to swim in the apartment complex's pool, as much as I could but I needed to step it up and join a gym. The pool was kinda full with screaming kids and chatterbox Moms one upping each other. Little Johnny learned to walk in 5 months one Mother would boast. Another one would chime in well My Suzy learned in four. It was ad nauseous after a while. There were so many gyms in town the decision was going to be based on finance, location and how comfortable I would be at the gym. I had many options so I figured I would start with Gold's Gym. Gold's Gym was offering a 30 day free membership and there was one close to the apartment, so I decided to begin there. I called

Gold's to schedule an appointment and I spoke to a woman named Shelley. Shelley was the membership director. She told me to come in right away and when I arrive to ask for her. I said OK.

So when can I expect you? She asks.

(I am thinking in my head pushy bitch "When I feel like it")

So I go Umm possibly today or tomorrow.

Can you be a little more exact? (I already don't like her)

(Again in my head I am saying -fuck off bitch. I will get there when I get there. You would think we were scheduling open heart surgery)

Tomorrow mid-day is good for me. I finally say..

1 pm works for me. See you then. **Click.**

See ya then. Wow she already hung up on me already?

I hang up the phone thinking to myself is there anything in this town that isn't difficult to do? I pondered it for a few minutes but it became exhausting to figure out.

All night long I keep thinking about the gym and my body. I have already psyched myself out about it already. Did I really need to join a gym? I could just keep up with the swimming and jogging. There was a small fitness center in the apartment complex I could utilize more. For the first time in my life an extreme amount of insecurities are beginning to surface. Am I fit enough to join a gym? Are other guys going to laugh at me or judge me? Oh shit is that a pimple coming in on my face? I need to go to the tanning salon before

I go to the gym. I feel pasty. Are the guys all going to look like "gorillas on the juice?" For those of you that do not know what Gorilla's on the juice is, it is when guys use steroids and look like a human gorilla. It is disgusting and they usually have pimples all down their back and God Knows where else. I know I drink alcohol but I do actually care if my liver shuts down by 32. Needless to say that I tossed and turned all night long, stressing about going to the damn gym. Ugh.

The next day I get up, go tanning, get a haircut and then go home to shower. I am trying to look as much like what I perceive to be an LA look. I must have tried on 15 different T shirts before I was ready to depart on my new gym adventure. I think I look cute though so it was all worth it! I am still so nervous that I think I am going to throw up.

I arrive at the gym at 12:45pm and I park my car right by the front entrance to Gold's Gym. I watch the people who are coming in and out of the gym, and that is when the panic really sets in. The guys look like they all are coming from a GQ photo shoot and the girls look like Hawaiian Tropics models. I can't do this, I just can't. I panic and start the car up, put it in reverse and start to backup out of the spot. I start to drive up the street and all of a sudden I think to myself, what a chicken shit you are Tate! Well I decide to have a battle within my head – with myself or inner chicken shit: I seem to do this rather often, just so you are aware of it early on.

I can't do it.

Yes you can.

What if they make fun of me?

What if they do?

As I find myself saying that, I actually say to myself…so what?

My mind is racing faster than the initial call I made to my Dad when I crashed his brand new car into a tree because I couldn't find a good song on the radio…So I start talking out loud to myself in the car. Which is always the smartest move while driving right?? Are you that much of a little baby that you are afraid of an LA gym? Did you pack your balls and send them back to New York? Turn the car around or you better Fed Ex your balls back to your Mother. LA is not going to change me into a self-obsessed, insecure mess that is constantly chasing ones tail and looking for constant approval from people around me. Get in that damn gym. If you are this insecure now what are you going to do when you actually start auditioning you idiot. As the left side of my brain is continuing to battle with my right side I finally say **Enough!**

I return to the gym and find a parking space further away from the entrance this time. I walk to the front desk, take a deep breath and I ask for Shelley.

Less than a minute goes by and here comes this tiny lady about 4'11" with these **huge** breasts walking towards me.

Tate? She motions to me.

Yes!

Welcome to Gold's Gym. Come on back and let's fill out some paperwork.

Paper work?? What paperwork? I say to myself still wondering how this lady is not tipping over while walking with those immense melon balls on her chest. I sometimes have a tendency to stare at things that confuse me by the way.

We get back to her desk and she asks me to have a seat. She is now asking me the small chit chat stuff.

Where are you from?

New York. I say.

I love New York. How long have you been in LA?

3 weeks.

How's it going?

Oh it's going….. Where it is going I have not got the foggiest idea.(I say as sarcastic as ever but honestly it is true)

Well let's get started. Do you want to pay upfront or monthly?

Huh? I have this coupon for a free 30 day pass. As I hand it to her with fear that I read it wrong or it is expired.

Shelley examines the coupon and says:

That's right she says you get the first 30 days free when you sign up for a 2 years contract.

What? Let me see the coupon as I reach and grab it from her. It doesn't say anything about any contract on it.

So now with this condescending voice Shelley goes:

You are getting the first 30 days free when you sign up for 2 years. That's what this coupon reflects.

Before I could even process what had just happened.

Will you be paying in full or monthly?

She is shoving a contract at me and has graciously highlighted where I need to sign.

Now I have had enough. So I growl…Lady you are shoving a contract down my throat and I haven't even seen the damn gym yet (with my defining NY accent.)

All of a sudden she has this look of bewilderment in her face. She asks?

Nobody gave you a tour?

Nope.

Oh my God. I am so sorry she says and hops up like a rabbit that just gave birth to 14 little bunnies. It's kind of the only way I can describe this little woman with these enormous breasts. I tried… can't be funny all the time! Maybe for the movie I will come up with something wittier

As she begins to show me around the gym I see some of the most beautiful and stunning people my eyes have ever seen. These people's bodies are incredible and within a few moments I do in fact, yup have a hard on. I am a little embarrassed but after about 10 painful minutes of listening to this bitchy twig yammer on and on about the gym and the endless possibilities I ask her:

Can I just work out and see how I like the gym? Do you think I could possibility check things out on my own? Sure she shrieks and I am sure she is over the moon, to get rid of my ogre self.

I need your California driver's license. (she did ask politely I will give her that)

I don't have a California driver's license yet I just moved here less than a month ago from new York! I told you this on the phone. (I say this extremely snippy to "My New Annoyance of the Day" Shelley or as some of you call her "The Membership Director.")

I will make an exception for you Tate but please come see me after your workout.

OK I say rather convincingly to Shelley and off I go to start my "Gym Bunny" journey in Gold's Gym in Los Angeles. This is going to be fun...I think...I hope... OK I am seriously praying....Please do not do anything stupid Tate.....

I go and purchase a Big Bottle of water and off to the locker room I go. As soon as I walk into the locker room my nerves have already set in and I feel like I am going to puke. First of all there are naked guys everywhere or half naked guys. People are aimlessly walking around the locker room. I will soon come to learn that while they are indeed walking around the locker room they are in fact cruising each other. Cruising is defined as 2 or more people checking out one other's physicality's, flirting and trying to decide whether or not sex is an option. I think that sums that up but it's basically the same as what I have done in bars and clubs for years. I start to think about it and it's a genius idea in a way. First of all you don't have to buy anyone a drink or sit through a boring dinner. I hate small talk as it is, you know the "Where are you from?" or "What do you do?" Plus you get to see what their bodies look like before...Ding Ding Ding! Let me tell you the worst thing in the world is to buy some one drinks or dinner and you get them into bed and they are "A Princess Lay-there" or worse...**Fat**! Man this is motivation enough for me to go to the gym – I have the possibility to have sex here at the gym. I am so **loving** this gym stuff even if my body is not ready to be shirtless! I find a locker in the corner, throw my stuff inside, lock it up and take one more look around. There is nothing sexier than a man with 6 pack abs I want 6 pack abs.

So off to the treadmill I go….Wait a minute! What the fuck? What is going on over there? Is that guy seriously blow drying his balls in the locker room?? **Ouch** that has got the burn the hell out of them!

I get on a treadmill between a rugged handsome guy in his mid-thirties and a pretty woman in her late twenties. I stare and squint to see the keyboard on the treadmill (because I couldn't possibly wear my glasses to the gym…. God forbid! I finally find the quick start button on the treadmill and off the belt goes. Soon I begin to feel more comfortable walking and I slowly begin to move the keypad to a much faster pace. All this time while I am walking and then eventually jogging, I am people watching and I think I just saw Angela Bassett walk by.

After about 15 minutes on the treadmill I begin to panic. All of a sudden I feel it coming on and there is **nothing** I can do about it because I am seriously going to fart. Damn diet pills I started taking them 2 weeks ago but what the fuck am I going to do now? I cannot hold it much longer and I certainly will not make it to the bathroom… It's too late now because the gas has passed my ass on the treadmill….Shit what am I going to do? At least it was silent and I have about 10 seconds to figure out what to do before it will become deadly to the people around me. Do I run and never look back? Do I do nothing and pretend I don't smell anything? Then in the brink of a second I have an idea. As the smell begins to loom I turn to the guy on my right and dramatically smell him. I then make this face of disgust and say **Yuck**!!!(Out loud.) I then turn to my left and do the exact same thing but even more dramatically. I then slam the Stop button on my treadmill and announce "**Someone farted**!! That's disgusting! I am leaving! Seriously fucking gross I yell. I then grab my water bottle, my towel and I march off the treadmill and proceed to get on another treadmill about 2 rows away. I look back after I am settled onto my new treadmill and the rugged handsome guy and the pretty woman are glaring at each other in disgust. They are both thinking the other one is an obnoxious pig who should be living in a pen but if they only knew it was me.

God that was genius wasn't it? A little bit suspect huh? Maybe? Maybe not? Ahh who cares what is done is done. I just hope that they don't know each other and figure out that it was me….Hey I can't see Angela Bassett anymore, there is this stupid beam blocking me now…Damn it!

I stay on my new treadmill for an additional twelve minutes gas free but now I am out of water. I don't want to pay another 2 bucks for water so I just figure I will fill my empty bottle up at the water fountain. I hop off the treadmill and search for the water fountain. I know I saw one here somewhere. I finally spot it and off to the fountain. As I am filling up my water bottle I hear this obnoxious loud bitchy screech behind me and next thing I hear is "Why don't I just give you like a dollar and go buy yourself another bottle of water?

Huh? (no she did NOT just say that to me?)

So I whirl around and say: "Why don't you take that dollar and go buy yourself a box of tic tacs?"

Your breath stinks you nasty bitch! (now I am waiting for her to hit me) Why would you say something that obnoxious to me I snarl?

She goes "Just get out of my way asshole and brushes me out of her way….

I couldn't believe it…There were actually people that go out of their way to be rude and nasty. Just shake it off Tate, she is a bitch.

Once I have filled up my water bottle, I proceed to go upstairs and work some of the machines. The gym floor was very bright but clean and VERY crowded. It was a Little overwhelming hearing the weights clank, people grunting and blasting music. I cannot really concentrate in the middle of the gym so I figure I would just find a machine in the corner, where no one else was working out. There was this contraption that apparently worked your arms and chest at the same time and it looked appealing. I figured I would start here first. I started to work out when this massive guy walks up to me and say's

Can I work in?

I say to myself… what does work in mean?

Um work in? Sorry first day here at the gym I say meekly waiting to get verbally trampled again.

A-l-t-e-r-n-a-t-e using the machine he snaps.

Oh oh sure…sorry I go but I was a little confused because he sounded so feminine almost like an obnoxious sorority girl.

As I am watching this guy work out he has the most amazing muscles and I cannot help but stare. I decide to step out of my comfort zone and ask him how he got that body. So I turn to him and say:

Your body is amazing! How often do you work out?

He says thanks and I work out about 4 hours a day.

I am in shock so I repeat to him 4 hours a day **every day?**

Yup….everyday as he smirks at me.

Wow good for you. It really has paid off buddy.

I'm Chase as he reaches out his hand to shake hands. He doesn't sound **that** feminine Tate

I am Tate as I now nervously shake his hand back. (Look at the size of those massive hands).

Welcome to Gold's Gym and I hope to see you around more often Chase says as he starts to walk away.

I smile and stare as he walks away. I start to think 4 hours? A day? Every day? Who has **that** much time to spend in a gym? I am a little discouraged but I just stare at Chase until he turns the corner and is out of my view. Wow what a body!

Well I continue to do a decent workout but I just don't know if I have the commitment for the gym. I make a valiant attempt to finish up my workout but I cannot get over how the gym is the second home to many of the people here. As I am eaves dropping or listening in on other peoples conversations I soon learn that the gym is like a family to many of these people. It is a friend club in a way and very Clicky. As I am walking back to the locker room, I notice Chase is also walking back to the locker room and I just smile. Well if there was a coincidence or luck involved we would win something. Our lockers were right next to each other's. We just laughed and Chase summons for me to go to the locker first.

So how long have you been in LA Tate?

About 3 weeks I go.

From where? Chase starts interviewing.

New York City. Actually Brooklyn born and raised I say proudly.

I would have thought Boston Chase says flirting.

No it is Brooklyn but I am just educated I say flirting a little back.

Well you look like Ben Affleck, Chase states…

Thank you people have told me that before I say and I am probably a little red in the face. Probably? You most definitely are Tate!

I think Ben Affleck is cute, Chase says.

Thanks…..I don't really know what to say but I am thinking I am not going to have sex with Chase, in the bathroom, at my first day working out at Gold's Gym.

Would you like to go out this weekend? Chase asks me dead on. I can show you around Los Angeles a little bit.

Um sure I say but I am thinking in my head, I would rather have you come over to my apartment and let me do an expedition on that amazing body.

Here is my number call me as Chase hands me his card with his number on it. Of course his business card also has his face and body on it. I guess I would too if I looked like that.

OK I will call I say. As I am getting ready to leave Chase has been undressing to shower at the gym. I was to chicken shit for that. Just the thought of me taking my shirt off at the gym makes my want to throw up. I guess baby steps for me with the gym. I pack all my stuff back into me bag and turn to leave. As I am getting ready to leave I look at Chase and say goodbye. As I am saying goodbye he drops his underwear to the ground and says:

I hope so…

I look down, I couldn't help it and his dick is perfect. Is there anything on this guy that is not perfect? I instantly get a hard on, turn red and run out of the locker room. Did this just really happen to me? I hope it **really** did!

I am racing to the door and all I want to do is get the hell out of that gym. I guess I talk a "Big Game" but actually I am probably a fucking prude after all. I go straight out the door and head to my car. Where did I park again? I start thinking about Chase, his body and what is down below. I come to the conclusion in my head that I would like to have sex with Chase on one condition. I would have sex with Chase if he didn't talk…**that** voice is so annoying….I wonder if he talks to his father that way? Mine would beat the shit out of me…..I think…Come to think of it, I am not really sure how my Dad would react but I know it wouldn't be good.

Ring…Ring…

Oh crap that is my cell phone that I stuffed inside my gym bag. I put the bag down and I rummage through the bag trying to find my cell phone.. I finally find it and I am frantically trying to open it before it goes to voice mail.

Hello?

Tate it is Shelley. I just saw you leave the gym without stopping by to see me. I am **very** disappointed in you. You gave me your word that you would come and see me when you finished your workout and I trusted you. You need to come back to the gym and discuss this with me. Do you enjoy wasting people's valuable time?

In my head I am like, **What**? Are you fucking kidding me? Do I look like an 8 year old who just got grounded for not playing nice in the school yard? Ok that is it….gloves are off with this bitch!

Click…yup I just hung up on her.

I really didn't like her anyway………

Ring…Ring…

Holy shit the crazy gym bitch is calling me back. What do I do? Do I answer it? Let it go to voicemail? Be a man Tate and answer the phone.

Hello I say.

Did you just hang up on me Shelley shouts?

Yes I did….

Why that is so rude Shelley snarls.

Because you were yelling at me like I was an 8 year old lady, I can snarl back too!

Well you were acting like an 8 year old. You told me you were going to come and see me when you finished your workout and you didn't. Doesn't your word mean anything to you? Does the word integrity mean anything to you Tate?

Integrity…. It is a fucking gym. It was my first time back in a gym in a long time. I was a tad bit overwhelmed today. Can you give me a break already? Shit what is wrong with you people, why does everything have to be so much drama?

Are you coming back to the gym she asks me but much more calmly this time?

No I am not. Not after that verbal attack you just gave me. I just wanted to try out the gym and see if it is me.

Well why don't you come back to the gym and we can discuss various options that we have to offer here at Gold's Gym... I am sorry I was a little stern with you but I do not like people that are not straight with me.

I am thinking in my head...Straight??? Do not go there with her Tate, she does have your address after all and she is crazy.

I do not want to come back and I do not want to join your gym I state to Shelley. I thought I would have 30 days to try out the gym, to see if it was something that I was comfortable going to. Clearly you made it uncomfortable after one visit.

So you wanted 30 days free right?

Yes!

I gave you 30 days free Shelley says, very sweetly now.

Only if I sign a contract for 2 years and I am not very comfortable signing a 2 year contract when I have only lived here for 3 weeks.

How do you expect us to stay in business if we gave everyone free 30 day memberships?

Than you shouldn't pass out Free 30 day Membership cards, that say anything about a 2 year contract? Nowhere on this card does it say Free 30 Days with a 2 year contract. It doesn't say that anywhere on this card Shelley,

It is the industry standard Tate. So let me ask you: are you going to come back into the club and discuss membership with me?

No (now I am pissed)

Yet you told me you were going to stop by and see me when you finished your workout today, am I correct?

Yes

But you didn't stop by Shelley quizzes me?

No…

So you are not a man of your word are you Tatey? So basically you are a liar who likes to waste people's time aren't you Tate?

First of all it is Tate and second of all you are a nasty bitch. Who the hell do you think you are talking to me like this?

Shelley Schwartz Gold's Membership Director ….. You know what Tate? (saying it really obnoxiously)You are an asshole and a liar. Why don't you just move back to New York, with the rest of the assholes because clearly you do not belong in Los Angeles…**click.**

Did that bitch just hang up on me? Holy hell what am I doing wrong? No matter what I do or say it blows up in my face. These people are aliens here. I don't know what to do anymore. So let's see I spent over $60 bucks between a haircut and a tan today, I went to a gym I clearly wasn't ready for, I got propositioned in the locker room. I got emasculated by Shelley, the insane membership director of the gym. Well at least I liked the proposition part and his body was amazing, but then again there is that voice. Hmm not sure, gotta think on this one. I guess I should just chalk it up to experience, cut my losses and just find another gym. Do I have the strength to go to another gym tomorrow? Sure I am an old pro now. I look down at my watch and it is only 4:30pm. Should I drive around and see what other gyms are in the area or should I just go home and hide? Who are you kidding Tate? You tanned, got your haircut and worked out today; there is no way you are going home. I think to myself 30 minutes to happy hour woo hoo!

I joined Crunch a week later and I kind of like it there. I think Crunch is more me and just for the record, I never did call Chase. I just couldn't do it. It would have been like having sex with a masculine debutante or something like it and I already did that in college. I didn't enjoy it then and I most certainly would not enjoy it now. I wonder if he works out so much, to not get beat up. I hope not because I do not believe or condone in any sort of physical violence, but where I grew up, if he talked like that, the guys and even some of the girls would have kicked the crap out of him.

He was nice though….he did say I looked like Ben Affleck after all. Now where did I put his phone number again?

He was nice though….he did say I looked like Ben Affleck after all. Now where did I put his phone number again?

That body was incredible……

Chapter 5

Working and Adjusting to LA

I have now lived here in LA for a month and I feel like a seasoned Californian. I have the apartment, car, gym membership but money is running out and I have to find a job and quickly. Money and opportunities are not throwing themselves at me so I need to venture out and find a waiter job. WOW what a big difference than NYC where you can find a restaurant job as far as you can throw a nickel but not here in LA. Restaurant jobs are hard to come by. Everyone here is an actor or in the entertainment industry and **everyone** wants to find a good waiter or bartending job, so that they can audition during the day. Everyone wants to book jobs and go to "acting class." It is not always a reality and I am learning that this is something, that they do not teach you in NYU film school. They don't teach things like how to pay your rent while looking for your next acting gig. Also where the fuck are all the NYU alumni's that NYU promised me, that would help me when I ventured to the West Coast to start my career?? Where I ask you?? OK I will tell you...

Taking all the fucking waitering jobs in LA that's where the Fuck they are!!!!! Ahh that great Alumni Association every college graduate learns to love and soon comes to realize that they are full of shit! NYU should teach us less about Uta Hagen, Checkoff and Strasberg, and more about how to survive the real acting world. I'm not bitter about this but just unemployed.

I loved NYU but I don't think they fully prepared me for the Los Angeles acting world. Why didn't I apply to UCLA again?

Wow my Dad would so be proud of the 200 Grand he spent on my Higher Education at NYU right about now. Why you ask??

I am so excited **I found a job!!!!!!!!!!!!** Waiting tables at the newest, hottest restaurant on the Sunset Strip! It is the brand new hot spot in West Hollywood. I have a flashback to my Mom's old National Enquirer and realize that that is the place, where my favorite gang from Beverly Hills 90210 used to hang out. I feel so cool now! I fill out my application, aced my interview and I am now off to get my uniform somewhere on "Sepulveda Blvd." I finally find my uniform, buy it and now I am reveling in the fact that I have my first job in LA!! I am excited and nervous because I am going to be meeting a whole bunch of new people. So far most of the people I have met have not been that gracious to me. Well I am going to think positive and for the first time in a month, I feel things are going to work out. I am going to get a good night sleep tonight.

The next day I report to training, the day before the restaurant opens. I arrive at orientation at my new job and there must have been 40 people there. I say to myself that this must be a HUGE place and that I am at the "it" place to work. If I had a tail between my legs it would have been wagging now. I look around and I notice that everyone is gorgeous. Some of these girls have to be models and the guys…some of them just **have** to be gay right? There is one guy that is so visibly stunning and I just have to be friends with him. Remember good looking people are friends with other good looking people. It is like a law or something. Before I can make it to the other side of the room, one of the models has already set her sights on the gorgeous model. Damn…bitch, you move quickly!

Before I can plot my next move, a tall blond woman comes in and says that the orientation will start in 5 minutes and to have a seat. Instantly when I saw her she reminded me of Big Bird. Within seconds I was humming the opening segment to Sesame Street. Come and play, everything is A-OK. I start to notice people looking at me strangely. It takes a minute for me to realize why but I quickly realize that I am indeed humming Sesame Street out loud… Yikes what a way to make a first impression huh? I can just see it now…aren't you the dude who was humming Sesame Street before orientation? Yikes, snap out of it Tate, you can back pedal and fix this, just smile and breathe. The orientation starts off great with some guy congratulating us on after carefully selecting over 400 applicants, we were the chosen ones. (My ego as well as my head is just filling up more and more as he speaks) He outlines our day on what we were going to be doing from training to eating. It is going to be a pretty rad day and I am sure very, very intense as well.

First up he groups us into groups of 5 and we are assigned to various computers throughout the restaurant. We train on the computer for about an hour. My group is not very bright at all, pretty yes but kinda stupid. This one girl must have asked over 50 questions and you could tell the trainer and the rest of us wanted to stuff a cloth napkin down her mouth. She just couldn't grasp how to punch in an order into the computer, after being shown like 20 times. Another guy comes over and hands us each a menu and when the actual menu arrives, I think this stupid girl is going to have a stroke. She keeps saying Oh my God, Oh my God there is so much stuff on here. She is pacing back and forth staring at the menu, one hand holding her forehead and I think she is crying. The trainer looks at her and says it's a bit extensive but don't worry you will learn it. I look down at the menu and I am a "bit" shall we say confused. I can understand why Little Miss Questions is going bat, shit crazy because this menu is huge!

There is a ton of stuff to learn on here. There are over 100 appetizers, soups, salads, entrees and desserts to learn. There is a gigantic wine and drink list as well. The trainer informs us that there will be a test before the Grand Opening and anyone that does not pass will not be working here. He goes on:

Guys I know the menu is a bit daunting with the amount of menu items. I know you only have 2 days to study it but most of you guys are actors right? (most of us shake our heads) Well if you cannot memorize this menu in 2 days than you probably shouldn't be an actor. Actors get pages and pages of dialog to memorize, on a daily basis, so this is nothing! If you cannot learn this menu, you might as well go back home to where you're from and get a union or office job. If I sound harsh, too bad you will make a lot of money here and it will be worth it.

Wow I like this guy and I think his name is Jake. He is cute too. I wonder what side of the street he shops on. Oh I hope it's the boy side but honestly if I think he is cute, he probably shops on the girl side of the street. We shall see but how the hell am I going to memorize all this shit and all the ingredients in 2 just days! I cannot get fired already. I need this job and holy crap rent is due in 9 days and I haven't even gotten new headshots yet.

Jake continues:

People breathe…we are going to make it a little bit easier for you. We will be tasting items from the menu in just a few minutes. I suggest you take notes… lots of them.

As the food starts to come out, certain people just start grabbing plates, pushing people out of the way, like complete savages. It was so disgusting to watch, it was almost like they hadn't eaten in days.

Jake announces:

People calm down; there will be plenty of food for everyone! Don't push and shove because we are watching everything you do. This includes the way you interact with your fellow servers and coworkers. There is more to working here than just memorizing the menu and learning the computes system guys. I hope you all realize that.

You could tell some people were really embarrassed while others became fearful of losing their jobs already. I am just grateful that my Mother did instill some manners into us as kids. Not many but at least some!

As the food kept pouring in, there were various conversations going on and it was becoming fun. I was starting to meet some really cool people from all over the place. It was becoming a great afternoon with great people and amazing food. Jake was becoming cuter as the day progressed. Everything was really good and I began to get excited about my future in LA again. The staff was talking about their careers, where they came from, why they moved to LA and other little tidbits of information; all while munching on some pretty great food. I like everyone…well almost everyone.

You know in every crowd there is always one. You know the guy who knows everything there is to know about everything! That guy that if you have done something, no matter what it is, he has done it bigger, better and faster. The guy who loves to force his useless bull shit down your throat without you even asking for any of it. The guy who takes credit when things go right but he would be the first to place blame if things went wrong. The guy who sucks up to who he thinks he has to and talks down to the people he thinks he is better than. Yup we all know at least one of these guys. This guy is called the bona fide asshole and there is one in every group.

Jeff who is the bona fide asshole in this group is a real winner. He is telling the Chef how amazing the food is. The best he has ever tasted in his entire life. He makes sure that everyone knows he has vast knowledge of food and what wine to pair each entrée with. He rattles off his restaurant resume trying to impress anyone with in ear shot. After every bite he will rattle things off like I taste cilantro or there is the perfect amount of wasabi paste in this dish. It becomes increasingly more obnoxious as more and more dishes come out of the kitchen. When Jeff turns to the Chef and says: I am going to have to up my gym workout tonight from 3 hours to four after eating this entire amazing food chef, I have had enough.

Shut up dude I say as sarcastic as possible. (laughter throughout the room including cute Jake)

What bro? The food is amazing, he retorts.

I know but do you have to put your nose that far up the Chefs asshole? (Laughter again including the chef)

I don't wait for the bona fide assholes explanation or response. I just roll my eyes at him and turn and walk away. This girl Amanda that I met early in the day comes up to me and whispers in my ear: Thank you, what a douche. That guy is such an "I am the guy" guy. Guys like that drive me crazy!

Me too as I nod my head in agreement. I look back at the table and Jeff is still glaring at me so I turn around and give him thumbs up. I am trying to make light of what I just said and it worked because he smiled and gave me a thumbs up back. Another thing to know about the bona fide asshole is that they are clueless to how much of a bona fide asshole they actually are.

After another 10 minutes goes by Jake announces:

Hey people now it is time to try some wine and also test our specialty drinks so let's all head to the bar. Now take it easy I don't want to see any of you drunk and messy on your first day so maybe you should sip. (He laughs) Kidding guys have fun but I wouldn't suggest getting smashed because you have a test to take tomorrow afternoon.

I trained to be a sommelier when I lived in Italy, Jeff boasts.

I again cannot control myself or my big mouth and I sing out loud **of course** you did Jeff......**Of course** you did!

Jeff is again glaring at me again and I just smile and walk towards the bar. As I am walking towards the bar cute Jake comes and taps me on the shoulder. My heart starts pounding. Is he going to fire me or maybe ask me out on a date? Before I can over analyze anymore Jake asks:

Am I going to have to separate you two?

Who? I ask. (but I know damn well who he is talking about)

Jake looks at me with those are you fucking serious eyes and says: Jeff...Tate you know who I am talking about.

Ahh Jeff.... nah he is fine. I have worked with guys **just** like him in the past. I will leave him alone....I am sorry. It is just he goes on and on and on.

It's cool Jake says with a smile. He is that guy who knows everything there is to know about everything. Trust me I get it and between you and me I cannot fucking stand him. I didn't even want to hire him but it wasn't just my decision.

Good than we can torture him together I say as we both walk and laugh about Jeff as we enter the bar area of the restaurant.

As the bar managers and bartenders start talking about and making the drinks my brain starts to wander. Jake is really cute. I wonder if he was just flirting with me or was making friends. I didn't get a gay vibe but I also didn't get the ultimate macho vibe either. I am going to drink little as possible so that I do not do anything stupid. Last thing I want to be is Snooki on her first day at the Jersey Shore house now do I? Well I am going to let this play its course. If he is gay he is gay and if he is straight than he is straight. My Mother always told me to never shit where you eat but then again when was the last time I listened to my Mothers advice?

I make my way up to the bar and just like when the food came out; people are grabbing drinks like it is the last 2 minutes of open bar at the club. I look over at Jake, I motion towards the bar and I roll my eyes. Jake laughs and he has a beautiful smile. He looks like he is about 28 or so...perfect age for me.

I eventually get to the bar and take a few sips of the Creative Cosmo and the Magnificent Mojito. They are good but again I do not want to drink too much because with every sip I become much braver, better looking and desirable to all. I know this because it has happened to me more times than I would like to admit, but I will not do this here. At least not until after my rent is paid.

I stay at the bar, making small talk with people until the bar starts to thin out. I figure it is time to go home and study. I say my goodbyes and I start to head out. I looked around for Jake but he was off doing other training probably but I did bump into Jeff. Jeff reaches out his hand and says:

Looking forward to working with ya brother!

I shake his hand and say me too...brother! I smile and turn to leave.

As I am walking through the restaurant I see Little Miss Questions sitting on the owners lap. She is being all girly and giggly with him. I say to myself hey whatever works...works....look Madonna fucked Mick Jagger and look at her now. No judgments and if she slept with him for the job or will sleep with him to keep it...good for her. I would sleep with Jake but only because I am attracted to him. To be honest I wish I could sleep with people I was not attracted to. It would probably make my life easier and I would probably get ahead quicker. So basically I can't give head to get ahead…..what is wrong with me?

I will pull an all-nighter tonight if I have to but I will learn this encyclopedia of a menu by the time this restaurant opens. I just wish I could not stop thinking about Jake. He had a little accent but I couldn't figure out from where. Spain? Mexico? Maybe South America….Me encanta!

As I arrive home and open the door I find Tommy in the same place he always seems to be, on the couch, which we purchased at the thrift store, watching TV. I turn to Tommy and I say:

I am soooooooo fucked that I lied my way through my interview and pretended that restaurants are my life! Look at the size of this menu I have to memorize all this by tomorrow afternoon. I have to take a freaking test and if I fail I am fired!

Tommy barely takes his eyes away from the TV and says Wow…

I head to my room, plop down on the bed and start studying.

Crab and avocado and rice sounded good so think hard hmmmm, study, study ahh **California Roll.**

Now only 34 more fucking rolls to remember! What happened to the days when would ask "would you like fries with your burger?" Or say ketchup??

OMG what have I gotten myself into? I am studying for a minimum wage job waiting tables! Is it worth it? Do I want to be in this business bad enough? I could be making $ 19.75 an hour selling Geico insurance on Long Island!!! But In the back of my head I kept thinking to myself: **but the tips must be**

huge!!!" I will pay my rent, pay for acting school and become a working actor. Plus I met a really cute guy.

Boy……… did I have **A lot** to learn.………

My father's voice came into my head (which has happened a lot throughout my life – sometimes good, sometimes not good but always looking out for what **he** thinks is best for me. My father worries on where I will end up and how I will support myself. He just has no concept of this life. He thinks I should have a 9 to 5 job, with health benefits, 401 K and 2 weeks a year vacation. I can still hear him now "Kid… Get your head out of the clouds and get a real job.……..please"

At that precise moment I say to myself …my head is exactly in my own cloud and it is exactly where my head should be. Whether or not he will agree with me is another thing all together. I have learned over the years that my Father and I rarely ever agree on anything. I know deep down that my Dad is proud that I had to the guts to try and make it in this world of show business. Something I think he regrets, never trying with his own singing but he will never admit to it or at least admit it to me. I think his fear is what keeps me pushing forward. When someone tells me I cannot do or achieve something, it makes me work 5 times as hard to prove them wrong. Maybe that is my Fathers way of pushing me, I doubt it but I will continue to prove him wrong.

I am going to learn every fucking Item on this menu including every sushi roll known to man. I will prove to me that I can do it, but also to prove to any doubters in my life, including my father, that I was meant to be more than just ordinary. A word my father still has trouble understanding but is learning to accept.

I love my father but he is the constant force for me to succeed here in LA is to prove him wrong. That you do not need a 9 to 5 job with benefits to be his definition of successful. I am a success already and I will continue to be a success throughout my life. My success for today will be to memorize this menu, pass my test and start following my dream. I am going to pass this test one way or another damn it!

I stayed up all night studying like a mad man. I am going to ace this test.......

All of a sudden I open my eyes.....**Fuck I fell asleep while studying!** What time is it? Why is the sun out? I am desperately squinting to find my watch or cell phone to tell the time. There are papers and clothes everywhere and I usually have to call my cell phone from the landline to find it anyway. Who am I kidding the cable box is the best bet for accurate time? Ouch as I trip over my shoes that I left right in the door way as I run to the living room. Tate what a brilliant place to put my shoes huh? I look down at the cable box and it says 11:14...Crap and I haven't even learned desserts yet. OK calm down you still have 3 and a half hours, so relax! Go make some coffee.

I head to the kitchen and put on a pot of coffee. I still have the menu in hand and I am trying to go over what I memorized last night. I think I will be OK, my memorization skills are pretty solid. I think about what Jake said about having to memorize pages of dialog as an actor.....ahhh Jake! Once the coffee is brewed I start to head back to my bedroom and I can hear Thomas snoring. Does that guy ever leave the apartment? I don't think he has left the apartment complex in like a month. I mean he goes to the pool or the apartment gym daily but nothing much beyond that. He is constantly on his computer and he does have um... shall we say, nightly visitors. He finds these visitors on the internet. Need I say more? We are not that close and as more time passes he grows more and more distance from me. I guess he thinks I am the bona fide asshole! Oh well I do not have time for that right now, I gotta learn desserts!

After about two hours of studying, I think I have the menu down pretty well. I better be because I didn't make it to the gym and I have to do 300 or more pushups now. What? don't mock me….I **have** to look buff for Jake. I pray that he is gay, please God let Jake be gay! See Mom I really do pray, ahh if she only knew, she would be so proud of me!

I finish my pushups in about 45 minutes and in between each set I would test myself on the menu. I would do pretty well and my adrenaline is pumping now. I jump in the shower and shave. I know people think it is odd but I shave and brush my teeth in the shower. What? It saves time. After about 10 minutes I hop out of the shower and get dressed. I put on my jeans and find a tight T shirt to show off my chest and arms. As I am doing my last minute touch ups in the bathroom I look down and Spencer is staring at me. He starts meowing and I know what that means. Are you hungry Spens? Before I can even blink he is already in the kitchen. Such a smart cat and so friggin cute! I wonder if Jake likes cats. As I am finishing feeding Spencer, Thomas comes staggering in.

Is that coffee fresh Thomas asks as he points to the coffee maker?

I made it about 11:30 this morning I inform Thomas.

Good enough for me, as he already grabbed a mug from the cabinet and began to pour the coffee into his Disney mug.

I am so nervous about the test I have to take. I stayed up all night or at least until I passed out while studying the damn menu. I tell Thomas.

It's a fucking restaurant Tate! Stop being so overdramatic and save the drama for an audition or something dude!

Wow someone woke up on the wrong side of the bed this…..afternoon Tommy! I do say as dramatic and sarcastic as ever.

Yeah…go take your stupid test Thomas snarls at me.

I need this job Thomas, rent is due in 9 days!

Well you should have moved out here with more money or maybe you shouldn't go out as much, or joined a fancy gym or bought a car or…..

Shut up Thomas… Maybe you should….You know what? I don't want to fight with you right now. I gotta go and take this fucking test!

Dead stare from Thomas.

I wonder where Thomas gets his money from. I heard internet porn is expensive these days…ha! Tate do not focus on his negativity, you have a test to conquer and then possibly a date so focus! I grab my keys and the menu, give Spencer a scratch on the head and off I go. I yell out to Tommy as I close the door "Wish me luck"

Crickets crickets….

Dick…..

As I am driving to the restaurant I am still quizzing myself in my head. The sushi rolls are hard to remember but I think I have the jist of them all. As I pull up to the restaurant I see Jake getting out a Mini Cooper. That is a good sign; it is one of the top 5 Gay Cars in America. Don't ask me how I know this but I just do. I park right next to him in my shitty Black Volkswagen Cabrio convertible.

Are you ready for the test? Jake inquires, all while flashing that beautiful smile.

I hope so….I really need this job!

Well good luck Tate I have a good feeling that you will do great on this test. Plus I would like to get to know you better. You seem like a really cool guy, Jake says as he winks at me.

Thanks I say as I look directly at him and then nervously turn and walk away, as fast as I possibly can walk, without making it obvious. All the time in my head asking myself what did he mean by getting to know me better? And what was with the wink? He has to be gay now right? Is he into me or maybe I am reading into this wrong. Fuck what is in a California roll again?

As I enter the restaurant, one of the managers smiles and says sign in and then grab a test. Leave all of your papers over there and she points to the bar area. You can take as long as you need. Once you are finished you may go into the bar area and wait for your results. You will find out tonight whether or not you will be employed here.

I gulp hard, grab a test and find a seat in the restaurant. There are people all over the place taking the test. The managers are walking around I guess to make sure no one is cheating. I feel like I am back in high school taking my SAT's right now. I sit down, take a deep breath and start the test. As I begin to read the test I breathe a sigh of relief. It is not **everything** on the menu and some of it is in multiple choices. The sushi roll descriptions were a little bit rocky, but I think I got them all pretty down pat. The drink portion was a breeze and I hope while we wait for the results at the bar we can have a drink. I reread the test and my answers over 3 times. I think I did really well. I get up and hand my test over to the manager and smile. She looks down, smiles and says go have a drink in the bar.

I go to the bar and there are a lot of people already filling into the bar. I see Amanda and of course I hear Jeff boasting on how it was a piece of cake. I walk to the bar and this stunning bartender named Sean immediately asks me what can I get for you?

After a 2 second pause of staring at his face, I say vodka soda with a splash of cranberry and can you make it tall?

He smiles, nods and goes off to make my drink.

I then hear it. The sound I dread. The voice I dread. Here is my bona fide asshole Jeff standing right next to me. How did you do?

Well he sounded genuine and sincere so I decided not to be a sarcastic dickhead and answer him as cool as I possibly could. So I tell him:

I think I did well. I thought it would be more! I studied and studied all night but I am relieved that it is at least over now and we just wait.

And drink Jeff raises his glass.

My drink arrives from Sean and I graciously thank him. He tells me it is free and I go to tip him and he say nah keep it. Well I was down to my last 300 bucks so I didn't insist.

Jeff continues on about where he came from, why he needs the job and that he has a daughter to support back in Texas. That he moved out here to make a better life for him and his daughter. He tells me how his girlfriend died in a car accident and his parents are caring for his daughter till, he gets settled. Well now I feel like the ultimate shit head the way I treated him. That was until he just turns to me and points at this girl coming down the stairs: Check out the rack on that chick....Woa man I want to work next to her....Before I can even say anything in regards to what this bona fide asshole just said to me, I hear Jake yelling as he is coming down the stairs Jake enters the room and he has a look on his face that just announces to the room that he is upset. Jake walks to the middle of the room and announces:

I did tell all of you that if you did not pass this test, you would not be working here right?

(We all say yes)

Well than there are some pretty stupid people in this room. Either that or did you think that what I say doesn't matter to you? I gave all of you a simple task to go home and study the menu. I don't want to hear excuses and I didn't expect all of you to pass but this ratio are disgusting. So if I call your name, you need to come and sit in this booth (as Jake points to a booth just outside the bar area) Melissa, Jeff P, Amanda M, (I am shaking in my pants right now) Drew S, Sabrina, Neil, Kristie and Tate.

As I am walking towards the table I am still not sure if I passed or failed and I am so fearful that I just put my head down and walk towards the booth. Just as I sit down I hear Jake go:

You eight people have passed the test and will be on the floor for tomorrows Grand Opening. Congratulations and thank you for taking this serious. Now I cannot fire over 30 of you, the day before we open this restaurant. I will be posting a chart with your names on it. It will list your names in alphabetical order. Next to your name it will say one of three things. It will say retest, hostess or terminate on it. If it says retest you must be here tomorrow at 10 am to retake the test. If it says hostess than you must be here at 11am, to meet with Maxine and train on the hostess stand. If it says terminate than have a nice fucking life and get the hell out of this restaurant. I don't want to hear any excuses and the owners of the restaurant support this decision 100%. I will have the list posted in about 5 minutes. Oh and by the way you have to score a 90% or better on tomorrows retest.

You can tell that Jake is still not happy. He probably ended up looking really stupid to the owners and chef who were grading these papers. Even when he was angry he was still so damn cute. He might even be possibly cuter. I could tell he had a fiery Latin persona and of course I am even more attracted to him now. He walks over to our booth and says:

OK you guys need to be here tomorrow at 4pm. We are scheduled to open at 7pm tomorrow night. It is a soft Grand Opening so it shouldn't be that crazy. Most of the people coming are friends and family of the owners and management. I am going to really need your help tomorrow because as you can see there are not many of you that passed. What a bunch of fucking idiots. This is going to be one of the busiest restaurants in Los Angeles and they couldn't even bother to study. You guys all did really well and I really appreciate that you took the time and effort to do what I asked of you.

I cannot believe all those people failed, Jeff chimes in.

Believe it! Jake kinda snaps at Jeff.

Oh I do I um kinda um just shocked that's all Jeff stammers.

I am just looking at Jeff like shut the fuck up, you douchebag, nobody want to hear you right now. As I look around I think pretty much all of us are thinking the same way, towards Jeff. We all start to get up to leave. As I push my way out of the booth, I make eye contact with Jake and he is smiling at me. I walk up to him and say see you tomorrow.

I knew you would pass Tate Jake says in a sarcastic but yet flirty way.

I **had** to pass dude I have rent due in 8 days ma**n.** I am down to my last $300 bucks and being homeless is really not that cute for me.

Ha Ha where do you live? Jake asks.

I live on Alta Vista between Sunset and Fountain, I inform Jake.

We are neighbors Jake states. I live on Martel between Sunset and Fountain. How long have you lived there?

About a month....I say with a sigh.

From where did you move from? Jake is quizzing me and he seems to be genuinely interested in what I have to say. He has such intense eyes.

New York City. I was born and raised in Brooklyn. Went to high school and college in Manhattan I graduated from college about 4 years ago. I always wanted to move to Los Angeles and now I finally did it. How about you I ask Jake?

I was born in Bogotá Columbia. I moved to the United States when I was 26 years old. I started off in Miami and then kind of moved out here about 3 years ago. I am not an actor though so I might end up moving to New York someday. I have never been to New York.(Jake looks down at his watch) Hey I have to go grab that list. Listen do want to maybe go grab a drink. I could kinda use one right about now.

My mind is racing. This cannot possible be happening to me right now. I mean I imagine these things happening in my delusional head but to really hear them coming out of his mouth. I am in ultimate shock and I just blurt out....

Sure! (I think I just sounded like a hyena)

OK give me like 5 minutes or better yet, why don't you meet me at El Compadre; they have the best margaritas in this town. Have you been?

I actually have. It is only about 5 blocks from my house. I will park my car in my garage and then shoot on over. It is 6:30 right now so shall I say we meet there at 7?

Perfect Jake says and he dashes out to get the list of doom for the failed test people.

As I walk back to my car I still can't believe how my luck is turning. I have an apartment, a job and now a possible new boyfriend. I feel like I am floating on air but hey I deserve it after the first few days I had here in LA. It was torture for me. If it could go wrong, it did go wrong but I was brave and fought my way back. As I walk to my car I debate on whether I should drop my car back home. On one hand if I take my car I will be responsible and not drink that much. On the other hand I am nervous and when I am nervous I tend to suck drinks down quicker. I don't want to risk a DUI but I also don't want to look stupid. Ahh fuck it, let me drive the car home, this way I can freshen up. I make a left right out of the parking lot on Sunset and start to head home. Traffic is a little thick this time of the evening but I maneuver quickly and I get home in less than 10 minutes. I pull into the parking garage and race upstairs to freshen up as fast as I can.

I open the front door to the apartment and guess where Tommy is. You guessed it…in front of the TV…surprise, surprise!

I passed my test Tommy I start my job tomorrow I boast to Tommy but I do not think he is listening to me anyway. I head straight to the bathroom and as I do I hear Tommy mockingly say Yippee you passed your restaurant test woo hoo as sarcastically and downright mean as he could possibly say it.

As I am freshening up in the bathroom I think to myself I do not have time to go out there and get into an argument with him but I have no clue what the hell I did to him. I don't know what I could have possibly done to him besides the disastrous first day here in the apartment. I have apologized for that over and over though. In the last week or so he has turned into such a dick. We were friends in New York. We were not best friends by any means but I thought he was a cool guy and that we would get along really well here in LA. I am learning that I am not right about a lot of things here in LA but I did pass my restaurant test and I did meet a guy, so are looking up. I will try and have a conversation with Tommy tomorrow about what is wrong but for now I am off to El Compadre to meet Jake. I leave the apartment and I do not say a word to Tommy, he probably didn't even notice me leaving anyway. Did he move out here to watch TV and have internet sex? He could have done that in New York or anywhere for that matter. Ahh screw Tommy, I have a date!!!

As I begin to walk down Sunset I start to notice all these beautiful cars. BMW's, Audi, Mercedes and Lexus's are everywhere. I notice there are very few Chevy's and Fords in this town at all. I say out loud to myself "There is a ton of money in this town!" As I start to approach El Compadre I look down at my watch and it is exactly 7:00 pm. Good I am on time. I think Jake is probably coming directly from the restaurant. As I walk in I see Jake standing at the bar. He waves me over and flashes that amazing smile at me. I walk towards him as he says:

You made it.

Yeah I wanted to take the car back to my place since it was only a few blocks from this place and then walk over.

He motions to this gorgeous Hispanic bartender behind the bar. She comes over and Jake leans into the bar and gives her a gigantic kiss. Once he is finished he turns to me and says:

Tate I would like you to meet my wife Sofia. Sofia this is the guy at the restaurant that I told you was really funny last night.

I am in shock but I try and hide it as much as I possibly can. I reach out my hand, smile and I say nice to meet you.

What can I get you two handsome guys to drink? Sofia asks so sweetly and I can tell she has a Spanish accent as well.

I will have a frozen Chambord Margarita with no salt please, I tell Sofia

Jake chimes in OOO that sounds good make it two but I will have mine with salt.

As Jakes wife goes off to make our margarita's my mind starts racing as fast as the Indianapolis 500. I should have known he was straight. I should have known he was straight. Why? Because I was attracted to him, that's why. Look he is good-looking, funny, great smile, intense eyes and Latin... how could he **not** be straight? It is a good thing I didn't do anything stupid yet. He probably doesn't even know that I am gay either. He probably just thought he was going to meet a buddy or a new coworker for a drink. He wants to be your friend dumb ass. Tate why does it always have to be about dating or sex with you? Maybe if you stopped being so fucking desperate for a boyfriend you might end up finding one. Remember this is good because now you won't shit where you eat and could end up making a really cool friend. You do not have many of those out here either Tate....friends! I look across the bar and I see Sofia coming back with our drinks. The silence between Jake and I is beginning to get a tad bit awkward so I turn to him and say:

So you never have been to New York City huh?

He looks at me with those intense eyes and says: Have you ever been to Bogota Columbia?

OK fair enough. No but I would like to someday.

I would like to go to New York one day as well. I told you earlier that I might want to move there some day. We shall see. (He picks up the drinks, hands me one and gestures to a Cheers.)

Cheers and we clink margarita glasses.

Sofia comes back over and asks if we want that table over there on the other side of the bar. Jake looks at me and asks:

Are you hungry at all?

I could eat something. Sure I say enthusiastically, I have a job now.

Jake turns to Sofia and gives her a thumb up. Wow he is even cuter now because he has a corny side to him as well. Oh well... I look over at Sofia and she is really pretty. Long wavy brown hair and like bona fide asshole Jeff would say..... a nice rack as well. They make a really good looking couple I must say but I still can secretly hate her right? Bitch....

When the table is finally cleaned off we take a seat and immediately look at our menus. Why did this suddenly become so uncomfortable? Was it when he introduced me to his wife? Was it my shock and look of horror when Jake kisses his wife? Did he pick up on that? Or did he finally realize that I am a big ole homo that wanted to have sex with him? I am not sure what it is. All I know is that I need to keep this job and I can still hear my Mother in my head "Tatey I told you not to shit where you eat," you should listen to your Mother once in a while. I gotta end this awkwardness before it gets really awkward somehow:

I am gonna get the chicken quesadilla with extra guacamole I state to Jake as he has already finished looking at the menu and is staring at me with this big smile. In my head I am saying why is this guy staring at me?

Yum Jake says. Are you excited about starting in the restaurant tomorrow night?

Yes I say like I am on another job interview.

I am too (as Jake looks around the restaurant) I wish I could work here. These guys make a killing but you have to be Mexican to work here. Plus my wife gets very jealous when she sees me flirting so it is better we work in different restaurants. You know what I mean?

I nod but I don't really know what he means. All I know is that I will probably go home tonight and beat off to the thought of Jake fucking his beautiful wife, Sofia the beautiful bartender from El Compadre. I glance over at Sofia again and she is busy making drinks, plus she thinks she has nothing to worry about with me. Now if I was a hot girl like her, with tits like hers, I am sure it would be an entirely different situation all together now.

So are you married, single or seeing anyone Jake inquires?

Nah I just moved here and I am trying to focus on my career right now. I am an actor and I am trying to get my shit together and make it in this town.

Have I seen you in anything Jake asks?

Mostly plays in New York, a couple of music videos and I did background work on a few of the New York soap operas.

AAH that is cool I can see you on a soap opera. All those guys are really hot. I can see why you would do soaps.

In my head I am like what the fuck did he just say? There is no straight man would ever call another guy hot especially not a married man who just introduced me to his wife. Maybe it is a language barrier but he speaks almost perfect English. What the hell is going on? Maybe Jake and Sofia like to have 3 ways? Or maybe....shut up Tate say something because Jake is looking for a response to his compliment.

Um thanks bro (yeah I know I said bro) so how did you meet your wife?

We met through mutual friends a few years back in Miami. So was there anyone that you found attractive at the restaurant? Jake asks very oddly

Dude everybody there is like a supermodel, I feel like I am in another realm or something. I thought I was intimidated at the gym but Wow. Some of those bartenders have probably been on the cover of GQ and Men's Fitness especially Sean. (I am visualizing Sean now)

Sean is very hot! Jake contributes.

(OK I guess Jake likes to use the word hot for good-looking. In the gay world hot means someone you would most likely sleep with)

So you would want to sleep with Sean Jake asks?

(Shit I am busted he knows I am gay. Fuck it I might as well put it all out there, plus Sofia has just brought us another round of margaritas)

As Sofia puts the drinks down she says: For two of the best looking guys in the entire restaurant. These are on me!

Ahh that's nice Sofia...thank you I graciously accept because I need all the liquid courage I can get right about now.

What can I get for you to eat as Sofia flirtingly asks me?

I will have the shrimp fajita's Jake chimes in.

Sofia snaps at him: I know what you are having. You have the same thing every time my darling guapo. I was asking Tate.

I will have the chicken quesadilla please I tell Sofia.

That's all honey (as she puts her hand on my shoulder)

Yeah that will do it….Thanks!

As Sofia smiles, winks and walks away Jake looks at me and again asks me: So you would sleep with Sean?

(Fuck it)Yes I would sleep with Sean but I wouldn't date him. I am way too insecure and because he is way too good-looking I state.

Oh huh Jake says (he is not even a bit shocked, that I just actually said that I would in fact sleep with a man.)

I know you are married but is there anyone at the restaurant that you find attractive I ask Jake?

Yes…..Jake says.

Who? I ask.

(After a long pause and big sip of his new margarita, Jake takes a big body sigh)

You…..he says with his head down.

What? Me? But you are married to a **Woman! A woman who is about 30 feet away from us!** Sorry man but I am not into 3 ways or helping you cheat on your wife man. That is so not cool. My Dad cheated on my Mother and it almost destroyed our entire family. I have a ton of issues when it comes to cheating man. I have no desire to have an affair or be someone's mistress. Woa this evening is fucked man.

Calm down Tate we cheat on each other all the time as Jake laughs. I know I said about the jealous thing. She just doesn't like to see me making out with someone in front of her.

So what Jake you guys don't rub it in each other's faces that you are cheating on each other? Have you ever heard of something called fidelity Jake?

Sure I have Jake pronounces. Let me ask you something Tate? Are you attracted to me? When you agreed to have a drink with me, were you attracted to me? Did you remotely think, at any point after you agreed to have a drink with me; from the time you left the restaurant; till the time that I introduced you to Sofia; that sex was an option?

I didn't know that you were married….to a woman Jake!

That is **not** what I asked you Tate. Answer the question: did you think sex or a possible connection to me was an option before I introduced you to my wife?

(Just as I am about to get up, throw some money on the table and run, the food arrives at the table. I am just looking at him. Why didn't I just go home and get a good night sleep I say to myself? I get up, put some money on the table and start to leave)

Wait Tate that is not fucking cool man and I can tell Jake is pissed. Don't leave you have got it all wrong man.

(Remember I witnessed Jakes temper in the restaurant. I didn't care; I was not going to have a 3 way with these two fucking people or help him cheat on his wife. Fuck I am going to get fired now. Wait no I am not. Let them try and fire me and I will tell the entire restaurant about Jake and his 3 way loving wife who both cheat on each other. Somebody has put a curse on you Tate....this does not happen to normal people. As I fling open the door I hear Jake yell)

Fucking wait Tate.

(I of course don't wait and just want to get out of here. What a disaster this night has turned out to be. What is Sofia thinking right now? Damn... no 3 way tonight? Or why is my husband chasing another dude down the street? Jake is in hot pursuit of me and grabs my arm and pulls me around)

So you are not going to answer the question Tate? Jake is looking at me with those amazing tense eyes but they are not very endearing right about now.

(Ok here comes Brooklyn)

Yes I did find you attractive, you fucking happy Jake. Is that what you wanted to hear Jake? I had a hard time studying for the fucking menu test last night because I kept thinking of you asshole. That was before I knew how much of a fucking shit head you are. I fucking can't stand cheaters Jake my Mother almost killed herself after she found out my Dad was cheating. Plus I have no interest in wetting you and your wife's whistles'. Did you see how she touched me when she was taking our food order Jake?

Wow you are an overdramatic little sensitive queen aren't you Tate? I thought you were a cool guy. I even thought that I could possibly date you.

Date me? Are you fucking kidding? Seriously date me? And let me ask you this: what would your jealous wife Sofia think about that huh? What did you envision Threes Company and Sofia would be Jack Tripper and we would be Chrissie and Janet?

Who are Chrissie and Janet? Jake asks confusingly. I don't know a Chrissie or Janet. I do know a Jack but I am not sure of his last name. Who are these people and what do they have to do with our conversation Tate?

It is an old TV show I say to Jake with utter frustration….I was just making an example. Can we just be done with this Jake? I am sick to my stomach and I just want to go home. I don't know if you are gay, straight, bisexual, a cheater, into 3 ways with your wife and I honestly don't care at this point.

Jake starts ranting in what I think has to be Spanish:

Este gringo no cerrará. El esta enojado. Yo no puedo creer que discuta con él en la calle. Esto es embarasozo. ¡Esto es donde Sofia trabaja!

I do not understand you Jake and I am going home. I say to Jake as I begin to calming walk down Sunset towards my apartment.

Jake roars back: You just told me you didn't know what or who I am right?

(I stop, turn and say)

Yup no idea….

Jake makes another rather large sigh and says:

The reason you do not know who or what I am is because you wouldn't answer my question first. Then when you finally did answer my question, not in the restaurant but on a sidewalk on Sunset strip, you wouldn't shut the fuck up long enough for me to tell you who and what I am. Is that about right Tate? Does that sum it up for you?

(I am so pissed right now but he is kind of right. When I get nervous or insecure my mouth seems to be my ultimate weapon.)

OK Jake talk I say as I throw my hands up in the air.

Jake reaches out his hand to me and says:

Hello my name is Jake Penzoni. I am a 31 year old guy from Bogota Columbia. I am a very kind, smart, energetic and witty guy who also happens to be gay. I happen to think you are a very attractive man that I would like to get to know better. Are you happy Tate?

Did you know you were gay before you married your wife Sofia, Jake? (I know I am such a bitch but come on…that is a valid question)

Jake smiles and says:

Yes I knew I was gay and so did my wife….Sofia….

What I say?

Jake comes up to me and whispers in my ear:

Can you please come back inside and I will explain it to you. We are starting to draw a crowd and this is really personal.

What do I have to lose? Plus I am fucking starving. The food is probably cold by now but yes I will come back inside and let you explain. Can you just give me a minute to compose myself?

Sure drama queen Jake teasingly yells as he walks backward back into El Compadre. You better not split Tate, I know where you live.

I won't I promise Jake.

(Once Jake goes inside the restaurant, I take a deep breath. So he is gay... with a wife. A wife that knows he is gay. They kiss on the lips. Wait OMG is Sofia a lesbian? Are they each other's beards for their families? That has to be it. I can deal with that. I hope that is, what it is. Why did you decide to quit smoking now Tate?)

(I walk back into the restaurant and go straight to the table. I look over at Sofia, who blows me a kiss and I sit down and stare at Jake for a second. He is smiling and I have no idea why he is smiling at me)

I knew you liked me...well I hoped you liked me....nah I knew but I had to cement it when I introduced you to Sofia... Jake teases.

I look at Jake confused and I say: so Sofia is not your wife (I look down at the table and notice the food is gone) and what happened to the food?

Jake says while continuing smiling...No Sofia is my wife and they are remaking our food. You cannot eat Mexican food cold especially fajitas.

Um OK Jake but I am really confused can you please explain to me what is going on. I feel like an asshole and all these people are still staring at me.... (I jokingly add) I am used to people staring at me but not while I am dining with my gay, married to a woman, co-worker who I am very attracted to, so can you just get on with it?

Very attracted to me huh? Cool... Jake says with a laugh while shaking his head up and down.

(I motion with my hands to just get on with it)

First off Tate I am sorry by the way I went around telling you this. I should have picked a different restaurant, probably one where my wife doesn't work at. Money is a little tight for me too and Sofia gets a discount here. Sorry for calling you an overdramatic little queen.

Oh I can be overdramatic…..trust me…I can be…Sorry to interrupt but fair warning, I use my mouth as a weapon of mass destruction.

Um Really? Jake perks up.

Don't get all sexual with me now buster you have some splaining to do. Wait you do know I love Lucy right?

Yes we did have I Love Lucy in Columbia Tate. So what I am about to tell you is very confidential and you cannot tell anyone about this conversation. Can you do that Tate?

You are not an axe murderer or on the run from the po po are you now Jake?

You use all these strange American words Tate but I am not an axe murderer and I am not on the run, from what you say po po.

(The food rearrives)

Now you are not going to run again are you Tate? Jake teases at me.

No I am fucking starving Jake. I don't think I have eaten a thing all day. Can you please go on with your explanation already? I say full of sarcasm.

Jake smiles: I love your Brooklyn accent!

Thanks Jake...well?

Ok (Jake says as he takes a bite into his fajita) so I have your word that what I am about to tell you will stay between us.

Yes I promise I say with my mouth full of quesadilla (I know so attractive)

Sofia and I have a marriage of convenience Jake tells me.

What is that I ask?

Let me start from the beginning....About 4 years ago I came to the United States for a visit. I came to Miami on a 3 month tourist visa from Columbia. When my tourist visa was about to expire, I didn't want to go back to Columbia so I was asking some friend for advice. My options were very limited. I would have to fly back to Columbia and apply for another tourist visa; get an American company to sponsor me, with a special skill I had or find a woman to marry me. Well I didn't have the money to fly back to Columbia just to fly back to Miami. Plus my family was very poor and the government might not issue me another visa. I had no special skills so my only option was to marry a woman. Tate are you following me so far? Do you want another drink?

Yes and yes I say.

(Jake looks over at Sofia and twirls his finger to show her we want another round)

My best friend's Juan Carlos's coworker told me she would marry me one night out but I was concerned she was drunk when she said it though. I figured when I called her the next day she would say she didn't remember saying it to me or that she would tell me she couldn't do it. I got her phone number from Juan Carlos and I telephoned her. I introduced myself over the phone and she said she remembered me. We chatted a bit about the night we met; she already knew I was gay because we met in a gay bar called Twist. I asked her about the marriage idea and she said that she would have to get back to me about it. That she had to think about it sober. I was for sure, sure that she was going to say no. What would she get out of it besides hassles from her family, doubting friends and not to mention the government and immigration laws?

(Sofia has arrived at the table with our next round of drinks)

Sorry Tate for the way Jake told you our lives. He wasn't sure you were gay and wanted to have a band aid in case you weren't. It back fired on him badly but he is a great guy. I am happy you came back into the restaurant.

(I look at Sofia and then Jake and then back to Sofia again)He told me a slightly different version of that story but it is OK, I get it.

(Sofia puts down the drinks and walks away)

I look at Jake with a smirk and say OK your band aid has left the table, you can continue with your story now Jake.

(Jake laughs)

OK well the next day my cell phone rings and I answer it. I answer hello this is Jaime…

Jaime? I am confused.

That is my birth name but I call myself Jake here in America.

Why? I ask.

Because it is easier, can I finish my story now Tate?

Sure, sorry I feel slightly embarrassed.

Hello this is Jaime, Jake continues the next thing I hear is this woman's voice and she says: ten thousand dollars. I was confused so I ask her who this was. She said this is Sofia Mercado and I will marry you for ten thousand dollars. I said that is wonderful but I do not have ten thousand dollars. I then responded as quickly as possible and asked her if I could pay her in installments. She paused for a moment and I was worried she was going to say no. I blurted out that I would also pay the rent and all household expenses while we were married. She agreed to it instantly. We met that afternoon and went over all the details. I gave her a thousand dollar down payment and we agreed to go to City Hall the next day. We told very few people but we got married two days later actually. One of her rules was I had to have the apartment before she married me. Once I got one she had to approve it as well. Well Queen Sofia wasn't happy with the first apartment but she agreed to marry me anyway.... Her Mexican Catholic Dad almost killed me when he found out 6 months later but I survived. We thought we were only going to have to stay married for a year but it turns out it 3 years actually.

How long have you been married now I curiously ask?

Almost 4 years but she is my best friend now. We both agreed that we would not divorce until someone serious came into one of our lives. Sofia is 28 now and we also agreed that by the time she is 30, if she has not met a guy, we would consider having a baby together.

Wow a baby I exclaim. So how did you two end up in California?

Sofia's father almost walked in on me having sex with my boyfriend at the time. He would have had me murdered, no doubt or question in either one of our minds. It was too close. Come to think of it he almost killed me for bringing his baby daughter to LA. We are cool now. I think he knows I am gay but would never ask. Sofia has a gay brother in Houston and her Dad is cool with him.

So Sofia is not a lesbian right?

No way! Look at her man. She is way too hot to be a lesbian. She might have tried it in college but no way. Actually Sofia doesn't have that many female friends come to think of it.

So no Lick-her license for her huh?

(Jake laughs out loud)

You are funny Tate, it was one of the first thing I noticed.

Really? Not my adorable face (yes my insecure ass had to ask)

You are adorable Tate and I would like to see you again. Can you handle me having a wife?

I sure can Jaime I say with a smile.

One favor or more like two favors Jake asks me. I would like to keep it hush-hush at the restaurant if that is cool with you. I am technically your boss and I think it would be easier for both of us. At least until we see where this goes cause we could end up killing each other! Second favor do not under any circumstances call me Jaime…I absolutely fucking hate my name. It sounds like Hiney and do you really want to talk to an ass…

HA I agree (as I look down at my watch and laughing) Holy shit it is 11:30pm. Where the hell did the time go? We should get the check.

(Jake tells me that the check is taken care of, but we need to leave Sofia a big tip. I go to reach into my pocket to get some cash when Jake reminds me that he already has my money from my first dramatic exit from the restaurant.)

Jake says I am happy we did this. I am glad we did this.

Me too I say and then I start to walk over to Sofia to say goodbye. Sofia comes from around the bar and gives me a big hug. She whispers in my ear "He likes you." I just smile and nod.

I hope to see you soon Tate Sofia yells as I am waving and walking out the door. I turned around and yell "You most definitely will!"

As we are now back on the sidewalk where it all began I laugh. I look at Jake and I am happy we did this after all. He grabs my hand to hold it but I am not really into public displays of affection but it is dark out so…I will let him for the time being.

When we get to the corner of Martel and Sunset, he just turns my body into his and wraps his hands around my body. He then comes in for the kiss and it is incredible. His tongue is rapidly, wrapping its self around my tongue and this kiss is amazing. I am enjoying this kiss so much that I don't care or hear the cars honking at us, people yelling homo or die faggots at us. If he asked me at this very moment to go home with him and have sex, there is no doubt in my mind that I would not have said yes. He finally pulls out of my mouth and says:

You can add good kisser to the list of what I find attractive in you Tate. Kissing to me is one of the most important parts of sex. Chemistry is so important to me and after that kiss we are going to have amazing sex. Not tonight though… but really soon.

I agree not tonight I stammer …but you are also an amazing kisser (I give him one more quick peck on the lips and off I go) See you tomorrow I yell. This was fun!

See you tomorrow guapo Chao (and we both walk towards our apartments)

As I walk home I feel giddy and I am actually happy. I am a little drunk from the four margaritas we ended up drinking but not too much. As I round the block I realize I do not even have his phone number. Well maybe that is a good thing because I have vodka at the house and I don't want to drunk dial.

As I walk in the door Tommy is not in his usual position but then I hear the sounds coming out of his bedroom. He is in his other favorite position… having sex with an internet stranger. Whatever I am going to bed, this has been one crazy day.

Good night.…Spencer is already in bed!

Chapter 6

Sunset Trash

So I started making a few new friends in LA and one night while we were not working at the restaurant, a bunch of us met at a bar, for a night of drinking and fun on the famous Sunset Strip. Since I worked at the new LA hotspot, which was also near the Sunset Strip, I knew where I wanted to go. I wanted to go to The Sky Bar inside the Mondrian Hotel. It was one of the hottest places in town (Or so I heard) Getting into The Sky Bar was extremely difficult especially for guys. I was nervous and I couldn't figure out why. I looked good and I was dressed really cool. I was even more nervous when I saw the large crowd waiting in line to get into The Sky Bar.

My new friend Amanda said not to worry and just follow her. She walks up to the doorman and gives him a big hug and kiss.

Hey baby Girl what's going on gorgeous the doorman asks?

Amanda leans in and whispers in his ear. I couldn't hear what she said to him but it put a big ole smile on the doorman's face. A few seconds later Amanda came over and says:

Hang tight, there is a private party going on right now but it is almost over. Let's go inside the hotel and have a drink by the pool or in the lobby. He said to come back in 15 minutes.

OK I say as we both walk into the hotel.

As we walk into the Mondrian it is really cool with flowing white tapestry everywhere. It is so modern and clean. There is not an ugly person in sight. We look out onto the pool area and it is packed so we decide to sit in the lobby bar area.

What do you want to drink? Amanda asks me

Vodka gimlet, straight up and chilled hard.

You are soooo gay as she walks toward the bar laughing.

I watch her walk away and I also watch all of the guys look up from their perspective dates, to stare at Amanda. Amanda was hot but not in that fake breasts, tight clothes, bleached blonde bimbo way. She was the girl you want to marry and also the girl you want to fuck. She is naturally pretty and does very little fuss to herself to get ready. In getting to know her I have come to realize that she has sex for sport and treats guys the way most guys treat girls....disposable. God I fucking worship her! After a few minutes Amanda is back with the drinks.

Here you go (as Amanda hands me my drink) you had to order a Martini, Amanda says laughing!

Sorry but this is The Mondrian, I say sarcastically

Smart ass Tate but I fucking love you Amanda says as she sits down.

I try I say as I wink at her.

Is Jake coming? Amanda asks.

No Jake is working tonight….as usual. I swear he would work 7 days a week, 365 days if you let him. He is obsessed with saving money.

Good I am glad, he is not coming tonight Amanda states.

Why? I ask confusingly to Amanda.

I know he is your boyfriend and all but he is kind of a dick. You don't work with him on the third floor Tate. He is an asshole. Always barking orders at people and always telling them what they are doing wrong. And you know what; he is a really shitty waiter too! Always fucking up his orders and blaming other people for his mistakes. I would rather work with Bona Fide Asshole Jeff, than work with Jake.

(Yes I taught her what a bona fide asshole is)

Wow Amanda I didn't know it was to that extent. I know he does have a temper and I have been on the receiving end of it, more times than I would like to admit. I work on the 2nd Floor so I don't see it at work that much.

Well I hate his fucking guts Tate! (Amanda states)If he talks to me the way he talked to me Saturday night, I am going to crack an empty wine bottle over his handsome boy head.

So you think my boyfriend is handsome? (Yup that is correct my insecure, seeking approval self only heard boyfriend and handsome)

Shut up Tate Amana sneers!

Kidding, I am kidding I say to Amanda as I am trying to redeem myself. Plus I don't think it is going to last much longer.

Why does he suck in bed? Or rather not suck as Amanda points to my junk.

Amanda???? No it's not that…well kind of….You see between his horrible temper, he is a workaholic and he has huge issues with money. He grew up poor and he has this fear that he will run out of money and be homeless one day. Plus he is a little bit selfish in bed….He is an amazing kisser but the rest is just very vanilla and generic.

So he is a temper tantrum prone, cheap skate who sucks in bed. Dump his ass Tate; you can do so much better. You are so cute Tate. Plus if my man didn't go downtown and treat my pussy like the Goddess it is, he would be given a direct ticket right out my front door.

(I am Laughing)

You are so wrong Amanda you know that?

How big is his dick? If he doesn't have a big Johnson and you are putting up with all his crap, you are fucking crazy.

Amanda!! I say (and I am blushing but she doesn't care because she wants an answer and she is staring at me until I give her one) Amanda he is 6' 2" and wears a size 12 shoe, so you do the math.

(Just as Amanda begins to open her mouth the doorman comes over and tell us we can start to go into the Sky Bar. Amanda thanks him and turns to me and says :)

This conversation is not over and we will discuss this later Tate.

(I nod and follow her to The Sky Bar)

How do you know the doorman I ask Amanda?

She turns and smiles at me with a wicked smile and it reads like pure evil. She doesn't have to say anything because I have already figured it out. She updates me later with the actual facts but I didn't care I was in The Sky Bar! I soon come to find out that my new friend Amanda had fucked the doorman several times, in the bathroom so getting in was really easy for us. It was told to me after we were seated the real reason why it was so easy getting into the hardest club in town. Amanda informed me that the waitress was the doorman's wife. I wondered if she was from Brooklyn too because she had the blackmail thing down really good. She had men falling at her feet and she knew how to use sex to her advantage.. God I worship this chick Amanda already and I love the fact that she knows how to spread her legs for the right opportunities. Then again I have a feeling she would spread her legs if the wind blew hard enough so...... she is just a nasty ho who got me into the "Sky Bar." I don't judge people for what they do but I am extremely happy to be in the bar. Who cares how she did it plus as my grandma Trudie used to say "Judging people leaves no room left for loving them" I didn't love Amanda but she was fun.

Once we were settled at our table and ordered our first drink I started to look around the room and to my shock these people looked AWFUL and tacky. I felt like I was at a Long Island Sweet Sixteen Party. For those of you who have never been to one just think big hair, cheap and polyester. What the hell is going on? I am supposed to be in the hottest club on Sunset Strip but it looks more like K Mart was having a sample sale at the bar. We soon find out that the Mondrian Hotel is hosting a convention for the Mary Kay Ladies and this is their meet and greet time. I couldn't believe my eyes there WAS pink EVERYWHERE and not that gay pride kind either; it was that Pepto-Bismol meets a bad can of egg shell paint. Chiffons and mo-moos for as far as the eye could see. The hair was BIG and they all believed in "Kitchen Cosmetics." For those of you that do not know what Kitchen Cosmetics means I will tell you? It either means you are too fucking cheap to go to a salon to have your hair done right or you're just tacky……. or both come to think of it.

Also as I peruse the room in horror I realize that either the women all went to "Ivan the tent man designs" or they never heard the saying "Just cause they make it in your size doesn't mean you should wear it." As I look at one woman I swear I can see through the dress and what she had for breakfast- about 11 muffins and a decaf coffee. I know I am being judgmental but I just don't like fat people or tacky people or cheap people or…. **Wait Arrrrr** look she has a cute little Yorkie in her bag. I didn't notice the dog right away. The dog was blocked through the fat rolls, the pink chiffon and the feather pink Mary Kay boa she was wearing. She has to know how ridiculous she looks, right? That poor little dog is scared to death and shaking like a leaf. I know most of you would say that the reason the dog is scared was because she was in a strange place or with all these pink people right? Not me. Nope I think that dog is scared to death that the restaurant is going to run out of food and mommy's gonna eat her later. Again it's just what I think. My opinion generally doesn't go with the popular vote now but I am sure you have figured that out by now. Come on guys…you know you are thinking the same thing.

As the night progresses I start to see more and more gorgeous people and less and less Mary Kay ladies. It is after all 9:15pm now and it is way past their bedtime.

All this time I am sitting next to this annoying girl from Ohio named Natasha. Somewhat of a pretty girl but kind of plain I guess. Natasha recently did a Dodge commercial and thinks that she knows everything about the business. She begins this conversation with me if you can call "it" a conversation.

So what do you do?

I'm an actor.

SO am I! She shrieks.

In the back of my head I am like "No shit really!! I couldn't have figured that one out on my own"

So who is your commercial agent? She asks.

Ummm. Before I could say anything else.

I'm with Innovative. Who is your theatrical? As she looks at me with pity.

Theatrical what? I asked.

With a sigh of disgust she says **Agent????**

Ohhh well I just got out here and I just took my headshots last week. I should be getting the proofs the end of the week. (I have already bored her as she looks around the room for someone or something more interesting than me)

Excuse me she says I see someone I **have** to say hello to.

Bye! She had no more use for me that I am sure of.

About 10 minutes later my new friend Amanda and this very attractive woman come over and Amanda goes to her friend This is my friend new Tate who just moved here from New York and he is very funny.

Hi I am Jill she smiles at me Nice to meet you.

Just as I am shaking this girl Jill's hand I notice that Amanda has locked her eyes with the married doorman.

She turns to us and says "I will be back I have to pee."

I reach into my pocket and grab a peppermint lifesaver and say to Amanda take this just in case while you are "peeing" you need fresh breath.

She laughs and off she goes to "pee."

I turn back to Jill and say nice to meet you also. I ask her how she knows Amanda and blah, blah, blah.

And then here it comes........ She asks.

So what do you do?

So here I go again already bruised from Natasha. I say to Jill, I am an actor. And before she can say anything I start to ramble I justtookmynewheadshot and I am shopping for a commercial and theatrical agent and everything is going exactly to plan. I am going on and on and on and I am sure she is thinking what a dork! Is he going for the Guinness Book Of World Records for talking or what?

Jill goes I think I need to use the bathroom also.

Bye she says but very politely almost like OK retard boy, I was nice to you now please don't dribble on me.

I order another drink and tequila shot from our pretty waitress. Just as I am finishing the tequila shot these two girls come over and say **Hey** there! How are you sexy? I smile and say HI but I am overwhelmed they both sound like girls from Long Island on helium. Wait did I hear right?

Did one of them call me sexy?

I start chatting away with Susan and Dora and they are from a place called "The Valley." Huh sounds nice enough but their voices are God awful. The conversation was going well since they actually seemed to like talking about themselves. Susan was in fashion school and Dora was a student/model. They were both Taurus's and felt like they were "the two hottest girls" in the bar. They told me this about 6 times as well. They were size 2's, were wearing tight dresses, both had long hair, too much perfume on and making sure everyone saw them. After about 20 minutes of painful "chatting" with the Valley Girls, here came that dreaded question that I have screwed up twice before already. I had heard it twice in less than an hour to be exact and both times it was a disaster.

So what do you do?

I couldn't do it again. There were 2 of them this time and it would have been double the beating so I look at them dead in the face and I say:

I choke chickens for the Colonel.

Huh? They say in unison.

Again I say louder this time...I choke **chickens** for the Colonel.

Dora goes what Colonel?

Colonel Sanders I say.

Who is he? Susan asks.

Finally some fun I think Ha!

He is the owner of Kentucky Fried Chicken I go.

Dora asks and what exactly do you do?

I explain how I pick up the chickens and I choke them till they die. I then put them on the conveyer belt and pick up another chicken. I am having fun as their faces turn to shock so I continue appearing proudly. My quota per day is 1000 chickens but after I reach that I get 75 cents more per chicken bonus and that's where the real money is I say.

Susan and Dora in unison squeal.

We need to use the **bathroom!!!**

They turn and run like Manolo Blanik is giving away free shoes in the bathroom.

I now have this grin from ear to ear and I say to myself "I am going to make a great actor here in LA." My mind goes off to my Academy award speech dream that I have recited in my head and mirror hundreds of times.

All of a sudden my new friend Amanda marches over and says "None of my friends like you dude, you gotta go"

Huh?? What just happened?

Maybe you and Jerk off Jake are meant to be together Tate. Amanda states. I don't like negativity in my life especially from friends.

What are you talking about Amanda?

My friend Natasha told me all about what you were saying earlier tonight. You were making fun of the sweet Mary Kay ladies, mocking their outfits and calling them fat. She started telling me something about eating a dog or something. That is fucking gross. Jill thought you were an absolute moron, who couldn't even put two sentences together. The topper to all this was these two chicks who pointed you out from the bathroom. They said you told them that you kill chickens with your bare hands for money. Is that true? Did you do all this?

(I look at Amanda like really you are really going to judge me? Didn't you just blow some guy in the bathroom? I can smell your cock breath even with the peppermint lifesaver bitch. So I turn to Amanda and I say)

Amanda I was kidding, trying to make a joke. Natasha is as boring as watching wet paint dry. She was so fucking condescending towards me. I have been here in LA for less than 2 months and she couldn't understand why I didn't have a fucking agent. She was rude to me and all I was trying to do is make her laugh. I am sorry that she is a homely, frigid bitch who doesn't find me funny. Something is definitely wrong with her if she thought I was serious about eating a dog. Jill just made me nervous and I acted like an idiot. So that I am sorry for but as for those two annoying valley girls, I own what I said. They just wouldn't shut the fuck up. I tolerated listening to them and then they asked me the dreaded question of the night "what do you do for a living?"

What was the question? How to act like a douchebag in public? Amanda snaps

No Amanda they kept asking me what I do for a living.

What do you tell them? Amanda asks.

That I am an actor I respond.

Are you an actor? (Amanda interrogates) and plays do not fucking count. This is LA and it is all about TV and movies. So are you an actor Tate?

Well Amanda (I am Pissed) I am trying to break into the business. It is why I moved to this fucking town Amanda!

Then say that Tate. Don't say you're an actor if you haven't acted. A painter would never say they are a painter if they never painted anything. I say I am studying to be a teacher but I have never said that I am a teacher. Get it?

I get it. I say to Amanda. It is just that this was my first time in a Los Angeles/ Hollywood scene and I just got really insecure. I am sorry.

Let's go get a shot. I would rather hang with drunken Tate than insecure Tate any day of the week. Sorry I was such a bitch just now but the doorman's wife just asked me, if I was sleeping with her husband.

Oh shit what did you say to her?

I told her to go ask her fucking husband.….Amanda smiles with that same evil smile that she gave me when we walked in to The Sky Bar. OK Tate but what is the deal with you killing chickens with your bare hands for money?

Ha!!!

It is my alias Amanda. I work for Colonial Saunders. I choke chickens for Kentucky Fried Chicken. I use my hands to show them how. They usually don't believe me so I go into what my chicken quota of the day is and once I reach it. Usually they are horrified by now because I say this as proud as ever.

I say it like I am a doctor or movie star. If this doesn't get them screaming away I go into the money I make for bonus dead chicken…..

Bonus Dead Chicken? Tate you are seriously not right…So you choke chickens for the Colonial…that is fucking hilarious. Can I choke chickens for the Colonial too?

Sure Amanda….No problem but you just have to have sex with the Colonial first.

Eww…..Amanda screams.

Once you get past the wrinkly age spotted pecker, it really isn't that bad and the Colonial is a really good kisser, especially when he takes his teeth out.

(laughter)

You are not right Tate?

Chapter 7

The phone calls from my Mother

So I have been living in LA for a little while now and things are starting to really take shape. The one problem I am still having is that my mother does not understand or grasp that it is 3 hours earlier here in LA than in New York. My roommate Thomas is ready to kill me about this also. I have tried **everything** I can to make her stop calling so early. I have told her time and time again about the time difference but she just doesn't get it. I have racked my brain trying to figure out a way not to be woken up so damn early every morning. I finally thought to myself Ahhh I have an idea! I found a way not to be woken up at 6:30 am, get yelled at by my roommate for waking him up or walking around like a zombie all day—I will just turn off the ringer. I am a genius I say to myself right?

Wrong!!

On one particular Sunday night we all go out late and have a blast! Even Thomas and I were starting to get along. I was pulling further and further away from Jake and I just needed a night out of fun. We hit The Abbey around 10pm and then went dancing at Micky's until closing time. What a fun night. Everyone was laughing, dancing and there was an extreme amount of flirting. Being not only an actor but a trained professional dancer I was able to garner a ton attention on the dance floor. As I was dancing on the dance floor I started to think about Jake for a minute. He was so good-looking but he didn't treat me very well. His Latin temper was horrible and few people I worked with liked him. I wasn't that happy with Jake but it was nice to say I had a boyfriend. I don't know why I needed the security of having a boyfriend but I just felt safe. Some of the guys on the dance floor were getting a little grabby so I felt it was time to get a drink. I glanced over and saw Amanda dancing like a hurricane so I decided to venture over to the bar solo. I glanced down at my watch and it was 1230 am already. Wow time does really fly when you are having fun. I walk over to the bar and I wait for the bartender. All of the bartenders are shirtless and their bodies are stunning. Of course I end up in the bar section where the bartender just happens to be Latin. Imagine that? After about 3 minutes the Latin bartender comes over to me and says:

What can I get for you handsome?

(Wait did he just call me handsome? Ah he probably says it to all his customers. It definitely makes for much better tips)

I will have a vodka soda with a splash of cranberry I state to the bartender.

Coming right up he says as he smiles and turns to make my drink.

(As he turns away I do what I always do. I compare him to Jake. They are both Latin but probably from different countries. The bartender is much leaner than Jake but Jake still has a much more handsome face. It would probably just come down to the personalities but I am a sucker for a good looking face.)

Here you go, that will be 8 dollars as the bartender hands me my drink.

(I fish in my pocket and I actually have a ten dollar bill. I hand it to the bartender)

Keep the change…thanks I say with a smile and take a sip of my drink.

Thanks…hey I haven't seen you here before. Are you visiting from somewhere or is this just your first time at my bar?

(My bar….I wonder if he is the owner….probably not…he looks too young to be the owner but you never know…)

I moved here about 2 months ago from New York City. This is only my second time here though. The music is incredible. I say to the friendly bartender.

I am Rodrigo the bartender says and he presents me with his very masculine hand.

(I extend my hand and say :)

Nice to meet you Rodrigo!

(As this is happening Amanda has spotted me from the dance floor and begins to walk over)

I thought you ditched me. Amanda says as she approaches the bar.

I would never do that Amanda.

Well I would….especially if the guy was hot…I would leave you a voicemail or a text though. As Amanda says with a laugh.

This is Rodrigo as I turn and point to Rodrigo. Do you want a drink? You were dancing like crazy out there.

Yes! Vodka soda and lets do a shot! Can we have two cock sucker shots?

Amanda!!!!!

What Tate it is a real shot (as she looks at the bartender for some back up on her cock sucker shot legitimacy)

They are good Rodrigo says as he winks at me.

OK why not…sure I will have one.

(Rodrigo goes to make our drinks)

(Amanda puts this smirk on her face and looks at me)

He is hot Tate…His body is incredible. I wonder if he is gay or straight/ I think he is straight…Find out for me.

Why would you think he was straight Amanda? This is a gay bar Amanda! Don't you have enough guys worshipping you on Sunset? Why do you have to go after the gay guys as well?

First off Tate…I never have enough guys and secondly there are tons of straight guys that work in gay bars. If they are hot they can make a fortune. I know for a fact that over at The Abbey the majority of the bartenders are straight….

Really? Wow I had no idea….

(Some of them probably get a kick out of it too….when a gay guy hits on a straight guy. Great something else to add onto my insecurities list)

Here you guys go (as Rodrigo places the shots and Amanda's drink on the bar) I am going to do one with you guys. (We all raise our shot glasses in the air) Welcome to West Hollywood Tate! (clink clink)

Cheers!!! We all say in unison.

(Wow this cock sucker tastes really good….the drink people…get your mind out of the gutter)

(We thank Rodrigo and he goes onto his next customer)

Do you want to dance some more Amanda?

Sure she says as we start our way back towards the dance floor.

(Amanda leans in to me and says)

The bartender is definitely gay Tate!!!

How do you know?

Because as we were walking away he couldn't stop checking out your ass! You should definitely go for it Tate! He is hot!

(I in turn whirl around and catch Rodrigo staring at me and he is smiling from ear to ear. I nervously raise my hand in a friendly gesture and then race to the dance floor. I was mortified because I turned around. I should have just listened to Amanda! Amanda eventually finds me on the dance floor deck which overlooks the dance floor. It is a great place to watch everyone dance)

What just happened? Amanda asks.

What? What are you talking about?

That you just ran away from the bartender staring at you like you just found out he has escaped from a leper colony. Amanda states.

I have a **boyfriend** Amanda!

Jake is an asshole Tate. He treats you like shit. Actually he treats everyone like shit. Get rid of him. Plus you are too young to just have **one** boyfriend! I have several. You have plenty of time to settle down after you hit 30. Our twenties are just for having fun. Go get the bartenders number Tate.

No Amanda…that is disrespectful to Jake. I don't cheat Amanda. It is not in my DNA.

Well then I will go get it and after you dump Jakes ass I will give you the hot bartender's number. This way it is not cheating Sister Mary Tate. Geez….what a little prude you can be. What is the bartenders name again?

Rodrigo I say…..

(Amanda turns and heads back to the bar and I didn't stop her. Why didn't I stop her? I know why… I wasn't happy with Jake. I knew it had to end. He really did turn into a bona fide asshole as well. Come to think of it I don't even think we have ever been on a real date. Is Amanda right? Should we not settle down till 30? I don't want to think about this anymore tonight. I just want to dance!)

I got his digits Tate! Amanda says as they are announcing closing time

So who is he into? I ask Amanda?

(Amanda whispers in my ear)

Dump Jake and you will find out….

(What a bitch Amanda! I know I had to do it but I am going to miss, Sofia so much. I think it will be harder to say goodbye to her **than** him. I really like her.)

Well it is the end of the night and all of us are pretty drunk. None of us want the night to end so we decide that its "After Party" time at our house and we invite about 15 people over.

We take cabs back to our apartment because Tommy has announced that we have liquor at the apartment. He as usual has some German man's tongue down his throat the whole cab ride home. The rest of the night gets a little foggy but I know that I did not cheat on Jake. I remember Amanda yammering on and on that I should have invited Rodrigo back to the apartment. I remember random guys making out all over the place that I had no idea who they were. It was all a big haze and man did I drink too much or what. I am going to drink a glass of water and go to bed. There better not be anyone having sex in my bed.

Finally around 4:15am everyone had paired off and went to bed or went home. I climb into my bed (solo) and start to pass out. Before I do I remember to make sure the ringer is off on the phone because I have a feeling I am going to be hung-over. I pass out and the next thing I hear is:

Tatey are you there? It's Mommy! Tatey are you there? Hello!!! Hello! Tatey where are you? Why are you not picking up the phone? Are you OK? \

(it is morning now and I cannot even focus my eyes on the alarm clock because everything is blurry)

Tatey!!!!! Now she is sobbing and I crawl across the room to answer the phone, My head is pounding, I feel like my entire body is going to explode. I hear Tommy yelling Answer the fucking phone, Answer the fucking phone. I reach for it and Click she has hung up. I turn to crawl back to the bed and the cat is hissing at me for my mother disturbing him too I guess......

I get back into the bed and throw the blanket over my head but before I have done this you better believe I have turned off that answering machine. Ahh **Finally** let me get some blissful sleep.

(An hour goes by)

Bang Bang, Bang, Bang On the door!

I am dreaming this noise I assume because this cannot be happening but to no avail Tommy is at my bedroom door.

Hey Asshole, the cops are here for you! Thomas sneers.

My mind races OMG what did I do last night? Ok I didn't drive; I pied in a bunch of bushes though. Was I on camera? Can you go to jail for that? I will never drink again God if you get me out of this. I didn't fight anybody right? Did I break something?

Asshole the cops are here for you!! Thomas screams.

(Gulp! Shit! Man my head is pounding.)

Did they say **why** they were here? I ask Thomas.

No Tate but I can only imagine what the fuck you did this time. You know I decided to go out with you last night but I had my reservations. I think

ncy call to the Hollywood Sheriff station stating that I was either
murdered, or being murdered or dead or dying.

I start to apologize over and over to the police officers and I tell them that
this will **never** happen again. In the back of my head I am saying to myself
"Why couldn't I be an orphan with a trust fund?" Don't get me wrong I love
my mother, but Hung-over and Hysteria just don't do well together.

(The officers just shake their heads and leave the apartment)

Next thing I hear is another knock on the door.

What the hell was that about???

Guess who??

Yup you guessed it! Only **me** right?? U-huh say it yup- The freakin landlady that **hates** me! Oh happy day for me.

I begin to explain about my hysterical NY mother. I can tell she has the look of contempt on her face and the utter disbelief that, I am going to explain to her how indeed this is not my fault either.

I ask myself is it worth it? Do I really care what this nasty bitch of a landlady thinks, when all I can think about is the throbbing headache coming from my brain? So I am staring at her like a slaughtered, beaten down, horror movie victim and I say:

My mother thought I was dead…

And why would she think that? She asks sarcastically, with a slice of nasty

(Because my mother just escaped from Bellevue Mental Institute I say to myself but out loud I just say very softly)

I don't know…………Sorry………..It will never happen again and I close the door.

What the fuck Tate????

Shut up Thomas let me deal with this.

Tell your Mom I said Hi! Seriously send her my love and tell her just **how much I have enjoyed this joyous fucking wakeup call!!!!**

(I am going to kill her) I shut my door and grab that telephone like a fat lady, has just discovered the phone is edible and tastes like chocolate cake. I dial the number.

Muh-tha what is wrong with you??

Tatey you're alive and you're OK! She yelps at the top of her lungs. I thought you were dead or something she says!

(Now mind you I can tell by her voice she had been crying and that she was genuinely worried, so I had to proceed very cautiously with this clinically insane mother of mine.)

Mom what's going on?

I thought you were dead.

Yes mom I kind of got that from the 2 police officers that were at my door.

Wow they got there quick Julia (Julia is my mom's BFF by the way and must be over the house} As I hear her say to someone else in her house

Mom why did you call the cops?

I told you because I thought you were dead.

Why did you think I was dead?

Who got there quick? I hear Julia ask my Mother in the background

The LA cops Jules.

O yeah Julia says with that Long Island accent that makes my skin crawl.

Mom why did you call the cops?

Huh because you didn't answer my phone calls. I must have tried you for an hour or so before I panicked, she laments to me. Why didn't you answer the phone Tatey?

Because I was trying to sleep in Mom. I have told you a million times that it is 3 hours earlier here in California, than in New York Ma.

Well my day started like 3 hours ago and I don't have time to wait for **you** to rise and shine in California! I wake up and I think of you. You see I love you and I miss you and I still don't know why you had to go and move all the way to California. You know you are 3000 miles away from me.

I do I think to myself......

Mom I have a roommate and it's not fair to him.

Isn't Thomas from New York and doesn't his mother still live here? She asks like the born prosecutor she should have been, if she actually didn't go to beauty school instead.

Yes Mom he is and his mom still does live in New York.

And **she** doesn't call in the morning? As she continues to talk to me like the prosecutor.

No Mom she calls in the evenings and weekends.

But don't you work evenings and weekends Tatey?

Yes Mom I do.

Thomas's mother must not love her son as much as I love you.

Ugh I give up Mom please just try and **Not** call so early.

OK OK I will try but don't you want to know **why** I was calling?

Why Mom?

Well first to tell you I love you, I miss you, I want you to come home desperately but besides the obvious I got a little worried.

(Again in my head I am like **really Mom** No shit? You got worried? Never would have guessed it! Wow this sarcasm is actually helping my hangover. Maybe I am on to something here. Hmmm..)

All of a sudden.

Tatey are you listening to me???

Ahh ye ye yes Mom what is it?

Well I got a little worried because I was reading my National Enquirer.

And what Mom? Did aliens invade Los Angeles again?

No....I **know** that is not real Tatey. There was this article about all these actors becoming scientists.

Scientists Mom?

Yes! they're a cult and they take all your money.

What are you talking about Mom?

You know Kirstie Alley's in it and Tom Cruise and John Travolta—is he really **gay** Tatey? Such a pretty wife he has. It is such a shame.

Mom!!!!

Oh but not you dear, I love my homosexual gay son. I'm so proud of you Tatey. We're here, we're queer, get used to us! Why won't you let me join PFLAG again? (I will explain later people!)

Time out, Time out Mom! Take a breather please!

It is Scientology and it's an organized religion bases off L Ron Hubbard's beliefs Mom.

I know **that's** why I called them scientists Tatey. What are you so dense sometimes? Get with the program. They are **all** over California and I don't want them taking you away from the Catholic Church now.

I say to myself" Yeah Mom that's what taking me away from the Catholic church MOM **–Fucking Scientology….**

No Mom I have no desire to become a Scientologist so you don't have to worry about it anymore.

Well good she says.

Father Flynn asked about you last week and I told him you went to California.

(Oh no I say to myself what's next? Somebody please just kill me now put me out of my misery.........)

And?? I say.

He says hello and God bless you.

Ahh OK.

Oh no its 11:04 and I am missing Judge Judy she say in a panic but a different type of panic I gotta go. I love you Tatey.

Bye...

Bye......

I hang up the phone and I say to myself" Does she **really not** know why I moved 3000 miles away from her? Certifiable but she is my mom and I love her no matter what. I should be very careful what I say to her no matter what though – God knows what's next.

I hang up the phone, take a deep breath and I decide to play the messages on the phone to gain knowledge of my Mother's hysteria.

You have 4 messages the answering machine tells me.

First Message: Hey Tatey it is Mom call me when you can. I have a question about scientists living in Los Angeles. It is very important.

Erase....

Second message a little more hysterical but basically the same!

Third Message Hey Asshole it is Jake. Thank you for fucking disrespecting me out in West Hollywood last night. I heard you were all over a ton of guys last night you fucking slut. I swear I want to bash your head in Tate. I do not want anything to ever to do with you again. Fucking whore bag. I wish I could fire your ass but instead I will make your life a living hell.

I turn off the answering machine and I lay back down in bed. What a great Monday this is turning out to be. I am staying in bed all day.

Chapter 8

Flashbacks to my childhood:

I decided on one beautiful sunny afternoon in Southern California to go for a walk in Griffith Park. It is in the Los Feliz part of LA and it is a really cool place to collect your thoughts. As I am walking through the park, I come across this family having a picnic. I can tell they are a family because they all kind of look alike. There is Mom and Dad, 2 brothers and a sister also. They kind of reminded me of my family for a brief second. That is until I realized that they were all getting along with each other and enjoying the day. **That** would never be my family. No. My family would constantly be bickering or fighting with one another, well all of them except me. I would just pretend they didn't exist and go off into never never land. I would pretend I had another family. I would always wish that I was a part of some TV family. I really did not like my family, especially my younger brother and sister. They were very close in age and **always** at each other's throat over something or another. I chose to pretend they didn't exist. My room was on the opposite side of the house so I did not have to deal with them as much. Whenever we went out I at all times, when it was possible, would go in the extreme opposite way they would be headed in. They would just embarrass me and just flat out ruin a perfectly good outing.

We all went to Catholic School and once I began the 5th grade I was on the second floor with none of my siblings. I would tell all of my friends, fellow

Classmates and teachers that I was an only child. What a glorious year the 5th grade was. I never had to apologize for their actions or break up a fight between the 2 of them (which happened on a daily basis BTW.) The 5th grade was a year of tranquility, an oasis of sorts for me and I never once all year dreaded having to go to school. The 5th grade was by far the **best** year of my life up until that point. Well when the following school year came around and my sister came onto my floor, I had some seriously explaining to do. Kelly would go around blabbing that I was her older brother and people started to look at me strange. I just became a mute and climbed under a rock for the sixth grade or though I thought I did. Every day I could hear her squawking at someone about something and always try and get me into it. I think back to all the friends I have lost due to this "impossible to please" person. People would ask me in the beginning why I told them I was an only child and I would respond "you'll see why" trust me "you'll see….." I made it throughout the whole year without actually answering the question as to truly why I told everyone that I was an only child. I remember overhearing my mother tell my aunt that my teacher told her, that I told everyone that I was an only child. My mother chuckled and told the teacher "I don't think he said he was an only child but that I wished I was an only child! My aunt and my mom laughed and she shrugged it off. God I loved my mother and I was definitely her son!!

When summer came around I was so excited to get the hell out of school but there was this looming dread that would follow me all summer long. When I go back to school in the fall, my brother Christopher would now be on the same floor as my sister and myself. I was going to have **a lot** of "splaining to do." The difference with last year was that after about a month of school I think people figured out "why" I lied about not having a sister. I think the kids and possibly the teachers realized that if they **too** were related to this loud mouthed, self-absorbed, blabbermouth they would lie about it also. My younger brother was a different story. Christopher was actually pretty normal and I didn't know how I was going to get out of this lie. All summer long I would think up ways in my head to get through what was fast approaching me and It wrecked me all summer long just thinking about it. The closer it would get to the end of summer, the sicker to my stomach I would get. Hmm I even wondered if he would go along saying he was my cousin???............ I would probably have gotten Christopher to agree to my scenario or plot, but that bitch of a sister??? HA she would have blown our cover before the first day of recess was over.

OK for the record. I didn't hate my sister I just didn't like her very much. Is that awful to say? I never wanted her dead but I never wanted her near me. As long as she stayed far away from me and I didn't have to hear her, my life was fine. My brother on the other hand, it wasn't that he was loud but he would do things to make my sister **loud.** He would pinch her and she would scream. Hide things from her so she would scream. Pull on her hair so she would scream. Give her wet willies so.... Do you get the fucking point? He lived to torture her and she lived to get him into trouble yet always at my expense. Ya see my parents had this odd and irrational idea, that with me being the oldest that I am "supposed" to watch my siblings. Now can I ask you... why is that? Did I ask my parents for a sister? No I did not. Did I ask for another brother? Nope. Did I ever ask for siblings? Never! So why should I be responsible for what they did? It is what my parents did...they had sex. Now because of their actions I am stuck with my sister and brother. They were always loud and ruining everything for me.

One Christmas we got an Atari to "share" for Christmas. I knew this had disaster written all over it. They could barely be in the same room with each other, let alone play video games with one other. We would get an individual half hour, each day to play video games and I was allowed to go first. Being the oldest had **some** benefits. I set up this arrangement with my mother because as soon as my time was over I would leave the room. This way my mother would have to deal with the everyday World War 3 that would happen, between my siblings. Every day I would hear things like:

It's **my** turn!!

But I'm on a high score my brother would yell!

It's **my** turn! My sister would screech louder every single fucking time she had to repeat it.

Then the inevitable would happen. My sister would pull out the plug or turn the game off while my brother would still be playing on his "high score." You would have thought someone just killed Christopher and the war would begin until my mother broke it up, Kelly was crying or one of them would brake something. It usually was either the second or third thing that would happen. Every single time it would happen we would be punished and no ATARI for a week. It didn't matter whether I was a part of it or not. Yup I too would be punished. My parents had this all for one type of punishment. It sucks right? Yeah I know....

One day my mother comes up to my room. I isolated myself on the other side of the house as much as possible.

I need you to watch your sister and brother for an hour??

(Hell no I am thinking in my head!) What? I say.

Tate it's just for an hour.... Please??(I could never say no to my mother no matter **how** much I wanted to).

OK "but if they fight it's not my fault" I go.(My Mom looks at me and say's) "just don't let them kill each other."

Fair enough Mom I say. My mother tells the two "Demons of Sibling try" that she has to go out and that I am in charge. I say to myself "Why mother? Why would you tell them this? Why????? The second you walk out that door bedlam is going to surely happen now. Do you think that the demons are going to listen to me? Ha… Mother you are more delusional than even I thought. These two children are the children of Satan and you are their Gatekeeper. Me? I don't even want a definition of what I am because I don't want to be defined remotely **anything** related to them.

My Mother's car is not even remotely off the block when Kelly starts screeching. I want to watch.……..My brother and her are already both lunging toward the cable box. We had a TV room that we used rather frequently and it was often where the latest and greatest battle between Kelly and Christopher would start. At this very moment they were both pulling at the cable box and pressing any and all channels at the same time. Mind you while my mother was home they were both content watching Tom and Jerry! The TV is flipping from channel to channel and I try and take control of this but it just becomes a 3 way battle for the cable box. Finally I take control of it and throw it to the back of the room. I scream" Do you want to lose your TV privileges for a week?" They both stop and realize that they don't want to miss the Part 2 of Dawson's Creek tonight. Or so I thought. They both go to opposite corners of the couch and just glare at each other. I plead with them to call a truce and they agree. They agree to a cease fire or so I thought they agreed. I ask them if I can go back upstairs and finish my homework. They agree and off I went.,,

I am not even on the 5th step when I hear Kelly scream **Ouch!!** "Chris that hurts!" she wails. I say to myself "It's not worth it" and I keep climbing the stairs and I close my door. I put my headphones on and continue doing my homework. About an hour later I hear this bang on my door so loud it scared the hell out of me.

Tate Connors Get your ass down here now! It's my Mother and I know I have done **something** wrong because she is using all my names. I know that when she uses my full name that I am in deep trouble. I opened the door and she says: **Get down here!!**

I walk down the stair with this "what did I do" look on my face.

Get in here she screams!!

I walked into the TV room and my neighbor Mildred is sitting in our trashed den staring at me in disbelief. I look around the room and it is trashed. The coffee table to broken, pillows are everywhere, a lamp is on the floor, Kelly is crying, Christopher is bleeding. Apparently things got so out of hand that my neighbor had to come over and break this up. It seriously looked like World war 3 erupted in the TV room.

My Mother is screaming at me. She is telling me I was supposed to watch them, make sure they didn't fight and keep the peace!!

I was just staring at the room and everything that had transpired and ignored her yammering. Finally I looked her dead in the eye, put my hands on my hips and said

"Well at least they didn't kill each other right?" –(I gotta be the fucking smart ass right I say to myself but it's **way** too late the damage is done.)

(My Mother just pointed to my room with this look of "I am gonna kill him!") I can't even rely on you for one hour to watch them, she says angrily.

Mom the second you took off they started with the cable box. I had to separate them within 2 minutes of your departure! I had them on separate sides of the couch and they agreed to a truce. Mom I have homework and I cannot sit here and referee them, I just can't!

By the way whatever did happen in Part 2 of Dawson's Creek? Did Dawson and Joey finally express their true feelings to one another?

I never found it………. Guess why? I was punished.

So let's go back to the first day of school when all 3 of us are going to be on the same floor. I am in 7ᵗʰ ᵍʳᵃᵈᵉ, Kelly in 6ᵗʰ and Christopher in 5ᵗʰ grade and we all go to our respected new classrooms. The day starts out great but by lunchtime my old 5ᵗʰ grade teacher, walks up to me and says "Tate I need to speak to you…

My stomach churns and this is **even** before the lovely school lunch food.

We have a very big problem she says…

Really, I say in disbelief. What kind of problem??

Your problem with telling the truth she scolds.

Huh?

I have your brother Christopher in my class this year but you clearly told me and your entire class two years ago that you were indeed an only child. I have also come to find out that you have a sister. I need to talk to your parents because clearly there is a problem….

But, but, but- I stammer please **no**! I am wailing, I am crying!! No… no you don't understand "They always get me in trouble! I hate them." I pretend I don't have any siblings because I hate them. Please Ms. Barouquo do not call my parents! I am sobbing Please!!!!!!

You have some serious issues young man and I will be calling your mother this afternoon. She informs me.

I soooo don't want to go home after school today! What is my Mother going to do? She knows I hate them and I think she knows I pretend to be an only child. I hope she doesn't punish me because the new TV season is just about to begin.

Well by the time I get home from school my Mother has already called a shrink and I have an appointment for Friday afternoon after school. She is looking at me like I have a big pimple in the middle of my nose.

Tatey we need you to talk to someone about this. You cannot go around school telling people you are an only child. You have a brother and a sister that love you.

Well I don't love them. I hate them. I angrily tell my Mother. They are always ruining everything! I am always in trouble for things **they** do wrong.

So you never do anything wrong Tatey? My Mother asks.

No I don't! I angrily retort.

My Mother laughs and says you are going to see the psychologist on Friday afternoon whether you like it or not.

Well I do not like it and I do not like you right now. How come you never take my side Mom? They do something wrong and we all get into trouble. When I do something wrong, how come only I get into trouble? It is not fair. I am an individual person Mom.

Well you can ask the psychologist that very same question on Friday afternoon Tatey. Now go upstairs and think about what you did. My Mother snapped.

So I went upstairs and plotted my next runaway attempt. I had $254 dollars and this time I was never coming back. I am going to Florida and I am going to get a job at Disney World. It is the happiest place on earth. I pack my duffle bag up with shorts and T shirts because it is always warm in Florida! I look up where in Florida Disney World is and I find out it is in Orlando. So tomorrow morning I am buying a bus ticket to Orlando and nobody is going to stop me. I will send my Mother a postcard once I get settled into my new life away from my brother and sister.

The next morning I set my alarm an hour earlier than I usually do. I shower and make a clean break for it. I scratch Pepper my amazing Labrador retriever on the head and tell her I love her and will miss her. Should I take her with me? No. I will send for her after I am settled. I look back at her as I am about to close the door. Her eyes are telling me please don't leave me. Please don't leave me. I reopen the door; pack some of her dog food, a few toys and lots of treats. I put the leash on her and off my go. As we are walking down the block towards the subway I tell her "Pepper we are going to have a great life" but all she is interested in, is where I have stashed her treats.

We enter the subway station and we take the # 1 train to 42nd Street. We get off the subway and walk one block to Port Authority. We walk into Port Authority and I start looking for the Grey Hound ticket office. I get goose bumps when I actually locate it. I look down at the dog and I say "Pepper we are going to ride Space Mountain 10 times a day!" I quickly walk towards the Grey Hound Ticket office. I walk in and go directly to the ticket counter line. I wait for my turn patiently on the line. We are getting a lot of attention because everybody loves Pepper and Pepper loves everyone! Once it becomes my turn I walk over to this gray haired lady in the ticket window and I say:

I want to purchase a one way ticket to Orlando for me and my dog please.

Where is your Mother Young man? She asks.

Oh she is already there. She lives there. She sent me up to New York to visit my Dad for a week bit now I have to get back for school.

So **where** is your Dad? She inquires.

He is at work I answer with sheer confidence.

How old are you? She asks.

I am sixteen years old (I lied…duh…I would have to be pretty stupid to be 16 and still in the 7th grade huh?)

Can I see some identification? The gray haired lady is looking at me kind of funny but she is at least still smiling at me.

My Mother has it in Florida. She forgot to give it to me when she packed my bag. She forgets to pack my lunch all the time too. I say cheerful.

What is your name? I need it to put on your ticket and I also need your Mother's name. She will be the one picking you up in Florida right? The ticket lady says as she is typing something into her computer.

Right (I am thinking **score** I am getting the hell out of here) my name is Tate Connors and my Mother's name is Jacqueline Connors. Do you need my dogs name too?

Sure she says.

Pepper Connors I say.

Thank you very much Tate. Now you can have a seat over there and we will call you when your ticket is ready.

Thank you I say and walk over to seat in the waiting room. I am so excited. I am getting away from my evil siblings. I will miss my Mom and I am sure she will be sad but she has two other kids to love. I am making the right decision. I am making the decision to what is best for me and my dog. I will go to school and get an after school job. I will get a job at Disney World. I will make enough money for Pepper and me to go on the rides every weekend. After about 45 minutes I am starting to get impatient because I think the bus is leaving soon. Maybe she forgot about me? All of a sudden I hear the most dreaded sound ever heard in the English language.

Tate Connors what do you think you are doing?

I turn around and I see her. I start to shake because she looks pissed. Boy am I in trouble now. Yup it is my Mother. I am busted. How did she finds me? I thought it takes 24 hours to fill out a missing persons report. Is it different for kids?

So I **live** in Florida huh? She asks as she approaches me.

What? I stammer (everyone knows that by saying what it gives you a few seconds to think up an excuse or a lie to the question)

Do not what me Tate (OK she is pissed, she never calls me Tate) so you and Pepper are planning to move to Florida?

Yes I say.

Where are you going to live? My Mother asks.

In Orlando…near Disney World I inform my Mother.

Really she asks? So **where** are you going to live in Orlando near Disney World?

I am going to rent an apartment Mom! (Why is she asking me all these questions? I am running away and she cannot stop me)

And may I ask with what money Tate? (She is softening up)

I am going to get a job after school at Disney World Mom. I say clearly annoyed at her for asking such stupid questions.

You have to be 18 years old to work there and you are not even 12 yet! My Mother says very calmly.

Just as I am about to answer her I see my Dad barreling his way down the hall right towards me and he is really pissed. As he enters the room I hear:

What is going on Tate? Where you going Tate? Going somewhere? Did you forget to ask your Mom or me permission? What is going on Tate?

(My Dad is clearly not happy but Pepper is very happy to see him)

Dad I can't live in that house anymore (I start to cry) All Christopher and Kelly do is fight. I hate them. I hate them. Now Mom wants me to go to a crazy doctor because I tell people I am an only child. I wish I was an only child. So I am going away to be alone so I don't get in trouble, because of them. All my life I get into trouble for **things** they do wrong. When I do something wrong they don't get into trouble. It is not fair so I am leaving.

Where are you going Tate?

He tried to buy a bus ticket to Orlando Florida, my Mother states.

Jackie I asked Tate not you, my Dad snaps.

I want to get away from them Dad. I hate them!

You don't hate your brother and sister Tate. Do you want to come home and live with me, Ellen and Roger?

(The utter feeling of fear and panic has just encrusted my face. I hate his new wife Ellen. She is an evil bitch and my half-brother is the ultimate brat.)

No Dad I hate **your** wife too I say while still sobbing.

Well you have two options here Tate. You either go home with your Mother or you come home with me. You can chose either one but you are not getting on that bus to Florida. That is for damn sure. So what's it going to be Tate?

(The fucking crazy bitch wife my Dad has married or my two obnoxious siblings, man those are not really great options)

Tatey just come home and we can talk about it my Mother says very calming.

Do I still have to go and see the psychologist Mom? I ask.

Even **more** now than before kid as my Father chimes in. Do you want to go live in an orphanage where there are hundreds of Kelly and Christopher's? That can be arranged as well!

Tate! My Mother yells. **Stop it!**

Listen here Jackie I don't know what the hell goes on in that house any more but I am sure as hell not going to let this shit happen again my Father screams at my Mother. **What kind of Mother are you, that your almost 12 year old son gets all the way to fucking Port Authority? The ticket agent stopped him from getting on that bus. What would have happened if he would have gotten on that bus? Seriously Jackie maybe if you weren't fucking every man in the 5 boroughs, you would have noticed your kid trying to run away. I am sick of it Jack. You are a bad Mother. I should take all your kids away from you.**

Stop Dad! I plead please stop!

Yeah just stop because you don't want to throw rocks at the glass house you built, now do you? Do you want your son to know the real reason we got divorced? Do you Ex Husband? (My mother is now in my Dad's face and she is not backing down) Do you My Baby Daddy? (My dad is mocking her now) So you want your son to know that you fucked another woman, got her pregnant, all while you were married to me. I am tired of being the villain all the time asshole.

(An unfamiliar voice says ;)

Child...I would run away too if I had those parents...that poor baby.

(I whirl around and it is a chubby black lady watching as all of the action goes down between me and my fighting parents)

Mom and **Dad** please stop fighting, please. I will go home and I will go to the psychologist I promise just please stop fighting.

Kid you pull something like this again you are going to military school. Do you understand me Tate? If you **ever try** anything like this again you will be in West Point before you can say I am sorry. Stop your fucking crying and be a man.

(I shake my head yes)

That is also part of the problem Jackie. You baby him and look what he goes and does. This is insane. My 11 year old kid just tried to run away to Florida because he hates his brother and sister. This never happened when I was in that house. Fuck Jackie get it together with these kids. I cannot afford to miss work because you cannot control our kids. I will take them from you, I swear if this happens again.

(My Mother starts to cry now and now for the first time in my life Pepper is growling at my Father.)

(My Dad turns to my Mother) Look I am sorry. I was scared. Call me after his therapy session and let me know how it goes.

(My Mother just wipes away her final tear and just shakes her head. My dad turns to me and says I love you Tate. I hope you know that. I nod but to be honest I didn't really know that. I just thought he was pissed off having to leave work. My Dad walks out the door with his head down.)

Let's go home Tatey my Mother says (as she grabs my bag from the floor and starts to head toward the door)

You keep your chin up baby! (The chubby black lady yells)

(I just grab Peppers leash and head to the door. I feel so ashamed and I have given my Father another excuse to make my Mother cry. We walk all the way through the Port Authority terminal and into the parking lot in complete silence. As we approach the car I turn to my Mother and I say :)

I am sorry Mom! I really am.

(She just looks at me with a blank stare and says) Just get in to car Tate. I am very angry and I do not want to talk to you right now.

But Mom I really **am** sorry!

Tate get in the car (She is really angry) I do not want to say something that either one of us are going to regret later.

But Mom I plead…..

Tate Connors just get in the fucking car and shut the fuck up. Do you hear me? Just shut the fuck up and get in this God Damn car!!!

(Gulp) Ok Mom

The whole car ride back to Brooklyn we sat in silence. I knew I was in a lot of trouble especially when my Mother wouldn't even look at me. As we started to drive over the Brooklyn Bridge, I could tell my Mom was trying to hold back tears. I felt like the worst son in the world. How could I do this to her? Sometimes I can be so selfish. For the first time in a long time I wasn't thinking on how I was going to get out of a mess but how I was going to make this up to my Mom. By the time we got home, I knew I should not press my luck and say anything. I just went into the house and directly to my room. About an hour later I heard my Mother drop the duffle bag in front of my door. I fell asleep sometime after that and was awoken to a knock on my door.

Knock knock dinner is ready Tate! Mom said to hurry up down and I processed it that it was my sister Kelly banging on the door.

I am not hungry I yell out to her.

OK but Mom is not going to be happy Kelly sings out.

Not even a minute goes by and there is a loud bang on the door. The next thing I hear is my Mother yelling at me:

Tate get your ass down stairs and eat. All I need right now is more ammunition for your Dad that I am not properly feeding you kids. Get your ass downstairs in two minutes.

Yes Mom I will be right there I stammer.

I slowly walk downstairs and I can already smell it. Yup we are having the dreaded spaghetti and clam sauce. Yup it is right out of the Campbell's can and I hate it. (That should be punishment enough)

(As we sit down my Mother hands me a stack of papers and says ;) These are your homework assignments from school. As soon as you finish dinner, you go directly to your room and do them. No TV for you.

For the next two days I get the silent treatment from my Mother and it is the worst punishment I have ever gotten from her.

So the dreaded Friday came and I went to the psychologist. I told him everything that was wrong and guess what happened?

For the next five fucking months I had to go and see a psychologist every week because I couldn't stand my brother or sister. I made the mistake of telling the shrink that I wished they never existed. I don't know if everyone had the fear I was going to kill them or what.

For the record I never wanted them dead but just to shut up, stop fighting and stop getting me into trouble.

Well after 5 months did anything change? Yes I lied to my Mother, my Father and the shrink that I loved my brother and sister very much. I think it was the first time I thought about acting to be honest. I was very convincing and I no longer had to go to therapy. After that I just pretended in my mind that I was an only child but didn't dare tell anyone that.

Damn therapy….I could have gotten a new bike for what they spent on my "recovery!"

Chapter 9

Day to Day Direction

So here I am living in LA for a while now but I haven't really achieved much in the acting career so far. I actually haven't been too focused on it to be honest. I have been more interested in having fun and partying but that is about to change. I was still waiting tables on Sunset, still fighting with Tommy and still hanging out with Jake. I was beginning to get frustrated but I also wasn't doing anything to advance in my career here in LA. On evening I was waiting tables on these two really cute girls. They were very sweet and I could tell that they were actresses. It was a Tuesday night and the restaurant was kind of slow so I struck up a conversation with them. So what do you ladies do? Are you from LA?

Girl # 1:

We are actresses and we just moved here from Ohio she enthusiastically cheers.

I ask them so what are you working on? Anything I have seen?

Girl # 2

CSI, Jane the virgin, Brooklyn Nine-Nine and I am doing Arrow on Thursday!

Wow that is amazing! How long have you been living here again? I thought you said that you guys just moved here?

Girl # 1

We did!

How did you book so many jobs so fast? I have been here for over three months and I haven't done fiddly squat.

Girl # 2

Oh it's just extra work she says as she lets out a sigh. We are doing extra work to break into the real show business here.

Extra work I never heard of it. What is that?

Girl # 1 and Girl # 2

They both in tandem say **Background Work**!

Girl # 1

It's the people in the background sitting in the café, or riding a bicycle, or standing in line somewhere. It's really fun! She says with so much enthusiasm. It doesn't pay very well.

Girl # 2 (cuts her off)

Unless you get a commercial!! Commercial extra work is amazing. You can make over a thousand dollars for the day!

That is incredible but don't you have to be in the union I ask?

Girl # 1

No they have Union and Non-Union Jobs. It is really fun and you meet a ton of people that are already in the business. It is a way to get your vouchers to join the union or even get upgraded to a principal. You should check it out.

So how can I do this extra work I ask with utter excitement?

Girl # 2

Call Central Casting and ask for this really cool lady named Lizette. I will write down the number for you. Can I borrow a pen?

Sure here you go. Thanks guys (as I look at them with such genuine appreciation) I gotta get back to work.

When the girls left they reminded me to call Central Casting and I said I definitely would. I thanked them again. I went over and picked up the check and they left me an awesome tip. So **now** I am even more excited because extra work must pay really well. They left me a 30% tip…nobody leaves you that much in this broke ass West Hollywood…unless you're a celebrity…or they want to have sex with you. I said to myself that I wasn't going to tell anyone about this. I wasn't going to tell Jake because he will do anything to make more money and I definitely wasn't going to tell that bitch Tommy about it either. I cannot wait for this night to be over so I could go home, get a good night sleep and call Central Casting in the morning.

As the night comes to a close I finish up cleaning my tables, do my side work and do my cash report. As I start to climb the stairs to the third floor where the office is I start to dread the thought of seeing Jake. I usually do not see him that often because he works on the third floor and I am on the second floor. I don't want to see him tonight. I just want to cash out and go directly home. I don't want to hear him bitch about his night especially if he didn't make a lot of money. I don't want to go get something to eat. I don't want to go to a bar or club. I have zero interest in drinking and I definitely do not want him to come to my house tonight. I get upstairs, I quickly look around and the coast is clear, so I dash for the office. Once inside the office there is nobody waiting so I get in and out pretty quickly. As I leave the office I glance around and I still see no sign of Jake. I am just about at the top of the stairs when I hear Jakes Voice:

Hey baby where are you going? Are you finished? Can you help me finish cleaning my station? (he is being sweet because he wants my help)

I am done. I am tired and I have a busy day tomorrow Jake. All I want to do is go home and climb into bed. I need a good night sleep and I am off tomorrow so I want to start fresh.

So you are **not** going to help me clean up? Jake barks.

No Jake I am not. Clean up your own station. I told you that I am tired and I need to go home and go directly to bed!

Why are you always such an asshole? Jake scowled at me why can't you help me?

I am not fighting with you tonight I say (as I start walking down the stairs)

Fuck you Tate Jake screams (but I do not care, I do not react and I just continue walking down the stairs very slowly) you are going to be very sorry if you don't get your ass up here and help me!

(I hear Jake being reprimanded by someone and I soon here a lot of fuck you's and screaming but I don't care. I just continue my way downstairs and out the door. I walk to my car, get in and drive away)

As I start to drive down Sunset I come to a final realization. Jake is part of the reason that I haven't pursued any of my acting. It is not 100% his fault but he is a problem. If I do not do what he wants then it always turns into a fight. If he is hungry and I am not he expects me to go with him and keep him company. It is the same with almost everything in our relationship. In general I am very easily influenced but that is usually to do fun and exciting things. These days I find myself agreeing with Jake just so that we do not have another fight or he doesn't throw an epic Latin tantrum. They start with him yelling in Spanish and it always goes downhill from there, if I do not agree to do what he wants to do. Well I have had enough and let him try and have me fired from the restaurant. He is universally hated by everyone at the restaurant except me and I guess management. He is the most selfish, self-absorbed asshole I have ever met. He has **never** once come down to the second floor to help me finish my station…never! I have helped him dozens of times but when I have needed help he is usually having a drink at the bar and cannot be bothered.

As I pull into my parking garage I say to myself. You know it is not just the tantrums, the verbal abuse or Jake always having to have his way. No it is the fact that he is so God Damn cheap. He never makes enough money no matter how much he makes on any given night. Somebody has always screwed him out of a good tip….always. It is never his fault. I will not ever go through a fast food drive thru with him anymore. It is always that he forgot his wallet and will pay me later or he only has a twenty and will break it and pay me later. For the record he has never paid me later…I know I am stupid for not asking for it but it is just not me. So I am done. I will call him tomorrow and end it. I don't want to do it at the restaurant because he might cause a scene. It wouldn't be the first time he caused a scene with me at the restaurant but tonight was definitely the last. My Mother's voice is haunting me right now… see Tatey? See this is what happens when you shit wear you eat.

I open the door to my apartment and I immediately hear that Tommy is entertaining one of his internet "friends." I go directly to the kitchen, open the refrigerator, grab a bottle of water and head to my bedroom. Spencer is already sitting on the bed waiting for me. I look at me and I think that he is pretty much the only genuine pure thing that I have in my life at this point. I immediately turn off my cell phone because I do not want to go round 2 with Jake tonight. I change into a T shirt and I get right into bed. Spencer immediately cuddles up to me and I think I was a sleep before my head hit the pillow.

The next morning I awake and I am so excited to call Central Casting. I immediately get the number out of my pocket from my work clothes. I sign onto my computer to check out their website as well. After browsing a few minutes I call. I try and get Lizette the woman the girls recommended through the automated prerecorded message but I cannot get through. I try and try but it just keeps repeating the same message over and over again. I am frustrated and confused but I finally figure out where it is and when I can go from the internet. They have open castings on Tuesday and Thursday's from 10am to 12pm. Shit its Wednesday but I can go tomorrow…cool….I am going to work out like a mad man today and starve myself so I can look awesome tomorrow! I am going to be an awesome extra and make tons of money!!! I am so freaking excited!! Oh and btw I am **still** not telling anyone about this……..I don't want them stealing my spot after all huh?

All day long I was so excited thinking about being an extra; exhausted from working out like a crazy man today and fucking starving myself by not eating anything all day. A few times throughout the day I would get dizzy. I wasn't sure if it was from the excitement or the lack of eating anything. Errr besides protein bars of course! I kept imagining being on sets, studio lots, talking to celebrities and on top of everything else……..all the money I was going to be making. Man I cannot wait to quit this shitty waiter job and it is not just because I do not want to see Jake. Extra work is going to be so glamorous and amazing I just know it is………

For those of you that know the business you have to at least endear my naiveté's right? I was about to find out what extra work really was.

I woke up extra (get it) early on Tuesday to get to the gym before my appointment at Central Casting. I went tanning and got my hair cut last night so I was looking pretty darn good! After the gym I drove home, showered and dressed myself pretty sharp. I checked myself out in the mirror and I was satisfied with how I looked.

I drove to Burbank, which is in the San Fernando Valley and I gave myself plenty of time to get to Central Casting. It was really kind of interesting in the valley, especially when I was driving past the Warner Brother and Disney Studio lots.

All of a sudden as I am cruising through the valley, I am like why is it so much hotter here? The temperature has jumped 23 degrees higher in the past 10 minutes since I left my apartment and made it over the hill. I was melting faster than the crayons I left in my Dads brand new car when I was a kid one hot August day back in Sheapshead Bay. Ahh another story, another time but let's just say that didn't go over to smashingly either. The car that I was driving had no air conditioner and it was a convertible. I was beginning to soak from head to toe in sweat. I looked like someone had dragged me up and down the river and the worst part yet was that my hair gel was ungluing faster than when a hooker spreads her legs. **Shit, fuck** what am I going to do? Should I turn around? Reschedule? But what would my excuse be for rescheduling? That my dumb ass self didn't know that it was like 30 degrees hotter once you go over that hill. hmmmm….I could tell them my Grandma died/ That always works. After all she did die 4 times while I was in college for various reasons…I am almost there as I remember that I have a new shirt in my trunk and they have to have a bathroom right?

I spot a Rite Aid as I turn onto the street central casting is on. I pull into that parking lot and I run in and buy more hair gel. As I am waiting in line to pay for my new hair gel I start to drive off and I start thinking "You see nothing is going to stop me from being an **extra**"………….nothing is going to stand in my way…absolutely nothing…The crisis has been averted.

Well I get myself all cleaned up in the Rite Aid bathroom and I return to my car. I drive to central casting and I am directed to park almost 2 blocks away from the actual building. I will be soaked to the bone again but there was nothing I can do but pray they have a public bathroom. I am a little relieved when I walk in because everyone looks like a drowned rat.

The office is really cool and big, with lots of glass windows. I didn't expect it to be this big of a place. The building is really nice but it is almost under a highway. I think it is the 5 but I am not sure. Once I fix myself in the bathroom again I head to the registration line. I am instructed to fill out my application and then I am told to wait for them to call my name. They call my name rather quickly, I pay $20 dollars for a picture, they snap the picture and they give me a booklet on how to call in to check for jobs. That's it. Didn't talk to anybody, Got no advice and it was like a chain gang type of deal. Even so I was so excited to get home and call the numbers in the booklet.

I raced home full of excitement and no longer caring about the heat. I get to my apartment rather quickly and go directly to my room. I close the door because I don't want Tommy to find out about this. I read the Central casting booklet from cover to cover and I am finally ready to call the numbers listed. I pick up the phone and dial the Men's number but line is busy. They tell you in the booklet that if the number is busy to just hang up and press redial so I did.

Well I sat there for the next 2 hours pressing redial. Just as I am about to give up and think that there is something wrong with the phone I get through to an automated casting line. It seems all of these different casting directors say what they are looking for and then give you **another** phone number to call. I listened to all of the different castings they were looking for. I wrote down as much as possible. There were about 3 shows that I would be perfect for.

I hung up and began calling all 3 of the different casting directors that had given descriptions of what they were looking for. I alternated between the 3 phone numbers I had written down and finally about 20 minutes later one of the casting directors answered the phone.

Social Security number please this particular casting director asks.

079-44-8746 I said as fast as I can.

Ok call 818-541-5874 for location and wardrobe. You are booked.

I hung up the phone. I was so happy. I immediately called the third number of the day and I got through immediately. The message told me where I was going, what wardrobe I needed, and the time to be there and where to park. I couldn't contain my excitement after I hung up the phone. What am I going to do with all this nervous energy? Who am I going to call and tell about my debut as an extra tomorrow? I think I will wait till after to tell people. My shift at the restaurant doesn't start till 7pm tomorrow night so I should be OK. Shit the restaurant…Jake…ugh I forgot about him for a brief moment and my mood changed dramatically. I started to get nervous and a little agitated just thinking about Jake. Five minutes ago I was so happy and excited about my new adventure until I started thinking about Jake. I knew what I had to do. There was no question to it. Jake was poison in my life and I need to detoxify Jake from my life if I wanted to succeed with my career. As I am sitting there contemplating how I am going to end it with Jake, the phone rings and it is Amanda.

Hello I go.

Hey honeys how are you? Amanda says very sweet and cheerful but I can tell by her voice she has something she desperately wants to unleash to me.

I am good no actually great. I just signed up for extra work and I just booked my first gig for tomorrow and I am really excited.

That is great Tate! Good for you! You will be amazing and you will be a big star someday! I just know you will sweetie! Amanda charms me

Thanks Babe what is up with you? I ask.

I just got out of class and I am so tired. Do you work last night at the restaurant? Amanda asks in a very curious voice.

Yes I did why? I ask Amanda

So you know what happened last night then? Amanda asks.

Besides the fact that I got my 100th verbal beat down from Jake last night because I would not help him clean up his station and that was my last beat down by the way. I was just sitting here trying to figure out a way to end things with that selfish asshole when you called. I have been running scenarios in my head all morning long. I am done with him…. I am seriously fucking done with Jake, Amanda. I say it like I would state an actual fact.

(Amanda laughing) Well I think it will be a lot easier for you now to dump his loser ass Tate?

Why? I ask Amanda.

(Amanda was still laughing) Jake got fired last night and then he was arrested Tate. He hasn't tried to call you Tate?

What? No he hasn't tried to call me as far as I know. What the hell happened? I ask with a little worrisome tone in my voice.

(Amanda starts explaining) Jeff called me this morning to tell me all about it, so this is just Bona Fide Asshole Jeff's version of what went down. Apparently he was screaming at you or someone by the stairwell after closing. Sean went up to him and asks him to stop screaming and I guess words were exchanges. Supposedly Jake took a swing at Sean and one of the owners saw it happen. Once the owner saw what was going on he **fired** Jake. Well Jake didn't take that...um very well (Amanda is giggling) He got into it big time with the owner and security had to be called. He was fighting security and they basically dragged him out of the building.

So they arrested him for that? That doesn't make sense Amanda. People are escorted out of the restaurant all the time and they don't get arrested. (I say confused)

No honey it was what happened after he was escorted out of the restaurant.

Oh no what did he do? I ask Amanda almost in fear.

Well Jeff told me that he went and did Jakes cash out for him. Jake was not going to leave without his money!

Of **course** not I interrupt Amanda.

(Amanda continues) So Jeff cashes him out, gets his bag and car keys. He brings them down to Jake who immediately starts counting his money. He accuses Jeff of stealing sixty bucks. Jeff and Jake get into it for a few minutes but security broke it up quickly. Jeff went back inside but Jake was still in a full on rage.

Was he drunk Amanda? (He usually is when he gets this extreme). I couldn't tell when I left. It was slow for me so I got done early.

(Amanda gets all serious now) I do not know but the next thing that happens is Jake goes onto the patio, picks up a chair and throws it through the glass doors on the first floor. Melissa was cleaning up her station and got glass all over her face and body. Security tackled him and the cops were called. He was still trying to fight everyone while security was holding him down. The police came and took him away in handcuffs.

Holy shit how is Melissa doing? I ask Amanda.

I am not sure but they did take her to Cedars last night to check out if there was any more glass in her face Amanda says with a sigh.

Oh my God! I cannot believe it but yet I can. His temper is psychotic and it seems to get worse and worse. I don't know what to do?

Stay out of it! That is why I am calling you. When the police arrived Jake was asking for you. The owners started asking questions about you and if you guys were a couple. Even Jeff said that you guys weren't and that you were mad cool. Even Maxine said that she didn't think that you had anything to do with Jake anymore.

Work is going to be fun tonight! I am fucking dreading it Amanda but thanks for giving me the heads up and letting me know. I really appreciate it. I gotta go.

(Amanda very sternly goes) Do not call him Tate. Do not get involved in his mess. I love you and I will see you tonight. Bye.

I hang up the phone and I am in utter shock. I have been watching Jake become more and more unglued by the day. He seemed to be spiraling more and more out of control. He has been drinking a lot the past few weeks but to put a chair through a window…holy shit….something is seriously wrong with him. How am I such a bad judge of character? When I met him I thought he was sweet, charming, good looking and the total package. Wow was I wrong and poor Melissa, she is one of the coolest girls in the entire restaurant. I hope she is OK. I sit there in shock for what feels like eternity. I decide I am not going to call Jake. I am not going to find out how he is doing and I am certainly done with this disastrous person and this relationship. I look down at my watch and it is 4pm…time to get ready for work. I hope I don't get fired because of this.

I dreaded walking into that restaurant. I felt like I was going to throw up but I need the job. I had saved some money but not that much yet. A cannot believe a day that started out with such full excitement and happiness had turned into this. Was I drawn to disasters? Did I subconsciously crave and need chaos but my brain didn't give me the memo about it?

As I enter the restaurant I can feel the energy suck the life out of me. I see the boarded up window and now it has become real. I walk directly up to the third floor and head for the office to pick up my order checks for the night. I enter the office and I immediately lock eyes with one of the owners Gary. Gary smiles at me and says:

You left last night before all the fun started Tate. You missed an eventful end of the night. Have you heard from your buddy Jake? Gary asks.

No I haven't heard from Jake, Gary and he is not by buddy. He hasn't been my buddy in a long time and he never will be again.

(Gary is looking at me kind of funny and says) I heard that it all started because you would not help him clean his station. Is that true Tate?

(Oh no I see where this is going and I am so getting fired) Yes it is true. He never cleans my station and I work on the second floor. He is on the third floor anyway. Why should I help him he never once helped me. (I am getting a little upset)

You used to help him all the time Gary states..

(Ok I am going for broke here what else can I do) Yes I used to help him…. when we were sleeping together. Anything else you want to ask me Gary?

(Gary laughing) Here are your orders checks get to work. Make me a lot of money tonight and I won't fire you. (I turned around and gave him a look like you better be kidding with me. I know Gary likes me a lot but not because I am a fun guy but because I make him a lot of money. At the end of almost every night, the first words out of Gary's mouth to you are what did you sell?)

I walk down to my station and I set up my area. Throughout the course of the night every employee comes up to me and either wants to tell me their version of what happened last night or ask me what happened last night. Fucking gossip…

The night is pretty busy and goes rather quickly. As the night winds down I start to yet again get excited about my day tomorrow. My first day of extra work is just a few hours away and I am so excited! I go directly home from work and I start to get my wardrobe together. I get home and I go directly to my bedroom. Tommy is in his usual place on the couch but I do not bother even saying hello to him anymore. It is not worth a fight with him. We have barely spoken to each other in the past few weeks and I think we both like it that way. I start organizing my outfits for tomorrow and about 3 minutes later Tommy is at my door. He says to me:

Call Jake. He said to call him no matter what time you got home. He said it is extremely important. He has called three times tonight. He said your cell phone is turned off and going directly to voicemail. He has been trying to call you all night.

Tommy I have no intentions of ever calling Jake again. We are done. We are finished and if he calls again I will let him know that I am done. I am shooting tomorrow so I need to finish this and get my ass to bed.

What are you shooting? Tommy inquires.

I am doing extra work tomorrow on Greys Anatomy. I am playing a dog walker in a scene and then a waiter in another scene. I inform Tommy.

(Tommy scoffs) You are doing fucking extra work. What a fucking loser you are dude. Only fucking losers do extra work…unless it is commercials. Is it commercial extra work Tate?

No it is TV. I tell Tommy.

You are an idiot (Tommy says as he walks out of my room laughing at me)

What is so wrong about doing extra work Tommy? (I bark at Tommy) It is just background work and it is easy and fun.

You will see what is wrong with it Tate….you will see. Oh and easy and fun? Have a good night, get some sleep because you are in for a "Fun" time (Tommy says as sarcastic as ever)

Don't you want to know why I do not plan to ever call Jake again? I ask Tommy almost forgetting that he has no heart or soul.

I don't give a shit about your life Tate. I could care less about all the twists and turns in your fucked up relationship. You will be back in love with the obnoxious Mexican by tomorrow. I do not want to hear it. I live my life simple. I have sex with the guy and then they leave. If we mutually want to have sex again we do and if we don't we don't. We are guys Tate and guys aren't supposed to want romance and love. All I want is to get off and then they get the fuck out. No fuss and no drama. Can you for a second stop being such a damn girl Tate? I am surprised you haven't painted your room pink by the way you behave. Have fun on your loser extra work tomorrow.

(I officially hate my roommate now I am going to bed)

Let me tell you how it all went down the next day for my first day of extra work. I got to my destination on time which was a parking lot away from the location. I was informed that I had to walk 6 blocks to the set. I had to walk this distance with the 8 required different wardrobe selections the stylist requested. Once I got there I was immediately herded into a small room with about 50 other extras. We were informed rather rudely that we were to wait there for the stylist to approve our outfits. About 2 hours later we were sent for approval to the stylist. After getting our wardrobe approved we were moved to another area but much closer to the set. I couldn't believe how many professional extras there were on this set. They all knew the ins and outs to extra work. A lot of the extras were in the union. People were talking about things that I had never heard of. I didn't want to feel stupid so I just sat there and listened. I found out you need these vouchers to join the union.

Everybody wanted vouchers if you were not in the union. I would learn that vouchers are like tickets to get in to the Screen Actors Guild union.

We were used throughout the day to sit in a café, walk up and down the street or just be office workers. It was interesting and very cool to be on my first LA set. I just didn't like people yelling at us to shut up between takes especially when it wasn't us doing the talking. By the end of the day I have learned that extras are the lowest form of life on a TV set. By lunchtime my initial excitement for extra work was pretty much gone but it was definitely a learning experience, I took some of the advice from other extras about how things work in Hollywood. Extras are very good at giving advice it seems. I learned about the Screen Actors Guild or as they call it SAG, where and how to get an agents and what showcases to do that day. The only thing I really didn't like was being screamed at all damn day. This little short guy who I learned was called the second AD was such a dick. He has this little Napoleon complex and I couldn't stand him. My waiting table's job is not that bad after all. After about 9 painful hours I was released and I didn't get to be a dog walker either. Just some guy who had walk back and forth across the street over and over again. I can just hear Tommy laughing at me now. It wasn't the worst day of my life and it went rather smoothly. I will do it again. The actual extra work is kind of boring and lots of down time. You spend hours upon hours just sitting around waiting to be called to set. I definitely need to bring a lot more reading material to these extra job sets. I heard tons of stories about the different studio lots and shows. I found out where certain shows are taped and all in all a decent day. I am exhausted but now I have to go and wait tables on a busy Friday night at the restaurant. I have to stop at the store and get a couple of shots of red bull because it is the only way I am going to be able to get through this night. I don't even have enough time to go home and shower.

Two weeks later I got my check from Central Casting for $49.71. Yup I received $49.71 for my full day of work as an extra. Tommy is so right, I am a fucking idiot!

Chapter 10

How I got my second pussy............cat!

So I have been in LA for a little while now and things were moving in various directions. Some great…some shitty….some nobody would ever give a shit about but the one thing I loved in LA was my apartment. Coming from NYC where a rat infested 300 square foot studio apartment would cost me around a $1,000.00 a month, if I was "lucky" to find one but here in LA it was quite different. My roommate and I were paying $700.00 each for a 2 bedroom/2 bath 1,600 square foot palace in the heart of Hollywood. The apartment had parking, a gym, a gorgeous pool and even a hot tub! This was the first time since I graduated from high school that I had my own room. When I first moved to NYC I lived in a 5 floor walkup with four other guys! Did I tell you it was a studio apartment? Or that there were no direct path's to the bathroom without having to jump over a body? I won't even bring up my sex life…who am I kidding…what sex life?? Here in LA not only did I have my own room but…. I…. had…**my…own….bathroom**!! Can you believe it? My own bathroom!!! In all my life I never had my own bathroom….If you haven't figured it out by now I can be a bit…….particular….It drives me crazy when people make a mess **especially** in the bathroom. I don't like cleaning up after other people's shit marks on the toilet, left over tooth paste in the sink, hair everywhere and just products all over the counter. This is not going to happen in this apartment, because this is heaven. Sharing the kitchen was a bit challenging but besides that, I loved it here. It is technically a penthouse apartment overlooking a glamorous pool. Screw Disney World…this was the happiest place on earth….well at least I thought it was….

One of the biggest distinctions I noticed between New York and LA is that you don't really socialize with your neighbors that much here in LA. I mean if you pass each other in the hall you smile or say hello but you're not borrowing a cup of sugar from anyone. Actually I think that expression stopped happening in the 1960's….damn hippies were smoking it instead. In my situation I had these annoying bitchy girls to one side of me and this weird couple on the other side of my apartment. They were really opposites though… The guy was really gothic and shy who rarely looked into your eyes. I would say hello when I would see him and he would kind of grunt at me. He was actually really rude to be honest. I would only see him during the day, come to think of it, but he always looked like he should be going to a nightclub. The woman that lived with him was this over the top costume wearing freak. She would always call me sugar pie or honey but man was she ugly. She wore makeup to enhance the ugliness….seriously…She was like a clown going to "The Circus Ball," and she was dressed up to win a prize! Every time I saw her it was one over the top outfit after another but she was fun. I secretly wanted to befriend her but I always chickened out. I always wondered where she was going and I actually thought about following her though. That would be kind of stalker—restraining order ish shit right? I did notice that she only went out at night though……

Well it was a super-hot late summer evening in sunny California and all of a sudden the building starts shaking and the power in my apartment goes out. The lights, air conditioning go out and shit starts falling everywhere. The TV is rattling, books are flying off the shelf, and the closet doors are swinging back and forth.

We are having an earthquake!!! I squeal out loud.

Get between a doorframe my roommate yells...

The cat just seriously flew into my arms. Ouch...why didn't I get all 4 of his damn claws removed...Now I don't want to hear from any of you cat loving freaks that tell me it is inhuman to declaw a cat and that he is traumatized for life....He has had a good life.

Are you circumcised? Are you traumatized for life? I am circumcised and probably traumatized for something .....But not for snipping my dick when I was an infant. Go find another cause...Cat people drive me insane. I love animals but there are people that go to the extreme with their animal causes. I actually like the animals over most people anyway.

Ok where was I...see I tend to go off subject for numerous reasons...OK cat in my arms, building shaking, things falling everywhere but then it stops......

There are going to be aftershocks...my roommate yells. Let's get out of the building **now**...

So off me go, out the door, down the stairs and outside. By this time many people have gathered onto the street and are pretty freaked out. People are saying it was a 5.0, others are saying 5.5 and then my roommate who is also an ex New Yorker goes it felt more like a 6.0. I look at him like how the hell do you know so much about earthquakes. What did he take a class or something?? I don't know but he is starting to really bug me...He keeps going on and on like he is the fucking professor of earthquakes at UCLA. I have to walk away because between him jabbering on and on as well as the dang cat wanting to just take off somewhere. I basically have to keep Spencer in a headlock to keep him from running away in fear. He has never really been outside before and I think he is really freaked out from the earthquake we just had.

I see my gothic next door neighbor and I go over and ask him how he is. How is it going neighbor? A little freaked out?

I am a little shook up but OK I guess…he says.

I am looking at him saying to myself does this guy **ever** not where black? He even has black eyeliner on.

How is your roommate? I ask.

He looks at me funny and I am thinking oh shit did the cat just pee on him or scratch him??

What roommate…I… I… I… don't have a roommate he stammers almost appalled and shocked that I thought he did…

(I am very confused) Then who is the woman I see all the time coming out of your apartment??

Woman? he goes Yes I say.

Ohhhhhhhhh he says with a chuckle…That is "**Sparkles Bottoms!**"

Sparkle Bottoms? I say staring at him.

All of a sudden his roommate's voice comes out of him…Darling I am Sparkle Bottoms and I am a female impersonator. I am thrilled to all Liza that you thought I was a real woman. You have just made this a splendid earthquake.

I panicked and just started blurting out random things. One of these days I will learn that once a word has departed the runway of my mouth there is no emergency landing and you cannot take what you just said back.

I am not going to lie to you but I did think you were a real woman…not a very attractive one… but a real funny one!!!

(His face just went from 0 to 60 and angry….)

Sparkle Bottoms is gorgeous she **roars** and storms away…There I go again with my mouth and I wonder why I still do not have many friends in LA….I cannot keep blaming Jake for scaring them all away for that much longer.

I try to stammer and tell him or her (still confused) I'm sorry but it is to late…. the damages have been done….so I sigh and think to myself…what a dumbass I am…I have been living in LA for almost 5 months now and I couldn't tell I was living next door to a drag queen….what is wrong with me? It took the whole state of California rattling to figure out that I live next door to a drag queen…no wait… I didn't even figure it out…I was told…I don't even know the difference between a real woman and a drag queen is??? What is wrong with me? Well I am definitely not the most observant person in the world huh? Or the brightest bulb in the chandelier for that matter…I was born and raised in New York City and I couldn't tell that my neighbor was a drag queen? I basically grew up around them. I walk back over to my roommate who is still talking earthquakes and I go:

Did you know our next door neighbor is a drag queen?

Yeah… Sparkle she is so funny he says and then Thomas turns right back into his Earthquake 101 Lecture for the masses.

I am so fucking clueless…………………pathetic and **now** on top of everything else she hates me. The drag queen hates me…good job Tate!

After about an hour later we all head back into the building. The aftershocks have stopped or at least the earthquake ones that is.

I can't believe you didn't know Sparkle was a drag queen you dumb ass my roommates says almost mocking me.

Nope I didn't know but don't worry Thomas she hates me now anyway…our neighbor Sparkles hates me now.

What did you do now Tate?

I just, just, just

Spit it out now Tate!!! (Thomas is pissed)

I just said that she was an unattractive female but, but, but very funny.….

You're an asshole dude…seriously you are…who do you think you are? Do you think you are God's gift to the planet? You better apologize dude…Last thing we need is some fucking psycho drag queen pissed off at us. They tuck their dicks with rubber bands dude…they don't mind pain douche bag….have you **seen** the shoes she wears? My roommate says angrily.…

You are so stupid….You better fix this.

I will…I will…I reassure him.

You fucking better.… (Thomas growls)

So now I am saying to myself…hmmm.. How am I going to fix this mess? I have to think about this one because it is a disaster that is not easily fixable. I might not know drag queens but I sure need to be dragged.…..like maybe to the shut ya big fat mouth institution!

Ugh......... It seems my life has been one constant after another with me digging myself out of another mess due to my big fucking mouth!

Well the next morning I wake up to "I am Beautiful" by Christina Aguilera and soon come to realize that the drag queen next door is playing it over and over again. This song is on repeat over and over and over again.

This is my fault….I have got to make it up to her in some capacity so I get dressed and go knock on the door.

The door flings open and there is Sparkle in head to toe gowns and jewels…

Oh it's **you** she snarls…what do you want?? Do not ask me to turn down the music because I will do no such thing.

I just wanted to apologize for what to you I said yesterday…

She puts her hand in my face and sings along with Cristina:

I am Beautiful in every single way…no matter what **you** say!! And then proceeds to slam the door in my face.

(Slam)

Bitch….fuck her…I was being genuinely apologetic about what I said. And for the record…she **is** butt ass ugly…apparently you just don't **tell** drag queens they are…I am from New York and I have seen stunning drag queens and she is far from stunning. She is funny…isn't that enough? Hey and I thought drag queens were supposed to like Barbara, Judy and Madonna….who am I kidding—I couldn't even tell she was a drag queen and now I am analyzing what music she listens to? Hmm well I guess that is good for Cristina….I wonder if she like Britney? That's it!!!! I will bring her a copy of the new

Britney Spears…maybe that will work…shit at this point I will try almost anything… almost… Ahh I so need mental help..

The following day I wake up and "I am Beautiful" is still blaring from her apartment…Ok so if first you don't succeed try again right? Here I go again. I got to try something because Tommy has not spoken to me in 2 days now. Wish me luck….

Knock Knock on the door. I go thinking to myself… I cannot believe she is still playing that song. It has been almost 2 days straight now and from morning till night it's Cristina Aguilera "I am Beautiful" blazing out of apartment 405. Crazy, crazy, crazy huh?

What she snaps? As she answers the door the snarl deepens from the really angry drag queen inside her apartment door.

I made this CD for you.(As I hand it out to her) She snatches it and slams the door in my face **again**.(Slam goes the door) Not even a thank you or an acknowledgement that I spent hours finding music for shim!!(I am standing outside her door in shock) Now I am mad and plotting my next move…what am I going to do? Do I call my drag queen friend in New York and ask her for advice on what to do? Do I just continue to kill her with kindness? Who am I kidding that won't work for either of us. If she doesn't respond soon I know me….I will turn spiteful and evil…I cannot help it…It's in my DNA after all. Have you met my mother?? This is going to need further thinking…that's for sure. I thought about it all day and night and finally came to the conclusion that she is just a bitter old witch that regardless of what I do she is going to hate me. I need to focus on more pressing matters like my career rather than pleasing the shim next door. I am done….well…at least for now that is.

The next day I wake up and yup….the drag queen is **still** playing Cristina Aguilera's "I am Beautiful." My roommate comes in and says the whole building fucking hates you dude.

What? Why? Because I hurt the drag queens feelings? How did they know it was me?

I told them….

What the fuck Tommy why would you do that?

I was in shock…it just slipped out of my mouth he says knowingly mocking what I said to him after the incident 2 days ago.

I seriously need to un-bruise a drag queens ego don't I? This sucks Tommy all my life people have said mean things and you do not see me going off the deep end.

Are you sure about that Tate? You have done plenty of shit stupider just in the 5 months we have lived together. Yup dude…fix this man…fix this.

I am trying but this is not easy…man mocking him right back.

Fix this **man** or **you** might have to move he yells.

The thought of having to move makes me physically sick and I start to get dizzy. I need to get some fresh air. I am heading down to the pool. I need to relax I am going to have a nervous breakdown. Plus I cannot listen to that fucking song one more time.

I throw on my bathing suit and grab a towel and head down to the pool. Well down in the pool I am getting really nasty looks from just about everyone because from down here "I am Beautiful" is blazing all around the courtyard and pool area. It is in full on stereo mode because the drag queens balcony on the 4th floor overlooks the pool. Ahh shit I don't want to move I say to myself…plus I am going to kill the fucking drag queen if she keeps playing that damn song. I am sitting there when all of a sudden I hear:

Meow!!!!!

Holy Shit!! The drag queens cat has just jumped off the balcony…No freaking way. That is 4 freakin floors….and she is alive…Wait…this is it!!! I tell the drag queen I saved her cat! This is genius and everyone in the building won't hate me anymore including the drag queen…Oh happy day. Come here kitty, kitty….

The neighbors by the pool are watching me "save" the drag queens cat so I should get some points for that. I pick her up and she is actually a really sweet cat. She starts purring almost immediately after I pick her up. How do I know it is a female cat? No idea I just assumed. So I bring the cat upstairs and proceed to knock on the drag queens door which is **still** blaring Ms. Aguilera. Sparkle opens the door and doesn't snarl at me but she is not exactly embracing me. I found your cat down by the pool and I then hand her the cat.

Bad Judy…Bad Judy…and shuts the door on me this time…

Well I am getting somewhere I think …she didn't slam the door on me this time right? Ok let me get my things from the pool and celebrate my little small victory….I feel like the cat that ate the canary right about now and I cannot wait to tell my dick head roommate Tommy what just happened. How I was the hero that saved the drag queens cat. Woo hoo…..Even back at the pool I am now not getting as many glares as before but they are still not going to be throwing me a neighborly reception anytime soon…Why is she still playing that fucking song??

Meow!!!!

The damn cat has jumped off the balcony again. Holy shit!!! Again? What the hell is going on? And then all of a sudden I see the drag queen in a full on pageant wardrobe including a tiara...of course scream"

Fine Judy! I don't want you here either. I am beautiful in every single way and you are not. You have hurt me for the last time Judy! We are finished....Our relationship is over!

Now there are about 10 people staring at her like she was auditioning for fucking Romeo and Juliet or something over the top, dramatic role in a really bad dinner theater. I know she is trying to channel Norma Desmond or something.

You!! She growls .....**Ah shit** she is pointing at me, flailing her arms and bouncing her head back and forth like a crazy person.

There are 9 other freaking people down here why is she just pointing at me? Why? Why, why, why?

The drag queen continues her rant and all I can think about is if that tiara falls off her head and into the pool I will **never** stop laughing...never. I am pinching myself because this honestly cannot seriously be happening to me and has to be staged or I am getting punked or something...Ok where is Ashton Kutcher and then I remember they only punk famous people and I am not famous...yet.

You two are meant to be together....Go Judy live with the inconsiderate New York asshole for the rest of your life...

Wait... she knows I am from New York??

I have fed you…cleaned your fucking litter box, gave you **all** of my love and this is what you go and do? Well the hell with you Judy you are a nasty and hurtful cat and then storms off the balcony and yup slam goes the balcony door.

I am sitting there trying to wrap my head around what just happened. So basically this cat had been listening to Cristina Aguilera's "I am Beautiful for the past 3 days, from morning till night. The cat was willing to die not to have to listen to that fucking song one more time. Imagine having to listen morning till night for 3 straight days to "I am Beautiful." The cat was like I can't take it. I cannot hear that damn song one more fucking time. I am done. I would rather die than hear that damn song again. Death sounded better than hearing that song one more time.

I pick up the cat again and begin to pet her. She starts purring again. I like this cat. I am going to keep it but I am changing her name to Stevie. If she is going to be named after a music icon than it should be a bad ass chick like Stevie Nicks…Hello Stevie…wait till Tommy finds out about this…he is **not** going to be happy at all…trust me. He is not really happy with anything I do these days so I don't care…fuck him I am keeping Stevie. I wonder how Spencer cat is going to react to the new addition to the family? I am sure he will be cool.

By the time I get up to my apartment all of the cats belonging including her dirty kitty litter are dumped on my doorstep…Ok now I am fucking pissed. This drag queen bitch has gone too far…I think I am going to be going to jail real soon. This is not going to be one Sex in the City episode where you fight with the drag queens and the episode ends with everyone at a roof top barbeque loving one another. No fucking way. OK that's it she/he whatever it is… has gone too far now. Brooklyn is about to come out all over her ass in a minute. I open the door, bring Stevie to my bedroom and bring everything that the drag queen has graciously left me inside. I clean up the kitty litter mess she left on my door step and head to the trash shoot. That's when I hear screaming and yelling and again it is coming from the drag queens apartment.

What now? Who is she fighting with now? I am a little thrilled to be honest. There are more people she hates and I could possibly have some allies. Maybe we could start a club or something I say out loud and then the unthinkable happens.

The music stopped. No more Ms. Aguilera's classic and Grammy award winning song "I am Beautiful" blaring from the apartment. If I never hear that song again it would be too soon.

Oh shit I need to hide; God knows what this crazy bitch is going to do next. I run into my apartment and lock the door. The screaming was endless and was going on and on for hours and I guess the sound must have lulled me to sleep because I was awoken to the sound of my roommate's loud knock on the door.

Guess what? Thomas asks almost like a Jeopardy question.

What? I say still a little groggy from being awoken…

Your best friend, the drag queen, Sparkles Bottoms has been evicted from her apartment for not paying rent for the last 5 months!

She is gone?

Yup he says.

Oh….thank God….thank God…phew I really didn't want to go into battle with an angry drag queen but I would have.

Any excuse for drama Tate Thomas spews.

By the way Thomas … we have her cat.

What??

Long story....long, long story dude....................

Un fucking believable Tate. I cannot wait for this lease to be up on this apartment so I can get the fuck away from you. You are the biggest loser I have ever met. Do we really need **another** cat in this apartment Tate seriously?

What did you want me to do? Just leave it outside to fend for herself? I couldn't do that. I will try and find her a home, (I am lying to him because I have no intention of giving her to anyone)

Just take her to the pound or shelter dude. Tommy says as he is disgusted with me.

(I am angry) Listen Tommy if I can deal with the constant revolving door, of your internet dates coming and going throughout the day and night, then you certainly can deal with an additional cat in this apartment, can't you?

I **knew** it! Douche bag Tate is jealous that I am getting laid and he is not. Poor blue balled Tate had to go and get another cat because he can't get laid... Boo hoo...you are going to become like one of those old spinster ladies with 8 cats living in a studio apartment. One day you will die alone and the cats will eat you when they run out of food.

You are such an asshole, Thomas you really are. I snarl at Thomas.

Hey Tate...I might be an asshole...but at least I am an asshole who is getting laid...At least I am not some loser who has to get more cats for affection.

Please Thomas go cruise the internet for your next shallow one night stand and leave me the fuck alone.

I was just about to anyway and you should think about doing it yourself.…. you have been a bit cranky the past few days Tate.

Thomas I have been at war with an ugly pissed off drag queen for the past few day. How the hell would **you** feel?

You did it to yourself Tate…well you and that big fat mouth of yours. You have nobody to blame but yourself big mouth. (Thomas says laughing) You seriously need to get laid and stop fucking obsessing over the drag queen… unless that is what you are into. Is that what you are into Tate? Are you a tranny chaser?

Fuck you. Get out of my room. (Hey at least I am laughing now)

I never did see Sparkles Bottoms again for now. I am sure one day when I least expect it I will run into her or her alter ego Gothic Guy. I was glad he didn't know what type of car I drove. He would probably have put a bomb under it for all I know. It wouldn't be the type of bomb filled with glitter, boas and lots of bedazzles either.

For the record I did go online and I did find someone. His profile said he was a 6'2", ripped 32 year old Latin Guy from Mexico that loved to kiss. When he showed up at my door, he turned into a 5'2" pudgy Indian guy who smelt like body odor.

Many, many lessons learned in the past few days. First off never call a drag queen ugly and secondly people lie on the internet for sex.

What the hell did I do with that bartenders phone number from Micky's again? I cannot even remember his name….good grief Tate…get it together already.

Chapter 11

Conversation with my Mother

Now I have been living in LA for almost 6 months and I really feel like I am becoming a Californian. I am not crashing cars anymore; I have the gym down pat, started making some friends, no more bus rides and my body is in the best shape of my life. Well Thanksgiving is coming up and my Mom has really been bugging me to come home for the Holiday. So I figure it is the perfect time to go back east and flaunt my new fabulous body! I will not eat that much turkey no matter how good it is. It probably won't be that good anyway because my Mother is a horrible cook. My Grandma was a horrible cook as well so she basically had no one to teach her. I haven't taken on an eating disorder but I am just more aware of food and calorie intake now. I read the back of the packages before I buy something now. I don't really want to see my family but I would love to make them jealous of my 6 pack abs. My brother has a 6 pack but it's probably in the refrigerator by now and it is named Budweiser. I look online and find a round trip ticket for under $300 dollars so I immediately book it. I call my Mom to give her the news that I am coming home for Thanksgiving. She is thrilled that I am coming back east for Thanksgiving.

When are you coming? (Mom is excited)

I am coming Tuesday November 23rd.

When are you leaving Tate?

What??? I am not even there yet and you already want to know when I am leaving.

Yes......she snaps.

The following Monday Ma...

Oh good!

Good? Why is it good? Weren't you the one that was all upset when I wanted to move to Los Angeles in the first place? Now you cannot wait for me to leave or to over stay my welcome. Thanks a lot Mom!

Oh stop with the drama Tate I was just asking....I have a life too you know? It's not ALL about you kids anymore. None of you bothered to ask me how I felt when you moved away so I don't need to explain myself to you kids either. You're all grown up now and have your own lives to live and it was time for me to rejuvenate my spirit. My life is all about rejuvenation of my body, mind and soul.

(Rejuvenate her spirit? Body, Mind and Spirit is **she** serious?) OK who is this and what have you done with my mother?

Ha Ha brat! What am I going to do with you Tate? (My Mother is in a weird mood)

O No she said my full name something is cookin in Brooklyn and I need to get to the bottom of this one. What is she up to now? Mom what is going on?

I am just saying that I need to do things to enjoy **my** life and stop worrying about my children's lives 24/7. I have a young spirit that needs to thrive in this eccentric city that I chose to live in. I am taking the second half of my life and exploring all paths and journeys. I am going to conquer the universe of tranquility and substance.

Ok what's her name Mom?

Who?

Come on Mom the new friend that you have made recently. Rejuvenate? Do you even know what Tranquility means? Seriously Mom who is it? Do you have a thesaurus in front of you? Possibly reading a dictionary? Who is programming your speech?

I thought you would be happy with me for not butting into your life anymore or at least not as much. You kept telling me to find a new hobby besides you,,, so I did.

Was I happy with my Mom? I thought to myself…. She hasn't been calling me as much but I thought maybe she started taking another ceramics class or something. I just need to make sure this new friend is not getting my Mother into a cult or something. My mother tends to do things in extremes and experimentations. My Mother is not afraid of change. I honestly don't even know what her real hair color is anymore. It's been every color of the rainbow to be honest. She is a hairdresser and does own two salons. I stopped letting her cut my hair when I was old enough to pay for my own hair cut. She would never listen to what I wanted. When I was 15 she gave me a perm and I looked like Tom Jones. You can imagine all the kids in school singing "It's not unusual" to me all day long. My Mother will dive into a pool from a high diving board and never even bother to look to see if there is water in the pool. I love my mother dearly but recently I feel like our roles have been reversed. I have become the parent and she is becoming the child. I don't know whether it's because I have gotten older, I have matured and moved away or the fact that she is getting older....She has always been "Out There "but...

(OK this is going to drive me crazy)...Rejuvenate my spirit –my ass! Who is the new friend Mother?

After a long pause and I deep sigh....her name is Dot...

Dot?

Yes Dot, it is short for Dorothy.

Mom where did you meet Dot?

I met her at this new church that I am going to now.

(Oh shit I knew it...it is probably a fucking cult.)

Where did you find this new church mother?

I didn't find anything, they came to me-- she snaps.

Why so snappy mother I am just concerned?

Oh so now you are concerned? You weren't so concerned six months ago when you decided to move 3000 miles away from **your** mother now were you?? Tate please save the bull shit because you are being so ridiculous.

Mom... seriously are we going to go down this road again? I told you why I needed to move to LA and you.

(she cuts me off)

You know they shoot that new Juliana Margulies show right here in Brooklyn. You know she is the one from ER...

I know who she is Mom. Can we get back to this new church that you are going to?

Why?? And now she is getting mean and defensive so I know something is not right. There is more to this new church that you are telling me and I am going to get to the bottom of this....Because I am your son and I love you and I just want to make sure you are ok and protected.

Tate..You want to make sure I am protected?? From what? Who are you going to protect me from 3000 miles away? Yeah right.....

Please Mom I beg! Tell me about your new church.

It's for all empty nesters.

Empty Nesters? What is that?

It is a church where woman can go to for support when their children have abandoned them. They can go and get the love and support that they need. It helps us on our spiritual journey to find love after feeling betrayed by people or children who claim to have loved us...

Mom we didn't abandon you... we just kept living our lives. So this church.... is it all women? Or do some men fell abandoned as well?

Pretty much all women she says as if she was standing on a platform.

Are they lesbians??

Tate ---**no they are not lesbians!!** Why do you always turn everything into sex? You turn everything into sex no matter what I say. It's that damn Madonna you listened to growing up that did this to you…I just know it! I know you are a man but can you get your mind out of the gutter and sex for a second. Jesh… I needed this church group and these women are helping me with the second half of my life. Why is everything a joke with you?

(I am thinking to myself who told her that this is the second half of her life did she get a letter in the mail? I know she has just learned how to email and God knows what she is reading on the internet! I am not going to go down that road of second half of her life…..at least for now. Shit she is 50…is she planning on living to 100? I hope she does because as much as she drives me crazy I cannot imagine my life with out her.)

Mom I don't turn **everything** into sex. I am really sorry to tell you this but when you get a large group of women together to talk about feelings, emotions and empty nests it sounds like a big old clam bake to me…..

Clam Bake Tate? We don't bake clams… We go out to dinner after church. You think you know **everything**…

(I had to chuckle… I love my mom but she is sometimes clueless. She is not a dim bulb but also not the brightest bulb in the chandelier.) **Mom** I just want to make sure that it is not a cult or anything. Are all the women single, divorced or widowed? Are you giving them any money?

It is **not** a cult Tate and yes there are dues but it's the same as the passed basket at St. Anthony's so I don't want to hear another word about it. (She is rambling and talking very fast so I am automatically assuming she is hiding something from me.) I haven't taken any sort of survey on who is or isn't divorced either Tatey.

Are you worried about your inheritance or something? **And** they do have a cross…**And** they do have Holy Communion…**and** we do pray for all of our children….**and** did I fail to mention that they have a cross??

What's the name of this church Mother?

I am not telling you Tate because you are going to mock it like you mock everything else I do. You are afraid of change or maybe you are fearful that this will become more important to me than you and your sister and brother. I **love** you kids but I have to live my life. I am becoming a strong independent woman who is living life to its fullest. I am marking my territory and nurturing my footprint to this world that we live in and I praise the Lord everyday…

This doesn't sound like you Mom… I sigh

Judging people leaves no room left for loving them Tate.

What's with these entire quotes mother? It's like you just threw up a dictionary or worse…. religious proverbs. You know how much I despise religious rhetoric mom! Who is feeding you all of this crap Mom? I am really worried about you. Do Kelly and Christopher know about your new found friends and church??

(Silence on the other end of the phone….)

Mom this sounds like a cult or one of those really freaky whack job radical church groups you read about in the papers or see on TV. They have suicide pacts and they steal your entire bank account Mom. I am really worried about this but I will keep an open mind about your church and I will see for myself when I come home to visit. Is that fair enough?

It's not a cult Tatey...it is a women's church group and just because it is **not** St. Anthony's it doesn't mean it is not a real church. I needed a change and I was tired of the same old church and faces. They don't treat me the same way since all my kids are gone. You know once your kids are grown or they don't go to their school anymore they look at you differently. Once the Catholic Church can't get any more money out of you they have no use for you. I just felt so alone going to St. Anthony's with all of you kids gone.

Mom...stop.... I don't think that is true but I am not the biggest proponent or fan of the Catholic Church either so I am going to leave that alone.

It is true! Do you remember the Flanagan's and there 8 kids that all went to St. Anthony's?

Of course I do Mom I went to school with Sean Flanagan and he was kind of a dick so I don't really care about the Flanagan's. Kelly didn't get along with Anne Flanagan either; they are losers....and bullies.

Can I finish? Why do you always cut me off? I swear I can never get a sentence or word in edge wise with you kids. You all know everything about **everything** and you all think that your Mother is an idiot. Well I am not...

Mom I.....

Can I finish? (She is now yelling)

Yes...

Well Mary and Joe Flanagan put all 8 of those kids through St. Anthony's. Joe worked 2 or 3 jobs sometimes to make sure they got a proper education whether you liked their kids or not Tate. Well every year St. Anthony's would deliver the Flanagan's a huge gift basket for Christmas. It would have food and desserts in it and they always got it on Christmas Eve. Do you remember the huge Christmas basket they would get? It was **huge** and I was always so jealous of that basket. Not that we needed a Christmas basket of course.

Vaguely Mom what's the point?

Well Paul Flanagan who is their youngest child graduated from St. Anthony's last June and you know what?

What Mom?

They didn't get a gift basket for Christmas last year. Explain that??

So…maybe it's because of the economy Mother…

Nope it is because they stopped giving St. Anthony's money…

Mom ----how do you know that is true and not just a rumor?

Well Mary Flanagan heard from Pastor Doyle's old assistant that they were to be taken off the list because their boosters were way too low and…..

Mom I am not going to debate the Flanagan's, the Catholic Church with you or who did or did not get a fruit basket. I honestly don't really care. This is long distance phone call Mother and I want to know about the cult.

It is **not** a cult and if you call it that again I am going to hang up on you. **And** by the way I should be the one worrying about you and that cult in Los Angeles!!

What cult? The Scientologists again Mother? I thought we went over this last time Mom

All those actors are in it and they give all their money to **that** cult. I read about it all the time in my magazines…and I have done some research

What magazines mother and what research?

My Star and my National Enquirer Tate…Kirstie Alley, Tom Cruise, John Travolta, the girl from Darma and Greg they are all scientists…

Did you notice that she calls the magazines "My Magazine" Like they write them just for her…

They are actors Mom!

Who are **scientist**s!!!!!!!!!!!!!!!!!!!!!!!!!!!!!!!

No Mom -- I am not mocking you and I am not going to become a **Scientologist**. I promise…

Good. That L Ron Hubbard guy has been trying to sell me his book for years. Did you know he is even on the internet? Don't even get me started about the cult where they wear the red ribbons. You know the one with your friend Madonna in it. She snarls at me. Puhlease you want to talk to me about cults…HA!

I joined a nice church for women who are **not** lesbians, who pray for their children health, support each other emotionally and they are not after my money. Why are you so judgmental Tate? You and your sister…You are just like your Father I swear. I will not make you feel superior to me. I am your Mother and you must respect me. I am not your friend. I am your mother and I deserve to be treated as such….and you wonder why I take blood pressure pills…it's because of you kids Tatey. She is talking at 100 miles an hour.

Mom calm down. I love you very much and I was just concerned, worried and curious about the church…that's all.

Well you would know all this if you weren't 3000 miles away from me. Your brother Christopher knows all about the church and he is very supportive to me having all of these new friends.

(I am thinking to myself that first off… my brother Chris is an idiot and secondly he wouldn't know the difference between a women's cult or a Girl Scout troop. Please that is such Bad Defense Dear Old Mother.)

OH OK that helps I say as sarcastically as possible. Mom I gotta go. I love you and I will talk to you soon. I will see you in 2 weeks. I am really looking forward to it. I miss you and I love you.

You better not be coming home to spy on me now Tatey.

Mom I was coming home before you even told me about your cult I mean church group.

Good. I love you. Bye.

Bye.

OK I am fucking exhausted after that phone call. I think it would have actually been a better conversation if she told me she was actually becoming a lesbian. At least I would know what to expect right? I wouldn't mind if she had her "Lick-Her License" I could deal with a shaved head, tattoos and flannel shirts. I could deal with two Mommies but this? A fucking religious cult? I **have** to call me sister she is **never** going to believe this shit. And fucking Chris... that dumb ass can't even keep an eye on his mother that lives 3 blocks away from him.... Wait till I get a hold of him.

I cannot believe that my dear old mother still wonders why I live 3000 miles away....Ugh Family but ya gotta love them right? No.

Right? I do have to love them right? Come on...by now you know that I am an insecure asshole and I need reassurance. So help me. No lesson learned here today. Unless you didn't know my Mother was crazy...or where I get it from. I love my Mother and she is crazy but now you know where I get my craziness from....not the milkman.

Chapter 12

Preparing for my First Trip Back to New York

As my trip back to NYC was approaching I was starting to get very excited about it. I had been spending longer hours at the gym and building an amazing tan in November to show off to everyone back east that I am fit and live in sunny California. I don't know what it is but I secretly get a thrill knowing people are jealous of me in some form or shape. I know that sounds bad and it is probably due to my genuine insecurities but...I am being honest. I am not the best looking guy in the world but I am also not the ugliest either. There I go again with my damn insecurities....I try to justify everything... Just shut up and finish the story...

Well the day before I am set to leave for New York I get up at 7am because I have lots to do. I am going to sound so Jersey Shore when I say this, but I do have to do Gym, Tan and Laundry. Plus I have to get a haircut and still pack. Was I always this vain? What has LA done to me? Let me just ignore that question.....for now. That will take **a lot** of time to figure out how much of a mess I actually am.

I start with the gym because we all know how much I just adore the gym. Ha! I throw on shorts and my Made in Ireland t-shirt and off I go to pump up my muscles for my New York visit. I arrive at the gym and I cannot believe my eyes. The gym is packed and it is only 7:20 am! You heard I said "am" right? Where the hell did ALL these people come from? The locker room is jumping and every treadmill is being used. I don't recognize one single person, which is good because this way my jaw won't get the best workout. Here in LA the gym is a very social network to meet people but I think today I will just "hit the gym hard." Yes I know… it's another LA slogan I have come to acquire. I am becoming a Los Angeles dictionary of cheesy slogans and anthems. Yippee a treadmill has just opened up **run!** Ahh got it!!! 30 minutes of cardio should suffice.

Now I am a people watcher and the gym is a great place to indeed people watch! I keep looking at all these different faces and notice that everyone is pretty serious and there is very little socializing going on. People keep looking at their watches and seem to be on a schedule. All of a sudden it hits me OMG these are the "Professionals." I know I claim to be on the ball and have street smarts but come on we all know I am fucking clueless. These are the people that actually "work." What I mean by this is they are the lawyers, accountants, doctors and just people that work in offices. I guess you would say 9 to 5ers or what? Not really sure what to call them so let's just stick to "Professionals" OK? I haven't really met many professionals, unless you consider my agent a professional. Hmmm….nah he's not. Of course I am envisioning him on the phone talking with his mouth full of burrito yelling at me, that I have to be in Santa Monica in 15 minutes to audition for "Fun Friend Number 3" for some anti-depressant drug commercial… Anyway as I look around there are a lot of attractive and well fit professionals. Who knew? I have become so accustomed to working out with all the out of work actors, bartenders and waiters that I actually forgot that these people existed. These are the actual people that pay their rent on time. These are the same people that don't wait outside the mailbox all day praying for a residual check or are the people that worry the restaurant will be slow and tips will suck tonight. As I continue to observe I say to myself I **bet** none of these people get final payment notices, disconnected cell phones or have a piece of string cheese for dinner cause the car insurance is due. I am fascinated by them almost mesmerized. The woman on the treadmill next to me must think I am a crazy person (**we all know I am but she doesn't know me…yet**)

I mean I am turning my head right, left, up and down. My eyeballs are **all** over the place. I am jogging at a 5.0 on the treadmill but my head and eyes are at sprint speed right about now. I am fascinated….I just **have** to meet some professional people!!!

But how am I going to do that????? Hmm

The woman next to me is looking at me like I am going to have a seizure. She is looking at me like I am nuts or need to be medicated, but I don't really care. Half the people that meet me think that way too. As I am pondering how I am going to meet these "professionals," the woman next to me stops the treadmill, gives me an utterly nasty on purpose look and takes off. Yup its official another person added to the "Thinks I am Crazy club" but I don't care I am on a mission…To meet "professionals." All of a sudden my treadmill stops and I am like O Shit she so told the manager there is a crazy man on treadmill Number 6 and is scared for her life. For once though it wasn't worst case scenario but actually I was so engrossed watching the "professionals' that I got distracted and did the maximum time on the treadmill. I did an hour and 10 minutes and that's a first for me….Look, see I am **even** getting a better work out with the "professionals." It's been a good day so far and it's not even 9 am yet Let me go towel off all this sweat so I can map out my plan of action to meet "professionals."

After I towel off and freshen up I walk over to the weight room and contemplate my next move. I see that one of the machines I like to do for shoulders is free, so I immediately hurry over to it. I am not even done with my first set when there are these two queens behind me, cackling and carrying on. Now before

I go on, let me tell you what a queen is. A queen is a really nasty, bitchy gay man. They snarl at you and think they are better than everyone else. They can be really rude and very insensitive. The world is all about them and they have no problem telling you that. By the way this is just my definition and if you look in the dictionary it would probably say, lives in London. Oh shit wait… Am I a queen? No no I am not rude….hmm makes me wonder…Anyway so these two 20 something queens behind me are cackling on and on with:

Girl, hmm look at him oooooo- ahhhh –he is fine, - wow I'll take some of that and they are just making noise, mostly for attention though. These are not professionals!

Hey Baby you are so cute, you are fine, you wanna train me? They are clapping their hands and just causing a scene. I am thinking to myself it is barely 9 am, do I shut the fuck up but I just say nothing.

They are ogling the trainer in front of me and carry on like little school children. By the way Girl is another word queens say to one another also. I don't really know where the word "Girl" came from nor, have a definition because I am sure they do in fact have a penis. Baffles me! You're on your own on that one. Halfway through my second set an older gentleman walks up to one of the queens and says

Hi remember me I am Steve

The first little rude queen says Yeah I think so in such a demeaning voice.

We met at Barry's party last week. I asked you if you wanted to have coffee and I gave you my number. Steve says.

The little rude queen says to Steve: Oh yeah I think I lost your number he says in this condescending holy than thou voice. Can I have it again he barely musters

Sure I will go write it down again he says cheerfully and Steve walks away

Now I am thinking to myself "clueless bastard" Are you kidding me? Why would you subject yourself to that little hyena? I know so many great gay men why would you want that obnoxious troll? Then all of a sudden I hear:

Rude Little Queen turns to the other Rude Little Queen and says: **Ugh** like I would ever go out with that old man! What is he like 38? Oh God…yuck…. it's a curse I know. I am stunning but come on he is **old** maybe even 40. Why does this **always** happen to me? Why can't I meet a hottie like that trainer over there? (He is directly pointing right at the trainer they have been "flirting" with for the past 20 minutes)

The second queen chimes in "Maybe he will take you to dinner?

Well it better be expensive he whines. Gross, Yuck ekkie…

(OK I cannot take it any longer….)

I turn around and look directly at the whiney queen and there is no stopping me now. I turn and say to the rude little queen:

You should take it as flattery because you are really **not** that cute.

In unison both Little Rude Queens go. **Fuck you asshole!**

(I am not stopping) Seriously no thanks I go and continue. There is no need to be so obnoxious and rude and one day you will be that guy. It comes sooner than you think. Age is cruel enough without you having to make a fucking 38 year old guy feel like a dinosaur. If you don't want to go out with him just fucking tell him. And if you want to know why you don't meet the hottie's? I will tell you. As I told you before you're **not** that cute and that personality makes you nauseating and ugly.

Of course they are sticking their hands in my face saying **whatever** and Hmmm but I have said my piece and start to walk away.

The little queen yells "You're an asshole!

I turn around and say with my full on Brooklyn accent "that's all ya got?" My mother has called me worse names jackass. Grow the fuck up.

As I am saying this Steve is scurrying back to give his phone number and I turn to him and just say **Run!** (In my head I am saying as fast as you can but he just kinda- sorta smiles at me and hands his number to the obnoxious queen.)

Poor sucker. Wow I cannot believe it…there is in fact someone in this gym that **is** more clueless than me and his name is Steve.

So far I am not off to a good start with the professionals huh? Those obnoxious queens cannot be professionals or can they be?

I am in a pretty foul mood for the next 20 minutes but I continue to lift weights. I decided I am going to finish with flies to really boost up my chest for New York. The pissy little queens are still glaring at me from across the gym but I could give a shit about them. I need to be pumped from New York and they are certainly not going to deter me.

I haven't even done one set when this huge, huge, huge bodybuilder comes up to me and in the most feminine voice I ever heard goes:

How many sets do you have left?

I go about 4 or 5 more.

Can I work in with you? He squeals

Sure let me just finish this set I said with a smile because he was extraordinary to look at. His chest was perfect and his arms were the size of my legs. Um it would be **both legs together** actually to make up one arm. He had to be using steroids but I am not going to place judgment on him. He seems nice. He does his first set and then he asks:

Where are you from?

(Wow that is one feminine voice man I think.)

Born and raised in Brooklyn but I have been out here for almost 6 months now.

Oh he goes

After I finish my third set he asks me this time in a real Snarky, nasty tone "Can I ask you **another** Question?"

(Now mind you this guy could split a Cadillac in two) so I say:

Sure….

Why is it that you said that you were from Brooklyn but your T shirt says Made in Ireland?

I look at him first thinking is he fucking serious? Is he trying to be a dick? Is he flirting with me or does he genuinely want to know? So I decide to believe he is either genuine or flirting so I say to him again with a smile cause I don't want to upset she man:

I am Irish. My mother was born in Ireland and my Dad is British. My mom immigrated to the United States when she was 12 and my Dad when he was 22. They met here in the states.

(As I am saying this he is rolling his eyes and pretending to yawn)

Oh he goes **whatever**...

Now I am irritated again and ask myself what are all these professionals so rude? Is it me? Oh I am not finished with muscled Barbie.

So I say to him, Can I ask **you** a question?

Sure she exclaims (Yes I am becoming a bitch and I did just call him a she.)

So I look at him dead in his eyes and I ask, Ok why it that you indeed look like a man but yet talk like a woman?

Hey that's not very nice he yells.

(So I look at him with a very serious face and I say to him…Hey I answered **you**r question now answer mine.

It's the voice I was given He snarls at me

(OK I don't want this entire gym to hate me before I leave so I just say jokingly)

OK shut up, finish your workout – hurry up!

Well I guess he liked that because then I couldn't get him to shut up. On and on about his life, career, contests he won, you name it. The kicker to this was I kept telling him to shut up, hurry up, faster –faster but the meaner I was to him, the more he talked and talked. I couldn't believe it! He finally finished and looked at me and said

Bye…Friend….and walked away

What universe am I in? This is insane!

All of a sudden this other guy leans in to me and says

Dude I seriously just threw up in my mouth when you said that to him. That was the funniest thing I ever heard. Did you see his face? I will laugh for days about that. Fucking hilarious…brilliant…so deserved… I am Greg nice to meet you.

We talked for a little while and I might have made a friend. Let me hurry up and get the hell out of here before I get my ass kicked. So let me see: I enlisted a new person into the "Is he Crazy" club, two enemies, a "special" friend and Greg. It is not a win win but I will take it, plus my ass will not being getting up at 7 am anytime in the future again. I mean seriously its only 930 in the morning and I am exhausted. You can keep the "professionals" that for sure. Leave me with the unemployed actors, bartenders and waiters. Ok off to tan…

So now I know tanning is not the healthiest thing to do but in my opinion it is safer than the actual sun. I don't over tan and I am a white boy so I have to be very careful with the sun. I have been building this tan for a couple of weeks so I just need to seal it off for the grand finale. I arrive at LA Tanning quickly and pretty much right when it opened. There is this orange looking guy that must have been waiting outside for it to open because he was acting like a drug addict joansing for a fix.

(I hear him say) I feel so pasty he says to the guy behind the desk.

You are fine Matty you just missed one day he said trying to comfort Orange Man.

Can I go in for 40 minutes instead of 20 since I missed yesterday? He asks.

No Matty it would be unhealthy to do that.

Why I could just go to another tanning salon after this Orange man argues.

Matty you don't need to spend 40 minutes in the tanning bed the guy behind the desks says very sternly but sincere.

What is it your business? He yells.

Matty do you want to tan or go somewhere else? You can only do 20 minutes a day here. If you want to go somewhere else after you tan here I cannot stop you from doing so. I don't recommend it but again I cannot stop you.

OK he murmurs and off he goes to Room 3.

I walk up with a smile on my face and he just looks at me like Can you believe that freak. I decide to play with him a little bit.

What bed do you have that I could do 40 minutes in?

He laughs and then looks at me and says My Bed.

Huh?

Would you like the address?

What you lost me I say very confused?

He then looks at me in this certain way with a charming smirk and then I get it. I just smile and say write the address down.

We then go back to talking about tanning and I ask him what bed I should use because I am going back east and want to look good. He recommends the "Magic Bed" and a lotion to go with it. He explains it will give me a dark deeper tan and I will not burn.

It's not going to make me look like that guy? As I point to Orange Man's room.

He laughs and says no bed, lotion or tan could make you look like **that** guy!

HA! Well let me think......

Deep, Darker, Tan and No Burn? Sold! Duh?

The guy behind the counter that I think just propositioned me pointed me in the direction of the "Magic Bed and off I went. I get undressed except for my underwear because I don't want to burn my ass or my Mr. Pecker. I lather myself up and lay down in the bed. OK 20 minutes now let's see some magic.

As I am laying there I start to think about New York and all the people and places I want to see and go. Do I really want to see all my cousins? I wonder how long on Thanksgiving before my sister and brother start to fight? Hmm I guess it depends on when they start drinking. Which of my friends do I want to see? I didn't tell everybody I was coming because I won't have enough time to do everything I want to do. I know I am being selfish but if I don't like someone, why do I have to spend time with them? That's right I don't. I am an adult and besides I am sure there are people out there that can't stand me either and hate spending time with me. I know.. I know.....it's hard to **believe** but it's true. There are people out there that don't like me. Crazy huh?

After a few minutes I start to think back on my morning. The gym started off well but maybe I didn't need to start a war with those 2 cackling little queens. They are young and were having fun. The older guy "Steve" I think his name was. He was clueless and will find out on his own anyway. When am going to learn to play nice? I just feel sometimes I try to be the anti-stereotype of LA. I mean I am a gay man but I don't want to be defined by that. I want people to say that Tate....phew he is a riot, lots of fun, a great friend, smart, intelligent oh and by the way he also happens to be gay. I don't want to just be known as gay Tate. Do you understand what I mean? I don't want to be identifiable as just gay and I do try to be multifaceted or at least I tell myself I do. I know I am a working project but at least I can recognize my faults and work on them. I have this wicked tongue but I think it just protects me from all of my insecurities. The tanning bed shuts off and I continue to think about the morning, I say Ok maybe I was wrong with the queens.........but I had fun with Feminine Hulk Hogan! Not going to apologize for that. Nope he deserved it....

No Matty you cannot go for **anothe**r 20 minutes!!! I said **No!!!**

Why not? Matty wails

Get Out!! I don't want you to come back here anymore. You are sick in the head and I have had it.

Why can't I go for another 20 minutes????

Why??? (Matty is screaming it over and over again. You seriously would have thought that the front desk guy just ran over his puppy or something.)

I am so not getting out of this tanning room right now. That crazy ump a lump a is going to kill somebody and it is **not** going to be me. I have to go back to New York and look fabulous after all. I wonder is there a back door? I stop myself and say Tate grow a pair. Do you really want to hide in the tanning booth? What could he possibly do? Blind me with his orange-ness?

(I hear the front desk guy yelling) Get Out of this salon or I am going to call the police. Matty you are fucking crazy. Do you know that? I have tried to be nice to you but get the Fuck out of my tanning salon **now!!!!!!**

I **am** never coming back here **ever!!!!!!** Matty screams

Good as I hear the salon guy opening the door.

Ok I am dressed now. Do I go out and pretend that I didn't hear anything? Why do I over analyze everything?…gesh.

(So I walk out and head back to the front of the salon as the tanning salon guy is boiling. His face is all flushed and he is shaking his head.)

It's not worth it buddy, he is crazy I say to the front desk guy trying to comfort him a little He just looks at me with this wounded face and says;).

Yeah but for the past 9 months it's an everyday fight with him as he sits down and sighs. I am probably going to get fired now.

He is crazy man I say again trying to be comforting. (After all he was cute and apparently wants to sleep with me. Anyone who boost my ego I gotta help right?)

Do you know how much money he spends in here a month man? He asks almost "not nicely"

How much?

About $750.00 a month he whispers

(I look around wondering why he is whispering. There is nobody else here…)

I gotta get out of here because this is insane asylum # 2 and it is not even lunch yet.

So I tell him goodbye, good luck and I will call him when I get back from New York. He nods and waves. As I am putting the key in the door to my car, I hear a familiar voice behind me; can you take me to Sunkist Tan on Melrose? I turn around and yup….it's Orange Man…,

Huh why?

I don't have a car he says.

What????? You spend $750.00 a month on tanning and **you** don't have a car? What the hell is that? No I cannot take you to Sunkist Tan you freak and besides you would probably stain my seats with all that lotion and shit you have on. Sorry man but you ate too many pieces of crazy pie and I am not dealing with that. $750 dollars a month on tanning and no car….

Would you seriously want me behind the wheel of a car? Matty asks.

I actually laughed out loud.

Funny but I am still not driving your crazy ass to Sunkist Tan dude, now back away from my car.

As I am backing out the parking spot crazy Orange Man yells:

You're an asshole!!!!

So I roll down the window and I go

I Know!!!! I have been told… but thanks for reminding me and I drive away.

Next stop has got to be better than this Right? Oh God I hope so. What could possibly go wrong at the hair dresser? I mean….things **could** go wrong; she could maybe cut my hair crooked or bald me! This day has got to get better but now I am a little scared! I now know why I don't get up till after 10am that's for sure! I think I am going to get something to eat first and calm my nerves, before I get my hair cut. Maybe if I break my schedule or pattern today things will get better.

Well I stop and grab a sandwich at New York Deli. I figured I might as well get into the spirit of New York right? Pastrami and mustard plus a Snapple Ice Tea – it's just what the doctor ordered and my favorite lunch to eat. I ordered my lunch from a very pleasant Russian guy and I received my order rather quickly. The sandwich was hot, it looked great and the Snapple was cold. Hallelujah Things were already starting to look up and I decided to put a positive spin on the day so far. I still had 10 hours left before I was going to go to bed. I have gotten the gym done, tanning and now I was going to get my hair cut. I am almost halfway done and maybe I will even have time to stop in the Beverly Center. Ok that thought just cheered me up! HA! I finished my sandwich quickly and off to the hair salon I go. I pull into the Supercuts parking lot and I find parking right away. I walk in and my favorite stylist is working!!! Yeah!!! I am so excited!

Hey Ruzanna how are you?

Ruzanna is staring at me like who the hell are you but then quickly puts a smile on her face and says:

Good how are you?

She obviously doesn't remember me but it's OK she has probably cut 1000's of heads and she has only done mine like 4 times. I am memorable but who knows… I don't care because she cuts my hair awesome. After this cut she will remember me…..trust me!

Have a seat I will be with you shortly Tate she says.

Wait she does remember me? Then what was that look for? I couldn't possibly have done or said anything to offend her could I? I don't think so. My mind is racing trying to remember the last few times she has cut my hair but I am drawing a blank….Ruzzanna is this little southern bell that has this really cute and funny southern accent. She is always Miss Manners to me or at least the last 4 times I got my hair cut. She was always smiling and laughing. Almost felt like she had sunshine in her purse or something. Please don't tell me I pissed off the sweet hairdresser because they can get **even** with very sharp objects and quick too.

Ugh…I hope not!

Well I gotta find out right? Ruzzanna are you OK? Did I do something to you?

No she mumbles and then sighs

We were silent for what felt like an eternity and then she said do you want me to wash it?

Yes please I say as cheerful as possible

OK...... this comes with another sigh.

Ruzzana are you sure you are OK?

No I am not

As she directs me to go sit in the chair by Sink 2 and then she starts:

My husband left me. Cocksucker left me....for another man. 8 years we have been married. He cleaned out the bank account! I knew he was cheating on me but I just couldn't catch him. Sure as hell didn't think it was with another man. Supposedly he has been stuffin the little gay boy who walks the dog. Oh by the way...He **took** the **dog** too....Only thing in that damn house I actually liked. I should have cut his dick off when I first thought he was cheating. Mother **fucker** and he left me with these 3 nasty kids that I would like to leave on some church's doorstep I swear. The church would probably close its doors and move instead of looking after these damn hellions. They eat, curse and swear all day. Can't leave em alone for 2 Jesus minutes before they be fighting. I cannot take it anymore and I am gonna go to Walmart, apply for gun and shoot the sons of bitches.

That would make you a bitch Ruzzanna I say hoping for a laugh or to lighten the tension.

Mister Smart Ass I will drown YOU in this sink do you hear my boy? Don't try and act all cute on me. You asked me what was wrong so I am telling you.

Are you one of that people that asks someone how they are but really doesn't give a licks ass?

No I care…. but you are getting madder and madder at me Ruz

I know I am directing my anger at the wrong person but you are the one in front of me. You shoulda just mind your damn business and shut yer mouth and you be off by now primping in the mirror. Admiring yerself in the mirror, all you fags do it ya know right?. I used to like the fags but now I hate em. Hate every last one of y'all. Don't y'all have a parade and bars and the internet to meet **other** gay men? Why y'all gotta go and take our men?

She is scrubbing my head like she has a piece of sandpaper and is sanding a piece of wood smooth. She is shaking my head like a lunatic and I am starting to fell dizzy now. I need to get the hell out of here.

Ouch! Ouch Ouch!

She stops and realizes that she went into a rage on me. She rinses off the rest of my hair and dries it with a towel

It's good I say as I try and escape.

I need to get away from this woman

Would you like any product?

Are you crazy bitch? You almost guillotined my damn head! I yell at Ruzzanna

Do I want any product? She asks me back in that sweet Southern voice

No! No thanks….

Thank God she didn't tell me what was wrong **before** she cut my hair. Imagine what I would look like. I just want to get out of here. Let me just pay. Of course there is someone in front of me but I patiently wait my turn. Patiently of course is me pacing and tapping my foot and doing a lot of tuts. Finally when it is my turn I hand the cashier my credit card and she asks me:.

Would you like to leave a tip?

A Tip?

Yes...

Seriously a Tip?

Here's the tip - go tell that crazy bitch over there 9 am pointing to Ruzzanna) she needs to be medicated and has no business working with the public.... there's your tip!

I grab my credit card back and I storm out the door.

That was insane and ordinarily I would feel bad but I think the bitch gave me whiplash.

Do you think I should tell someone about the Wal-Mart gun thing? Hmmm where is there a Wal-Mart? Never been to one and I think they are mostly in the burbs. I think it is like Target on steroids though. She wouldn't really kill her kids now would she?

I wonder if her husband is cute. I never knew so many straight guys cheated on their wives with men until I moved to LA. I wonder how crazy Darlene is doing and maybe her and Ruzzanna could start a support group or something.

I know, I know I am going to hell but thank God I am outta there. I am exhausted. Why does everything have to be so difficult….**today?**

I get back in my car and start to head home. So far this day has been a success. Yeah successful…. that I am not dead, injured or hospitalized in any way, shape or form. I am not going to even run the risk of going to the Beverly Center after the day I have had. A clothing rack would probably fall on my head or I would get stuck in an elevator…**again.**

I get back to the apartment around 230pm just as my roommate Tommy is arising from his bed. I don't know how someone could move 3000 miles away from home, sleep all day and then party all night. It baffles me but it's none of my business. As long as he pays his share of the rent I don't care what he does anymore and our relationship is almost like strangers that live together. I go to my room, grab my laundry, soap and quarters and head down the hall to the washing machines. What I liked about this building is that there are 4 washer and dryers on every floor. If the ones on your floor were being used you could go up or down and always find a free one. Saturday afternoons could be challenging but weekdays…..never a problem.

Ahh awesome all 4 were empty so I loaded my clothes into all 4 of the machines. Three are for colored clothes and one for whites. No I don't wear a lot of clothes I just hate doing laundry! 45 minutes to kill. Let me go take a nap because I need it! As I head back to my apartment I notice that new people are moving into Sparkle Bottoms apartment. I try and avoid eye contact with them because I just want **tha**t nap. I will be friendly when I get back from New York. My universe cannot take anymore crazy. It has been maxxed out and I cannot take the risk. Even though I find it douchey when people deliberately don't make eye contact with me…. I get it sometimes, I guess people just need to be alone and just be.

Once I get back into my apartment and bedroom I take off my shirt and shoes. As I look in my bed Spencer is curled up in a ball and he looks so freakin cute! As I get into bed, I carefully move him a little so I can inch in to the bed. He actually moves very easily and then gets up and looks at me. He waits for me to settle in and then he contours his body into my side and begins to purr.

Arr how cute! He must know I am going back to New York without him and he is going to miss me. I set the alarm clock for 330pm so that I don't sleep too much. I don't want to sleep a ton now and then toss and turn all night tonight.

Ahh this feels so good…..

Oh my God how the hell is it 615pm? How did I not hear the alarm clock? Holy Shit my clothes!! I race down the hall… and yup they are there….but they are on the floor….in a pile….**wet!** Now who the hell would do that? I never could or would do that to someone. I would go to another floor or come back later but technically they were left in there for almost 3 hours. Couldn't they have put them on top of the washers and not on the floor? Screw it….I just picked them up and threw them in the dryer. What am I gonna do? Rant and rave or curse and swear? I did think about waiting to see who comes back for their clothes but it wasn't worth it. I had too much to do and I didn't want to waste the energy on this stupidity. I bet you it was the new tenants in Sparkle Bottoms place though.

I specifically look at my watch to check the time so I wouldn't have dry clothes on the floor next.

Time to pack for New York Yea! I head back to the apartment, go to my closet and grab my suitcase. I haven't had any use for it since I moved here. I carry it to my room and open it on the bed of course forgetting about Spencer.

Meow!!! oh Someone is pissed! I hit the cat with my suitcase and he is **none too pleased** with me!

I run to go say sorry but he has already taken off under the bed and I am sure he is really mad at me now.

Sorry Spens I didn't do it on purpose good Boy! I try and say to him as I am bending down under the bed. I am sure he will forgive me but the true test will be tonight when I fall asleep. He has a way of getting even with me for some of the things I do while I am sleeping. Ok back to packing….Most of the stuff that is in the dryer are summer clothes.

So 7 days -late November in New York hmmmm what to wear? What to wear? I go through my closet and pick out Fall/Wintery things and begin to pack. I remember to go get my clothes out of the dryer at the perfect time. Guess who is there?

Yup my new next door neighbor who I think dumped my clothes on the floor.

Hi I say

Hi he says with a southern drawl

Did you really have to dump my clothes on the floor I said I decided I was going to be quick, blunt and straight to the point?

Hey man I am sorry. I ran back to the apartment to get more quarters because I was going to put them in the dryer for you and by the time I got back the clothes were all ready in the dryers. Sorry Man didn't mean to disrespect y'all clothes.

It's OK it's cool I say.

Thank you and again Sorry. I am Antonio as he reaches out his hand to shake.

Antonio is very good looking mid-thirties Spanish/Mexican guy. He is tall and has an amazing body from what I can tell. He had this smile that I instantly fell in love with. Antonio had a big confident smile that could light up the entire Rockefeller Center during the holidays. It was clean, white and bright and when he smiled his dimples would just connect with his amazing cheek bones.

I think I stared just a little too long because he started to slant his perfectly groomed eye brows at me.

Oh hey I am Tate did you just move in?

Yes my boyfriend and I just moved in today.

(I say to myself **Boyfriend**? Seriously can the universe throw me one freakin bone today! There has been no one since Jake).

Ah well welcome to the hood. I have only been here 6 months but the building is cool. Did you know a crazy drag queen used to live in your apartment?

Yes we heard and it explains the feathers we keep finding. Antonio says with a cute laugh

HA I go. Well I am leaving for New York in the morning so I gotta run and finish my packing.

You're from there right? New York that is. I hear an accent from back east, he says again flashing that amazing smile

Yes I was born and raised in Brooklyn. Let me guess you're from Texas right?

Close… Albuquerque New Mexico we left the old Mexico for the new one!

HA and he is funny too…..Just put the knife in right here I say to myself as I point to my heart.

Well when I get back maybe we could grab a drink. I mean you and your boyfriend and I and um and maybe my roommate or maybe not. It depends on your schedule **and** your boyfriends. Or maybe just see ya around the pool. I know its November but it is heated. Or maybe we will bump into one another in the… the… lobby or even the gym downstairs. (Shut up Tate Don't say another word I am pleading with my brain to tell my voice to shut up)I am tripping over my own words, I am turning red and I am mortified by all this. Am I flirting with the Hot Mexican guy who just moved in next door…with his boyfriend? Yup….u-huh…..I am….shit!.

Ok bye I say and race away. That went well…**not!**

Have a great and safe flight neighbor! Antonio yells out as I am scurrying down the hall in utter and sheer embarrassment.

He probably already forgot my name. You see I can talk to almost anyone. My mom used to tell me I could have a conversation with a dead corpse because I could talk to anyone about almost anything. I was always really good adapting to different peoples hobbies, interests and views. The only time I am not is when I find someone attractive or I am attracted to them. Well guess what?

I was tripping over my words faster and more times than trying to figure out how to play double Dutch on the streets of Brooklyn as a kid with one leg.

I get back to the apartment and as I walk through the living room Tommy is there.(Surprise surprise!! Tommy in the living room watching TV)

I met our new neighbor. I tell him and I think it is the first thing we have said to one another in days or probably this week.

Yea?

He is hot but he has a boyfriend.

Your "Hot" or my "Hot" he asks me sarcastically

Shut up Tommy I am not in the mood and I go into my room and close the door.

I finish packing; I shower, heat up a frozen pizza in the microwave and watch a little TV in the living room with Tommy.

Are you excited to go back to New York? Tommy asks me

Kind of…there are a few people that I miss.(Are Tommy and I really going to have a conversation right now?)

Like your mother who cannot grasp that it is 3 hours earlier here than in New York? Tommy snaps at me.

Yes Tommy like my mother who cannot grasp that it is 3 hours earlier here in LA and is possibly in a religious cult.

What? As Tommy looks at me with this scowl wondering what new conspiracy I have looming in my brain today..

Nothing dude, don't worry about it I am off to bed. Good night!(I didn't have the energy to get into with Tommy tonight)

Have a safe flight and Happy Thanksgiving. I won't miss you one bit. Tommy says with that ever loving sarcasm that I have come to loathe.

You are going to feed the cat right? (as I stop, turn around and look at Tommy for his next witty response)

Don't you mean catssssss it plural now remembers?

Yes the cats Tommy.

Did you buy food? He moans

Yes there is plenty.

Then I will feed the catssssssssssssss!

Thanks Night.

As I close the door I say to myself out loud what a dick he is. How did I wind up living with such an asshole? I need to start booking more jobs so I can live on my own. I am going 1000% percent when I get back I swear. Miserable piece of shit you are Tommy.

It is 1130 and my flight is at 9am so I set the alarm for 6 am. That should give me enough time to get ready in the morning. The cab is coming at 630am.

For what seems like eternity I toss and turn. I am reliving my day. From the gym queens, to my haircut with Ruzanna, all the way to my hot new neighbor with the boyfriend. I keep trying to make myself sleep but nothing is working. I finally must have dozed off around 3am. I think I would sleep better if I wasn't so obsessed with finding someone besides my Mother to actual love me. I have this constant fixation on not spending the rest of my life alone. I desperately want a boyfriend and it shows. I do get asked out but I am only attracted to a certain type of guy. That type is usually unattainable assholes who think they are God's gift to the planet.

Wait that is not true, they also have to be poor, broke, gay but married to a woman for a green card, have fieriest tempters or already have a boyfriend. Thanks God for internet porn these days or I would be climbing the walls.

You know what I do miss the most about New York? The men! In New York they are not all actors or in the business. There is nothing sexier than seeing a hot Latin man in a suit, carrying a brief case to the office. A stock broker with a sexy accent, A British doctor on his way to St. Luke's to perform an operation on someone, an Italian lawyer on his way to court, or just any ruggedly handsome natural guy **not** wearing mascara.

Chapter 13

MY First trip home.....and more!

Holy Shit!!!!! OMG

How can it be 10:15am???

I missed my flight!!!!!! **Shit!!!!**

What am I going to do???

Well the first thing I want to do is throw that God damn alarm clock out the window but I think I will call the airline first.

American Airline how may I help you?

I missed my flight…I overslept

So sorry sir where were you headed? (The woman on the phone sounded so genuinely upset for me).

New York City

And where are you now?

Huh?

What city are you departing?

Oh oh Los Angeles LAX

Well everything is booked really solid sir. It is 2 days before Thanksgiving. Today and tomorrow are two of the busiest travel days of the year.

So I am stuck here in LA now?

Well **No** not necessarily sir, the good news is there are A LOT of flights to New York from LA still today. They are all booked solid but what I might suggest is going to the airport and put yourself on the stand by list.

Stand by? what is that?

It is when people don't show up or cancel their flight last minute. People get stuck in traffic, they over sleep like you, (ugh remind me) people change their minds all the time. Things like that. The next flight is at 1245 but that is over sold as well. Let me check the 215.

Over sold? How do you over sell a flight? What do you put the extra people in cargo or something I ask?

NO no during the busy seasons the airline expects people to not show up or miss their flights like you.

(Does she seriously **have** to keep reminding me?)

The American Airline woman on the phone continues: We sell more tickets so that no seats go empty. So go to the airport and put yourself on the standby list. You might have to hang around all day but you might get lucky.

I never get lucky trust me I will be there all day but thank you, you have been very helpful. I graciously thank her for all of her help. It is not her fault, my stupid ass overslept my flight

Happy Thanksgiving sir and thanks for flying American Airlines Good bye!

Bye

So I race around and get ready. I call the cab company.

I need a cab to the airport.

Phone number please this guy who you could tell has probably smoked 3 packs of cigarettes for 30 years asks me.

310-578-2143

There was a cab there at 630 this morning and nobody showed up for it.

I over slept my flight sir. I am sorry.

But you scheduled it for 630 am.

I know sir I overslept.

Well you shouldn't do that. The cabby sat out there for 25 minutes waiting for you and no one came out.

I know I am sorry I overslept can I please get a cab?

Are you ready now? He says sarcastically

Yes I am!!

Not going to over sleep again now are you? (Why is this man torturing me? People can over sleep sometimes!)

No, I am going to be waiting downstairs sir. How long?

5 minutes he says and he just hangs up.

I double check that I have everything. Suitcase, carry on, wallet, money, keys and tickets. Check! I am all good to go.

As I open the door, who is standing in the kitchen.......Thomas?

What... dude you missed your flight? As he shakes his head in disbelief.... you are such a disaster dude.

(Why is **this** the one day that I have ever seen Thomas out of his damn bed before noon?)

Yes I am painfully aware of that Thomas. The alarm clock didn't go off. Or if it did go off I didn't hear it man.

Well you know it's like Thanksgiving and the airports are packed right? Dude you are screwed but you cannot stay here.

What? Why could I not stay here? Is the apartment being fumigated or something like that. I thought you were staying here for Thanksgiving?

I am staying here. I have a buddy from college coming to visit and I told him he could stay in your room.

Where you going to at least ask me?

No I thought you would never find out. Do you mind?

Fuck you Thomas!! No I don't mind but you could have asked me if a stranger can use my room while I am out of town. I would never do that to you.

But I never go anywhere Tate. Thomas has dealt me his daily dose of sarcasm at me already and I just want to choke him.

Yes that is something I am painfully aware of Thomas. Have a **Great** Thanksgiving as I say in a tone that he knows I am pissed.

You better feed the fucking cats Thomas as I slam the door.

He yells to me bye…. Bye… now, off you go!

(As I get out of the elevator the cab is just pulling up.)

(I have gotta get on a flight….My mother is going to **kill** me!

American Airlines please and hurry!

My mind is racing and I am trying to figure out how the hell I am going to tell my mother that I over-slept the flight. She is going to be so pissed at me. I can already here the speech about responsibility and being on time in life or how rude it is to keep people waiting. Oh please God let there be no traffic.

No such luck it is bumper to bumper as we get close to LAX. Ugh what else could go wrong? Shut up Tate! Don't even say that because you know more can wrong right? Yes brain yes.....

I arrive at the airport and it is not as mobbed as I thought it would be. Everything seems to be moving along. There is a line at the ticket counter but not that bad. I wait on the line for about 10 minutes and I am watching all the ticket agents and deciding which one I want to get. Some are nice and sweet while several look like that would rather be anywhere else than at American Airlines ticket counter. As I get closer I start thinking please, please, please let me get a nice ticket agent.

Next......

I look up and it is actually from what I have been observing for the past 12 minutes the sweetest ticket agent. I rush up to the window and I say:

Hi there how are you?

I am wonderful she says with a big smile and how are you?

Well I missed my flight this morning I um... um overslept. I know it's the worst day in the world to over sleep a flight

You did? Well let's see if we can get you on another flight dear where are you going?

JFK I say meekly

Oh there are still several flights going there today, let me check. (She is being so sweet to me.)

Well she starts typing in the computer for what seems like an eternity with a lot of "On no," "tisks" and "wows." Finally she comes back up from the computer screen and says well we have three different options for you today. I can get you on the 4:15pm flight but there is a $50.00 booking fee and

Done…. I will take it please!!!

Sweetie do you want to hear the other two options before we do this?

Are they any better? I ask kind of in a funny yet sarcastic tone.

Well the standby is not better but you wouldn't have to pay the $50.00 rebooking fee for that flight.

That's OK

I could tell I was beginning to annoy her by cutting her off but I just **had** to get on a flight

And the third option….is the red eye flight tonight at 10pm.

I will stick with option 1 because the sooner I get to New York the better. What time does it arrive at JFK?

A little after midnight but by the time you taxi to the gate around 12:30 am.

(I am dreading that phone call to my mother….she is **not** going to be happy with me, that is for sure.)

How many bags are you checking in? She asks me very chipper

Just one I say very cheerful especially now that I am actually getting on a plane today and not stuck in LA.

Ok doll she says and off she goes to get my new ticket. She comes back and presents me with my new boarding pass. That will be $50 dollars please.

I reach in my pocket and hand her exactly $50.00 in cash. Remember I am a waiter after all and I live off cash tips.

The American Airlines sweet ticket agent gives me my receipt and hands me my boarding pass. Now you go and have a nice Thanksgiving honey.

Thanks you so much! Thank you, thank you, thank you. (As I am bowing to her) You have been amazing thanks!

Now off you go and don't miss this flight. It leaves from Gate 24 and boarding will start in about 40 minute's darling.

OK and I wave to her as I walk away. Let's hope security doesn't hold me up. I need to get my magazines for the flight! Well security was OK and I got through rather quickly actually. Maybe things were turning around for me today. I mean with all the bad luck I have had in the past 2 days, it seems like the universe was finally throwing me a bone. Man I am starving….I have some time so I might as well get something to eat before I board the plane.

I grab a burger at Applebee's and start doing my favorite thing to do at the airport…people watch! There is every walk of life at the airport especially at Los Angeles Airport. I see some of the most gorgeous people at this airport. There is this beautiful woman walking down and **she** has to be a model, I see a bunch of families and then I see a bunch of Middle Easterners. I am sure they had a rough time at security but do they really need to where the towels on their head… at the airport? I know it's a religious thing but it really makes people uncomfortable. It makes me uncomfortable actually and I am sure they get a lot of resistance everywhere they go. I have met some really great people from the Middle East. Anyway I will shut up about this for now.

I then see this guy who has to weigh like 500 pounds…no joke. I feel sorry for the poor bastard that has to sit next to him on the plane. Watch it be me. Of course he is eating McDonalds… of course! Why would anyone get that fat? The guy looks like he is in his mid 30's to top it off. I don't want to hear that shit about it could be his health or it's a medical condition my ass. He is just some lazy fat slob who doesn't exercise and eats like shit. And McDonalds?? He should be arrested for public fatness. Hey now don't lynch me because I don't like the fatties because there is a difference between gaining a little weight and **that!** I think if he wasn't scarfing down a Big Mac, I might not be affected the way I am.

Did you know I worked at McDonalds when I was in high school? I got fired…. I flash back in my head to what had happened. I remember my outfit was a blue stripped shirt with a red clip on bow tie like it was yesterday. I fucking hated that outfit and no matter how many times you washed it, it would still smell like fries and grease.

They put me in the drive thru as the cashier…which was the manager's first mistake. They also didn't have anybody to take the orders over the speaker, so I had to do that too. Did I mention that it was 7:30 pm on a busy Friday evening? The food runner "Jane" (the person who brings the food into the booth) was a bitch and is fighting with her boyfriend, who is the cook. She is not helping me with anything but I will deal with her later. So basically I have to take the orders, get the money, make the drinks, put napkins and straws in the bag, ask them how many ketchups or what sauce they need all by myself. I did mention it is 7:30pm right?

Well the drive thru lane is wrapped all the way around the building and cars are starting to beep. Fuck!! The manager's in the back talking on the phone, Jane is fighting with her boyfriend, we have no more fries and customers are yelling at me where their food is. One of the cars got tired of waiting and got off the drive thru line. Now the computer just basically says the next car gets the next order in line. It doesn't say that the brown car gets the hamburger and the blue one gets the Chicken Mc Nuggets. It was a mess and it took a while to fix but eventually things calmed down but man was it crazy.

Well I ran out of the plastic covers for the drinks and I ask Jane if she could get me more from the back? I think she said yes but I was completely out by now. All of a sudden this lady in a brown Cadillac comes screeching up to the window.

Do you know how long I have been waiting on this fucking line! 40 God damn minutes!! Where the fuck is my order? Now you know she is screaming at the top of her lungs to me.

Mind you she had two little kids in the car with her. Great mother huh?

I am sorry ma'am it is coming I stammer…

Hurry the fuck up she spits.

I hand her the bag with the food and tell her the drinks will be a second.

(Mind you her drinks are a vanilla, chocolate and two strawberry shakes.)

I yell Jane where are the lids for the drinks?

I am **looking** for them **calm down**! Jane sneers

The crazy bitch, in the brown Cadillac, with the two kids in the car is summoning me to the window. As I approach the window she reaches in and grabs me by my clip on tie. It is a clip on so that if we ever got caught in an ice cream machine it would just pop off. Well that theory didn't work because she dragged my head all the way out the window and screamed: **Give me my fucking shakes!!**

All while shaking my clip on tie and my neck back and forth.

I finally pulled away with my neck throbbing and still no Jane with the lids for the shakes.

You want your fucking shakes lady??

Yes Asshole. she screams at me

Well here are your fucking shakes!

Without the lids in a cup holder I thrust the four shakes out the window and straight into her and her car. There is strawberry all over her and the car, vanilla made it all the way to the back seat and the chocolate was all over her dashboard.

Enjoy!!!!!!!And I slammed the window to the drive thru shut!

Well this certainly caused enough commotion now for Jane to come up from the back and the manager to finally get off the phone.

What happened? The manager yells.

I quit, I am fired, I don't care as I am walking to the back. I want to get the hell out of here.

By this time, the crazy bitch in the brown Cadillac, with the two kids in the car, is inside the store and she is going to **kill** me. She has strawberry shake everywhere and even the manager can't keep a straight face.

I am going to kill that little fuck I swear!!!! I can hear her yelling as I am walking downstairs to get my coat.

Calm down ma'am the manager yells!

In the meantime the assistant manager comes downstairs to ask me what happened. Wait we had an assistant manager? Where the hell has she been for the past two hours?

What happened?

So I tell her everything. How the line was around the corner, Jane fighting with the cook, having to take the orders, get the money, fill the drinks, napkins, straws blah blah blah and Jane disappearing for 15 minutes to get the lids for the drinks. I tell her about the abuse from the woman and how she assaulted me with the clip on tie. I told her how she kept pulling and pulling the tie from my neck out the window of the drive thru.

She pointed to my neck and said those marks are from her?

Yup

I will be right back she said **stay here!!!**

I went back in the break room and called my Dad.

Dad, you gotta come pick me up now.

I thought you don't get off till 9pm he quizzes.

I am off now can you come and get me?

What happened?

I will tell you when you get here.

It's going to take me about 20 minutes to get you because I have to pick up your brother from practice before I can get to you.

Ok please hurry up Dad?

Is everything OK Tate?

YES! Just see you soon.

(Over the loud speaker)

Now boarding Flight 286 to JFK

What huh? My flashback took entirely too long. Shit I still have to get my magazines and call my **Mom!** The magazines come first of course though. I could always call my Mom when I board the plane. Ok so I want People, Star Magazine and US Weekly and that should do it.

$23.50 please the cashier tells me

What? Three magazines cost over twenty bucks?

Yup! She did say it with a smile though

OK here you go as I begrudgingly hand over the cash and thinking I already spent close to a $100 bucks and I haven't even **left** the airport yet.

To lie or not to lie to your Mother, that is what is going on in my head right about now. I am torn between telling her the truth and getting a lecture or just lying to her and blaming my late arrival on someone else. What a dilemma!

Ok quit staling…time to call my Mom.

Mom?

Hey Tate are you here? I am just parking the car at the airport. I will meet you at the baggage claim.

No Mom I am still here in LA.

What did you just say **Tate**?

I am still in LA Mom

What? Why? What is going on? Are you Ok? Is something wrong? Are you hurt? You are supposed to be at this airport now! (My Mother is starting to get a little hysterical and I need to react really quickly or this is going to be an epic meltdown. She is afraid of flying as it is and she very quickly goes to doom and gloom.)

(As I start to tell her what happened I pause….think hard for a second…. and then I continue. I had a very good reason why I did this by the way….)

There was a problem with the airplane Mom.

Oh My God you didn't crash Tate did you?

(She is now hysterical and it is full on scene stealing epic. I thank God that she is at least still in her car for this meltdown.).

Mom **calm** down! Everything is fine (Man I feel awful and I am such a horrible son) There was a problem with the engine and we have been delayed but everything is fine now. We are boarding the plane right now. Everything is fine so just calm down.

Why didn't you call me? She asks

(Hmm OK next obstacle....)

We were stuck on the plane and they wouldn't let us use our cell phones until we were back at the airport gate.

Oh how long were you on the runway?

3 hours Mom! It was just awful. No food or water and they wouldn't let us get up to go to the bathroom either.(That should keep her calm for a second, make her feel sorry for me and it usually works like a charm.)

Oh that is awful. We should write them a letter.

OK Mom we will do that.

The nerve! I am going to call them right now. They have no right making my son, stay on an airplane for 3 hours with no food or water. I never....

Mom calm down they bought everyone a nice lunch when we got off the plane and were waiting for the mechanics to come and fix the problem.

Why didn't you call me then? I could have stayed home and not have to make two trips to the airport now?

Shit! (Why can't I ever get a lie to work?)

Mom I forgot my cell phone on the plane. I am so sorry.

Don't they have pay phones at the airport? Honey you know you can **always** call me collect. You know that right?

I know that Mom but this is Los Angeles and nobody uses pay phones here anymore. Everybody has cell phones and most of the pay phone companies have either gone out of business or are bankrupt. I am so sorry Mom. (The only thing that is bankrupt is my morals right about now.)

It's OK as long as you are OK and safe. That is all that really matters Tate. What time does your fixed plane get in now?

Um midnight....Mom

Midnight? I am in bed by then.

I know Mom, I will take a cab.

A cab....that is nonsense I will pick you up. It is like $45 dollars for a cab. I will come and get you. I love you Tatey. I am looking forward to seeing your sweet face. Now have a safe flight. I love you and kiss kiss.

I love you too Mom. See you soon. I am very looking forward to this visit, sorry for worrying you and I love you very much.

Bye.

I feel like total shit. I have just lied to my mother, I know she is a nervous wreck now because of me; she will be worried sick that the plane is going to crash. I know that once the week is over it is going to become the ultimate and she is going to try anything to get me to stay in New York. What a dumb ass I am and how the hell did you oversleep your flight in the first place? What are you in the second grade? I feel **awful**.

All of a sudden this guy leans in with a look of curiosity and asks me what flights were you on that had the engine trouble?

I just looked at him and said the flight that I just lied to my Mother about because I over slept the flight and forgot to call her.

Dude seriously….that is just wrong as he shook his head in disapproval and gave me the dirtiest look as he walked away. He turned around as he was walking away and said Man that is **bad** karma. You better hope your plane doesn't go down man because you are going straight to hell.

(I just looked at him, nodded and then finally said: I am already going to hell, trust me the list is a mile long.

Finally I board the air plane, find my seat, (Hey Cool it's an Aisle Seat) put my carry on in the overhead compartment above me, grab my magazines, sit down and buckle up. What a day it has been and I have nobody to blame but my stupid self. I cannot believe what I just did to my poor sweet Mother. That guy is right, I am disgusting.

Ahh **finally** I am on the plane headed back to New York for the first time since I moved to LA. Airplane please don't crash, I promise I will make it to my Mother. Plus she is used to me being a fuck up and an occasional liar. Occasional?

Next thing I know is I look up to see some of the other passengers boarding the plane and I am horrified! The obese man from the airport eating McDonalds is on my plane! He is headed straight for me and the **seat** next to me is still empty. No, no, no, please no. I will never lie to my Mother again. Oh God no…Please, please no. I closed my eyes as I was begging and when I opened them in fear I looked up. Wait where did he go? I look back and I say Oh **awesome** out loud he is further back phew! About 4 people later this 20 something petite girl comes to my aisle and says

Can I squeeze by ya? That's my seat by the window.

Sure can! I say very cheerfully as I pop up to let her in.

As we settle down I hear this woman about three rows back start to yell. I can tell she is Asian by her accent but I had to turn around and double check. Presto she is a little old Asian lady and she is yelling at the Obese Man with her broken English.

You too fat, you too fat..you hafta buy 2 seat. I am a little woman and your fat is in my seat. I pay fo my toll seat….Just fo me….No me and not fo you fat too. You hafta buy 2 seat….Look…. (Now she is grabbing his gut) You too fat…you crush little woman….I **little** woman….No you hafta buy 2 seats…I need help!

By this point it is getting loud and the flight attendants are trying to calm the little old Asian lady down but she is not having it.

He too, too fat. I no share my seat wit he fat. He need to buy 2 seat. I no share wit he fat. No fair. I pay $312.45 fo my whole seat. I am little lady and he too fat.

The obese guy is trying to argue with the little Asian lady and you can hear him pleading with her. I will hold all my fat in my seat. (He is gripping all his fat rolls with both arms)

No, No you let go and it flies into seat and you crush me. I a little lady. No You buy 2 seats. You no sit here. No fair!

I as well as several others passengers actually laughed out loud when she just said he would crush her. I didn't feel bad laughing because it was a group…. actually I probably wouldn't have felt bad if it was just me laughing. Who am I trying to kid?

After what had been about 20 minutes the obese man was taken off the plane.

Did I feel bad for tubby? No fucking way…That little Asian lady might have just saved his life. I learn valuable lessons from being humiliated all the time. Maybe he will go on a freakin diet now. Or at least stop eating like crap but I have a feeling he will probably be buying 2 seats from now on.

Finally Take off. I need a drink….or several

After about 5 hours, six cocktails and a rather smooth flight we land at JFK. The captain comes on and says he had a great tail wind so he got us to New York 45 minutes early. The time in New York is 11:30 pm. We taxi for what felt like forever and then de-plane the aircraft. I immediately turn on my phone and call my Mom.

I am here! I tell her excitedly

U huh I am at the baggage claim (**click**)

Did my Mother just hang up on me? Uh O what is wrong now? What did I do? I have been in the air for 5 hours. I say to myself

I get to the baggage claim and my Mom and sister are there waiting for me. As I approach I get a big hug from my sister as she whispers in my ear:

Mom knows….

What?

Well my sister quickly jumps off of me and I immediately hug my Mom! I get a half hug back from her and then she goes:

How was your flight?

It was great Mom!

(Now having consumed 6 cocktails on the plane --I kinda "forgot" About the conversation I had with my Mom before takeoff. Completely forgot about the engine problem story and pretty much everything else I told her.)

Really? Much better than your first one right? (I have heard this tone many times over the years and I know I am in trouble but I am not sure why….yet.)

(I look at my Mothers face and Oh shit….I am busted and it all comes crashing back through my vodka soaked brain.)

I love you Mom….I am so very excited to see you. You look so amazing Mom. Have you lost some weight?

(Nothing…stone cold….she is not buying it. Plus I think I am slurring my sentences to her…you think Tate? You know you are!)

She angrily looks at me and says:

Remember Tate you had me write down the flight number so I would know which carousel to meet you at... remember? (I am nodding) Well to my shock and dismay, I saw people coming out of the airport earlier today when I came to the airport for the **first time** to pick you up. I noticed the tag on their suitcases said flight #286. I thought maybe there was a flight #286 from every city so I asked some of the people. Where are you folks coming from? And guess where they said they came from Tate? (Sarcastic voice in full affect) LA....Imagine that. So I ask what time was the flight. **and guess** what time their flight was Tate? Yup 9am.............Hmm Strange huh?

Mom I am sorry it just that.....

Tate you scared me half to death...What's with all this lying again? I thought we were past the lying Tate? Are we past the lying Tate? Do you want me to treat you like a child Tate? Your sister managed to get here from Chicago on time Tate **and** without scaring her mother half to death. Now I am wondering what else you are lying about Tate?

(My sister is looking at me with that same smirk that I have always wanted to slap off her face. It's like I am a child again. I just had another Flashback to my childhood - with my Mom yelling at me and my sister enjoying every second of it.)

(Thank God I'm Drunk!)

I am sorry Mom! I will tell you all about it later. Can we just get my bag and go home please. It has been a really long day. I plead with her.

We will discuss this in private Tate. I am very tired as well especially having to make **two** trips to the airport in one day!

This is going to be a real fun car ride back to the house that's for sure. Not even here 30 minutes and I have already pissed her off.

6 more days….6 more days…I just need to keep telling myself that 6 more days and my family sentence is over and I will be free.

We are home! I hear my Mother cheer

I fell asleep in the car to avoid any more lectures and why I lied to my Mother. Wow the car ride wasn't that bad after all as I stagger out of the car clutching my suitcase. I turn to my Mother and I say to her:

Mom I am sorry for lying to you…I really am. I was just so embarrassed that I over slept my flight. I love you and I didn't mean to upset you…

I love you too Tate…Now go to bed because you smell like a God damn brewery. Did someone spill a drink on you Tate?

(Don't lie now Tate I say to myself in my head. You promised your Mother you would not lie to her anymore)

Yeah Mom the girl next to me had like seven cocktails on the plane and the flight attendants had to cut her off. She spilt a drink all over me.

(She is looking at me like I know he is full of shit but I am way too exhausted to go another round with him tonight.)

Take a shower then because she spilt the drink on your breath as well.

OK as a walk away feeling like an 8 year old that has just be punished and told to go straight to his room….**again.**

Chapter 14

Spending the day with Mother

It had been about 6 months since I had been in my Mother's house. A lot has happened to me over the last 6 months. I moved 3,000 miles away, I have had an array of adventure; as well as a slew of misadventures since the last time I was in this house. I have a hunger for the world. I have dreams that I must conquer. I was not built or created for status quo. I am not a 9* to 5er, a time clock puncher or am comfortable getting up and going to that same job for the next 30 years. I want to see and do everything that the world has to offer. As I look around this house I think I had an epiphany...nothing in this house changes.

As I start to look around it's like nothing has changed or moved in the last 6 months. The living room is exactly the same as I remember it. There are chach-skies and kitsch everywhere. All of my Mother's ceramics of various animals are throughout the house. She has a real hankering for ceramic cats which would explain why she has 3 live ones now. Twiddels, Candy and Marshmallow were their names. I do understand why my Mother named Marshmallow though. That has got to be the fattest white cat I have ever seen in my life. Actually it is the fattest cat ever regardless of its color. The pictures on the wall are all the same. Same ole furniture, same paint, same ole carpeting, same smell

Tatey **get down here we have things to do today!!!**

Same ole Mother......

Ma I am coming

Well hurry up we have things to do.

I am coming.....

Tatey you are going to make me late for my day.(she yells from downstairs)

How do you make someone late for their day ma?

You just do! Are you ready to go?

Where are we going?

To the City....

Mom we are in the city. (I smartassingly declare to my Mother)

To Manhattan smart ass!! Let's go!

OK OK!!

Well out the door we go and I stop dead in my tracks.

It's freezing Ma.

Its 58 degrees and **beautiful!!!**

I need to go get a jacket. I will be right back, I say as my Mother looks at her watch and groans for me to hurry up.

I run back in and grab a jacket in a matter of 18 seconds.

You are making me fall behind on my day already she snaps, as I am trying to walk and put the jacket on at the same time. She just keeps looking at that watch over and over again.

Do we have an actual appointment somewhere Mom?

Yes we do Tate.

Where Mom?

Bergdorf Goodman.

Really Mom Bergdorf's?

Yes Tate Bergdorf's. The church had a raffle last week and I won. Yup I won a huge shopping spree for $250.00 at Bergdorf Goodman's and the girls were all really jealous. It was the Grand prize that everyone wanted. I have been dying to go there. I waited for you to come home before I went there. I want to buy myself a nice dress, a pair of shoes, a purse, get my hair done and maybe if there is some money left on the gift certificate we can have lunch there too.

I just look at my Mom and I smile. I say to myself I wouldn't trade you for any other Mom in the world. My poor, sweet naïve Mother but I just love her so, so much. I cherish on how she has been able to remain so unaffected with life. She is so simple, innocent and pure and doesn't have a mean bone in her body. She genuinely at this very moment believes that she is going to get a dress, shoes, a purse and a haircut for $250.00....At Bergdorf Goodman...I just look at the excitement on her face and how much she has been looking forward to this. I just don't have the heart to tell her what in fact she is going to get for $250.00 at Bergdorf Goodman.

I am so excited for this Tate I truly am.

It will be fun **Mom!**

I miss you – you know that Tatey

I know that Mom I love you.

She just smiled and grabbed my hand and said **faster!**

We were walking to the subway at a pretty brisk pace but I kept looking for something to be different. The restaurants, grocery store, the pizza parlor, the movie theater were all the same and the people working in them were the same. There was slutty Jolene, who would spread her legs if the wind blew hard enough, for almost any guy, still working as a cashier at Gristede's. Across the street there was Gumba Joey still making the pizza and by the looks of him, he has been on a pizza and beer diet for many, many years now. As we crossed the street I get a wave from Old man Louie who is still in the ticket booth at the two screen movie theater in Brooklyn Heights. He is such a nice man. He used to let me into R rated movies when I was 12 years old. Don't let me miss guide you here-- they haven't just been working those jobs for the past 6 months, they have been working them for over 10 years. Louie since before I was born.

We get to the subway, my Mother whips out a Metro card; swipes the card and walks through the turn style and says swipe it after me.(as she is handing me her Metro Card)

Huh?

(I stood there confused for a brief moment)

Get on the subway Tate! Swipe the damn metro card my Mother says angrily

Oh sorry Mom wasn't thinking. Cool!

Well after 2 attempts at swiping the card the card finally works and the turn style lets me walk through it. Yea!

Mom we are going to take the 1 train to 59th and walk I tell my Mom.

No we are going to take the red train to Columbus Circle and **then** walk she states.

Same thing Mom

Oh....

(It is funny on how certain people equate to colors while others to numbers huh. It's very interesting).

As we are walking down the stairs the train is coming! Perfect timing I say.

As the train doors open all these people come pouring out. Next thing I know all of these other people start pouring onto the train.

Mom maybe we should wait for the next one.

Why?

Because this train is really crowded Mom.

This is a New York City subway train Tate they are **all** crowded she snaps. What the hell has LA done to you boy? Get on this train before I

Ok OK I am coming as I squeeze on.

(She is just shaking her head at me now.) What has LA done to you? You took a subway to high school every day and **now** you are afraid of a crowded subway train? Tisk tisk and she shakes her head.

Mom even when I lived in Manhattan I didn't take the subway that often. I would walk everywhere or take a cab.

Well the subway is quicker than a cab and far less expensive.

I hear her under her breath even has the train rattles away

Walk to Bergdorf Goodman that boy is crazy. He would never walk to Bergdorf's from Brooklyn. He is insane.

After about 18 minutes of standing on the train squished up against every walk of life, we hit Columbus Circle station.

Columbus Circle we hear through a broken speaker and we squeeze our way off the train. As we start to make our way up to the street my biggest nightmare has come true. It is raining outside and the Umbrella People are out in droves. I hate umbrella people. Umbrella people have no regard for anyone else on the street or how to use an umbrella correctly. They poke you in the head with the umbrella, hit you in the back, splash water at you, they think the sidewalk is for them and their umbrella only. They have a total disregard for anybody who isn't an Umbrella person.

Have there always been this many people on the streets at this time of the day Mom? It seems awfully crowded for this time of day.

Yes Of course Tate why?

It just seems there are **a lot** of people at the crosswalk Mom.

There are **a lot** of people Tate…its New York City after all! It is the greatest city in the world and you better promise me that as many mocha soy lattes you have out there in Hollywood you won't forget it.

I won't Mom

This is **still** your home.

I know Mom I know.

Look there is Bergdorf Goodman she shrieks let's go! (I have never seen my Mother move so quick!)

Now Bergdorf Goodman is what you would call a high end department store. It's on the same caliber as Neiman Marcus and a step up from Macy's or Bloomingdales. Now Bergdorf Goodman sells very high end couture from fashion houses like: Versace, Chanel and Gucci. It is where the wealthy or the people pretending to be wealthy shop. It is not a place that my Mother from Brooklyn visits that often. Actually I think it is her first time in the store.

(As we enter the store the store is breath taking and it looks amazing)

The store is already done up for the holidays and it looks magnificent! There are beautiful trees and lights everywhere. All of the store windows have different themes to them. A winter wonderland in one, Santa's North Pole in another and they just go on and on with one more magical than the next. Simple and gorgeous with an impeccable attention to detail is the best way to describe them.

Excuse me where are the dresses? I hear my Mom ask.

This snooty saleswoman goes Couture? Gowns? Evening Wear? Casuals?

Um yes…she says with enthusiasm that I haven't heard from my Mom in years

Well which one? She saleswoman snaps

The one that has dresses my Mother says as innocent as possible.

Dresses? (Saleswoman is clearly annoyed)

Yes Dresses

What kind of dress? What is the dress for?

Thanksgiving my Mother states

Oh for God sakes try the third floor but I doubt you will find any "dresses" for **you** up there but I think that is where the sales rack is.

(Did this retail bitch just mock my Mother? Yup she did.)

What did **you** just say to my Mother? Lady you better dial back the tone. That's my Mother you are talking to. Do you understand me? (I am pissed)

Sorry and she rolls her eyes and walks away.

Come on Tate let's go to the 3ʳᵈ floor and stop picking fights with the sales girl.(as she looks at me like don't ruin this for me.)

(OH I dread what is going to happen within the next 15 minutes. Wait how the hell did my sister get out of this? Is this my punishment for missing my flight?)

My Mother immediately leaps off the third floor escalator and starts going through all the dresses like an excited school girl looking for her first prom dress.

Wow much for this dress? (I hear my Mother exclaim as she is holding this beautiful dress in her hand and examining the price tag)

This has to be a mistake. This price cannot be right. Let me find a salesgirl. Oh miss…**miss**! This tag **has** to be wrong!

UGH……

Mom I beg you, can you please come over here for a minute.

Hold on Tate I am trying to get the sales girl she exclaims

Mom….(pleading)

All I am thinking to myself is this is going to end up bad. I just hope the new sales girl doesn't insult her also.

All I can hear is my Mother's voice approaching one of the sales people:

This price tag is wrong my Mother states to the sales lady.

(Btw Thank God it is a lady and not some snotty little girl bitch)

It is?? She says cheerfully to my Mother Let me go and checks the price.

The woman scans the tag on the dress and returns smiling to my Mother. The price is correct dear it is $1,100.99.

How can a dress be a thousand dollars? My Mother says almost demanding to the sales lady.

Its Balenciaga darling she says sweetly but almost like how could you **not** know who it is and what this dress is worth.

Who? My poor Mother asks.

All I am thinking is how I am going to get my innocent Mother out of this store in one piece. My Mother is far from poor and is actually a very successful hairdresser. She owns 3 salons in Brooklyn and they are all doing well. She just doesn't know high end fashion or designers. The people that work at places like Bergdorf live for fashion labels, it is what they breathe.

Mom let's go look at some shoes OK?

Fine I am **not** going to pay a thousand dollars for a dress that is just plain **ridiculous** as she storms out of the department…Just **ridiculous!** Who would pay that much for a dress? Well maybe Sofia Loren would have paid that much for a dress but certainly not me. Have you met Sofia Loren Tatey?

As I sigh I say No Mom I have not met Sofia Loren……….yet! Let's go find you some shoes.

OK

Well as we approach the shoe department it was just as I feared. Big selection of Prada, Gucci, Louboutins, Jimmy Choo's and every other expensive name brand shoes as far as the eye could see. Yup there goes my Mother straight for the Jimmy Choo's.

Can I try these in a 6 please? My Mom asks another sales girl

Mom you are a size 7 aren't you? I ask kind of curious on why she would ask for a smaller size shoe than she actually wears.

Shhh Tate ladies don't wear size 7' shoes they wear 6's.

Who told you that Mom?

Everybody knows that Tate?

So I am thinking to myself that this has to come from my crazy grandMother. The same grandMother who also told my Mother that girls that wear glasses don't get passes. How I know this is one of my Mother's "isms", is because my sister almost failed the 7th grade because she couldn't read the blackboard and my Mother refused to get her glasses. Thank God for the invention of contacts because if not for contacts my sister would probably be 25 years old and still in the 7th grade. This "ism" also explains why my Mother was constantly crashing the damn car and still hated to drive at night.

Mom can you just please get a size 7 shoe, I beg of you.

A size 6 is just fine Tate! I know my feet. I am going to be the one wearing the shoes after all. As she leans into the salesgirl she says **"Kids"**!!

Well the salesgirl comes back with the Jimmy Choo's and I must say they are beautiful. I watch my Mothers face light up with excitement as she comes back with the size 6 shoe. I also watch my Mother squeeze her size 7 foot into a size 6 shoe. She gets up walks back and forth, looks from side to side and puts her hands on her hips and says "I will take them."

What credit card would you like to use Ma'am? The sales lady asks

I have a gift certificate she squeals.

Again in my mind I am saying please God let them not be a $1,000 bucks. I don't think they will be but I am sure they are not going to be under $250.00 dollars. I just hope she reacts better this time than with the damn Balenciaga dress fiasco. She had to have read the price on the bottom of the shoes right? I really hope so.

(I watch as the salesgirl heads to the register to ring up the shoes)

Ma'am there is a balance on the shoes after the gift certificate. The salesgirl informs my Mother as nice and polite as possible.

Oooohhh How much? She says trying to act all calm and collective. (Me.... I have been playing out in my head on how this scenario was going to play itself out).

$172.48 is the balance, the salesgirl informs my Mom

(And you know my Mother is now trying to add in her head how much money the shoes actually cost).

You took off the gift certificate my Mother asks quizzing.

Yes Ma'am the salesgirl says who is still being sweet.

So these shoes cost $422.00?

Yes and they are 25% off today the sales girl cheers

(Oh girl shut up I am thinking…please just shut up.)

But they are Jimmy Choo! My Mother states pointing to the label on the shoes

Yes they are and fine Jimmy Choo's they are ma'am.

But….they are Jimmy C-H-O-O's? My Mother continues

Yes Ma'am she quips

OK she is starting to lose it.

Choo's??? Get it? My Mother asks annoyed

No ma'am I don't get it the salesgirl states.

(I get it …but it is way too late for me to do or say anything at this point. My Mother goes on while I want to run and hide or crawl or bury myself anywhere in the world, besides the Bergdorf Goodman shoe department right now.)

Choo's? There Chinese …so it is impossible that these shows cost $422.00's. We send everything to China to be made cheaply. It is the American way. Everything that comes out of China is cheap, so you see these shoes cannot possibly cost $422.00, there must be a mistake. Nothing Chinese costs this much money. My Mother is angry now

(Did you hear that gasp? No? Well I did. It was the entire shoe department gasping at my Mothers "Facts.")

Ma'am that is how much they cost and I take great offense to that.

Why? My Mother asks

Crickets, crickets, and you could hear a pin drop.

Well I don't want them and again she has her hands on her hips.

Fine I will get the manager.

I am trying to make eye contact with the salesgirl as she marches to find the manager to mouth I **am sorry** but to no avail. I am mortified because everyone is staring at my Mother. I do get a particular nasty look from this Upper East Side looking bitch but I will ignore that for now. The shoe manager comes by and is actually very sweet. She graciously gives my Mother back her gift certificate and actually apologizes. Not all people want to spend this much money on shoes she smiles. I am thinking my Mother doesn't want to spend that much money on a Paris vacation. I mouth the word I am sorry and the manager just smiles at me. As we turn to leave The Upper East Side looking bitch says:

Real classy lady I think there is a TJ Maxx down the street – you are pitiful.

What? **Wow?** What did she just say? "Oh no she didn't just say that to my Mom." I sound like a drag queen in my head but I don't care.

What did you just say to my Mother? I whirl around and ask the nasty bitch

She turns and snaps at me. This is Bergdorf Goodman and maybe you should educate your "Mother" about Bergdorf Goodman is all about.

Educate my Mother? I asked and let me tell you I was pissed.

Yea she snides at me

(I am sorry I couldn't help it.) So I go:

Well tell me what Bergdorf Goodman is all about and while you are doing so can you educate me on who the fuck did your makeup? You look like a fucking clown lady. How dare you? Did you get dressed in the dark this morning? It doesn't matter how much money you have lady because you are one tacky bitch. What no mirrors in your house? So I turn to the crowd (which is increasing by the second) and say, spends all her money on shoes and can't afford a damn mirror.

Go ahead say something else lady, I dare ya.

The woman turns her back to me and is now making faces and hand gestures like I just drowned her cat or something.

That's what I thought.(as I look over at the tacky bitch to make another comment about my Mother) Mom let's go!

(I take my hand and reach out to my Mom for us to go)

Why do you always have to embarrass me Tatey?

What? Me? Embarrass......... You? Thank God this was in my head but as I look over she is getting all teary eyed as we are walking out of the shoe department

Mom it is OK this is just one snotty pile of bricks.

Can we just go?

Go? **No** Mom? We came here to get you something fabulous from Bergdorf Goodman's and that is just what we are going to do. We will just accessorize OK?

Accessorize?

Yes we can get you a scarf, some gloves, maybe some perfume maybe a necklace and now I am sounding just like a flamboyant wedding planner but I don't care it is working because she is starting to smile again. Off to **accessorize** we go! As I grab her hand and off to the first floor we go!

Once we are down on the first floor I direct her to go look at some scarves and I say I will be right back. I go and I find what I am hoping is a nice sales woman and I ask her for her help. I explain what has transpired over the last hour and how my Mom is really upset. I explain that she is not really a Bergdorf shopper but I want her experience to at least not be as awful, as it is turning out to be. She looks at me and says:

My Mom is the exact same way and I even get a 40% discount here and she flips out over the prices.. Absolutely I will help. Where is she? (So I point over to my Mom who is trying on scarves but she is checking every single price before she even tries anything on.)

Hi I am Vanessa. I heard you are looking to **accessorize!**

Um Yes as she turns to look for me.

I just smile and mouth **Go** Have fun **Mom!**

272

Vanessa goes so I hear we have $250.00 to spend huh?

Yeah I know… I have learned it's not a lot of money here at Bergdorf Goodman she sighs….

Nonsense Let's go shopping!! Vanessa cheers.

My Mom looks back for an OK from me and I just nod, smile and wave for her to go. I watch as Vanessa brings her around the store and the two of them were laughing and joking like two little school girls. It brought tears to my eyes. I swelled up right there in Bergdorf Goodman and I will never forget that moment. I will be eternally grateful to Vanessa for everything she did because about 45 minutes later my Mom was back and she was beaming.

Tate I cannot wait to show you **al**l the things I got. I am so happy. Let's go have lunch on me! This was **so** much fun.

(I look around to thank Vanessa but I do not see here anywhere.) Mom where did Vanessa go? I wanted to thank her.

She went on break Tate my Mom informs me

(I bet she probably needs one after that! It figures…..)

Let's go Mom and maybe after lunch we can go to Macy's and I will buy you a dress.

Tate I love you but no thanks…as she just belittles me a bit with her response

Why Mom I can afford it?

I know you do honey but shopping…with you…Is just not something I ever want to do or live through again.

Huh?

I start thinking about this day and this Bergdorf experience and the damn gift certificate. I then remember where she got the gift certificate from. Yup that damn raffle from her new fucking church. Boy I cannot wait to go to **this** new church of hers. Seriously can't fucking wait!

(I am starved. I forgot how exhausting my Mother can be!)

OK Mom where do you want to go for lunch?

How about Planet Hollywood?

It's closed Mom.

What? No it isn't.

Yes it is Mom. It closed years ago.

It did? She asks so innocently. How about Hard Rock then?

Closed too….

Now Tatey don't you start that lying again and if you didn't want to go, you could have just said so. Planet Hollywood and Hard Rock closed – I don't think so. Your Mother is not as dimwitted as you think. I actually saw in my US Weekly that they both even have hotels in Vegas now.

Mom they….(as she cuts me off)

Even Britney Spears stays there. She exclaims.

Well if Britney says its true than it must be true Mom. They closed a lot of their restaurant chains but not in Vegas. In Vegas there are enough people who still aren't tired of Planet Hollywood. Any other restaurant choices you have **Mom?**

What about that nice restaurant that you used to work at on 42nd and Lexington – across from Grand Central?

Houlihans?

Yes she says very exuberation

Closed.

Tate really….must you keep playing this game?

No seriously Mom it is a discount clothing store now or at least it was the last time I was here in New York. I think they closed the whole chain about 2 years ago. The real estate in New York has become more lucrative than the actual businesses Mom. With the real estate boom a lot of small businesses are selling and making the money quick verses having to work 10 times that time to make the same money. Why do you think Woolworths went out of business Mom?

Woolworths didn't go out of business because of real estate Tate they went out of business because they sold crap!! I mean the last few times I went in there they were always rude. They brought in all these Mexican's and Puerto Rican's

Mom!!!!!

You cannot say that on a crowded New York City street corner someone is going to shoot your racist ass.

I am not a racist Tate I like black people. There are 2 members of my church that are colored.

Mom, Mom, Mom I am trying to make her stop.

A whole two people in your church huh? Impressive Mom! What is one the cleaning lady and the other in the choir?

Who is the one being racist now Tate? She stammers

I am not being racist I am being sarcastic. There is a difference Mother.

What did they teach you that out in LA also? Did you take a class on the difference between the two Tate?

Wow she is getting sassy in her older years.

No Mom I didn't. I am getting hungry. Are there any restaurants in New York City that you want to go to that are actually open Mother?

Ohhh the look she just shot me.....classic

I bet you are going to tell me that the Olive Garden and TGI Fridays are closed too?

Nope they are both open and both have locations in Time Square.

So we have to walk 10 blocks?

Yes Mother is that a problem?

I guess not.

Mom there is a restaurant on almost every street corner. Look there is one (as I start to point at various restaurants) there is another.

I don't know them.

What?

I don't know them?

Now I am confused.

So you know Mr. and Mrs. Olive Garden? or…..Mr. Friday's? I think he is divorced Mom. Let me guess ---they go to your new church too.

Don't be silly Tatey.

Then how do you know them **Mom?**

They are on TV Tate!

So you know them from TV?

Yes they play them during my stories and they always look so warm and inviting. We have an Olive Garden on Court Street now. Did you know that? And also a Fridays on Montague now…

So which ever we hit first we will go to?

Yes Tate and when did you become so difficult? Shesh(My Mothers favorite word from my childhood)

(Now I'm the difficult one)

As we are heading into Times Square I notice that my Mother has become oddly quiet and this worries me. I never know which way she is going to go these days. I think she is in the process of "the change" but I would never dare ask her. For God sakes I honestly don't even know how old she is. I can guess but it is just safer to just smile when she says she is 39. She has been 39 since I was a sophomore in high school so if that's what age she wants to be than let her be. I am not going to be the one to question it anytime soon.

Look Mom there is a Fridays!(as I point)

Good because I am thirsty and hungry. This has been an **exhausting** morning as she glares at me with that…just evil look.

I say to myself right back at ya you, evil witch but I smile and open the restaurant door, like a good son is supposed to do for his Mother.

We are greeted at the hostess stand by this really perky little blonde girl.

Welcome to TGI Fridays where every day feels like a Friday!

Ok her perkiness is already irritating my Mother so I just say:

Hi! Table for two please!

Right this way folks!

As we are walking to our table Little Miss Perky starts right in with the questions.

Where are you visiting from? Where are you staying? What sights are you going to see? Are you going to the Statue of Liberty?

OMG she is not going to take a breather. How does she get air in there? I have a headache. Finally my Mom stops Miss Little Perky and turns around and says:

We are from here! My son has spent his entire life in New York, well up until he abandoned me and moved to LA. He is 3000 miles away from me now.

Well Miss Little Perky looks at my Mom like she just ran over her cat with her car. I am sorry ma'am we don't get many locals around here.

Is this our table? I ask

Yes! Enjoy your lunch as she scurries away to go find her next victim of lunch harassment. We sit down and immediately both open our menus. It has the traditional chain restaurant food. Chicken Fingers, Nachos, Burgers, salads. Etc.

Can I take a drink order I hear someone ask.

I peer up from my menu and there is this 6 foot gorgeous guy standing there with these adorable suspenders with buttons on them.

Hi folks I am Antonio and I will be taking care of you guys today. Can I start with a drink order? Ma'am?

What kind of diet soda do you have?

Diet Coke Ma'am

Oh No Diet Pepsi? My Mother has this wounded look on her face.

Sorry ma'am just Diet Coke.

I will take an Ice Tea then she says all disappointed because they didn't have her beloved Diet Pepsi drink. (I would swear that woman would have stock in Diet Pepsi the way she drinks it.)

And for you Sir? (as the gorgeous waiter looks over at me)

I am staring at this man and he has the most amazing blue or are they green eyes? He has to be my age but I cannot figure out what "team" he is on. Team is a gay term for whether he is gay or straight. Not that there is an actual team but it is more of a saying. It's not like Oh you are gay so you go to the Pink Team and your sport is shopping and floral arranging. It's nothing like that.

Sir anything to drink?

Oh sorry Yes I will have a white wine do you have a good Chardonnay?

Robert Mondavi?

Good I will take that.

I look over at my Mother and her eyes are literally ready to pop out of her head.

White wine? Chardonnay? It's not even one o clock yet Tate!!!

So?

You are **not** supposed to drink wine during the day.

Say's who Mom?

Everybody knows that unless it's a Holiday.

What?

Only alcoholics drink during the day Tate. Are you an alcoholic now Tate? I just love what LA has done to you. Now my son drinks wine during the day. What's next?

(She is now dabbing her eyes looking for sympathy from just about anyone by this point. People are walking by and seeing her cry and of course they are looking back at her horrible son, like what did you do to your Mother?)

Mom it is a glass of wine, not a bottle but a glass.

I am thinking to myself I wonder how she would react if I ordered a martini? I think we would be rushing her to a hospital.

Here are your drinks folks. Are you ready to order?

(He looks Italian or Latin. What a great smile. He has flawless skin with a 5 o'clock shadow. This guy has to be a model or an actor. Stunning yet masculine an...)

Tate are **you ready to order? and can you please stop staring at the waiter...**

Huh sorry um yes I am ready to order. Sorry was off in another place (as I am trying to save face with the handsome waiter)

I can hear my Mother mumble "yea I know what space he was in…hmmm."

Yes I will have the Chef Salad please.

Great and you ma'am

(There goes that great smile again. God he is hot!)

I will have the Chicken Cobb salad and Tate would you split some Zucchini sticks with me?

Sure Mom…

Great I will put that right in for you guys and off he goes.

(You know I am watching him as he walks away and guess who is watching me? Yup that's right…..My Mother).

Really Tate could you make yourself be any more obvious? You are worse than your sister. Now I love and support your choice but the waiter Tate? Really?

Sorry Mom but he is gorgeous.

Ahh he is OK she goes.

We sit in silence for a couple of minutes and I can tell she wants to ask me something. What is it Mom?

Um, well, never mind it is nothing…

What is it Mom?

Silence for what felt like eternity....

What? As I stare directly into her direction

Did you move to Los Angeles to get away from your Mother?

(OK do I tell the truth or do I lie to her I ask myself. My heart is pounding and I am beginning to sweat. I told her I wouldn't lie to her again but....)

No Mom please do not be ridiculous I moved there for my career. Honestly I did.

They shoot movies and TV here in New York too Tate.

Mom plus the weather is better and I just get more for my money in LA.

Well you would save a lot of money here in New York. You wouldn't need a car and you could live with me for free. My Mother states

(In my head I am visualizing living with my Mother and the next scene I am jumping through a plate glass window of the 79th Floor of the Empire State Building.)

Mom I like it in California, please do we have to have this conversation again? We have had the same conversation like 50 times in the last 6 months Mom. I needed the change and I really like it out there Mom. Can't you just get onboard with this and maybe come out for a visit.

(Did I just say that out loud?) It would have to be after I got my own place because I could just picture how well my Mother and Tommy would get along.... I look over and she is starting to get teary eyed again.

Mom can we change the subject?

Yes what do you want to talk about?

Anything you want Mom just not California OK?

OK so are you dating or seeing anyone special?

That waiter I see bringing us our Zucchini Sticks looks mighty special to me Mom.

Oh Tate and she laughs.

When the waiter brings the zucchini sticks to the table my Mother whisks her hair back and in her best Ann Margaret impression and says thank you handsome and winks at him.

(I am freakin mortified as the waiter shuffles away, but that's my Mom and it was actually kind of cute. You never really know what she is going to do or say next. He smiled and was probably saying to himself, just smile because the two crazies will probably leave me a good tip.)

So no one special in your life right now Tate? She says this a little louder so that maybe the hot waiter will here this, come running and whisk me away to…..probably Queens, where he lives with 4 other struggling models. Who am I kidding I would go in a second. HA!

So Tate as she is chopping on her first zucchini stick do **you** give or receive?

What?

You know with the man sex.

What?????Is my Mother seriously asking me if I am a top or a bottom? OMG I want to crawl under this table and just die.

Mom??? I say with a whispered shriek

What you see I am showing some interest in your life. Well do you give it or receive it?

Mom I don't ask you your sex life do I?

No because I don't have a sex life. You are practicing safe sex?

Yes Mom.

Well?

She is looking at me like a dog wanting a bone. Almost like I was holding a bone over my head and making a dog jump for it.

Mom I guess I am both. It's called versatile.

Oh does it hurt?

What???

When the penis goes in your bum, does it hurt? Years ago your Father wanted to try it and it hurt like a bitch. It was like trying to put a baseball bat into a mouse's ass. It was a complete disaster.

Nah nah nah nah Mom I don't want to hear about your sex life with Dad.

Do you think that is why he cheated on me? That son of a bitch cheated on me because I wouldn't take it up the ass she exclaims!

Mom shhhhhh the whole restaurant is staring at us.

(How I wish we were talking about LA again).

Here comes our main course Mom.

We are not done with this conversation Tate. I need to know these things about you. I am your Mother and I worry. Don't you worry about it tearing or blocking what has to come out of you naturally?

What is tearing or blocking, I ask her with utter confusement?

Your ass Tate. She snaps and loudly too I might add. Don't you worry that when you put a man's tally whacker up your butt it's going to block "other" things from coming out of your ass Tate.

OK who had the Chef's Salad?

(No say it isn't so. NO, No! No please do not tell me the hot waiter has heard my Mother ask me about my sex life. Please no. I look up and he has a smirk on his face and is looking at me in a way I cannot even describe).

Right here I say as meekly as possible.

And here is the Chicken Cobb Salad for you ma'am Will there be anything else he says again with that damn smirk.

No thanks as I try and wave him away.

Too bad.

What why?

Because I wanted to hear the answer to the question your Mom asked you. – The waiters smirk has gotten bigger.

Please go away as I look down into my salad and I know my face is as red as the tomatoes in this salad.

Please.

Ok well if there is **anything** else you need, you just ask and he walks away backwards still smirking at me.

I hate you – you evil woman and this time I said it out loud.

What Tate? What did I do?

Just eat your salad Mother…..

As we sit there eating in silence I begin to wonder where my Mother comes up with these things that come out of her mouth. I never remembered her being like this when we were younger. I start to think back on all of the things that we did throughout my life. I start to smile and then laugh a little out loud. I remember all the things that have come out of my Mother's mouth throughout the years. I am definitely my Mother's son that's for damn sure!

What now Tate?

Huh?

What are you laughing at now? What do I have food stuck in my teeth or something? She asks.

No no no Mom it's nothing.

It is never nothing with you Tate Connors now spill it she demands!

Mom honestly I was just remembering the time with Pepper when we were at Grandma and Grandpa's house.

That dog my Mother says with a laugh. It would eat **anything** she says with a laugh. She was a good dog but she was like a little nanny goat. She would eat anything no matter what it was (and now my Mother is laughing again… phew)

Do you remember when we were at Grandma and Grandpa's and all of a sudden Pepper is yelping and running round and round the pool Mom?

Yes Tate that stupid dog got in the garbage the day before and ate everything in the whole damn trash. What a mess?

Mom do you remember why Pepper, the dog was actually running around the pool, like a maniac and crying?

Yes Tate because she has cerran wrap stuck coming out of her ass. Half was in and the other half was out. Ahh that poor dog. We kept trying to chase her but she was determined to get that saran wrap out of her butt one way or another.

Mom I remember I finally had to jump on her and hold her down while you pulled the saran wrap out of her ass and I remember Pepper making the biggest Sigh I ever heard – like Thank God that is out of my butt.

Would you like a refill folks?

Ugh it's **you** again (the waiter is back) Why do you always manage to come over when we are talking about an ass of some sorts? Don't worry this time it wasn't mine we were talking about but the our family dog…

Um…..O----k Good to know I guess….Well that is…. that your Mother wasn't pulling saran wrap out of **your** ass.

(We all laughed this time)

(Wow he is good looking **and** funny. Something has to be wrong with him I think to myself. Nobody is this perfect. Typical me though when I like someone I become a mute so what do I do? Yup? U-huh!)

Can we get the check please? I ask the gorgeous waiter

Um sure I will be right back and off the waiter goes. Damn he has a nice ass too!

The waiter comes back with the check and he kinda seems like he wants to talk. So where are you folks from he asks in a very "I am really interested" voice.

We are from Brooklyn my Mother states as proud as a patriot coming home from battle.

I live in Los Angeles now and I am just back for Thanksgiving to see my family I tell him acting all hoity tootle

I **love** LA he say's I am thinking about moving there in the spring. Where are you in LA?

I live in West Hollywood I say and if by now you didn't think he thought I was gay he definitely does now. Then again who am I kidding how many straight men would talk about their ass.....in a restaurant....with their Mother!

I have **a lot** of friends in West Hollywood he exclaims. Let me get your number.

Are you on Facebook? I ask.

Yes he says my name is Antonio Vargas ---friend me.

So now my Mother knows nothing about Facebook but I can see she is about to inject herself into the conversation one way or another. I can tell this after all these years of her... in fact being my actual crazy Mother.

So what side of the street do you shop on Antonio? (My Mother prides herself on learning gay lingo but it is just **wrong** when it comes out of her mouth.)

Excuse me? He asks

Do you shop on the boy's side or the girl's side of the street?

He laughs but in a polite way

Well I would like to ask your son out on a date, so I would like to say the same side of the street your son shops on

(Before he could even finish the sentence she **blurts** out:

He is single and his eyes have been following you around this whole time we have been in this restaurant. Are you from Mexico?

Mom!!!!! You cannot (Antonio the hot waiter cuts me off but with a smile tells me Mother)

No ma'am I am Cuban.

Oh

Sorry but My Mother thinks that any person of Latin descent is either Mexican or Puerto Rican. I inform Antonio

It's cool. So you have been watching me throughout lunch huh? Antonio has that big smirk again

Shut up I say trying to be funny and I know by now I am probably redder than an apple. I haven't been watching you like a stalker but I just told my Mother that you were attractive. Is there anything wrong with that? (as I am now full on flirting)

Attractive please you have been watching him like a fat lady waiting for her pies to cool down so she could eat all 10 of them in one sitting --my Mother blurts out.

Woman when we get out of here I am going to…and I just give her this look. I have an idea that will piss off my Mother though…

Cuando estas libre?

Ahora guapo (his Spanish is perfect)

No ahora, luego.

No tienes escuela!

Mañana?

Mañana es Thanksgiving.

Ah Claro

Sabado?

Perfecto!

Mi nombre es aqui (as he points to this piece of paper he has just put into my hand).

Llama me.

OK as I smile, sign the credit card receipt and still stare at his beautiful eyes.

Ciao he says

Bye!

Did Antonio just wink at me as we were walking out the door? I find that so sexy.

Are you done with you love connection Tate? Can we go? My Mother clearly annoyed that we switched to talking in Spanglish.

Yes Mom but we are taking a cab home.

I thought you said you were taking me to Macy's to buy a dress?

I thought you didn't want to **ever** go shopping with me again Mom?

Oh yea but let's go see if there is a sale!

Taxi!!!

We get a taxi rather quickly and I tell them 34th and 6th please. I say it with my full on Brooklyn accent, so that the cabbie doesn't think we are tourists and try to screw with us. This has been an eventful day as it is…..

As we approach Macy's I am like Holy shit Mom!

I never told Antonio my name!

Who is Antonio?

The waiter Mother. The waiter at TGIF! I forgot to tell him my name.

He gave you his phone number so just call him.

And say what? (I ask her as we both exit the cab)

Tate he will remember you…trust me….you are very memorable! Let's go inside, it is chilly out here. She moans

I guess your right Mom.

Macy's is done up in Holiday Decoration even more the Bergdorf's was. Wow it was beautiful but could I really take another department store….with my Mother? Oh God please grant me the strength to get through this next shopping excursion.

Surprisingly my Mother knew exactly where she was going in Macy's. She knew where the dress department was and even where the sales racks were.

In less than a half hour she had about 4 dresses to try on. I was impressed because she even knew where the dressing rooms were. She waved at me to follow her because after all I was being a good son and holding her purse while she shopped. I would give her thumbs up if I like the dress or just shake my head if I didn't like it. I followed her to the dressing room and I would stand outside. About 25 minutes goes by and I am now starting to worry. Where is she? Is she OK? Should I go ask the salesgirl if she is OK? Maybe she ditched me. No I have her purse but what the hell? As I start to approach the dressing room, out comes my Mother.

I am going to take this one Tate as she holds up a royal blue dress that is actually really pretty.

Why didn't you come out and show me the dresses Mom?

Why?

I wanted to see them on you. Have you model them for me.

I am not a model Tate do I look like Cindy Crawford? Shesh your a pain in the ass to shop with Tate. Let's go. Are you still buying this dress for me Tate?

How much is it?

$89.50 she boosts and it is on sale!

Sure Mom of course.

Can we just find a cashier and get out of here Mom, I am tired.

Tired Tate? Already, you are too young to be tired???

I wanted to say you exhausted me you crazy woman but I just smile and say I think I am just jet lagged.

She smiles very sweetly and says OK.

Wow she bought that one because it is kinda true. I am exhausted but it is more that I hate to shop. I really do. I know you want to take my gay card away or something but I didn't get the shopping gene…that or floral arrangements to be honest.

We find a cashier nearby and I purchase the dress on my Macy's card. Please don't decline. Please don't decline.

Sign here sir!

Praise Jesus the card went through!

Let's take the Red Train home Tate. Hurry up Tate it's 4pm and I want to beat rush hour, plus it looks like it is going to rain again.

I double time it with my Mom because I don't want a return engagement of the umbrella people! We get to the station quick and this time the switcher -roo with my Mother and the Metro card goes smoothly, It only took me 3 times this time to swipe it verses the 5 failed attempts this morning-**impressive** huh?

The train wasn't as crowded as this morning so we were able to find seats right away. As I look around there is every walk of life on the train. I miss this.

You got 5 dolla for me?

What? No get away from me I stammer.

My Mother reaches in her coat pocket and takes two quarters out.

Here is 50 cents and that is all you are getting from us she states. Now **go!**

Well the panhandler goes away and I ask my Mom:

How many quarters do you have in that coat pocket Ma?

I go to the bank and get a roll of quarters every time I go to the city. This way I don't get mugged or anything. I learned the idea from my new church she says (and looks directly at me) Do you have a witty banter about that also Tate?

No I think it is pretty smart actually Mom.

She looks at me like hmmm where did that come from? What have you done with my son?

We ride back to Brooklyn and we are just kind of people watching and a little small talk. I am trying not to fall asleep on the train but it is getting harder and harder to keep my eyes open.

Brooklyn Heights I hear and I am startled because I have in fact fallen asleep on the subway.

Did you have a nice nap? My Mother inquires very sarcastically.

I was a sleep for like 3 minutes Mom.

That's all it takes Tate. That is all it takes. She makes sure to repeat it twice just in case I didn't hear it the first time.

As we walk out of the subway all of a sudden I am like **damn** it is freaking cold!

It's always like this once the sun goes down Tate. You haven't even missed a winter yet and you already aren't used to the cold weather and she laughs at me… wimp!

Mom even when I lived here I hated the cold.

Yeah and even when you lived here my Mom explained whether a kid or an adult –getting you to wear a hat was next to impossible. Always worried it was going to mess up your hair…HA!

Ring Ring Ring oh that is my cell phone. Hold on Mom.

Hello?

Where are you guys? My sister asks.

A few blocks from the house.

"Oh good" Ask Mom what we are having for dinner?

What are we having for dinner Mom? as I look over at my Mother

You guys are on your own for dinner tonight I have to cook a Thanksgiving meal tomorrow for all of you guys. My Mom states in a way trying to tell us we are not children anymore and we can most certainly feed ourselves.

Let's just order in --I say to Kelly.

I can cook…..

No that's OK I say as I remember all those childhood failed attempts Kelly would make to cook and me being forced to eat it. I even remember one time that Pepper, the dog, that would eat anything wouldn't even eat Kelly's food. I ended up having to put the food in my pocket. I also remember forgetting to take the food out of my pocket and my Mother washing it and then of course continuing to dry it. It took me a week of scrubbing that dryer to get the smell of burnt beef out of the dryer. I think even after that we all smelled like beef stew for about a month.

I don't mind Tate. Kelly states very sincerely

No no let's just order from Grimaldi's Pizza. It has been forever since I have had a good slice of Brooklyn pizza.

What about Mr. Body Conscience, who doesn't eat carbs because he has to have a ripped stomach for LA? Kelly torments

It will be fine for one day Kelly.

Oh OK don't worry I won't tell LA that you had a couple of slices of pizza Tate. HA Pizza actually sounds good right about now. The Chicago pizza is good but I am kind of sick of the pan dish pizza all the time. What do you want on your pizza/

Just cheese! I say already savoring the taste of a good slice of cheesy Brooklyn pizza

Just cheese how boring Tate?

I know but it is what I like.

OK I will order a couple of pies. Do you have any cash? I need to go to the ATM.

(Of course you do Kelly I say to myself)- **typical...Yes Kelly I have cash!**

How soon before you get home?

We are about 6 brownstones away.

Great! How did it go today?

Don't ask. I will tell you all about it when I get home. Gotta go! Bye!

My Mother is up a head a bit but I know she is listening to every word I am saying. It is best that I tell my tale of shopping in New York City with my lunatic of a Mother, to my sister later. I also need to get to the bottom of how the hell my sister got out of this Mr. Toads Wild Ride shopping extravaganza with our Mother! I gotta give her props for getting out of this but I just need to learn for the next time. She is so going to deal with the church cult thing with me, if I have to drag her kicking and screaming all the way there and back.

The wind is starting to pick up and we turn the corner to our block. We are right on Columbia Heights in Brooklyn and it is right on the water. Actually we are higher up and we have the Brooklyn Queens Highway which is better known as the BQE as a buffer but even now it's not helping much with the wind. Hurry up my Mom yells! It is getting colder by the minute Tate. We reach our brownstone and my Mom and I both actually run up the stairs like there is a tornado chasing us through the streets of New York.

Brrr and I am blowing on my hands waiting for my Mother to unlock the door. In we go.

Ahh we have just went from 30 degrees to about 150 degrees inside this house. I forgot about my Mother's issues and the heat. I would have to open my window all winter long just to be able to breathe. 4 more days, 4 more days….

Here comes Kelly….

Mom how was the day? Kelly questions

Your brother met a gay Mexican guy at the restaurant we went to and now they are going on a date with each other.

What? Seriously Tate?

He is Cuban…

Huh? What happened today? I want to hear all about your day and your future date with this gay Cuban guy.

Give me 5 minutes Kelly it has been a day! I need to take a hot shower. Please I will tell you all about my **fab** day later.

Tatey can you bring my bags upstairs?? I hear my Mother yell from upstairs in the back bedroom

Huh all day it is Tate and we are not 2 minutes back in this house and we are already back to Tatey….ugh classic

Coming Mother…..

As I am walking up the stairs with my Mother's bags I remember that my Mom had the hallway bathroom redone and it has a huge tub. So fuck the shower, I need a bath and I sooo deserve one. How did I survive with her all these years? Is it me? Have I changed as I have gotten older? Or is my Mother a certifiable lunatic?

As I reach the top of the landing and reach her doorway it seriously has to be about 160 degrees in her room, no exaggeration!

Mom it has to be about 160 degrees in this house. I am boiling Mom. Are you trying to slow cook the turkey outside of the oven Mom? I can barely breathe up here. Can we lower the thermometer to maybe 100 degrees?

Quit complaining Tatey it is very cozy up here.

Cozy Mom? Are you on crack Mom? I feel like I have a flesh eating virus eating at my skin and the air is trying to boil it off.

It is 87 degrees in here Tatey stop being so damn dramatic. Gosh everything with you today has been like a soap opera and you certainly won the daytime Emmy award for best dramatic actress….oh I meant actor.

Very funny Mother I bet you have been saving that one all day huh?

Saving what?

Never mind, I am going to take a bath as I sigh and leave her room.

OK honey but use the hallway bathroom. It has the new tub and the jets are just amazing! You are going to love it. Just don't stay in there forever I am going to need your help in the kitchen.

What? How about you ask Ms. Princess Kelly to help Mother I have been helping you all day.

She has helped!! She helped me all day yesterday and did all the grocery shopping with me. And wait now where were you yesterday??(Now here comes the sarcasm I can feel it) Let me think…hmm….where was Tatey???hmmm…. where was Tatey?? Oh yeah… oversleeping in LA and scaring his Mother half to death….**That' s** where you were…

What about Prince Christopher now where is he?

He helps me the other 51 weeks of the year Tatey. He is the only one that hasn't abandoned me and plus he has kids. You know the only son who is going to give my grandkids Tatey.

Gulp….

OK Mom I will be done in 20 minutes and I will come downstairs to help.

Thank you my son she says like the cat that just ate the canary.

I turn and I walk back towards my room. I feel like I need a scissor to cut through this heat. When I reach my room, I immediately open all the windows because it is unbearable in here. I am feeling like I am trapped in a New York Subway car in August. I actually stick my head out the window to get some air. Phew I don't miss living in this house one bit. I actually opened up the window in the bathroom as well because as much as I bitch about the heat I cannot take a cold bath.

I start the water and I then begin to undress.

Knock knock……

Yes

Pizza is here my sister says

OK I will be down in 15.

I need cash to pay him Tate….You told me you had cash she snaps.

I do hold on. How much is it?

$48.25 plus tip

For two pizza's?

Yes my sister states as I can clearly tell she is extremely annoyed that she has to talk to me through the bathroom door or talk to me at all.

Wow $25 bucks….for a pizza!

I give her $55 dollars under the door and she snatches away yet again, like she is the one being inconvenienced and she is clearly trying to tell me she is annoyed about it.

Finally some peace and quiet but who the hell knows for how long. I place my right and then left foot into the tub and it starts to feel amazing. By now the outside air has filtered in to the heat and it has made it bearable to be upstairs in this bathroom, taking a hot bath in this sauna we call my Mother's House. As I submerge into the water I begin to relax and close my eyes. I start to look back on the day I have had. It's called reflecting people and you should try it….Bergdorf Goodman's….TGIF and the hot waiter Antonio…Macy's…. the rain…the subway and most of all **my Mother!**

My Mother has been all over the place and it is baffling to me because she never was like this before I left for LA. I never had a day like this in my life that was so all over the place. It's like she runs hot and cold with me. I know she was angry about me lying about the over sleeping the plane but this is more. I know she was not happy about me moving to LA but I thought we were passed all that by now. I talk to her on the phone every couple of days. I have taught her how to email and I do tolerate all the "cat jokes" she emails me but something is off but I just cannot put my finger on it….yet! It's like one minute she loves me and misses me and then the next she is so mad at me. I know it has something to do with me moving far away and at some point this weekend, I will ask her but I so do not want to provoke her….**again** Maybe I should lay off the church comments tonight or until I actually go and see for myself. The next thing I hear is

Tatey are you OK in there. Is everything OK??? Tatey????

Yup I have gone and fallen asleep in the tub. I am that emotionally drained that I actually feel asleep in the tub.

I am Ok….I am coming….Be down in a minute…

Brr the water is cold and it is freezing in this bathroom now. I know, I know I am never satisfied. It's too hot and now it's too cold. I am all over the place in my brain. Maybe I actually had a good time with my Mother today and I am just imagining that it was a bad day. We did laugh a lot today also. Maybe it is me who is struggling with not being near my Mom and my family. I could be the one creating all this chaos in my head as well. I tend to create a lot of chaos. I am an over thinker as well.

Tatey the pizza is getting cold, get your ass down here now! Both my Mother and my sister yell in unison.

Coming…..

Well there goes that theory…I am not struggling with missing my Mother. I hear her down stairs saying to God knows who:

He is probably still fixing his hair. Ever since he was a kid it was always about "**that** hair" and you know he has never, not seen a mirror he doesn't love. Let me go get him.

As I am drying myself off I hear footsteps on the stairs I just know my Mother is on her way up to get me. I am now frantically trying to dry off and get ready. Well it is too late because I hear the knock and don't wait for a response open of my bedroom door. Next I hear:

What the….no, no, no

Tate Connors get in here!!!! I cannot believe you are <u>still</u> doing this!!

I know you all must be wondering what my Mother is upset about now right. Well it is not that she found porn, or sexual objects. I am not having sex in there or jerking off. The room is clean and the bed is even made. So why is she so upset? Stay tuned….HA! I throw on my shirt and I open the bathroom door.

Slam, slam and slam I hear. I open the bathroom door and she is standing there glaring at me with her hands on her hips.

What do you think I am supposed to heat all of Brooklyn Tate?

Yup she is mad – she is calling me Tate again. You see my Mother has 3 names she calls me. Tate when she is angry, Tatey when she reminisces about my childhood/treat me like a child or Tate when she is trying to be cool

I was wondering why the house was freezing when I had the heat on. My Mother snaps at me

Mom the house is **not** freezing and it's been a boiler room since we got back from shopping. I couldn't even breathe up here and soon you are actually going to have the real oven on too. It is totally unbearable Mom.

Well you are the only one in this house that has a problem with the heat Tate

No Mom I am the only person in this house that will actually stand up to you and tell you that it is too damn hot in this house, with that heater on full blast.

Well now she has this mean scowl on her face and World War 3 is going to erupts in a few seconds.

It is my house and I want the heat on.

Mom nobody is saying the heat cannot be on Mother but you have it on full on blast. It is hotter than a sauna in here.

Like i said Tatey this is my house and if you do not like it you can leave!!

Well if I had a dollar for every time she said that I would have my own penthouse on Park Avenue. I have **had** enough for today. Ok woman you want to fight like that, I am bringing out the big guns.

That's fine Mom I will go and stay with Dad. Do you have a train schedule… or has that melted from the heat as well?

Well now my Mother has this look on her face like I just ran over her favorite cat with the car.

Tate did you really need to go there, I hear my sister yell at me.

Yes I did Kelly! You haven't spent the day with her today. One minute she is my loving Mother, the next she wants to be my best friend cruising for boys and then a split second later she is this witch, who needs to wax her broom. **enough**!!! I am going to go pack and then I say something that I am going to regret for a very long time.

Hey Mom

What?

Remember this exact moment when you ask me for the 1,000[th] time why I needed to move 3,000 miles away from you!!!Remember this moment and moments like these and that should give you the answer to the question you so desperately wanted an answer to…I **have had it!**

I turn and walk upstairs fully prepared to pack my bags and leave.

As I start to pack I hear my sister…

Mom don't, Mom stop, please Mom don't let him get to you. It is him Mom, it is not you Mom stop….Mom please

Yup I did it…my Mother is crying.

Fuck…It is Thanksgiving Eve and I have been home for less than 24 hours and I have already made my Mother cry….Congratulations douche bag I think this might be a record for the fastest time ever. I clocked in at 21 hours this time to make my Mother cry. I brought up the two most sensitive things in the world to my Mother and in less than 4 minutes I used them as ammunition in an argument with her. Well obviously by now you know the first one is me living in Los Angeles 3,000 miles away from my Mother but the second one is one that goes deeper. I actually used it first in this battle tonight. By saying that I was going to leave her house and go to my Father's house is like taking a blade to her heart.

My parents were married for 13 years when it came out that my Father was having an affair with his legal secretary and she was pregnant. The woman who is actually my step Mother now called my Mother and told her. She told her everything like how long the affair was going, he didn't love her, he only stayed because of us kids, that my Mom has put on so much weight and is not aging well. This woman is a bitch and I have had several issues with her over the years. I despise this woman so much that this will be my only mention of this miserable cunt in this book. The relationship with my Father at first was severely strained and I actually told him I hated him. As the years have passed things have thawed and we have come to have a relationship. I have no relationship with the woman he impregnated and eventually married. I did not attend the wedding. It is a very limited relationship with my Dad and we have even worked through his gay issues with me. There were many rough years with my Father and our relationship will always be extremely tumultuous.

I promised my Mother that with this book I wouldn't bring up that part of our past because it is still too painful for her to bare or relive.

Anyway the one thing I know is that when I want to hurt my Mother, it is the quickest but yet the most cowardly way to hurt her. I don't get my way or she opposes something I genuinely believe in, than what do I do? Yup…I play the Dad card…It works every time and it is so not fair to her. When am I ever going to learn? Ok I have to go eat crow and make this right with her.

I walk downstairs and Kelly is just glaring at me. Are you happy? Good job Tate! You are so fucking selfish Tate…

Shut up Kelly I don't need it from you right now. Where is she?

In the kitchen asshole where else do you think she would be schmuck.

Kelly….enough OK

I walk into the kitchen and my Mother is over the stove filling what looks like a pie.

Mom?

She looks over at me and says what…did you miss the train? Don't worry I hear the trains come every hour…

(She is now crying again)

Mom I am sorry…I really am…I love you…you know that right?

How am I supposed to know that after what you just said to me?

You know I didn't mean it Mom…I am sorry (now I am crying too)

Tatey sometimes you can say some of the most awful things to me. I know sometimes that I do or say things, that you do not approve of. I know certain things today that I did or said were probably not appropriate but I am struggling….

Mom what are you struggling with, what? Mom? (Now I am concerned)

I am all alone Tatey. My kids have all grown up and left me. You are all the way out there in California, your sister is in Chicago and I never see your brother anymore.

What Chris lives 2 blocks away?

Yes he does Tatey but he has his own family now. He has a wife, he is a Father and he doesn't always have time for his old Mother. I don't want to be a bother plus his wife Samantha is not my biggest fan at all.

Sam's a bitch Mom. Don't ever forget that Mother.

Next thing I hear is my sister:

I agree Mom, don't ever feel alone again. You need to come and visit us more often. I think Tate got frustrated that you were picking on him all day today.

Maybe I was….just a little… and she cracks a smile and laughs a little.

It is going to take a little more than that to cheer her up but at least it is a start. I give my Mom a hug and then Kelly joins in and we are all hugging each other.

This is going to be a great Thanksgiving Mom. I love you how can I help?

You can start by peeling the potatoes Tate…um I mean Tate

I want to help too Kelly chimes in

You can start by making the salad my Mom says sarcastically.

As I look at my Mom I finally get it. I get it all… the issues with me being so far away in Los Angeles, her new church, trying to understand me being gay, the panic when I don't answer the phone etc etc. She feels like she is losing us. My Mother has spent the better part of her life being an amazing Mother. She did everything that a good Mother was supposed to do. She loved us unconditionally, told us every day how beautiful and special we were, gave us such a sense of confidence and was always there when we needed her. Our house was always the house that all of our friends hung out when we were growing up. So many of my friends and my sibling's friends would end up calling my Mother Mom because they spent so much time here.. They were at our house more than at their own house sometimes. You could talk to her about anything…you wouldn't always get the answer you wanted but she always explained why. She wasn't the best cook in the world but we ordered in a lot of takeout and delivery as a family. All my Mother wanted out of life was to be a Mother, a good Mother in fact. She was always reading parenting books in between her National Enquires and Star Magazines. My brother and sister fought like cats and dogs but my Mother would always be the referee. I often wondered where she got the energy from.

I get it.….

We have all grown up and have moved on with our lives. She doesn't know what to do or how to react. It explains the new church and the fact that subs conscionably she is a little angry that we have all grown up. I think she would have been perfectly happy if we were kids forever. I am really going to make an effort to help her transition. I just hope she doesn't get another damn cat. 3 cats Mother seriously? What next?? Are you gonna live in a shoe?

The three of us small talk for a while and drank what we thought was a little red wine but in turn out it was about 3 bottles. Let's just say I am a quicker drinker than the women as well.

I look down at my watch and I cannot believe my eyes!!Holy crap it is midnight and I am drunk.…again! 2 nights in a row I am drunk. You know tomorrow I am going to be getting the Alcoholics speech from my Mother. Especially after she said "You're opening **anothe**r bottle of wine Tatey?"

I gotta get to bed before she realizes I am drunk again!!!

Mom I am going to bed I love you and again I am sorry for what I said.

I know I love you too. Did you notice I lowered the heat Tatey?

Yes Mom I did I say and I kiss her cheek and go upstairs.

Did I notice she lowered the heat? Not really. Still was sweating like a whore in church but I kinda was getting used to it.

Kinda got used to it or kinda got drunk?

Either way you know I am so opening up those fucking windows in my bedroom….

Night night…

Chapter 15

Thanksgiving Day

Well after a really peaceful nights rest I arise and I already hear noise coming from the bathroom. By the sound of the noise, I can tell it is my sister painting on her face and making a miserable attempt at that birds nest she calls her hair. You would think being raised by a hairdresser she would have learned but alas…no. My sister has a really pretty face, I just wish she would take better care of herself. Maybe if she did she would get laid every now and again and not be such a witch most of the time. We live in different cities now so we tend to get along better these days. I just will never fully understand that after an hour in that damn bathroom that she still comes out looking the way she does. Don't even get me started on her clothes. Let's just say Rainbow Shops, Strip Malls and Payless. She tries to call herself "Imelda Marcos" but I doubt the majority of Miss Imelda's shoes only cost $14.95. Ahh I know I am being a bitchy, catty queen but I haven't had any caffeine yet, plus I would never say any of this to her face because I just love, **love** my sister….Oh who am I kidding…yes I would. I have told her a thousand times how tacky and cheap she is, but she doesn't listen. It has nothing to do with sibling rivalry I just….don't like her sometimes. I am being honest right? Hey there are plenty of people out there in the world that don't like me, including my sister. We pretend to like each other for the sake of my Mother. I try and get along with her but my brother Chris and her actually full on despise one another. I rather enjoy the snipes they make at each other but only when my Mom isn't around.

My Mom tries to make them get along but it never works and then she gets upset. That is when I usually step in and play referee but it is exhausting. Yup things haven't changed much because I still play referee; in fact I wish I was an only child. Oh well…..wait… did I really just say that? If I was an only child I would be my Mother's 100% focus **all** the time. At least I split the insanity with the two of them…Hmmm ya know what??? I sooooo love my brother and sister when I look at it **that** way! HA!

(Ok she has been in there over an hour now….)

Kelly what ya doing in there? Getting ready for the circus? Kelly come on now!! As I bang on the door really hard.

Wait your turn dickhead she yells. Or why can't you go and use the bathroom down the hall you lazy loser!

(Ahh can you feel the love??)

This is **my** bathroom Kelly Marie! Happy Fucking Thanksgiving to you too sis, I smart ass reply back to her.

Now I could have walked down the hall to the other bathroom and I was probably being a spoiled brat but this was **my** bathroom after all! It is the bathroom right off my bedroom and the natural one for me to use but I do know it has the better water pressure.

How much longer Kel?(I asked her very nicely)

(silence)

Kelly?

Crickets

Kelly come on it's only 930 in the morning and you have all day to work up to being a complete bitch. How much longer?

Next thing I hear is the blow dryer turning on…

Bitch I am gonna go piss in your bed I swear --I yell.

Blow dryer stops and the door swings open.

Don't you fucking dare! She yells

Then let me use the bathroom Kelly. I have been up for over an hour waiting for you to get out of the bathroom.

How was I supposed to know that? How would I know you have been waiting for over an hour? Oh my crystal ball **must-must** be broken she snaps.

Go use Moms bathroom Tate!

All of my shit is in this one Kelly….please I do not want to start the morning out fighting with you.

OK I will be out in 3 minutes I promise Tate.

I really need it now….like right now…as I visibly grab my tally Wacker and jump up and down and from side to side.

Just hurry the fuck up asshole she says

Thanks! As I scurry in already dropping my pants and mooning her.

You're disgusting she yells.

Why you have seen my ass before? I taunt her as I am waving my ass in the air like I just don't care!

Hurry up Tate my hair will frizz out here. Kelly pleads

Frizz? I think and say to myself shut up Tate and don't even open that can of ridiculous up. Frizz would be a step up for **her** hair.

I pee, brush my teeth, slap some water on my face and open the door. My sister is standing there glaring at me. I turn to her and I say:

See was that so hard?

Just go douche bag she yells as she points her finger towards the stairs. I scurry out of the bathroom and she immediately goes back in the bathroom and slams the door.

Slam!

What is going on up there? I hear my Mother yell.

Nothing Mom I yell back down …Kelly is just being her charming self or riding the cotton pony. I will be down in a minute to help.

Are you torturing your sister with her stuffed animals again Tatey? My Mother asks

What? What stuffed animals Mom? I ask confused

Well you said her cotton pony….

Cotton pony means when you get you're…um…women's….flow….um… never mind Mom and I am so not torturing her cotton pony. I will be right down.

OK Tate she yells clearly sounding annoyed

As I come down stairs and into the kitchen I notice that my Mother must have 10 things going on at once in the kitchen.

Good Morning Tate. I have coffee made because I am sure you are gonna need **a lot** of it she snides looking directly at me.

Huh? Whatever….I say to myself?

So I bet you crazy peeps reading this book want to know, why my sister flew open the bathroom door so quickly when I threatened to pee in her bed huh?

Yup I thought so. I have never actually peed in her bed but….Ya see when we were teenagers my brother and sister shared a bathroom and I had my own bathroom. At some point my brother and sister were fighting so much and my Mother was at her wits end with the two of them. My Mom decided to move Kelly to the guest room which adjoined the bathroom I used. I was **not** very happy about this at **all**! Well upon Kelly's arrival into her new bedroom, she began to use my bathroom. Now Kelly has always been a bitch but….she is also a really messy one. Within days we were constantly at war in regards to her cleanliness. There would be makeup and hair everywhere. Who needs 6 different types of deodorant? She would use all the toilet paper and never replace it. I swear I thought that maybe she thought there was a Toilet Fairy that came about 3 times a week to replace the toilet paper. Well after about a month I had enough of Mary Kay Kelly and we were going to have it out when she got home about **my** bathroom.

When she finally got home and before I could even approach the subject about the messy bathroom she starts right in with me:

Hey Tate look? Mom got me this brand new Nexus shampoo for **my** hair. You hear that Tate, for **my** hair. Do not even think about using it. I need it for **my** hair and it's for my hair only. You don't need it for your slimy hair Tate. If you use it I am telling Mom.

Kelly I don't care about your stupid shampoo but can you just try and clean up the bathroom a little every once in a while?

She responds but not to the way I wanted her to:

I **do** Tate – you are the pig not me, leaving your dirty underwear with the skid marks on the bathroom floor. Don't worry Tate I told everyone at school about your skidded draws. You're disgusting.

She places her new Nexus shampoo in the shower and again looks at me and yells **my shampoo** right into my left ear.

I don't want it! Can you get lost I gotta take a pee. (As I begin to slam the bathroom door right in her bitch face.)

TMI she goes while placing her hand in my face and turns around and prances off.

Well I am pissed. I cannot believe she told everyone at school I have skid marks in my underwear. That is why people keep coming up to me and pretend to screech and break in front of me. That bitch, I will fix her. I thought they were making fun of my driving or something. Bitch I will get even with you I say to myself...

I look over and see her damn new Nexus shampoo. Ahhh I have an idea. OK Kelly you wanna play with me?

I reach into the shower and I grab her Nexus shampoo. I dump half of the shampoo into the toilet and I then unzip my pants. I pee into the shampoo bottle until it is nice and full again. I shake the bottle nice and good, to get the shampoo and piss to blend. I then put it back in the shower in the exact same place as it was before. That'll fix her telling people I have **skid** marks.

For the next 3 weeks all I would do is compliment my sister on how beautiful her hair looked. I would ask her if it has an odd smell to it and she would snap at me:

That's the product!!! It is for special hair duff-us. God you are so stupid.

Oh OK I go....

About two weeks later while we are having dinner my sister turns to my Mom and goes:

I need another bottle of shampoo Mom. I just **love** the shampoo Mom and **everyone** at school has been complimenting me about my hair...even **all** the boys.

Well I can't resist.

So you love the shampoo Kelly? I inquire

Yes Tate I **just** said that.

OK OK. And I just left it alone.

So for the next 2 years I peed in every new bottle of Nexus shampoo she ever got. Oh and you know I told everyone at school that she was shampooing her hair in my piss **btw**. Poor troll didn't get a single date throughout high school. HA that will fix her for talking about my skids…hey she started it.

Tate are you going to help me or what? (It was the sound of my Mother's voice interrupting my funny trip down memory lane)

(Shit) I am coming Mom (I was in never, never land **again**! My sister just brings back all of these awful things in me. One of these days I will actually tell you how she found out….Hint – she caught me!)

I pretty much jump down the stairs and exclaim Happy Turkey Day Mom.

You still smell like wine did you shower yet? She asks

No Kelly is still in there. I will before company arrives.

Just use the other bathroom Tate.

Does **anybody** in this house remember **that** is **my bathroom**! (I say to myself.) Mom it's OK what do you need me to do? I can wait for Kelly to finish painting her face and blowing out that mop that she wants us to call hair.

Tate please do not start with your sister already. First off you are probably going to want those and she points to 2 aspirins on the dining room table. She says like a school teacher who is disappointed I didn't study for the test.

What for Mom? I ask

For your **hangover** Tate she states like a judge with her gavel.

What hangover Mom?

Um the hangover for drinking all **that** wine last night.

Oh please Mom I am a professional wine drinker I say with a laugh.(Thinking that she would take it as a joke)

A professional wine drinker Tate?

Oh shit I shouldn't have said that as I replay it in my head.

Mom I am kidding. Lighten up it's the Holidays.

So do tell me Tate what makes up a professional wine drinker Tate? I really, really want to know as she glares at me. Are you an alcoholic Tate?

No Mom….**stop**….It was a joke….seriously a joke Mother.

Are you planning on drinking today Tate?

Um yes are you kidding me Mother do you know what house this is and what family I am with? (My kid brother hasn't even shown up yet. I say to myself).

Mom please stop I am fine -I say almost like I am before a Superior Court judge pleading for a much lesser sentence.

You know because if you did drink today it would be 3 days in a row now.

Mom **stop**!

Is that the real reason you overslept your flight Tate?

Mother I am begging you please stop!

Stop what? Oh great Princess Bathroom bitch has arrived. (in case you forgot…it is Kelly)

Mom thinks I am an alcoholic.

You are but so am I Kelly states like a queen over seeing her disciples. It is the only way we can survive the Holidays Mother. Have you met the rest of our family? Do you know that mongrel of a brother we have? Plus he has those 2 hellions of children. He has never heard of the word discipline at all Mom. How do you think we get through all of it? We drink Mother…we drink lots of wine Mother.

Crash and all you hear is broken glass. I run and there is cranberry sauce **all** over the kitchen floor now and I mean everywhere.

My mother is just staring at the floor with cranberries everywhere and she is crying. So my children are alcoholics because of me.

Ok I panicked…..No, no, no Mom we are alcoholics because of Dad and only on the Holidays.

She eyeballs me and smiles.

This conversation is not over you two. Can you get me the mop Kelly and Tate I am going to need you to go to the store and get more cranberries.

OK Mom that won't be a problem and I will buy lots and lots of wine too?

Ha Ha smart ass the wine stores are closed today.

As I head out the door to get my Mother more cranberries, I think to myself ahh shit, that's right, in New York City you still have to go to liquor stores for all that fun stuff including wine but in LA it's all in the grocery stores.

I will find wine….I just **have** to….If I have to get on a damn train and go to New Jersey I am finding me some wine. There is just no way that I can make it through Thanksgiving Day sober, especially with my loving family.

As I turn the corner to the supermarket I see the liquor store and it is **open!** Oh Happy Day! I didn't know if I was happier the liquor store was open or that I get to prove my Mother wrong again. Not sure but it might run 50/50.

Ha ha Mother I say out loud as I skip on in to the liquor store.

Where is the red wine section sir?

He points me in the direction to the back of the store and I smile and continue to skip to the back of the liquor store.

I start picking up bottles and I am shocked by the prices. What??? They want $25 bucks for Columbia Crest Merlot?

This price has to be wrong right? I head to the front of the store and ask $25 bucks for this? The cashier just nods his head yes plus New York sales tax and turns the other way.

Really? Wow?

Geez God ….as I just have a flashback to my mother at Bergdorf Goodman's and the dress price being wrong to her.

I am definitely **my** mother's son. Who questions prices? Yup we do. I hope that is not what our family is known for....

Can I get a case of this as I hold up the bottle of wine?

Sure the clerk says and heads to the back of the store.

That will be $360.00

Hey it's cheaper than therapy I tell the cashier as I fork over my credit card.

So I am carrying the case of wine back to the house. I am seeing lots of familiar faces and saying hello to many.

As I am walking and carrying the case of wine the comments are flowing. That's a lot of wine there Tate! Spare a bottle! Where is the party? I just smile and fake laugh and walk faster with every comment. I get to the door and I open it using my butt to turn the knob on the door.

Surprise **Mom** the liquor store was **open**!

My mother comes out of the kitchen and glares at me and the case of wine.

Did you buy that case and then walk through the neighborhood?

Yes....why I stammer?

Because now the whole neighborhood is going to think we are alcoholics too Tate!

Well at least they won't think we are price checkers?

What Tate?

Nothing Mom…

Where are my cranberries?

Cranberries? Oh Shit Mom I forgot. I will be right back as I am grabbing for my jacket and running towards the door.

Yeah because you were only focused on something else that was red as she picks up one of the wine bottles.

Fuck! I can't believe I forgot the damn cranberries…..

As I am hauling ass back to the grocery store I hear

What happened did you run out of wine already?

I just look at my douche bag neighbor who I have known since I was 7. Fuck off Guartini I forgot the cranberries.

OK Mr. Tate Hollywood I think you have fried your brain out there in Sunny California as Guartini mocks me

I say to myself –Don't engage him it is not worth it. He is a loser that will never amount to nothing. He will probably get the first drunk girl who ever agrees to sleep with him pregnant and will be living with his Mother til he is 60. Better not let any of my female relatives drink too much wine with him around though.

I get to Da'gostino's in less than 8 minutes but sadly it closed four minutes ago for Thanksgiving. Damn Thanksgiving store hours!

Closed

What am I going to do now? My mother is going to kill me. I try and go to every bodega in Brooklyn but nobody has cranberries. I am never going to hear the end of this from my Mother….thank God I have the case of wine… right?

I walk home defeated and loser Guartini is still on his stoop. What happened Mr. Tate Hollywood did you lose something?

You're so not worth it Guartini…so not worth it.

As I walk into the front door of my house I yell:

Mom they were out of cranberries at the grocery store! I tried everywhere Mom…I am so sorry. Do you want me to go into Manhattan to look because I will

It's OK they are popular I shouldn't have been so clumsy…

Well I did it again. I **lied** to my Mom and now she feels bad. Where did I learn this from? I swear my Mother makes me feel like Pinocchio. If I don't get out of here soon I am going to have a 9 inch nose…I wouldn't mind a nine inch….

(Get out of the gutter Tate.)

Mom Can I help?

No go get ready because now not only do you smell like a brewery but now also a really sweaty brewery so **go shower**!

OK

I run upstairs and take a nice and long hot shower. As I am in the shower I start thinking about everything that has happened so far this trip. I am exhausted and I am only half way through it…not even half way…..yikes!

After I shower and get dressed I hear the voice from the top of the stairs.

Hey Fatty! How many of the deep dish pizzas you been eatin in Chicago??

(Yup it is my brother Chris and he is already torturing my sister).

As I head down the stairs I yell Hey Buddy How are you?

Hey bro how is my favorite homo?

Seriously Chris…do not go there! She is over there as I point to my sister. You fuck with her…not me. Do not fuck with me because you will lose and lose **big** time….Uh huh and I shake my fingers.

OK dude relax. Man you are looking buff. Looking good my brother. What have they been feeding you out there in LA? Chris asks

Apparently wine…..my Mother chimes in.

Mom? As I look over at her and I cannot hide that I am starting to get annoyed with her now. Enough Mother I am not an alcoholic. Seriously Mom enough.

Clean living Chris and the gym almost every day. I boast to my kid brother.

Cool, cool are you still a fag?

Seriously Chris? How about I kick the shit out of you and then you can go back and tell all your boys, how you got your ass kicked by a fag? Is that what you want??

Chill dude, chill? Aren't we testy? Phew

I laugh and say well if you spent the last 48 hours with these two (as I point to Mom and Sis) you would be testy too.

My Mother turns to Chris and says:

It hasn't **even** been 48 hours yet. He "over slept" his flight and lied about it. My Mother chants as sarcastic as ever.

And of course not to be one upped by my Mother my sister goes, Yeah he probably drank too much wine the night before. He just **bought** another whole case of wine for today.

Well that was a stupid mistake Kelly because what did you think that my little brother would do? Yup he chants.

Sweet as he hops up and down like a retarded monkey. Let's open up one of those bad boy wine bottles and get this Thanksgiving started!

We will but I have a question. Where is your wife and your kids? I ask

There not coming. They are going to Sam's sisters for Thanksgiving. Chris informs me very non- chalets and in a no big tone.

What? Why? I ask Chris.

Sam doesn't like Mom's cooking Chris tells me very matter of fact.

What are you fucking kidding me? You are kidding me right? Questioning Chris and I staring directly at my little brother.

Nope no joke Sam and the kids are not coming. You are just stuck with me.

I am speechless my sister goes.

I think to myself **now you are fucking speechless**? The girl that has something to say about everything from the crack in the pavement to what feminine product she is douching with this week, has nothing to say? Is this really happening? Is my brother's bitch of a wife disrespecting my Mother? I am being punked right?

And you are OK with this Chris?

Yeah I am fine with it and so is Mom. Tate don't give your bullshit holy than thou look or speech. We are here **all** the time. Just because you decided to grace our presence for Thanksgiving doesn't make it mandatory for every other single family member to attend.

Mom are you OK with this?

Yes she told me but don't worry we will see them all on Sunday. Samantha is cooking at their house.

Um Sunday? Nobody told me about Sunday....

Yes when Sam said she didn't like my food and wanted to go to her sisters I mentioned that you were coming and that you would want to see the girls. She mentioned Sunday and I thought it was a lovely idea.

I swear, I swear I am saying this to myself. Another **full** day with **this** family is so **not** going to happen.

I turn to my Mom and brother and say:

I have plans on Sunday but I will figure out a way to see my nieces. Thanks for the heads up people.

I am actually really pissed. The reason I am pissed is because I genuinely love my nieces. I adore them. They are the cutest little things in the world to me. Actually the thought of seeing them was what was going to get me through this day.

Maybe my Mom is right….I am an alcoholic….because I need a fucking drink pronto!

So who is coming to our Thanksgiving dinner Mom?

I thought it would be nice if it was just the four of us.

Just the four of us???

Are you on crack? (in my head of course)

Just the **four** of us Mom are you serious?

Yes Tate.

Only the four of us? As I point to my sister, brother, mother and myself. Where is Ron?

He is having Thanksgiving Dinner with his daughters on Long Island. Is there a problem with just the four of us? My Mom snap.

A problem Mother? Are you mad? Have you met your children Mother? The two of them have been at each other's throats since Chris came out of your womb. I can barely tolerate your daughter but when the two of them are together it is a nightmare. (Pointing at my brother and sister) We need buffers Mom. Your son and not your other son needs to be on the far end of the table and your daughter on the other.

Buffers Tate? She asks as if she is confused.

Aunts, uncles, cousins, nieces, neighbors......Mom why would you do this to us?

I thought it would be nice she snaps.

Nice? Did you live in this same house as me? It was World War 3 here 24/7 with those two.

I thought it would be nice....

OK Mom I am concerned- I have to ask...are you dying. Or sick? Is there something wrong?

There is nothing wrong with me. I just wanted to have a nice Thanksgiving dinner with my children. Is there something wrong with that Tate? (She is exasperated by now)Why do you have to ruin everything? You know I don't miss you. I thought I did but you are really a pain in the ass. Do you want me to cancel this dinner Tate?

No Mom I don't.

So we will have a nice Thanksgiving dinner Tate?

Yes Mom as I turn to the cat who is sitting on the dining room table and say we will have dinner but I am not so sure how nice it is going to be.

Sit down dinner is ready....

Well for the next hour we sit there in silence trying to chew through a turkey that is dryer than sand, mashed potatoes that tasted like eating paper. We continued to nosh on burnt stuffing. How does someone burn stuffing? All while every few minutes my Mother would say I wish we had cranberries and then follow it up with how is your wine Tate?

I am stewing in my head. Why did I do this? What kind of satinistic thing would make me decide to come home for Thanksgiving? Thanksgiving? I should have waited for Memorial Day or even July 4th. I can deal with a burnt hamburger – hell that is what ketchup is for. I could deal with the heat and humidity. But this...This is torture, the food is awful, the friction between us is awful but we will all feel awful, if we hurt my Mother's feelings. I do what any good son would do:

Everything is great Mom! I say as cheerful as possible.

Thanks Tate as she turns to my brother and says Tell Sam that Tate loves my food.

So Tate how is California?

It's cool I like it.

How are the chicks?

Did he really just ask me about the chicks??Gorgeous and stunning you should come for a visit. I say sarcastically

I want to but it won't be for a while now.....

How come?

Well we were going to wait til Sunday to tell you but.....

What is it Chris? I ask.

Sam is pregnant and it is a boy!Chris says like a gay cheerleader who just got drilled by the entire football team.

That is great Chris how far along is she? I inquire.

Almost 5 months he proudly states.

5 months and you didn't tell your Mother Chris? As my Mother states between her tears and the agonizing stares of disbelief. What did I do in my past lives to deserve such awful kids?

Mom we were just keeping it quiet until we found out the sex.

Why my sister quips?

Well......if we were having another girl we possibly...um....might....not have had....ya know the kid...

What my Mom screams you would have had an abortion?

No no Mom Chris stammers but we might maybe have put up for adoption.

I cannot afford 3 kids **Mom**. Not now at least.

You mean 3 girls Chris! My sister snides.

We just weren't ready for a third kid but we are all onboard now. The girls are excited they are getting a brother.

Even my grandchildren knew before my son's Mother found out, my Mom cries like she just accidently won an Academy Award.

Mom chill…please? Chris states.

So Chris let's get back to this. What would have happened if you were having another girl? I ask really wanting to know the answer.

I don't know… but we don't have to even think about it now. We are going to be really careful about sex after the baby comes Chris declares

Careful? My Mom asks. Aren't you always careful with a baby?

(Oh shit let me take this one before my Mother has a stroke)

So after you have the baby you are going to be careful as in wearing condoms? Samantha is going to go on the pill? You are going to actually win the lottery? Maybe you get a vasectomy or she gets her tubes tied.

Tubes tied? Vasectomy? Hells no…Chris is pissed now

Well than what are you going to do, I sternly ask my younger brother who I can tell is getting agiTated? What are you going to do?

Um I am just going to pull out quicker….Chris states like he just answered the winning Jeopardy question.

Are you fucking kidding me? Your wife agrees to this? I cannot believe you are raising 2 kids with a third on the way. You are an idiot Christopher.

Dude I have been doing this for a long time Tate my brother states. I am really good at pulling out fast.

Ok my Mother looks confused:

Chris you're going to pull out of where? Are you moving?

No no Mom it's when they…..my sister starts to educate my Mother

Kelly shut up…don't go there with Mom.

Yes Mom they are moving….they are after all….. Having a third child. I say as condescending as hell but I am not going to explain this one to my Mother with dry turkey still in my stomach. My Mother doesn't need to know that my brother's future method of birth control is to pull out of his wife's vagina and shoot any future children up against his bedroom wall.

I just shake my head and look at my brother, my sister and my Mother. This is seriously my family…..how?

Thanksgiving dinner is officially over. Now where is that wine opener?

More wine Tate? My Mother is looking at me in utter disbelief as I start to open another bottle of wine that I purchased.

Yes Mom… more wine.

Since when do you drink so much wine Tate I am worried.

I start to say in my head…since the second I walked through the gateway to hell…AKA your house Mother…but I just looked at her and said It's the Holiday Mom…knowing that it wasn't going to be a good enough answer but….what the hell.

I am going to go upstairs and take a nap Mom all the tryptophan from the turkey is making me sleepy.

Are you sure it is not all the wine you have been drinking and NOT the turkey Tate?

Mom I have only had a bottle….

A bottle? A bottle? My Mother is in hysterics you have had a bottle ALL to yourself Tate she shrieks…

Yes Mother I say as I walk up the stairs…

You have a problem Tatey….

(So we are back to Tatey now….I need to prepare myself for a reversal into my childhood now…I wonder where she will go…)

Yes I do have a problem but it is not drinking wine Mother. Wake me up in an hour. Are we still going to go to the movies?

Yup my sister yells, Nah my brother goes and I guess so, my dear old mother sighs.

Goody….wake me up in an hour….

Fine I hear in stereo.

I am exhausted after that dinner as I lay down in bed. My brother is having another kid…God save our souls….

zzzzzzzzzzzzzzzzzz

In what feels like less than 10 minutes later I am hearing Tate, Tatey, Tate, Tatey, Tate**…..Tate Connors get up!!!!**

All this in my **ear** of course….

It is the sound of my Mother ---screaming my name, with my sister as her backup screamer/tormentor.

You have been sleeping for over 3 hours!!! It is 9pm are you ever getting up?

9pm??? Why didn't you wake me up sooner?

We have been trying for over an hour douche bag my sister snaps.

Really? I say as I rub my eyes.

No we are fucking lying to you. Your Mother and your Sister are lying to you… (And here comes the sarcasm)

Kelly shut up. Why didn't you come up 2 hours ago and scream in my ear? I snap at my sister and I am severely pissed.

Because we were downstairs watching a movie dumbass. Kelly snaps at me

Oh I see..so when it was convenient for you to not wake me up it was fine but as soon as it is an inconvenience to you, then you come to torture me Kelly... what the fuck?

My mother is just watching us fight. I think she rather enjoys it to be honest. I bet she is secretly taping us so she can either replay the video when she is lonely, when one of us has a kid or as some sort of blackmail.

Listen putz I have been putting up with yer shit for 3 days now...**Enough** just get the fuck up and come downstairs she snarls.

Fuck her....I say to myself.... but out loud I continue.....

Hey Kelly next time you need to talk to me put a cert in your damn mouth – you breathe smells like you just licked the cat's ass.

Fuck you....Kelly screams like she is a bartender yelling last call for alcohol

And Kelly if ever in your pitiful life, you **ever** wonder why you are alone, bitter and single just call me....**because** I will tell you why...

Oh I see you want to make another family member cry Tate? What? Do you have a quota for the day or something? You are such an asshole....such an asshole....Kelly is glaring at me and I honestly do not give a shit.

Kelly wait....Can we not fight? You guys just woke me up and I was grouchy.

Kelly is pissed and here she goes:You know Tate you cannot take back the hurtful things you say once they have left the departure gate, of your fucking mouth. You know that right? You say these mean and hurtful things and then once you realize you hurt someone feelings, you say I am sorry. Did you think that is your get out of jail free card? Well you know what Tate? It still doesn't erase what you said. Seriously think about that. You hurt people deliberately and you thrive on that. What is wrong with you? I am so thankful that I only have to see you once or twice in a year because I don't like you…you are not a very nice person….

Wow **ouch**….did she really just say that to me.

Tate it is not always what you say but it is how you say it…yup now it is my Mom's turn….and she is not stopping there:

You love to pick fights Tate whether it is the salesgirl at Bergdorfs or the lady in the shoe department or your sister or…….

I couldn't take anymore….

Ok ok enough already (My time to fight back)

I am not going to be ganged up on. Are we going to the movies or not?

It is too late for a movie since you ruined it by oversleeping…my Mom says like I killed another one of her cats.

I say to myself ---Good thing you have 3 cats because 2 are dead already! (I know not nice but I am getting beaten here people)

We are going to watch a movie at home instead my Mom insists.

Please not The Sound of Music again….

What is wrong with The Sound of Music Tate? My Mother asks and has now placed her hands on her hips…which is never good

Nothing Mom but we have seen it a 100 times....

Make that 101 my sister chimes in...

I turn to Kelly and ask: **no way**.....is that....what.....um....movie you were..... um watching while I was taking a nap?

Yes Tate she says looking at me like she is ready to punch me in the face...

I walk up and whisper in Kelly's ear....No wonder you were soo bitchy to me as I run to the bathroom and lock the door.

Revenge is best when served cold "Tatey" Kelly yells.

I laugh as I am splashing some water on my face to wake up. I start to think about what Kelly said. Am I that mean and hurtful to my family? Do I get some sort of sick or demented enjoyment out of torturing people? I wonder if people think I could be a pre op serial killer. Hmm let me try and be nicer to my family especially tonight. They drive me absolutely crazy. I love my Mother very much but the distance is good.. I kinda love my sister. I don't really think about my brother too much but I will try and be....um gentler son and brother

(My Mother and sister have departed my room by now and are back downstairs)

(I don't care what they say about me but that salesgirl and bitch at Bergdorf Goodman, so **had** it coming!

Tatey are you coming already? My Mother is still so damn loud and we are back to Tatey again.

Coming Coming.....I grimace and yell back

So as I head down the stairs I can smell the popcorn popping and that kinda gives me a smile as I head down the stairs and into the living room.

What are we watching? I ask my sister.

Ask Mom she says with a sarcastic laugh.

Mom what are we watching? I yell to her in the kitchen

The Wizard of Oz she shouts enthusiastically

Really Tthe **Wizzzzzz**

Tate don't… let's just watch this fucking movie and our Thanksgiving prison sentence is over – my sister whispers.

OK I whisper back and sorry if I was being a dick upstairs. It is just being back in **this** house and…

It's cool, I am sorry too Kelly say apologetically, you are not always a satanically asshole minded dickhead either.

Well I think that is a compliment….I say to my sister

Do you think Mom would have a stroke if I opened wine? I genuinely ask my sister

Tate don't be silly….if you opened wine….she wouldn't have a stroke….she would go into full on cardiac arrest!

Your right Kelly….

Here is the popcorn my Mother says with such excitement as she comes running from the kitchen to the living room.

I am **soo** excited for The Wizard of OZ – it is a family tradition she says beaming at the TV.

OK let me get something to drink as I hop off the sofa and head to the kitchen.

My Mother has turned white and before she can say anything I go…Ma I am going to get some cranberry juice.

Oh OK I figured my Mother says almost embarrassed that I saw how white she had gotten, thinking that I was going to open up another bottle of wine. For the record her darling Christopher guzzled the wine all day like it was water.

See Mom Cranberry Juice I say raising the glass as I head back to the living room to watch the Wizard of Oz.

Cranberry juice is very good for you Tate and it tastes really good!

I know **Mom** I say to her, but in my head I say yes Mom it is…. Especially when there is vodka added into it….it would kill her if she found out…

Kelly is glaring at me….Guess who has figured it out? **Ha!**

I wonder if she is glaring at me because there is vodka with my cranberry juice in my glass or she is just pissed that she didn't figure it out first. Yup….you are right, me too…I will go with option number 2 as well…when is she not pissed or bitter….I wonder when was the last time she got laid or even had a date for that matter. Frigid B

Let's watch the movie I say and my mother hits play on the DVD player.

As the movie starts I wonder to myself, how the hell am I going to make it through this movie **again.** In years past, I usually by this point at Thanksgiving make an excuse that I have to feed the cat or something, to get out of this but I have no excuse tonight. I am staying with her, my cat is 3000 miles away and her cats could probably go a month without eating. Guess who is going to watch the Wizard of Oz again?

As the movie begins to chug along there are a lot of childhood memories that float in to my head but quickly and rapidly float out. As I watch the movie the more confused I get. Judy Garland is seriously a gay icon? She doesn't look like a drug addict to me. I guess this was before the drug years. You **can** tell it is Liza's Mother though...The colors and set design are fantastic even if the movie was shot in 1939. Was it originally in black and white? Those little munchkins give me the creeps. I wonder if before The Wizard of OZ what we called little people. um Little People. So the slang word for Little People which became Munchkins came from the movie The Wizard of OZ...huh? Never thought about that before.....

I look over and my Mother has embraced the TV like a baby drinking its bottle....My sister is still glaring at me because I am about to finish my first of many "Cranberry Juices."

Be right back Mom I am going to get some more Cranberry juice...but you do not need to pause the movie.

I will pause it Tate I don't want you to miss anything Tatey.

Miss anything? I have seen it freakin 50 times!!!

Bring me a cranberry juice too Tate? Kelly yells almost pleading from the living room.

I look back and I smirk...sure Kel!

I come back with the two cranberry juices. Now I refreshed mine just right but I fixed my sisters **really** good. Ya know I needed to make up for being **such** a horrible brother to her.

Here you go Kel,(as I hand the drink off to my sister who is sitting on the sofa) try it and let me know if it is cold enough for ya?

OK she says...

It was like taking candy from a child I swear. The dumb bitch started chugging the drink when halfway through the Nero surgeon has realized that it is 80% full of vodka. She wants to spit it out but if she does we will **both** be busted by our dear Mother.

I got to hand it to her...she turned every color in the face from blue to red but she didn't spit out that vodka...I am impressed.

Let's continue with the movie my Mother says as clueless as ever, to what has just gone down....

As we continue to watch I say to myself....How could we not know The Scarecrow was gay? Look at him? He is just a big old queen in Emerald City, with his fag hag Dorothy and her little dog. It could be any given Wednesday night in West Hollywood...without all the munchkins that is. I am sure he was just looking for the next scarecrow bar to pick up a trick or a hustler. As I keep watching I could swear I have seen a few old queens that look just like him...OK, ok stop Tate I say....**now** you are being mean...

Now I am starting to analyze every character in this movie. The Wicked Witch? Please the manager at the restaurant I work in would eat her for breakfast? Don't even get me started on the good witch…And while I am asking how do you fall under a house? Why do people love this movie or dare to call it a classic. I do not get it.

That cowardly Lion would get his ass kicked by a bunch of 3rd graders….And what don't I like about the Tin Man? Hmm he is alright I guess. I wonder if they had WD-40 in 1939.

I cannot even remember what or where they are in this movie by now. I have been analyzing the character for so long that I forgot to pay attention to the plot….That and….I am now on my fourth "cranberry juice."

OK there is the castle and the yellow brick road; she is going back to Kansas blah, blah, blah

The End

Shit I need to go brush my teeth before my Mother smells my "cranberry juices."

Gotta pee I yell as I hop over the chair and head upstairs to the bathroom.

Why does he have to announce everything he does? My Mother has just asked my sister expecting an answer

I feverishly brush my teeth. (Don't worry I took the glass with me upstairs—I am not a rookie after all.) I spit, smell my breath, take a pee and then run back downstairs.

I am exhausted my Mother states. I am going to bed.

Good night Mom, I love you, thanks for a great day. See you in the morning. **Kiss kiss**

Night Mom my sister yells as I can hear her pouring herself another drink in the kitchen.

Night Kelly. I love you. Sleep tight.

Now don't stay up too late we have a busy day tomorrow my Mother tells us.

What did she just say? Uh-uh my sentence is over.

Mom tomorrow? What's is going on tomorrow?

It is Black Friday…we have to start our Christmas shopping and doors open at 6am!

Wow Mom slow down I say. Black Friday? Tomorrow? Shopping? Tomorrow? 6am? Tomorrow?

Yes Tate we are going shopping in the morning and then your aunts and uncle want to see you guys before you abandon all of us again. Then the church is having a pot luck/leftover night.

Mom tomorrow I was going to see my friends. I was going to go to the Alumni Association at school to get some referrals. I had my own itinerary for the rest of the weekend Mom. Plus the waiter from TGIF was supposed to call me and we were going to set up a date.

The Mexican waiter from TGIF is **not** going to call you Tate. He knows you are only going to be here for a few more days. What possibly could you do in just a few hours or days with the Mexican waiter from Fridays? My Mother asks

I don't know whether it was my 4 "cranberry juices" or that fact that I was in shock that she had planned tomorrow also so I just blurted out.

Mom we could have a drink, we could go dancing **or** we could just have **sex!!**

Crickets…. And then my Mother yells:

Have sex??? How do you have sex with someone after just a few days?

(At least now I have smartened up and started being sarcastic in my head and my head only. A few days Mother? Try a few hours?)

Are you easy Tate?

Again in my head…..um….yes!

Mom I am kidding. Ha ha just laugh Mom but I still have plans for things I need to do tomorrow, there are people I need to see.

Of course Mr. Popular has to see his friends. My Mother again is at the top of the stairs with her hands on her hips.

Mom please stop?

I get to see you what once or maybe twice a year Tate?

Mom there are people I want to see.

Up there she goes again and she is crying again. She thinks crying is going to manipulate me into changing my plans....well guess what? It worked.

Mom, ma, Mom stop crying. I tell you what. Listen how about you go shopping with Kelly in the morning and I get my errands done. After all you don't like shopping with me anyway. I then will meet up with you guys for lunch with the aunts and uncle. Half of our cousins are going to be working tomorrow anyway Mom.

(I will then take the afternoon to see some of my friends. I am looking at her trying to make her nod her head.)

Around 6pm we go to your church's pot luck because you know I am **dying** to see this new church of yours and meet all your **new** friends. I will stay for an hour to an hour and a half and then I will meet my date or go into Manhattan to meet other friends. I will be home by 2am.

1am she goes.

Mom I am a grown man and I will be home by 2am OK?

I guess so. I cannot believe I have to schedule time with my oldest son. On top of that, I have to negotiate when I can see him and spend time with him. I do not think you are being very fair to your Mother but as you said you are a grown man and there is nothing I can do. It is not like I could punish you or take away your TV but I have thought about it **a lot** the past few days. Did I raise you to be such a damn selfish person?

I love you Mom Good Night. (I could not go another round with her tonight yet)

Goodnight Tate I will talk to you in the morning as she is walking up the stairs. Halfway up the stairs she turns and says I still want to talk to you about this sex thing you said. I am not so sure you were kidding about it.

My Mother starts to wobble like she is going to fall down the stairs, so my sister quick on her feet, runs up the stairs, grabs her in the nick of time and says come on Mom let me put you to bed.

My Mother leans over to Kelly and says is Tate a slut?

No Mom Kelly laughs and walks with her all the way to her bedroom.

Well I guess it wasn't just Kelly and I who were sipping vodka into something else. My good old Mom and her vodka and Diet Pepsi's....ah something's never change. At least she won't remember this in the morning....Maybe that is why we have seen The Wizard of OZ so many times and my Mom still acts like it is the first time she has seen it....too many Vodka's and Diet Pepsi's.

Maybe but ya never know....Next thing I hear...

You're an asshole Tate I hear my sister hiss....

What? What did I do now?

The look on Kelly's face is uglier than I have ever seen and she starts her speech: We won't even start with your stunt of trying to induce alcohol poisoning into me. It was amusing at first and I wish I would have thought of it first but....Mom is all up there worried about you having sex. You know you cram it down our throats about you being gay, accepting you for who you are and I think Mom has been really cool about it.

Kelly....

No you are going to listen to me.

(I am thinking to myself --listen to you? Cram down your throat? You wish you had something to cram down your throat...I mean besides a cheeseburger).

Tate listen she says softly with tears swelled up in her eyes.

What Kelly? What?

She is afraid you are going to get AIDS and die Tate. She has read every book, magazine and newspaper known to man about AID's and HIV. She used to go to a support group about mothers with gay sons. She loves you, you are now 3000 miles away and now you tell her you are going to have sex with a guy you just met? What is wrong with you? I just told you earlier how cruel you can be. I know you think it is funny but it is **not** to her. She is petrified about losing you. Do you know that? She calls me always worrying about you. When she tries to bring it up, you just make some stupid joke that usually makes her look stupid. Do you know how lucky you are to have a Mom like that who loves you? I have friends that parents have disowned them for a lot less. How would you like it if she was like Dad or that bible thumping bitch he has for a wife? How many times has that witch, our father is married to told you, that you were going to hell because you are gay? How many times Tate? 20? 40? Yet our sweet Mother, that you live to torture is scared to death for her oldest son's life. Do you fucking understand me you self-righteous faggot?

(I am standing there in utter shock...)

Kelly continues:

Um sorry for using the F word. I know it was wrong but you know I worry too. You are my brother and I love you...

350

(Now I am in tears….we love to make each other cry in this family huh?)

Tate please do the right thing by Mom, she is not as strong as you think she is. I worry about this new church too but maybe she turned to them because maybe she feels her own family, doesn't give a shit about her. I want you to just think about it. Seriously think about it because sometimes you can be such an asshole to her but yet other times be the sweetest son in the world. Which is it Tate? She desperately needs your love and to know you are safe. Whether I like to believe it or not but you are her favorite kid and always have been.

I am always safe Kelly

Not just practicing safe sex Tate, get your mind off of sex for one minute ya whore. Safe as in your environment, your job, your friends, your choices and of course sex….

Let me go up and talk to her Kelly. I don't want her to cry herself to sleep thinking I am going to die of AIDS on Thanksgiving night.

She is probably passed out already but go check. Kelly says in a genuine 3rd grade teacher voice that will annoy me to the day I do die.

Thanks Kelly --I mean that. I really appreciate that….honestly I do.

Quit ya crying ya Big Baby as she wipes away my tears with a tissue. Don't let Mom she **you** cry now- that's all we need. She will think you actually have a heart and then we are all in trouble.

Good night Kelly.

Give me a hug homo!

I give her a big hug and then run up the stairs.

I walk to my Mom's room and she is already snoring. I pull the covers back, turn off the light and give her a kiss on her forehead.

Through the window the moon shines in right onto her face. God do I look like her- the resemblance is scary. We have the same eyes and forehead and we even have the same skin which includes freckles. I don't really remember the actual real hair color of my Mom's hair but I think it is close to mine. As I just look at the moon shining over my Mother, my eyes begin to swell up. I have an amazing Mother and I am going to treat her like the queen she deserves to be treated like. For the next 3 days I am going to be the best son I can be. Whatever she wants I will do for her, whatever she needs I will get for her but for as long as I live I will not talk about my sex life with her....ever! I will make her think I am a priest if I have to. Don't laugh.....I could....if I wanted to. The one thing I will tell her is that she never has to worry about me getting HIV and dying of AIDS....That is my solemn promise, to you Mom as I grab her hand and lightly squeeze. I promise Mom. I kiss her forehead and head directly back to my room.

I didn't even brush my teeth. Went directly to the bed and nosedived in....

Thanksgiving is over!

Chapter 16

The day after Thanksgiving

Tatey get up already, I gotta give you the details on lunch!!!

Huh what Mom? Its 545 am I say as I try and adjust my eyes to the alarm clock.

I know but Kelly and I have to be at JC Penney's for their door busters by 6am she exclaims.

OK all I see is a ball bust…..(hold on Tate you said you were going to be nicer).

OK Mom whats the dets?

Dets?

Details Mom.

Oh OK we have reservations at Rocky's in Little Italy at 1230 pm. don't be late.

OH cool I **love** Rocky's I won't be late. See ya there Mom now go bust some doors Mom.

We don't really bust doors Tate.

I know Mom go see you at 1pm

Tate!!!!!!!!!!!

Mom I am kidding. See you at 1230, at Rocky's and Mom regardless of my joking you know I love you.(Yup I am yawning and yelling from my bed on the second floor.)

I love you too Tatey.

Well since I am up I am going to go to the gym, maybe find a tanning salon and do a little NYC shopping of my own.

It is good to be home….but ask me if the answer is the same, after the church pot luck dinner tonight, on whether it is still good to be home. Gosh I cannot remember the last time I was up before the sun came out.

I hope Antonio from TGIF calls I am horny… (sigh)

As I am turning on the water to the shower, I hear a massive **meow** like a cat has just been run over by a truck. Unfortunately for me it was Marshmallow the cat, who I guess liked to sleep in the shower during the night; because as I turned on the water out came this huge ball of white fur flying directly at me. I ducked but the fucking fat cotton ball scratched the hell out of my neck.

Meow, Meow, Hiss- Hiss!

Fuck that hurt! I am bleeding. The worst part of it was the door was closed and a really pissed off, not so furry friend was locked in the bathroom with me. Every time I tried to go to the door to let Marshmallow out, she would make these unimaginable growls that I was beginning to fear for my life. After the 5th attempt to open the door, she scratched me good. Fuck I am going to be murdered in my Mothers bathroom by a really pissed off wet fat cat.

Well fuck it… I might as well shower first. I could just imagine telling my Mom why I missed lunch.

Mom I was trapped in the bathroom with that demon cat of yours. I honestly would really like to know what my Mother is feeding that thing because I have never felt stronger paws in my life! Maybe "it" will calm down after I shower and by the way this episode has gone so far, I am pretty sure I am safe in the shower. As I jump in the shower for the second time there are no surprises until the hot water hits my neck. **ouch** what is that? Oh it is the water hitting my morning presents from the cat…4 scratch marks. I swear I am going to roast "a marshmallow" when I get out of here. Let's make this shower quick my neck is killing me!!

After I shower I grab a towel and it is freezing. This is the first time during this trip that I am grateful my Mother cranks the heat though. Even with the heat blasting I am still shivering. Thank God I brought my clothes into the bathroom with me this morning. I guess I have gotten into the habit of bringing my clothes into the bathroom when I shower, because of college, dorms and having roommates all of my life since I left this house. Ahh fully dressed….now how do I take down a wet puss?.

I get an idea to use the towel as mighty defense or shield to open the bathroom door. I lunged towards the cat and the one thing that I under estimated is how quick that fat cat can move. Shit, Ouch scratch number 5. Damn it cat I have better things to do than get my ass kicked by you. Just let me open the fucking door so we can both get the hell out of here. Well I don't know if she understood me or not but on the next attempt at escape, I actually got the door open without mutilation and flung the door open. Marshmallow ran towards the door and as she was leaving turned around to hiss at me one last time. I don't know if it was her final fuck you to me but in any case we were both free….Ouch my neck hurts….let me go see if Mom has any Neosporin.

As I am looking for Neosporin in her medicine cabinet I come across everything else except what I am looking for. How many half empty bottles of Midol does my Mother need? Just as I was about to give up I notice 3 Polaroid pictures turned upside down at the bottom of my Mom's medicine cabinet. Hmm what could these be…

ahhh no no my eyes!!! I am going to be sick!!!!!!!!!no no no!

I am sure by now you are wondering what has just made me vomit in my mouth huh? Well I will tell you but I need to calm down first and catch my breath!!

Foo-foo-foo-breathe Tate breath Foo-foo-foo just breathe. OK I am calm…

Let's just say that there are 3 very naked Polaroid pictures of my naked Mother doing various um "things" to her also very naked boyfriend Ron. It was like a car wreck and I could have just looked at the first one and shoved them back where I found them, but nooooo I had to look at all 3. I am now seriously traumatized for life I swear. I suddenly begin to panic because I cannot remember exactly where in the cabinet I found them. I need to put them back **exactly** where I found them because my Mother can never know, that I know that, she is a kinky sex whore. Wait…. that is not nice thing to say about my own Mother I shouldn't be calling her a whore….but **da-amn**…if you saw these photos….phew. OK wait I think they go under the condoms… Oh…my…holy…shit…my Mother has condoms. Why does my 50 year old Mother have condoms? I am in hell…I am waiting for a dildo or a vibrator to pop out of the towel closet next. Nah that is probably in the night stand…I have seen Sex in the City…that is my Wizard of Oz….OK anyway…gross now

I am visualizing my Mother having sex…gross…ugh…I am going to need therapy after this. I shove the pictures under the condoms and run out of her bathroom. Ugh I cannot believe what I just experienced. Naked pictures of my Mother doing "things" I cannot even believe she still does…or ever did. Well the one good thing I get out of this is…at least I know where I get being a whore from now…

I need to get **out** of this house. Mornings like these are the reasons I never get up before 10am. I am going to KILL that fucking cat! It is **all** that cat's fault that I now think my Mother is a dirty filthy whore.

Well it is now 730 am and I am finally ready to leave the house. I run downstairs to the dark kitchen. I grabbed a banana and had some toast with orange juice. I needed to give myself a little energy for the gym. I don't think I have **ever** worked out this early in my entire life…well stop procrastinating… let's go! I am going to go around the corner to New York Sports Club and get a good workout in this morning. I bring everything I need to shower there because I am not going Round 2 with the Mighty Fuzzball Ms. Marshmallow Balboa. I bet you want to know why I didn't just shower there in the first place huh? Well A. I was still sleeping when I turned on the water B. I didn't think there would be a cat in the shower and C. OK I am fucking stupid. Happy?

Well off I go. I make sure I lock up because I can just hear my Mother now. Tatey make sure all the doors are locked now…we don't want anyone stealing our TV. She never thinks about her jewelry…nope…just the TV. The same TV she has had for over 10 years.

Well as I am approaching the gym I begin to remember the beauty of Brooklyn Heights. The store fronts, brownstones and the promenade. As I am approaching the gym, I realize I forgot how beautiful a building this once was. The New York Sports Club is in a part of the old St. George Hotel. The St. George Hotel was a lavish hotel in its heyday. Marilyn Monroe, Humphrey

Bogart, Frank Sinatra all used to stay there or at least that is what I was told as a kid. As time marched on, the hotel began to decay and by the late eighties it had become a transient hotel and then pretty much a drug den. In the mid to late 90's it was closed off and sold to various businesses individually. The gym was on the North Side of the building. I think the rest were turned into condos or something. I am not really sure but my Mother would know…

I walk into the lobby and it is beautiful. I am happy they kept some of that 1920's charm the St, George had. The lobby is still all marble sculpted but it does seem a little cold…for a gym that is. I am greeted at the front desk by a typical Brooklyn meathead who when you looked at him, you would think he worked at a gym or was a bouncer at a club.

Hey bro what's up?

Can I get a weekend pass?

You don't live round here bro?

I used to live here but I live in Los Angeles now. I am just visiting my Mom for the weekend.

You an actor bro?

Trying to I say somewhat modestly.

Have I seen you in anything bro?

I have done mostly background for TV and a few commercials.

That is **so fucking cool** bro! He says so excitedly

What commercials?

Well I just did a Chevy commercial.

Yo bro I drive a **fucking Chevy Silverado.**

Cool so how much for the weekend pass? (I am trying to get back on subject)

Yo Bro it is on me as he hands me a 3 Day pass. You just promise me bro, that when you make it **big,** you come back here and give me an autograph… right?

Sure will um what is your name?

Gino…Gino Travasino

Thanks Gino. Will do!

As I am walking into the gym I turn back to wave and Gino who is nodding his head at me and smiling.

You know……Gino is actually kind of sexy…..Tate stop… get your mind out of the sex pool and focus on having a good workout.

Wow it is quiet in here. Everybody is actually just working out. This sure as hell wouldn't be happening if this was LA that is for sure. I do a great run around the track, I lift a bunch of free weights and I work on my abs for over a half hour. Why doesn't this gym have that many mirrors? Strange…Wow I look down at my watch and it is 1015am already. Shit gotta hurry up if I still want to hit Canal Street for some shopping.

I get to the locker room and shower and it is like a monastery in here. Nobody talks or makes eye contact with you. Now Brooklyn Heights is no West

Hollywood but it has its share of a gay population, I just cannot figure out where they all are today. I shower quickly, (which I seem to be taking a lot of quick showers on this trip) get dressed and do my primping in the **one** mirror they have in the bathroom. On my way out I thank Gino again and say I will see you tomorrow.

No bro I don't work weekends.

Oh well thanks again.

Hey bro do you know Pam Anderson? She is Hot.....

Nope but if I see her I will tell her you said so......

Really???? Thanks bro...

Bye and I wave as I walk out.

I glance back and he is still smiling and waving at me.

He is sooo cute.....Why is it that I find big and stupid guys so freakin attractive? What is it about them that do it for me? Ahh who the hell knows but Gino... uh..hmm...yummy but so stupid. Does he know that Pam Anderson is like 42 and he is maybe 24 years old? Hey to each his own...no judgments from me! Plus Pam still does look fucking amazing.

Let me drop this stuff off at the house and head into Manhattan. I quickly run home, primp my hair again, get another lovely hiss from Marshmallow, grab my jacket and run out the door. Have you noticed I haven't bitched about the weather? Well it is cold as hell but it just doesn't seem to be bothering me anymore. I must be getting used to it by now. I am still a New Yorker after all.

I go to the subway station and buy a metro card.

In what increment would you like your card the subway teller asks me.

Um in what increment do they come in?

Read the **sign** sir....she snaps

Oh what sign?

The one in front of your face......sir as she points to a sign in her glass cage.

Oh shit....Um $10 is cool. Thanks.

She looks down at the tray and nods her head at it.

Huh?

I am not giving you the card until you put your damn $10 dolla in the slot....
sir –she has now gotten real surly by now

Oh here you go sorry.

Don't apologize......... just pay attention and we will get along **just** fine......
sir.... Here is your card...now don't fall in the tracks now.

Thanks as I grab the card and slink away

As I am slinking away I am like what a mean bitch. What do they put on the
application for special skills to get hired as a subway clerk? Rude and Nasty?
Bitchy and **fuck** the train is coming. Well I manage to swipe my Metro card
on the first try and race down to the subway track and I slide right on in the

train, as the doors were closing....slick job Tate...slick job. You can take the boy out of Brooklyn but ya can't take Brooklyn out of the boy. My Mother thinks I am becoming so LA...what does she know.

Next stop Boerum Hall (I hear from a cracked speaker)

What? Nooooooo I **didn't**....Yup I got on the right train...yes..but wrong direction. What a dumbass I am. Ok this is fixable... I hop off the train and wait for another train on the opposite track...to go the opposite way towards Manhattan. Thank God my Mother didn't witness what I just did because she would probably disown me. Well 10 minutes later another train came going the right direction and I hopped on. As we hit the Brooklyn Heights station again it really bugged me that I got on the train, going the wrong direction but I will get over it. Well about 8 minutes later I was at the Canal Street station and couldn't wait to find all these secret hidden knock off to bring back to LA. I am sooo excited! I look down at my watch and say out loud How is it 1130 already?

I climb the subway stairs and head straight to Canal Street. In case you do not know, Canal Street is an outdoor market and the **best** place that you can go to buy Designer knock offs really cheap. Things like sunglasses, watches, leather bags etc and I am looking to find another leather bag because mine was stolen shortly after my move to LA. It sucked that it was stolen but it was kinda my fault for leaving it out at the gym and not putting it in a locker...Anyway.

Rolex, Rolex this guy has just rammed a suitcase full of knock off watches into my stomach.

No thanks I said politely because the dude looks mean.

Where did all these people come from? as I continue to try and walk through the crowd.

362

Rolex, Rolex but this time I was not able to maneuver around it so the suitcase with knock off Rolex's ended up in my gut.

ouch man!

Rolex?

No thanks man! With my full on Brooklyn accent.

I see the cologne place on the corner of Broadway and Canal and I say ahh Canal Street gets better after that. Down that way is where all the good stuff is.

But no….bam….Rolex, Rolex wanna buy a watch homeboy, you cannot tell the difference between the reals and this- This **huge** black man is trying to put one on my wrist.

No thanks man. No thanks man. Not today.

I start to walk over to the cologne place and I am not even there 30 seconds and this little Asian lady comes over to me and says:

Ju want to buy 3 or 4 colognes? I give you discount. Cheaper than store. What ju want? Don't waste my time….Hurry or scat and she waves me a way. I turn around and yup….

Rolex, Rolex?

No I say and I cross the street. This is maddening…What the hell happened to all the cool places on Canal Street? And where did all these people come from? Then I remember…Ah shit it is the day after Thanksgiving, **shit** I forgot about that…I think the whole state of New Jersey is here on Canal Street though.

Oh cool there is the sunglass shop I like! Phew…As I am making a bee line for the store selling the sunglasses guess what happens?

u huh go ahead say it

Rolex fucking **Rolex**

No thanks man!

Hey you're missing out. These are the finest pieces on this whole street bro. The Rolex man informs me.

I say to myself …what? Black guys say bro now? When did that happen?

Well I finally make it to my sunglass store and try on a few pairs of sunglasses. I buy a pair of Versace and two Armani knockoffs for $30 bucks. How cool is that? And for an extra $ 5 bucks I get the case included **and** they even say Versace and Armani on them. OK I am happy now.

Rolex, Rolex

Now I am angry.(yes I do go to extremes) More like pissed. These guys are ruining my experience on Canal Street. I should have just shut my freakin mouth but with me being the idiot I can be, that would have been next to impossible to do. So here I go:

NO. I don't want your fucking cheap ass looking Rolex watch dude. I have a real one at home (yeah I wish) and I don't want to be harassed 15 times every damn block. Where did all you Rolex fucking salesman come from?

Halfway through my rant I notice I am drawing a crowd.

So no thank you as I am now scared for my life.

Boy you better watch your mother fucking tone with me. I am just trying to make a mother fucking living out here. What ya got in the bag? Yeah I see you got some fucking cheap ass knock off sunglasses but- cho gonna disrespect me and my watches mother fucker?

Sorry man…really

You cool T? Another **"Rolex"** seller comes over and asks.

No man this cracker over here just disrespected me and my watches man.

Did you disrespect his watches? He looks over and asks me now.

No I just don't want to buy a watch.

He called them cheap ass looking watches! **Rolex Rolex** man just tells his friend.

Well now he is looking at me like he is going to kick my ass.

I think you should **buy** a watch from my friend.

Or what? I say as with my feet planted on the ground

I think you should **really** buy a watch.

Well now it has become a Fake Rolex convention right here on Canal Street because there must be 75 Rolex, Rolex sellers gathering around me.

I am **not** buying a watch.

Boy you gone and pissed me off now...

And? I know I am about to be pummeled if not killed by the Rolex sellers friend.

If you don't buy 2 watches now I am going to fuck you up cracker.

I am **not buying a fuck.....**

All of a sudden a NYPD Police Officer to the rescue and this officer leans in and says

Is there a problem??

All of a sudden it was like bomb went off on Canal Street..... Fake Rolex sellers were scattering everywhere:

Aint No Problem! Aint No Problem! **Aint No Problem**! Aint No Problem, Aint No Problem, Aint No Problem, Aint No Problem **aint no problem**!

The officer turns to me and says

Is there a problem?

No officer as I look at Rolex seller dead in the eyes, as well as his side kick. Yes...I am Mr. Tough Guy now...I got 5-0 behind me

I am late for lunch officer's thank you!

The one police officer looks me straight in the face and says:

Stay out of trouble tough guy. You will get you ass kicked down here.

Yes sir I say as I very very quickly cross the street.

As I cross the street to head to Rocky's I hear

Rolex, Rolex…..

Ok play it cool Tate.

Hey thanks man…Maybe next time…I am broke and I am late for lunch. Maybe next time? Have a great day. Take care. Peace.

And now I am running towards Little Italy. How the fuck is it 1245 already? I start to run and say to myself **shit** my Mother is going to kill me.

I run all the way to Rocky's and when I finally get there I am out of breath but I made it in one piece. I am late but I am in one piece.

I walk through the door….

Well look who decided to make it Jackie? It's Mr. Hollywood and he is only 24 minutes late. Thank you for gracing our presence nephew!

Fuck off Uncle Paul. Seriously fuck off.

I turn to my Mom and say sorry.

What? don't worry about it, we only got here like 8 minutes ago. The city is crazy today. We just sat a minute before you walked in… How was your morning?

I will tell you about it later Mom, let me say hello to everyone.

I kiss my Aunt Barbara and hug my Aunt Sally. I hug my cousin Jennifer and shake hands with my aunts husband Alex. I wonder why we never called him uncle but it was her third marriage after all. I then of course glared at my Uncle Paul and I certainly didn't shake **his** hand. I cannot stand that prick.

So we all sit down and chit chat for a bit, we order drinks and food. I ordered an ice T because I didn't want to get into it with my MOM and because I just really wanted an ice T.

So how is LA Tate? My Aunt Sally genuinely asks

It's great I am really adjusting to it out there. I have an agent and a manager and things are starting to go really well for me.

We saw your Chevy spot Tatey....I mean Tate my cousin Jennifer says...We were all sooo excited when we first saw it. It runs almost every day during Judge Judy.

The spot is retarded my uncle states. Like anyone is going to believe this fairy would be driving a 4 X 4.

Paul my Aunt shrieks.

I turn to my Aunt Barbara and say don't worry about it. Nothing he says would ever affect me.

I turn to my uncle and say:

Uncle Paul you're the one who is retarded and why would you come to this lunch?

To see your sister....he snaps

Yeah I am sure that is **what** it is…I think it is more like you knew my Mother would pick up the check, you cheap fuck. Get a free lunch out of it but I gotta be around my homo nephew.

Tate!! My MOM yells

Sorry Mom but I am not going to take any abuse from this asshole!

You make me sick. You people make me sick! Uncle Paul yells

What people? I inquire

You faggots….Uncle Paul hisses I hope you all die of AIDS!!

Paul!!! My Mother screams

I turn to my Mom and say: Don't worry I have handled a lot worse than this homophobic douche bag uncle Mom.

Paul I am so **happy** you wished death on me but I gotta tell ya… Keep drinking a gallon of rum a day and smoking like a chimney, you will be dead waaaay before me.

I am going to the bar. Uncle Paul hisses

Good….It was really nice to see you and catch up Uncle Paul! I swear I said that to him as pleasant as possible! Ha!

(Footnote: he died 7 months later and these were the last words I ever said to him. When my Mother told me he died I didn't shed a tear or attend the funeral)

The rest of the meal was very pleasant and I love my aunts, cousins and aunt's husbands. It was really nice to see them. We talked about LA, and my life but I was kind of starting to feel sorry for Kelly. No one was showing her any interest but then again nobody really ever has. I have always been the favorite and the center of attention. I **have** to learn to be nicer to my sister as well. To be honest…she is just not that interesting.

So you are all invited out to LA whenever you want I say to my relatives. It was great seeing you all. I have to go meet a friend for coffee in Chelsea.

The waiter from TGIF Tate?

No Mom he hasn't called. You were probably right and he is not going to call.

It's early in the day He still he might call you. She puts her best effort forward….

Mom it is Ok. I am going to meet Mary.

OH I love Mary. Tell her I said hello and to stop by the house anytime she wants.

I will Mom.

My Mom turns to my aunt and says I still wish he would have married Mary if it wasn't for the gay phase he is in.

Mom?

Sorry just sayin!

I kiss and hug everyone goodbye and as I turn to leave my Mother sees my neck and she gasps like I have just been hit by a truck.

Tate what happened to your neck?????

Well…..Marshmallow sleeps in the shower in the morning and…

Oh no my Mom says as she covers her mouth and shakes her head….you didn't?

Yup I turned the shower on…

Tate!!!!!

What Mom I didn't see her sleeping in the tub. Nobody warned me.

(Kelly is finding this extremely amusing)

And she scratched your neck?

It was where she landed, as she flew out of the tub…yup right onto my neck.

Oh dear….my Mom says as she is examining my neck

Wait there are more as I point to my leg and my hand. She wouldn't let me open the bathroom door Mom. Your freakin cat held me hostage in the bathroom for almost a half hour Mother.

She hates water. My Mother informs me like I am her idiot son.

Really Mom? Thanks for letting me know that she sleeps in the tub.

Well she usually is only in there till the sun comes out around 8 or so.

Well Mom someone got me up at 6am to tell me about door busters. I wonder who that person was now? Hmm let **me** think.

Who knew you would actually get up. I just figured you would grunt and roll over and go back to sleep. Who knew you would actually get up **that** early? And I wasn't even thinking about Marshmallow. You didn't hurt her did you Tate?

No Mom Marshmallow is fine but I hate **that** cat!

I look down at my watch and crap I gotta go! Nice seeing all of you and I wave. I catch my sister's eye and it's time to be a good brother.

Do you want to come with me to see Mary? I sincerely ask my sister. Mom is going to go back with Aunt Sally and play cards or something right?

Right…wanna come too? My Mom and Aunt say in unison.

Um no but I will see you two later.

Yes! I want to go with you. **Yes!** Kelly exclaims not even looking at anybody else but me.

Are you going to say goodbye to Uncle Paul? My Mom jabs

Fuck Uncle Paul Mom. Kelly hurry up I am late.

As we leave the restaurant Kelly turns to me and says:

I get the shopping experience you had with Mom. I totally get it. Wow is SHE a pain in the ass or what?

Taxi!

Well a taxi pulled over right away. We hoped in and I said Chelsea 21ˢᵗ and 8ᵗʰ Ave please.

I turn to Kelly and say Shit I am 30 minutes late I should call her. Well I pull out me cell phone and OMG. I have 2 missed calls and a message too!! Please let it be Antonio from TGIF….please… Well of course I forget all about Mary waiting at the coffee house for me. I dial my voicemail on my phone. The sweet voicemail lady says "You have one unheard message. Main menu…I immediately press 3.

Hi Tate it is your Mother. Please do not be home later than 530 I don't want to be er…..what do you call it? Fashionably late ---to the pot luck tonight. OK bye, Love you and don't fight with your sister. That was very sweet of you to take her with you. I thought Mary didn't like Kelly? OK OK coming Sally **click**

Was it him? My sister asked

No…it was Mother calling to make sure that we are home by 530 for the pot luck at her church

Oh Kelly sighs… it is still early and maybe he is working and will call when he is done with his shift. Didn't you say that you had two missed calls also?

That is true he could be working and O yeah I did say I had 2 missed calls. Let me check.

21st and 8th the taxi driver states and we are now in fact on 21st and 8th Avenue in the heart of Chelsea.

Oh look it is a 917 number as I start to show my cell phone number to the cab driver and I get a look like he doesn't give a shit, but just wants his money. I turn to my sister as I hop out of the cab and say Pay the cab driver Kel.

I am fixated with the number on the cell. It is the same number twice!! It **has** to be him. Do I call it? What should I say? Should I wait for him to call back? What if **he** was too nervous to leave me a message…it is possible…I think. Let me find Mary first and then I will figure out what to do. I start to case the coffee house but I don't see her.

Ring ring ring

Omg Kelly I yell like a little school girl It's him, It's him, It's him!

Answer it! Kelly screams almost like I had just won the lotto and it was our last chance to claim the winning ticket.

OK OK

So in the calmest voice I ever had I go

Hellooooo?

You're a real fucking asshole. A familiar female voice states through the phone.

What huh who is this? (I am confused).

I waited a half hour for you. I called you 2 times and you couldn't even bother and pick up the fucking phone?

Mary?

Yes....

Where are you? I am at the coffee shop with Kelly.

I am on the Long Island railroad going home.

Why?

Because I waited for over a half hour for you to show up. Mary screams. **you didn't call to tell me you were running late and when I called you-you couldn't be bothered to pick up the phone.**

Mary stop I yell. Did you get a new phone number?

Yes like 4 months ago she snaps.

And how would I know that Mary? We have been Facebooking for the past 6 months and we set up a meeting for coffee in Chelsea **through** Facebook email.

But I called you **3 times!!!** What Mr. Hollywood can't answer the phone anymore? You screen calls now Tate? How LA of you....You know I came **all** the way into "The City" just to see you Tate. You couldn't even bother to call and tell me you were running late? What a schmuck you are...You **know** I have kids Tate. I had to arrange for someone to look after them while I came to see **you** all the way in The City!!

Mary how could I have called you if I had the wrong number? Seriously calm down. What the hell is wrong with you? Why did you leave Manhattan already? I was just about to call the 2 missed calls when you called just now. I didn't hear the phone ring when I was in the cab. Can you come back?

No I cannot come back Tate I am already out of **Penn Station**. All you had to do was pick up the God Damn phone and tell me you were running late and I would have stayed. Some things never change with you huh Tate?

What? Hold On…

In the meantime my sister is mouthing something to me and I have no idea so I just say:

One large black coffee.

I turn back to my phone and Mary's heated voice.

What doesn't change? I ask.

You Tate….you! Everything has to revolve around you. Tate this and Tate that. You are the most self-absorbed person I have ever met in my entire life. I thought that when you moved to LA, it would knock you down a peg or something but noooooo

Mary seriously are you really saying this to me?

Seriously what Tate?

Mary what is wrong with you? You know I would be late to my own funeral so what the hell is really wrong. What are you riding the cotton pony or something?

Fuck you Tate…

Got too much clitty litter down there and are taking it out on one of your oldest and dearest friends? Huh Mary hmm?

Shut up Tate!! Mary says with a chuckle. You are such an asshole. I am pissed. I miss you and I really wanted to see you.

I did too but I was with my crazy family **and** you know my family. They are all crazy.

How is your Mother?

The same....crazy!

Tell her I said hello.

I will and she said to tell you to stop by the house anytime.

Oh I miss your Mom Tate. Mary oohs and ahhs.

So I guess I am not going to see you huh? I was really looking forward to catching up with you in person Mary.

Well it is not going to happen… Not unless you are coming to Long Island to see me. Come to Long Island Tate?

I can't I have a zillion things to do here. I haven't even seen my nieces yet. Oh by the way Samantha is pregnant.

Again? Mary says in utter disbelief.

Yup but they are having a boy this time.

Good than hopefully they will stop she laughs.

I doubt it…especially with the effective birth control they are going to put into effect lead by brothers extreme brilliance.

Huh?

Never mind it is a long story.

I am going to go through a tunnel is like 45 seconds and I will probably lose you. Mary says

OK I love you and I am so sorry Tam.

You're an asshole but I love you. Call me tomorrow if you can.

So this is your new cell phone number?

Yeah…Mary sighs

How long are you going to keep this one for?

Shut up…

Come visit me because I have so much to tell you about……………………………………..

She must have gone through the tunnel oh well.

You see Mary is a good friend of mine. **We** basically grew up together, went to school together, we worked together and we both even managed to get fired from McDonalds one week apart together. Our lives just went in separate directions after high school. I went away to school while she stayed locally.

She ended up meeting a guy, got pregnant, married the guy and then moved to Long Island. They bought a house, had another kid, got a dog etc. etc. Mary had one of the most amazing singing voices that I ever heard but she made her choices and now she has to live with those choices. She is a wife and a Mother and I can tell that it is not where she thought she was going to end up. She always wanted to move to California and in high school that was her plan. She claimed she had an aunt that lived out there but I would just yes her to death when she says she is moving to California. Mary is one of those people that lives a drama filled life. There is always some sort of turmoil in her life. She thrives on it and don't get me wrong, I love her dearly but she is a train wreck. Every vacation I ever went on with her was always a disaster. I even had sex with her and it was a disaster. Yes…..I have had sex with girls. Just not in about 15 years.

Tate what is going on? I hear Kelly say who is sitting at a table all by herself. She is giving me this dirty look like…what the hell is going on.

So I walk over and before I can even say anything Kelly blurts out:

Was that your Mexican date on the phone?

(I look at her in disdain):

No Mother it was Mary.

Oh where is she? Kelly asks

On the train… I sigh… She left because I was a half an hour late.

Here is your coffee as my sister basically puts the cup in my face.

You should have called her Tate instead of obsessing over some TGIF waiter. Kelly berates

I know you are right and she was pissed Kel.

I would be too Tate. You know she is still in love with you.

She is married and has kids Kelly!

She still in love with you Tate and always will be.

She loves me….yes but she is **not** "in love" with me.

I see it differently Kelly snarls

How do you see it differently? Have you ever been in love Kelly Ann Connors?

Yes….and that was a really nasty tone Kelly snaps.

Tell me who have you been in love with…..that um loved you back? I snap back.

In college with Teddy! Kelly states for the defense

Teddy was and always will be gay Kelly. Yea he is cute but he isn't and never planned to de flower you… my sister. Are you still waiting for Teddy Kelly?

No I know he is gay but he still has been the love of my life.

Ha!

You are the love of Mary's life Tate.

I am not! And she is **married** and has kids!

That doesn't mean **anything** trust me I know.

OK Professor Kelly can I ask you a question?

Sure Mr. Connors

Are you a virgin?

No Tate I am not **why?**

Well because you state things like you know all about these things, that have to do with sex and love, but I know for a fact that while….and I will use this word loosely….you were "dating" Teddy, all you guys ever did was do each other's hair and go shopping. You were his beard Kelly.

Beard? What the hell is a beard?

Yes Kelly it is when a gay man uses a woman to throw off the gay scent to heterosexuals, that they are gay. Usually the men are still in the closet and take the woman to dinners, events, social gathers to dispel the rumors that they like to suck cock.

Why do you always have to be so vulgar? Kelly says with such disdain in her eyes.

I don't know I thrive on the shock value I guess Kelly. A beard is say what you were to Teddy in college. Teddy didn't want people to know he was gay and so he dated **you,** to keep up appearances and such. He didn't want anyone at that point in his life to know he was gay, so he used you as his beard. The problem was that **you** didn't know you were Teddy's beard and that really must have hurt you, when you found out.

(Kelly eyes are misting)

I was devastated….it hurt me so bad. Even now when I actually do go out on a date with someone, I always compare the men to Teddy.

Kelly the difference… is that probably most of those guys actually want to fuck you.

You are so gross Tate pure vulgar!

Kelly can I ask you this? Did you ever wonder or ask yourself why that after dating for over two years, you guys still weren't fucking? Have you ever sucked his dick?

I am good Catholic girl who was and still is waiting for marriage. Like Mom always says once you taste the milk nobody wants to buy the cow.

I know many good Catholic girls that suck dick Kelly and have gone on to get married and have kids. So you are a virgin…there is nothing wrong with that Kelly.

I am not a virgin Tate. After I found out that Teddy was gay I went to a bar and got **really** drunk. I met this guy that night and I told him everything that had happened to me. I told him all about Teddy and he consoled me, by buying me shots. We ended up back at my place and the next thing you know he is inside of me. It hurt a lot but the pain Teddy inflicted was so much worse so I didn't care. I don't remember everything because I was so drunk. I kept saying in my head –take **that** Teddy…I am having sex with a man **too**. Somebody wants me Teddy, I am attractive Teddy. I was so angry at myself for not knowing that Teddy was gay and just kept replaying it over and over in my head. I was so disturbed that I didn't even notice the guy from the bar that I was having sex with was finished and was getting dressed to leave. When I finally realized what was happening he was gone. He barely said goodbye and I don't even remember his name.

Well you had your first one night stand Kelly good for you! I am proud of you. I still can remember my first one night stand!

No Tate what I had was my **first** abortion.…..

What? Kelly why didn't you tell me? I would have been there in a second. You know I tease you and play with you but you're my sister and I love you. OMG Kelly what happened? I never in a million years would have thought.…

Well obviously we didn't use a condom and I was too drunk to know or at that point care. The days or weeks right after I had sex, I didn't even give it a second thought. I engrossed myself in school and that's all the mattered at that point. Teddy finally gave up calling me 17 times a day to apologize after a while and I was just getting some normality back in my life. Then I thought I got the flu and after a week of it, I went to the university hospital. They told me I didn't have the flu but that I was pregnant.

I wasn't in shock this time I just went home, took out the yellow pages, found an abortion clinic; scheduled an appointment and had an abortion. I didn't tell a single soul before, during or up until now. You are the first person I have ever told Tate. Please do not tell Mom because it would kill her. She thinks I am the good one with the chastity belt. Plus she loves being a grandmother.

(I am in shock and I know I have to choose my words very wisely right now.)

Wow Kelly first of all thank you for telling me. I wish you would have called me because I would have been there for you. I am so so sorry that happened to you. No kidding aside I would have flown to Chicago in a second for you Kel. Did you go to therapy or anything after?

They make you go before the procedure to make sure you really want to terminate the pregnancy. They recommend you go after the procedure but I just wanted to block it out of my mind and never think about it again.

Looking directly at Kelly I ask: And how is that working out for you Kelly? Have you dated anyone since? Have you had sex since that first time?

I have dated men over the years and done sexual things but haven't had intercourse.

So you have French kissed?

Yes

Sucked cock?

Tate???????

Kelly continues: I have let a guy or **two** go…..um…..downtown.

Downtown?

Yes um down stairs…..

Down…..Oh OK good for you…I think.(this is not the conversation I thought I would be having right about now.)

I know I am in my mid-twenties Tate and I need to experience a little more sex with guys.

Mid? Oh shut up Tate she laughs I just always worry about what would Mom say.

I think she would say Go for it Girl. Ride that pony! Lick it real good.

You are ridiculous....that is our Mother...the prude.

Kelly no! You are never going to believe this:

Kelly I went into Mom's bathroom to look for Neosporin after the demon cat scratched me. I didn't find Neosporin but I did find Polaroid's

Polaroid's of (Kelly asks confused).....now you cannot say anything to anyone Kelly....

What Tate what?

Technically 3 Polaroid's of Mom......naked...

What?

Wait there is more.....One of them she is fondling her breasts with her tongue out, the next she is giving Ron head and the third they are fucking....

No fucking way!!!!!! You are **such** a liar.

They are still in Mom's medicine cabinet under her condoms?

Her Condoms?

Yup

Who do you think took the pictures?

Probably someone from her new church I say sarcastically as ever.

Kelly and I are both laughing so hard. We are actually enjoying each other's company. I cannot remember the last time we were this intimate with each other and had a deep conversation. We were actually enjoying each other company. I **know** I had to repeat it again. We told each other a secret...Well she did because I am pretty much an open book.

(Looking down at my watch)

OH shit Kelly the church pot luck!!! It is 520 pm and Mom is going to kill us. Let's get to the subway!

Well off we go running to the subway. **F**uck! Time has **Never** flown with my sister. **never!!!!!** You know I am going to have to lie to my Mother.....again...

I don't have a metro card Kelly yells as we are running.

I do Hurry up, you run like a girl!

So do you Tate Kelly snaps

We get into the subway and down onto the tracks lickity split. I read the sign to double check that we were going to head in the right direction this time.

Fuck train hurry up I say as I pace back in forth on the platform.

Finally the train arrives and it is packed. All these "Holiday Shoppers" are on the train and it is filled nut to butt. I don't care if I have to stand on someone's microwave oven or train set, I am getting on the damn train. Kelly and I squeeze on the train, bump some people but not one dirty look or tisk tisk. That is right I am in New York freakin City man!

Kelly you know we are going to have to lie to Mom as to why we are late.

Why can't we just tell her the truth that we lost track of time?

Because she **then** will think we **are** lying. Especially after she hears that we missed Mary as well. Do you think she would believe that you and I spent 2 hours talking, drinking coffee and getting along together?

Good Point Brother so what are you going to tell her?

Me why? Why does it have to be me that lie's to Mom?

Kelly says with a laugh: Well you're better at it Tate, so you do it and I will just follow along. What are you going to tell her the reason why we are late?

OK…hmmm That's easy…I will tell Mom that the subway broke down and we were stuck in a tunnel.

Really??? That is kind of lame Tate.

It happens **all** the time plus if we use anything else she will ask why we didn't use our cell phone and call her.

Good point. I told you that you were better at this than I was my brother.

Come on train move.

Brooklyn Heights

Well at 5:48pm we get out of the train.

Run I yell to Kelly **run!**

We are racing down the street.

Come on Kelly we gotta get home before 6!

I am coming. Sorry Tate I don't spend 3 hours a day in the gym like you do.

OK 602pm we run through the door that we grew up in.

As I enter the house I yell:

Sorry Mom the subway broke down under the Brooklyn Bridge. We were stuck there for over 35 minutes and it was hell.

Mom? Mom? Where are you? As I begin to look all around the house but no Mom.

I turn to Kelly and say did she leave us?

Then I hear her at the top of the stairs, with her hands on her hips **no** I didn't leave you two!

I swing around and my Mother is standing at the top of the stairs like Ava Peron in Evita, doing the scene Don't Cry for me Argentina but she is in a robe and has curlers in it.

Mom what is going on? We are late. The subway st

Save it Tate. The pot luck doesn't start till 7.

But you told us 6?

Yes but I also know how prompt my children are, especially when they have to go somewhere they are not exactly thrilled to go to.

Kelly and I just look at each other like seriously did Mom just pull one over on us?

Go get ready....and Kelly I **am** doing your hair and makeup. This is an important night for me and you need to look pretty.

What about Tate Mom? Kelly pleads

Kelly...Mom states...Tate is one of the most self-absorbed, vanity conscience guys I have ever met and remember I am a fucking hairdresser so I know. He would look cute at a Republican Anti-Gay Convention just to get a compliment.

Let's Move!.

Chapter 17

Friday Night

Get ready and Tate can you please not where a shirt that is 2 sizes too small for you. It makes us look poor.

Mom it shows my muscles….

I don't care what muscles it shows it makes us look poor. It makes me look like I cannot afford to buy my son a shirt that fits him. That he is wearing shirts he grew out of.

Mom it is the style in LA.

Well you're **not** in Los Angeles right now. You are in Brooklyn Heights, New York Tate. If you need a shirt that fits you properly, I am sure Ron can loan one to you.

No Mom it is fine. I am sure I brought something.

Well my Mother informs us that we are leaving in 30 minutes. Do you hear that Kelly? My Mother asks. It is 6:05 pm and we are leaving here at 6:35 pm **sharp!** You use my bathroom Kelly. The last thing I need is World War

3 between you and your brother in the other bathroom. Come on lets go, we leave in exactly a half hour.

A half hour Kelly whines.

Yup even if one side of your head looks like a rats nest we are leaving at 6:35 pm.

What do I have that is not tight…shit… I ponder to myself. Everything in my new LA closet has to be tight..

Well it is now 6:35 pm I am all ready and look spiffy and sharp. I head downstairs to the living room to wait. Ron my Mother's boyfriend is already downstairs.

Can I make you a drink Tate? He asks.

I hesitate for a second but it might be a good idea to lubricate some alcohol before I go to this cult church.

Sure I say!

What can I get you?

Vodka and soda

Coming up…

We small talk a little but the visual of the Polaroid of my Mother sucking on his wanker keeps distracting me. He already thinks I am a moron so he will never catch on to what I am thinking.

6:45 pm comes and the ladies are still not down. At 6:55 pm Ron yells Ladies lets go.

7 pm I yell Mom what happened to 6:35 pm sharp?

7:15 pm they grace us with their presence and they both look Beautiful!!

Tate and Ron will you grab the trays I made from the kitchen. My Mother asks

Sure we say in unison, as we both go into the kitchen and grab the trays.

7:22 pm out the door we all go. Off to the pot luck at my Moms new church. This is going to be so much fun!

Where is Chris Mom?

He is not coming

Why?

Chris has been to the church before; it is you two that I want to show off. They are sick of Chris. He comes with me **all** the time. I think they almost didn't believe that I had two other children.

Chris comes to church with you **all** the time Mom? I ask her in total and utter disbelief

All the time.

Liar I say under my breath. Who is the liar now Mother? Now I know where I get it from.

We walk for about 10 minutes to the church.

Here we are Immaculate Leadership. My Mother exclaims!

I look up kind of in shock.

It is a store front Mom….on Court Street…this isn't a church.

Tate don't you start with me. Don't you dare embarrass me! A church can be anywhere you make it. A church is where love is. It is a place where people who love each other go to rejoice God and bond.

Mom that could be a bathhouse, on any given night as well.

A what Tate? I never took a bath here.

I turn to Ron and my sister and say didn't this use to be a hardware store?

Shhh you are going to get us in trouble Ron says

On your best behavior Tate and you too Kelly, don't let him egg you on. My Mother gives us that look like when we were kids that if you embarrass her —wait till we get home looks. I will never forget that look, maybe because I was always getting **that** look as a kid. Wait I actually still do get that look and I think I am an adult now.

Mom just open the door, we will behave I promise.

As my Mother opens the door and walks in, a lot of people start turning around. They are hugging and kissing and calling my Mother's name. Jackie, Jackie, Jackie, over here Jackie, Jackie is here. Hey Jackie!

My Mother is like the most popular girl in St. Nuts and Bolts. This is surreal. Get the hardware store dig?

This herd of people starts gathering all around us like we have come to feed the poor or we are on the red carpet at a movie premiere..

My Mother starts the introduction saying this is my oldest son Tate, that stands for Tate and this is my daughter Kelly Marie. Tate lives in Los Angeles and is an actor. Kelly lives in Chicago and is an investment banker. Tate just shot a Chevy Silverado commercial and Kelly just got promoted to VP of International Affairs.

While my Mom has become the emcee of the Tate and Kelly Beauty Show, Kelly and I are meeting people and shaking hands. Everybody seems so nice and normal and….**old.** My mother has to be the youngest person here. Is this a church or a nursing home? As I am about to start to make fun and tear it down in my head I hear.

Jackie your son is **Gorgeous** followed by lots of echoes of agreement from all the other old ladies. What a hunk! Look at those muscles! What I would do with those back in my day. I bet the girls just throw themselves at him?

Yes they do my Mother says but……so do the boys. And Tate seems to let the girls fall flat on their asses and catch **all** the guys…

Oh that is too bad Jackie. What a shame but it is the boy's choice, one of the sweet old lady says. She then turns to me and says If you ever change your mind I have a granddaughter for you.

I just smile and nod.

And…..

What about your pretty daughter? She is not um…..gay also?

I can't resist….No ma'am she just looks like a lesbian!

Crickets crickets

Kidding Kidding!

Do you have a boyfriend dear?

Yes….yes I do Kelly exclaims.

No you don't Kelly. (I am such a dick **I know**) Your cat doesn't count as a boyfriend Kelly. I am sure Mrs. Murphy has a grandson that would be **just** perfect for you, as I jump up and down and clap my hands.

I look over at my Mother and even she finds it slightly amusing. I look back over at my Mother and I almost burst into tears. My Mother has this look of pride on her face over my sister and me. She is so proud of us and I just wanted to go over there and hug her. I have to wait my turn because she is very popular at Church of Nuts and Bolts though. Finally I hug her and I whisper in her ear, I love you Mom.

Say cheese! Suddenly I felt like Lindsay Lohan crawling out of a bar at 4 am. There were cameras everywhere taking pictures of me and my Mom. It was like Geriatric Paparazzi. We obliged all of them and took pictures as a family, just me and my sister and took turns with Mom. About 9 of these people asked me for my autograph. This was cool and then one of the men asked me:

Would you like a beer?

Sure I would love one. I say thank you as the man hands me the beer.

It's Michelob Light…..very cool.

As I look around the um…church I see there is **a lot** of food here! I couldn't believe how much good food can be at pot lucks. Well this is my first one unless you count going to Grandma's for leftovers when we were kids.

For the next two hours we had an amazing time. Everyone was so nice. They ALL loved my Mother. They would tell us stories that my Mom would have told them about us. It is strange that they know all these really great things about us. Well I see she certainly doesn't tell them **everything** about us, especially me! They told us that when they have dances my Mother dances all night long. All of the men want to dance with Jackie. Ron likes that because he gets to play cards in the back.

There was a lot of love in this room even if it did smell like old people. I couldn't believe the amount of genuine love in this old hardware store. I was relieved that my Mom has found a group of friends that seem to really enjoy her. Even if some of them were substantially older than her, it still made me feel good to know that she had a support system. Nobody here was looking to steal her money and it certainly wasn't a cult. I am really happy we came to this. The people were great; the food was amazing and free beer. Who could ask for anything more?

OK it is time to go home guys my Mother informs us. My Mother is leaving a party that isn't fully over yet? She is not offering to clean up? **Wow** is it possible that my Mother has changed?

Don't you want to get your night started with your friends or your date Tate?

He didn't call Mom

Hmm I told you and then she pinches my cheek and laughs. Thank you Tate you were a proper gentleman tonight and everybody just loved you.

Kelly how many grandsons phone numbers did you get? My Mom asks genuinely.

A few Mom and even one that lives in Chicago. Mrs. McFarland showed me his picture and he is really cute.

We spend the next 15 minutes saying goodbyes and taking more pictures and then we finally exit the Church of Nuts and Bolts.

Mom that was a lot of fun, they were great!

I told you.

Empty nesters....

Yes you did tell me but I really had to see it to believe it Mom. You are like the prom queen in there. Everybody loves you Mom! Hey what about we all go to Armando's and have a drink?

I thought you were going to go into Manhattan Kelly asks... to see your friends.

Nah I will go tomorrow Kelly. I want to spend time with you guys tonight.

Tate, Ron and I are exhausted and all we want to do is go home and get into bed why don't you two go and have some fun.

Nah Mom I don't want to go to Armando's as Kelly sighed.

I look directly at Kelly and say: Kel don't you want to go and see who got bald, fat and old. We both look amazing. Come on the drinks are on me.

OK let's do it.

I thought you were going for a drink and now it is drinks Tate? As we are saying goodbye to my Mother and Ron..

Mother.....

Go, go have fun, just be safe. I love you both very much and it is nice seeing you two get along. Thank you and she hugs and kisses us both.

As we watch my Mother and Ron walk hand and hand down the street, I hear my Mother lean over to Ron and say what a wonderful night this was.

Ahhhh I love my Mother so much.

Come on Kelly off to Armando's we go!

So we arrive at Armando's and it is as dead as a mortuary. We walk in and there are a few people eating at the tables but the bar is empty. So here we are at the bar and no one is here.

What happened to this place I say to Kelly?

I hear a voice from the back of the bar saying Gentrification of the Heights. I turn around and it is a guy that kinda looks familiar but not sure where from.

Hey what's up would you guys like a drink?

I look at the bartender and say: Not sure, it is kinda dead in here, what happened to this place? I ask. This used to be the "it" place to hang out.

They have made it more of a restaurant now and less of a bar crowd now the bartender we assume just told us.

Oh well we used to live here and now we are just visiting our Mom for the weekend. I inform the bartender.

You went to school here?

Yup Kelly goes and she brushes her hair back. (I think she is flirting)

Where did you go to school? (I think the bartender is flirting back)

We both went to St. Anthony's Kelly says as she flips her hair back again! (yup she is flirting and she is kinda embarrassing herself))

It is closed now the bartender says all informatively

We heard I say (let them flirt on their own time) so where does everybody go to have fun on a Friday night now?.

I look down at my watch and it is only 1115pm on a Friday night.

Go to the Ale House or Last Exit Bar both have cool crowds. Ale House is much more locals though but then everyone moves over to Last Exit.

Thanks Man let's go Kel.

Wait Tate can't we have a quick drink here? (She is looking at me like if you say no I am going to rip something off your body and you are not going to enjoy it)

Sure Kel

Is the bar still open? As I turn to the bartender

Sure what can I get for you?

I bow to my sister with a nice hand gesture what would you like?

Do you have a nice Chardonnay? She asks.

Actually we have two of them. Why don't I have you try both and see which you like better? The bartender asks.

OK she squeals.........

Well the bartender is smitten with Kelly and why shouldn't he be, she looks amazing tonight. You know my Mother did her hair and makeup because Kelly couldn't paint it on **that** good. My Mother was a professional after all.

After Kelly decides on a wine he asks me what I would like to drink.

Absolut Gimlet, straight up and chilled hard.

Sure dude.

He makes my drink quickly and then Kelly and I do a "cheers".

We start talking to the bartender, actually Kelly is turning into Katie Couric with question after question and he doesn't seem to mind..

It turns out Kyle is from Pennsylvania and moved to New York City about a year ago. He went to Carnegie Mellon in Pittsburgh and is 24 years old. He came to New York to be an actor......Imagine that!

My brother here is an actor

I nod my head and before I can even say anything Kelly continues

He graduated from NYU and did Law and Order, the Guiding Light and One Life to Live here in New York. He moved to LA a little over 6 months ago and has a Chevy Silverado commercial running right now. I am so proud of him.

Well now of course the bartender has shifted his attention to me. I am looking at my sister and I am like no wonder you don't have a boyfriend. It is because you deflect all the attention off of you and then onto someone else. I don't even think she realizes she does it.

Cool man so how is LA?

I like it **a lot** but I do miss New York. I left Brooklyn at 18 but my Mom and brother are still here in the Heights.

I am thinking about moving to LA next year. What is your advice?

Well come to LA with a lot of money or have some sort of job lined up before you move there. The waiter and bartending jobs are not as easy to come by as in NYC. Everyone is an actor/musician and everyone likes to have their days free to audition and then work at night. I work as a waiter on Sunset.

Really? You wait tables? Even with having a national commercial running?

It is feast or famine buddy. Gotta put the money away for the famines and the waiter job brings money in consistently.

Good point! Do you have a card or something?

I am on Facebook just look up Tate Connors.

Cool I will man

Kelly are you ready for The Ale House?

I guess so....

Hey guys I am off here in a half hour. I can meet up with you guys.

Definitely !! Kelly yelps and is thrilled again.

Kelly why don't you give him your cell phone number, just in case it is lame or too crowded and we end up at Last Exit?

OK and she is already writing down her number on a napkin. Where did she get a pen that fast from?

OK see you guys soon!

We shake hands with the bartender, well I shake hands but Kelly gives him a big hug and then out the door we go.

Tate what side of the street do you think the cute bartender shops on?

She is learning my lingo....

Yours Kelly, I say with a little bewilderment.

I thought so...I was just getting a little nervous that he liked you.

Because you deflect....

I what?

Deflect....you see Kelly, I noticed something about you tonight.

Oh here we go what did I do wrong now Tate????

Just listen to me...

Go ahead....

Clearly when we walked in he was totally into you and I was invisible to the bartender. He starts showing you a ton of attention and barely acknowledges me. I am fine with that...it was actually nice to see you get some attention Kelly. I think that made you nervous though.

No it didn't! Kelly exclaims

Then why would you tell a struggling actor that is clearly into you that your brother, who is sitting right next to you, is an actor? Not only that but then you start reciting my resume. Guess where his interest has just gone??? Yup onto me! Then you will turn around and say I stole him or it is all about me, but it is not...you just gave him away. Do you get where I am coming from?

Kind of....and then she sighs

Kelly, I would have been perfectly content just sitting at Armando's listening to you two talk. You do it all the time with me being the attention whore I can be. You have to make situations like these all about you sometimes and stop deflecting off of you, and onto someone else. I think it is honestly a defense mechanism that you have built up to avoid getting hurt. OK so listen when Kyle gets to the Ale House and if he wants to talk about acting with me, I am going to say hit me up on Facebook and we will talk when I get back to LA.

OK?

Thanks Tate Kelly says and she actually hugs me.

We walk about 5 blocks to the Ale House and chit chat about the old neighborhood and some memories that we have of the old hood.

It has changed so much as I turn to my sister.

I don't think that the Heights has changed **that** much. I just think that maybe we changed that much. Kelly says to me.

Ahhh the Ale House and it looks jumping in there. We walk in and we see lots and lots of familiar faces. We find a table in the middle of the bar and all of a sudden Jolene from Gristede's yells:

OMG it is Tate and Kelly Connors!! How are you guys? OMG it has been forever! What a loooong time guys! How the fucks are you two? Haven't seen you two in a lawng time?

We are good. We are visiting Mom for Thanksgiving. Kelly answers really quickly

Holy shit how is ya Mom? I love her!

Kelly says she is good same old Mom.

Let me get the waitress we need shots! Jolene shouts

Before we know it Jolene is bring over the waitress. Maxine ya gotta meet my friends from elementary school. I graduated with Tate and his younger sister Kelly and I were girl scouts together!

Hey there what can I get for you guys? (She couldn't have cared if we were visiting from Mars)

Do you have a good Chardonnay?

I look at Kelly…Kelly?

Huh Maxine goes.

So I say a white wine?

Oh yeah we do! As I nod to Kelly to say yes.

And what about for you handsome?

Just a draft light beer! (My ego is popping)

And shots Jolene shouts

OK Jager or tequila? Maxine asks

Both Jolene shouts!

It is a good thing I have a credit card on me because this is going to be a long night I think to myself, but it will be fun. Crazy Jolene….she has not changed a bit. I figured she would be knocked up or have a litter of kids by now but nope.

So Tate when did you get all those muscles? Jolene inquires.

When he moved to LA Kelly taunts….

Holy Shit you live in LA?

Yup

Wow that is so cool! Jolene is really impressed with me.

What are you doing out there in LA?

Well you know he was on the soap here in New York Kelly interjects.

Yeah but you played like the doorman….Are you acting in LA now Tate? Jolene inquires

No not really….I muster

Oh my brother is being Bashful Jolene, he has a national Chevy Silverado commercial running right now! It is running all over the country. I just saw it during Monday night's episode of The Bachelor and it runs all day long too.

Really she squeals!!

Drinks are here Maxine states.

After Maxine gives us our drinks and our 2 shots a piece she asks if we want to start a tab and they all look at me.

Sure I say agreeable

I need a credit card, Maxine says clearly showing us all how much she hates her current job situation..

Jolene whirls around angrily and says I am good for it Maxine!!

I know you are J but I don't know him. (As she points right at me)

Jolene points at me and says he is an actor how do you not know him?

If luck would have it any other way the music stopped at the exact same time Jolene said this, so now the entire bar is looking at me like whom the hell is this douche bag??

Jolene it is OK. I turn to Maxine as I hand her my credit card and say.

It's cool I have been a waiter. I have been burned on a bar tab or two in my day, so I get it about the credit card.

Thanks sweetie shall I bring you another beer?

Sure by the time you get back I will be ready.

Let's do these shots guys! Jolene yells and very loudly

Jolene gets up and says To Tate and Kelly Back in the Heights!

Cheers!!!

I hate shots ugh….and I still have one more to do.

Tate you do the next toast!

Ok so I pick up the tequila shot and say: to old friends, Family and the Heights…. Cheers that you can still come home!

Cheers!!!!

Hey guys!!

(Kyle is here)

What's up? Can I join you guys?

Sure and before he can even make a choice of where to sit I gesture him towards Kelly.

Hi Handsome I am Jolene.

Kyle reaches out his hand and is very cordial. (She is blinking her eyes, pouting her lips and has probably got her legs wide open with no panties on under the table). Jolene would fuck a gnome if it had a penis.

That Jolene is still a whore…gotta love her though, as I look on and smile.

I case the bar from my seat and it is not as local as I would have thought. As a crowd itself it was definitely a 20 something crowd but it was very white collar. They might be locals now, but they didn't grow up here. Brooklyn Heights has changed dramatically over the past 10 years and it is a whole different place since I lived here. As the rents and property values in Manhattan started to soar more and more people started to explore the outer boroughs. Since

Brooklyn Heights was one subway stop away from downtown Manhattan, it became a very desirable place to live. Now don't get me wrong it had always been desirable but not as gentrified like the bartender Kyle told us earlier in the evening. The Heights felt like a community just a stone throw from the big lights of Manhattan. It was very easy to access with almost every subway line going through it. It was only a $10 dollar cab ride over the Brooklyn Bridge as well…

As I continue to case the bar I see a somewhat familiar face, Tony Ianucci. I have not seen Tony since probably the 11th grade in Dagostino's. He used to work there. I wonder if he still does. He looks good. Actually who am I kidding he looks as fucking hot as he did back then. Tony and I were actually really good friends until his parents forbid him from hanging out with me. Now it is not what you think….it is **worse**.

Tony was dating this girl Gina Lamendola and she was kinda a slut. She was always flirting with guy's right in front of him and **always** putting him down, like he wasn't good enough for her majesty. I felt so bad for Tony but he was like a lap dog, that would just keep taking it. I know he was taking it because he was getting laid but come on enough is enough. She would downright humiliate him and then turn it like it was always Tony's fault the whole time. Every last penny he made at Dagostino's he would spend on her and she wouldn't appreciate it one bit. Nothing was ever good enough for the Royal Princess and she really bugged me. So you can say that well Gina and I didn't exactly get along, it would only get worse when I saw her on the Promenade kissing another guy. I wasn't spying on her and it was totally on accident that I saw this, as I walked my dog Pepper. I told Tony about it but he didn't believe me and said I was jealous of the time he was spending with Gina. One day after another humiliating defeat Tony received from Gina and he stormed away, I ask her:

Do you really like my friend Tony? Or are you just using him? You are so mean to him.

Mind your own fucking Business Tate. Why are you always around? God get a life. You are such a loser. I will do, say and fuck anyone I want to and you cannot do a damn thing about it. I know you told Tony about what you think you saw on the promenade but it wasn't what you think it was. I was with my cousin asshole. Tate, Tony will believe anything I say to him, so stop trying to get into our shit. I will get rid of you soon, one way or another. What Tony doesn't know won't hurt him plus he is getting "some", so he is blind to any and all extracurricular activities I have on the side. Gina was beginning to win the battle so I just stepped away. I stopped calling and made excuses not to hang out with them anymore.

Tony wouldn't believe me that she was cheating on him. We fought about this for months and I finally just gave up. Gina **had** won. Finally about 3 months later he caught her cheating on him and broke up with her. He called me to apologize and we were cool again. We didn't see each other that much after that and soon would never see each other again.

You see Tony was my friend from the neighborhood but I went to high school in Manhattan. As time would pass I was slowly spending more and more time with my friends in Manhattan anyway. I was going to school there, taking after school classes at Broadway Dance and just embracing my life outside of Brooklyn.

Well one day I get a phone call and it is Tony.

You are never going to believe what the fuck Gina did now.

What did she do?

She mailed me a picture of her giving another guy head?

What? Who is the guy?

All you see is the guy's dick and her face with her mouth over his dick.

No way Tony! I have to see this. What a skank she is. Come over and bring the pic.

I will be right over and Tony quickly hangs up the phone.

Not even ten minutes later Tony is at my front door. I ask him in and he says his hellos to my Mom and we race upstairs to my room. He pulls out the picture and I couldn't believe my eyes. It is Gina giving this guy a blowjob. What a classless bitch…Who would do this? As I look at the picture I think --Wow she has a great future in porn ahead of her but …will probably be knocked up by 17. Tony is visibly upset about this and he should be.

Do you want to get even with her? I ask very calmly

Dude I am not going to have sex with a girl and have you take snap shot of it.

No way dude! Not at all what I was thinking Tony! Just leave the picture with me for a day and I promise you I will "blow" her out of the water. Notice the pun on blow?

OK but don't do anything stupid with it Tony barks.

Trust me I know what I am doing.

That is what scares me Tate.

Do you want to stay for dinner?

OK

Hang on….Ma can Tony stay for dinner?

Of course Tate just make sure Denise is OK with it.

My Mom said it is cool if your Mom is cool.

Cool let me call her.

It was nice to catch up with my friend through dinner. I actually really missed him.

Well the next day at school I snuck into the computer room and I made 20 color copies of the picture. I take one of the copies and I mail it directly to Gina's Mother. Now this is genius because this was way before the internet and social network were even heard of. Do I get some props?

I get home from school and Tony is waiting for me.

Well?

Here is the original back as I hand the picture back to Tony.

The original?

Yup I made a copy and mailed it to Gina's Mother….

What? That is awesome!! How did you think of that? Tony asks me while he is high fiving me and laughing

Tony the less you know the better. I tell him.

2 days later I get a phone call from Tony:

Someone threw a brick through our front window dude.

Ahh I guess Gina's Mom got the picture and someone is not happy about it! Ha Phase 2....is next!

What there is no Phase 2!

Just hang tight my friend, hang tight. What is Gina's phone number?

Why Tate?

Because --I am going to make things right with Gina.

You promise Tate?

Oh I promise Tony!

OK 718 242-5555

Cool talk tomorrow I will let you know how it goes.

Dude **please** don't get me into **any** trouble.

I won't.

Bye.

Now… what Tony doesn't know is that I made 20 copies of the picture and I mailed one to Gina's mother and I gave Tony back the original. That means I have 19 left. Well I took 10 pictures from my stash and wrote on them "For a Good Time Call Gina 718 242-5555."

I then snuck out of my house at 3 am and stapled the color copies, on every telephone pole in the surrounding 10 blocks of our neighborhood. I then went home, snuck back in and went back to sleep. I was gleefully happy on my way to school the next day because I was witnessing the telephone poles drawing crowds of curious passerby's and it was only 7am in the morning. I knew of at least 3 telephone poles that were going to be really hard to tear down the pictures easily!

I'll teach you -- you stupid bitch. Now everyone will know you are a whore. I say to myself, as I am walking to the subway.

Yet again when I came home later that day from school, Tony was franticly pacing up and down the sidewalk, as he was smoking a cigarette.

I didn't know you smoked Tony.

Tate what did you do?

What are you talking about? I ask but I knew what he was talking about.

The telephone poles Tate!!!

Oh yeah I say now everyone knows Gina is a whore.

Well I got jumped at school today and they were really going to fuck me up so I told them…I told them it was you….

OK.

That's all? You are not pissed at me? Tony asks with bewilderment.

Nope. I am not afraid.

Well the next day came and went with no incident or so I thought. That was until I heard my Mother on the telephone with Chrysler saying that someone snapped the windshield wipers off her car and I then knew **exactly** who did it. Gina Lamendola! Boy I was pissed and I said to myself, OK Gina you want to fucking play, let's fucking play. I took the remaining 9 color copies I had of the picture left and mailed them to all of her neighbors. I wrote on the picture "do you know you are living next door to a prostitute?" I sealed every envelope with pride and dumped them into the mail box on my way to school the next day.

About 4 days later there is a knock on the front door of my house and my Mother has answered the door. Well it is two police officers. **gulp**... I hear my Mom talking to the police officers and then I hear those 6 dreaded words:

Tate Connors get down here!!!!

What's up Mom? I say as calm and collective as possible while coming down the stairs.

Come down here Tate, you are being arrested for pandering pornography of a minor?

What?

Next thing I know I am handcuffed, getting my Miranda rights read and in a heap of trouble. I am down in the Brooklyn police station and I **know** it must be bad because **even** my Father is here.

Well the next thing we find out is that Gina is telling her parents that Tony and I forced her to pose for the picture in question while I took the picture.

Did she just say forced? I ask. Hell no! That is complete bullshit I yell! That little skank mailed the picture to Tony after he caught her cheating on him. We didn't force that tramp to do anything. (I am yelling now)

Tate Connors you better check yourself my Dad says to me very angrily.

Um yes that is true officer Tony murmurs but Tate decided to do everything else, he stammers.

You weasel I say to myself —you threw me in front of the bus. OK it is on now.

Is that true son? The officer asks me.

Do I need a lawyer?

Answer the question Tate because if you don't you going to need more than a lawyer, when I am done with you. My Father stated.

It is true I did it all, but we didn't take the picture. She did that with people other than us. I will drop my pants and show you that is **not** my penis. I don't think it is Tony's either but I am not a 100% on that one. She mailed the picture to Tony's house. Check with the post office I say sounding like a lawyer.

Gina is crying and acting all wounded, like she is the victim here. Stupid slut is just crying because she got caught.

I still have the envelope and the original picture Tony meekly says.

He opens up his book bag and hands the picture and the envelope over to the officer. The officer looks at the picture for a second and then starts analyzing the envelope. He turns the envelope over to Gina's Mother and asks:

Is this your daughters hand writing?

Mrs. Lamendola takes one look at the envelope and goes **Gina** mija how could you do this? You are going to the convent. I am so sorry officers but these boys still went too far.

Gina is bawling and crying now.

Stupid bitch, I say under my breath.

The officer turns to Tony, Gina and myself and says I want to speak to all of your parents, so you need to come with me.

We follow him and he puts all three of us in a jail cell and locks the door.

Gina is bawling, Tony is whimpering and I am shaking because my Father is going to kick the ever loving shit out of me. That is "If" I ever get out of here that is.

Are we going to jail? Tony asks

No they are just trying to scare the shit out of us just relax Tony I say as calmly as possible.

I hate you Tate Gina hisses.

Right back at ya Gina! You couldn't have just walked away a classy ho right? I knew you were a fucking whore the day I met you. I hiss right back at Gina.

Please Tate stop kidding yourself, you are in fucking love with Tony ya homo!

Fuck you Gina!

You wish Tate, you wish!

I thought you said I was a homo Gina, then why **would** I wish?

Just shut up both of you Tony snarls at us both.

I don't really remember what happened next, I do remember I got an ass whipping from my Dad, when we got home and that I was punished for what seemed like forever. I do remember Tony's Mom Denise, coming up to me and saying that I was a vial human being, who needs physiatrist treatment. She also said that she never ever wanted Tony to be around me again. She said she forbid him from ever being my friend again. I know at some point my Mother and Tony's Mom got into it as well but it is all fuzzy now. It was a life time ago..

Like I said I got into a ton of trouble, I never saw Tony again, till now standing at the bar. As for Slut Gina, I think she was shipped away somewhere. I did feel a little bad for Gina's poor Mother though. Every time she walked down the street or went shopping in the supermarket, people would stop and stare at her. She was the Mother of the whore whose daughter takes pictures sucking cock.

Tate, Tate, Tate

Huh what?

(Kelly is shaking me) You were off in space or in Tate's never, never land my sister said. Do you want one more beer before we go?

Sure I said and I look up and Tony is staring directly at me now.

Tony Ianucci is here, I whisper to Kelly.

Where?? As she then so obviously turns her head up and down like a crazed drunk lunatic. I cannot believe I am related to her sometimes.

My stupid sister (ugh) because now he is going to know I am talking, about him.

He got divorced about a year ago Jolene informs us. He is here almost every night. He is back living with his parents. His bitch of an ex-wife really did a number on the poor guy. She took everything from the poor bastard.

I say out loud to the table: I see something's don't change. He attracts the same type of women over and over. I wonder if she was a dirty whore too.

OMG like Gina Lamendola, I totally forgot about that!!! Jolene laughs

What? Kyle asks

Nothing it was a long time ago. I say

Are you going to say anything to him Tate? Kelly asks

Nope.

Let's get out of here. I am tired Kelly.

I ask Maxine for the check and it wasn't bad. $112.00 so I say, I got it and put it on my credit card. Jolene and Kyle offer to give me money but I honestly just want to get the hell out of there. I want to go home, it's been a long day.

Maxine takes what seems like forever to bring back the credit card receipt for me to sign. When she finally does I sign the receipt. I leave a 25% tip and I just want to get out of there.

Kelly you ready?

I am going to stay and finish my drink with Kyle.

I will walk her home, Kyle says.

OK

Do you want some company Tate? Jolene aggressive suggest sex.

I was so tired and was just whacked with a blast from the past so I just turned to Jolene and said:

No Jolene, I am gay…..

Wow didn't see that one coming. It's cool but around these parts when a guy pays for the drinks, he usually wants to be paid in…

It's cool. Goodnight and I give her a hug.

Be safe Kel and I will see you tomorrow.

She actually gets out of the comfortable wedge with Kyle and gives me a hug and kiss. I guess as grownups Kelly and I can actually get along. Yeah as long as we live in separate cites and we don't see each other that often. I guess it is possible.

I am trying to make it to the door without making eye contact with Tony. Did you ever have that feeling when you know someone was watching you? Well I was having it now. I heard him yell Tate as I got close to the door but I pretended like I didn't hear it. I opened the door and scurried out.

I was kind of in shock because after not seeing Tony Ianucci for over 10 years, I completely blocked him out of my mind. After seeing him from across the bar and having that flashback when we were teenagers, a voice started ringing in my head. It was Gina Lamendola and something she had said when we were sitting in that jail cell. It was like a tidal wave hit me and I was gasping for air.

Tony Ianucci was the first guy I ever feel in love with…...

Tate…...Tate…...Tate

I didn't want to turn around because I knew the voice like I had a conversation with him yesterday on the phone. It was Tony Ianucci. So I turn around and it is Tony.

Hey Tony how are you? (What else could I say?)

I am good. **Wow** it has been what 10 years now? Tony asks

I think a little bit more but about that.

What have you been up to? I see your Chevy Silverado commercial running all the time? I just saw it tonight.

You did?

Yeah! Every time in plays, while I am watching TV with my Mom, she just looks at me funny and sighs. He says with a laugh

Are you sure we are allowed to be talking to one another? I ask. Didn't your Mother forbid us from ever seeing each other again?

Haha we were kids back then man. My Mom says that she bumps into your Mom all the time at the market. I saw her a few months back on the promenade and we talked for a little bit. She keeps us up to date on what is going on with you with your move to LA and your career. She didn't tell you that we talk all the time?

No.

We always tell her to say hello from us.

Yup. Well nice seeing you Tony. I gotta go.

Where are you going?

Home, it has been a really long day..

Hey have a drink with me for old time sakes? Tony pleads

I am tired Tony and I really just want to go home. I have been up since 6am and haven't stopped all day, trying to stuff so many things in. It started with getting attacked by a mean giant cat and just ended with Jolene propositioning me.

Come on… please? I don't want to wait another 10 years to see what you are doing.

Friend me on Facebook. I tell Tony

Come one…One drink.

I look at Tony and God I forgot how gorgeous his eyes were.

Come on back in. Tony pleads

OK

Now it was getting late and the place had started to thin out a bit, so it was easier to find a space to sit and talk.

What do you want to drink? Tony asks me.

I couldn't have another beer because I was feeling bloated from all the beer I had tonight.

I will take a vodka and soda.

Cool.

He comes back from the bar with the drinks and we start to talk. I glance over and Jolene has moved on to her next male victim. My sister and Kyle are full on making out right where I left them. Good for Kelly I am glad she is getting some..

Tony looks over at Jolene and says something's never change huh?

We both laugh and it is just awkward now.

So.......what has been going on in your life? I ask Tony.

Well I got married about 4 years ago and divorced last year. No kids but I am back living with my Mom. Dad died a few years back from cancer. I am now the General Manager of the Dagostino's on Henry Street. Not as exciting as you but am I still young, so I still have some time but I turn 28 in January.

I just turned 27 in September. 3 years from 30 yikes!!

So how is LA? Tony asks

I like it Tony, I really do. There was a huge adjustment in the beginning but now I genuinely love it. Not every single thing about LA but for the most part, I do love it. Don't get me wrong, I love New York but I guess when you grow up someplace the opposite attracts. At least it does for me.

I see your brother and his little girls every once in a while. He is really good with them. He is not very friendly with me though...

Well they have a boy on the way and he is not that friendly with me either, so don't take it personally. He is just an asshole..

Wow that's great they are finally having a boy Congrats!!! Do you have any desire to have kids at all Tate?

Nope!

Not ever?

Nope…..um Tony I don't know but let me ask you, in your several vast conversations with my Mother, did she tell you anything else about me?

Like?

OMG this is hard and I really haven't told anyone from the neighborhood, nevertheless my first crush **ever** but here goes. I take a deep breath and say to myself that, if he tells me to fuck off you fag, I will just get up, leave and never ever think back on him again, but I had to see his reaction.

Tony I am gay.….

Tony puts this smirk on his face and says You gay? Never? Wow? That's a Shocker! And he is mocking me now. I have pretty much known since we were 14 Tate. Don't ask me how but I just did.

Oh Ok. (I am a little wounded)

Tony looks at me with this straight solemn face and says I think I am gay too. Actually I don't **think** I am gay, I know I am

What? You are gay???

Yes I kind of figured it out halfway through my marriage and it just went downhill from there. I experimented and was kinda on the DL but I just couldn't do it to my wife Michelle anymore. I told her the truth and it was ugly for a while. No woman wants to hear that there husband is gay. She hated me for a while but we are actually friends now. The divorce was pretty amicable. Her brother beat the shit out of me but I deserved it. I knew before the wedding that I was gay.

Wow does your Mother know?

Yea but she still hopes I will change my mind and thinks it is a phase.

My Mother has finally given up that hope. (We both laugh!) So Tony what are you doing at a straight Ale House on a Friday night in Brooklyn Heights?

Hey don't knock it…

I just looked at him like cut the bullshit.

To be honest….I was…um…kinda stalking you.

What?

I heard you were in town through my Mom. She saw Kelly and your Mom shopping on Monday and then I saw your Mom at Dagostino's the next day. She was so excited to see you. I think she was getting ready to go to the airport to get you.

Fast forward to how you ended up at The Ale House. I sarcastically ask Tony.

I "accidently" bumped into your Mom and her boyfriend and she said you guys were going to Armando's. So I was going to accidently bump into you at Armando's when I saw you and your sister walking down Henry Street and turned on Atlantic. I figured where you were going,

Well we were right over there for 2 hours…

I know.

Why didn't you come over Tony?

Will you have dinner with me tomorrow night?

426

Holy shit this is not happening. I gotta go home.

Tate please?

Even just as a friend. Tony is pleading again

You know begging is not attractive Ton, as I tease.

Please have dinner with me.

Come on let's get out of here before Kelly comes up for air and blabs to my Mother that I saw you. You know my Mother wasn't too thrilled with you either after what went down with Gina either. My Father beat me so bad I couldn't sit down for a week. The last thing I need is Kelly blabbing to my Mom about me talking to you.

Your Mother **loves** me. Will you go out with me tomorrow?

Will you just chill the fuck up and let me think. This is a lot to take in Tony! Man can you slow the fuck down. What are you Mike Gay-syn(trying to be funny with the Tyson tie in). I already got a punch in the stomach, that you are divorced and gay. What are you trying to do, knock me out?

Come on dinner. I will take you to The River Café.

No, fuck no, even if I agree to have dinner with you we are going far, far out of Brooklyn.

So you are thinking about it?

About what? I say.

That you will have dinner with me

I didn't say that!

But you want to!

(I am walking as fast as I can)

Thank God I lived around the corner from this bar. I stopped in front of my house and I asked Tony for his cell phone number. After we properly exchanged cell numbers, I turn to him and say I will call you tomorrow. Well I don't know if it was the combination of 3 Michelob Lights at the church, the Absolut Gimlet at Armando's, the 3 beers and 2 shots at the Ale House, plus the vodka soda with Tony but the next thing I know, I am full on making out with Tony right in front of my house. Wait it is **not** my house anymore, it is my Mother's. I don't know how long we were going at it but it was 3 am and there wasn't a soul on the street. It felt like it could have been a second but was probably more like an hour but he was an amazing kisser.

Wow it looks like both of us got lucky tonight….I hear the familiar voice.

Shit!!!!!!

We pull away from each other and here comes Kyle and Kelly sauntering down the street and Kelly is grinning from ear to ear..

Hi Tony Kelly cheers!

Hi Kelly Tony somewhat mortified says back.

I am frozen and I just say to Tony, I will call you tomorrow and we awkwardly hug and he starts walking backwards staring at me. I try and ignore him and I just say goodnight and nice to meet you Kyle.

Yeah you too Kyle cheers.

I am going in. I say to Kelly.

Me too and she slobbers a kiss all over Kyle.

Come on Kelly I don't want to wake Mom up twice hearing the door open and closing.

We slowly open the door and close the door behind us quietly.

Kelly turns to me and is like Holy Shit Tony Ianucci is freakin gay??

U huh? !!!

He wants to take me on a date tomorrow night Kelly!

So does Kyle! We should double!!!

No Kelly, I date mano o mano!

What?

Never mind, Goodnight!

Night!

Don't you dare tell Mom. I hiss at Kelly.

Tate and Tony sitting in a tree K I S

Kelly I will kill you in your sleep I swear…shut up. (Yelling but whispering)

I will I promise.

Night.

I brush my teeth and get ready for bed. Is this a dream? Did this night really happen? Do you know how many times I masturbated to the thought of having sex with Tony Ianucci…. Well I passed out before I could even answer that question….Or I was way too tired to count that high.

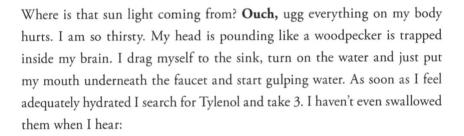

Chapter 18

Saturday in New York - somebody pinch me

Where is that sun light coming from? **Ouch,** ugg everything on my body hurts. I am so thirsty. My head is pounding like a woodpecker is trapped inside my brain. I drag myself to the sink, turn on the water and just put my mouth underneath the faucet and start gulping water. As soon as I feel adequately hydrated I search for Tylenol and take 3. I haven't even swallowed them when I hear:

Tatey are you up?

Yes Mom I am up.

Well do you want some lunch? She says sarcastically

Lunch as I look over at the clock

Holy shit it is 2:24 pm. I slept for like 10 hours.

OK Mom I will have some lunch. I will be right down. I pick up my cell phone and there are 2 texts from Tony. One at 10:45 am and one at 1:30 pm. The first one says how great last night was blah blah but the second one? You can tell by his tone that he is getting a little insecure, even asking if he scared me away. HA Tony Ianucci one of the best looking guys I have ever met, is getting insecure over me Ha…he needs glasses! I text him that I just woke up and that I would call him in an hour. He immediately texted me back…Cool…Ok.

Kelly is downstairs and she looks perfectly fine.

I heard you played matchmaker for your sister last night? My Mom leans in and kisses me. You smell like a brewery again Tate!

Mom after 1 beer you say I smell like a brewery.

Kelly is smirking at me but you can tell she is happy.

Mom is there any coffee left?

Who drinks coffee after 10 am Tate?

I do Mom!

Ok Tate I will make you some coffee! Just relax and have a seat. Are you sure you don't want decaf Mr. Snappy Pants has a hangover.

Sorry Mom.

Oh Tylenol please just kick in already.….. please.………I beg of you because I cannot take my Mother and Sister with a hangover.

So Mr. Matchmaker, Kelly has a date tonight. How did you introduce them?

I didn't introduce them Mom. I just taught Kelly how **not** to deflect off of herself and onto someone else. Plus you made her look great last night..

What does deflect mean? Is that a walk or a sex thing Tate? Please do not tell me it is perverted or something that is going to horrify me. Here is your coffee.

No Mom, never mind as I just give Kelly a dimwhit face to mock my Mother.

Mom Tate has a date tonight too. Kelly quirps in.

With whom Tate? The Mexican finally called you? My inquisitive Mom asks and she is going to stare me down until I tell her.

Just with an old friend that I bumped into last night.

What old friend? Do I know him?

Yes Mom you do.

Who is it?

I look at Kelly like why couldn't you keep your fucking mouth shut. I swear I want to tell my Mother she was making out like a cat in heat at the bar but she has waaay to much ammunition on me.

Tony Ianucci Mom.

Tony IanuccI Tate??? He is my grocer!

I know Mom, he told me he sees you all the time, why didn't you tell me that you and Tony talk all the time?

I don't know…so is this a date that you are going on with Tony?

Why Mom? Why do you ask?

Because you know he is gay right? That is why he got divorced from his wife. Did you know his father, died of colon cancer Tate?

Mom how do you know this and why haven't you ever told me? You tell me things like when the neighbors slip was showing at church but you don't tell me that Tony Ianucci is Gay or living back in the neighborhood!!

Because it is gossip….plus I just cannot see that big strapping, good looking man as gay. I just can't.

But you can believe I am, Mom?

Please Tate you forced me to believe it with you, you basically choked it down my throat. I just, just have trouble with Tony. I just cannot believe he is gay.

Kelly chimes in:

Well believe it Mom because I saw Tony and Tate making out first hand last night in the front of the house. It was full on tongue and all Mom. Kelly states with her breaking news voice that to this day still makes me cringe.

What? They were kissing in front of my house? Oh dear what will the neighbors think? I am now running a brothel!! My Mom shrieks

Kelly you better start writing your obituary now bitch because I am going to kill you.

I need to go lay down. My Mom says with utter defeat in her voice.

Hey Mom before you do.

Yes. Tate.

Kelly was making out with this guy at The Ale House for over 2 hours and he even had his hand up her shirt. (Take that bitch!)

Kelly Marie!!!!!!!!!!!!

Mom don't listen to him you know he lies….

I am going to lie down. You kids are going to put me in an early grave. You know you kids leave on Monday but I live here 365 days a year. I am never going to be able to shop at Dagostino's or have lunch at the Ale House ever again! Thank you very much!

Mom I love you….

I love you too Mom Kelly chirps in.

I am going to call your brother at least he knows how to conduct himself in public.

I turn to Kelly and I say yeah call our brother who knows how to control himself in public. Wait till his birth control method fails again and soon he has 8 kids!!!

We both laugh!

You are such a bitch Kelly why did you tell her? I ask

I learned from the best Tate plus I enjoy watching you squirm! I don't get to do it that often, so when I have a window to embarrass you I can't help it…I just **have** to open it…I just do.

But I had ammunition on you?

Yeah but I knew she wouldn't believe you…..

Well played little sis…well played!

Shit! I gotta go call Tony but where can I get some privacy in this house? Ahh the hell with it, I am just going to call him from the living room.

As I am fumbling in my pocket for the piece of paper with his phone number on it I then remember that he texted me already and that his name came up. When the hell did Tony Ianucci program his number into my cell phone? Let me find out. Man I hate drunk blackouts…

So I call and Tony answers on the first ring:

It's about time you called me back dude.

Dude what's with the word dude? I thought that word was reserved for heterosexual men drinking beer and playing pool?

Sorry…um what do you want me to say?

Not dude I state.

Well in the most effeminate voice I have **ever** heard in my life Tony goes how is this?

Hey Girl what ya doin? Wanna go shoppin and um get our nails done? Like right now Miss Thang....

Shut up dude....I say sarcastic as ever. If you really talked that way I **would** slap the gay out of you. Seriously I would!

Ha ha when did you get to be so funny?

I have always been funny Tony it's a gift....

So am I taking you out for dinner tonight?

Why don't we take each other out my friend?

Because then it will be more difficult to get into your pants. I am taking a page out of Jolene's playbook on sex. Tony flirts with me

OK I am staying with **my** Mother and you **live** with **your** Mother. So hypothetically where would this into the pants actually happen? I am not doing anything revolving sex on my front porch or **your** car Tony. I am not 16 years old and looking to go to Make Out Point. On that note I must tell you....I am really easy though and I have wanted to sleep with you since I was 16,.

Easy? Tony is confused What?

Um sex....

Ha you're a riot dude but I haven't thought all the way through this date yet. Maybe we could get a hotel room or something?

A hotel? If I do not come home tonight my Mother is going to have the National Guard out looking for me Tony.

Well...um...maybe we could get one of those hourly hotels or something?

Tony....I said I was easy....but I am not a hooker....

You kill me dude Tony says while laughing on the other end of the phone.

I had forgotten how cute his laugh was. It was very masculine but with a hint of a girl screeching. I missed that laugh.

Tony I would actually like to see a Broadway show tonight. Maybe we could grab dinner before the show and then after the show go have a few drinks somewhere. What do you think?

Hey I want to be the man in this relationship he says mocking me. Can we see Wicked??

The manly man...just picked Wicked....Wicked is his first choice to see on Broadway. Can you be any gayer? What are your backup's Momma Mia and La Cage? I taunt.

Quiet there Tate plus I already saw La Cage...

HA...cute!

Well Tony takes charge of the conversation and starts to say let me get the tickets and you pick up dinner?

Sure but it better not be no cheap ass seats Ianucci

BEEP BEEP

Oh shit that's my call waiting Tony hang on....

I look down at the call waiting and just about terded in my willies. It was Antonio from TGIF calling me. Shit when it rains it pours men huh?.

Of course I had to answer it. Would you expect anything less of me?

Hello....I says as I switch my call waiting on my phone

It's um Antonio...we met....last Wednesday at the restaurant. TGIF's? You were there with your Mom and I was your waiter and

Wow Antonio....you learned how to use a phone? A day late but you learned. I am so proud of you. (I can be such a sarcastic bitch)

Ha sorry I had to work a double yesterday and I left your number at home. You see I just had the lunch shift and I planned on calling you when I got home. Well 3 servers called in sick and they kinda forced me to work a double. It was insane and I didn't even have time to call one of my roommates to find your number in our room. By the time I got home it was 1 am. Now I saw how insane your Mom got after you ordered a glass of wine for lunch so I could only imagine how she would react if I called you at 1am.

HA she wouldn't have heard it. I was out and I probably wouldn't have heard it anyway but good call on the Mother thing. If she heard it she would have flipped. Did you say roommate and our room?

Yes there are 5 of us in a studio apartment in Astoria Queens...

Really? How did I know that?

Um what I don't understand. Antonio stammers

Never mind what's up? I ask Antonio.

Well I am meeting…

Beep Beep

Hold on that is my call waiting Antonio I will be right back.

Ok

Click…

Wow you have patience Tony. I annoyingly state.

I hate to be kept on hold Tate. So do we agree that I get the tickets and you pick the restaurant, is that a deal Tate ?

Agreed. Can I call you back Tony?

Who are you on the phone with?

Um….my Mother! (Ugh why did I say that?)

Isn't she in the same house as you?

Um yes…but she is at the store and wanted to see if we had enough coffee.

I am at work at Dagostino's is she here? I can pop out of my office and say a quick hey Mrs. Connors.

No...she is at Gristede's and is going to get really mad if I don't get right back to her.

Call me back Tate.....

OK

Click

You there?

I am here Antonio says. You were saying?

I am meeting a friend for dinner and then we are going to see a Broadway show. I inform Antonio

What show?

I think Wicked.

Ahh I loved it! I saw it when Kristen Chenoweth came back for 6 weeks on a limited run and it was awesome. You do know that Kristen Chenoweth won the Tony for it right? She was the original.

Yup got it.

So what are you guys doing after the show? Do you want to grab a drink?

I think we could do that Antonio. I could text you after the show or we could just plan a place and a time to meet.

Why don't we meet at the Marriot Marquis and the revolving bar? Antonio offers up. You get to see the entire city all while sitting in your same seat. It is an amazing restaurant but it is a little pricey, but so worth it.

Antonio you do **know** I am from this city right? I grew up here.

Oh yeah I forgot.

Well Antonio has now gotten a little nervous and starts rambling on well…. We could go to G Launge in Chelsea, Therapy in Hell's Kitchen, Don't tell Mamma's right by the theater, The Irish Pub, Bartini….

I cut him off.

The Marriot Marquis is just fine plus we could all talk there without blaring music… Then we could always go somewhere else? What do you think Antonio?

Sounds great! So who is your friend a boy or girl?

A boy.

Gay or straight?

Confused but leaning on the gay side.

Is he cute?

I am thinking to myself you fucking pig, you are supposed to be asking **me** out. I know I am going to regret this but I am going to be honest.

He is very cute and most people would call him Hot.

Does he live here in New York or is he a friend from LA?

He lives here…. (I cannot resist) with his Mother in **Brooklyn.**

Awesome that is great!!!

Wow show some excitement why don't you there Antonio? I bring out my sarcastic jealousy to the finest. (Am I jealous already and they haven't even met yet?)

Tate….Tate you are going back to LA on Monday. What can possibly happen with us? Let's just have fun. Plus if me and your friend hit it off, who knows we will name our first Labrador after you.

(I want to throw up)

OK I will text you after the show.

Bye

Bye Tate looking forward to seeing you tonight.

Click

Liar you are looking forward to meeting my Hot Friend. Yup it is official I am already jealous of Antonio and Tony hooking up..

Ring Ring

Hello?

I got us Row D Center! Tony Boasts.

That is awesome Tony you didn't have to spend a fortune because I was kidding about the cheap seats.

Nah I got them right through telecharge. The woman on the phone said I was lucky because they must have just released them.

Awesome so where do you want to go to dinner? Where is the theater?

It is at the Gershwin on 51st.

Well do you want to do like a Carmines or Sardi's? We could go to Restaurant Row? Or we could walk down 8th Avenue by the theater and find a restaurant because there are tons to choose from. (I am now informing Tony like Antonio started to inform me.)

Let's do that, I like the idea of strolling but can I pick you up at 5pm because I gotta park the car and all that. Plus City traffic will probably be a nightmare because it is a Holiday weekend and there will be tons of tourists.

Why don't we just cab it? I ask.

Because later on tonight it will get very difficult to hail a cab and when you do it is always becomes a fight to take you to Brooklyn. Before you say anything else can you just do me a favor and let me be the "man" on this one?

Sure man!

Can I come in and see your Mom before we go Tate?

Sure but don't plan on being out of here anytime soon if you do.

Why?

HA Because Big Mouth Kelly told her all about last night.

No?

Yup.

Did she freak?

Not really Tony…..I know I was a bit surprised too…

(Yup I am lying again….I think I really do have a problem)

Well that's Kelly… Tony laughs and adds some things will never change. She has always been a tattle tale on you.

More like a bitch Ton.

Hey be nice to her! I will see you in an hour.

An hour? Shit is it 4 o clock!!!

I start racing upstairs to get ready but once I get up there I realize I have another dilemma. If I don't wake up my Mother and Tony comes she will be angry. If I don't wake up my Mother and she wakes up and doesn't feel like she is presentable she will be angry. If I wake up my Mother now and tell her that Tony will be here in an hour, she will be angry but not as bad as the other 2 scenarios.

Ma! Ma! Wake up.

What is it Tate? She barks as I am opening her bedroom door.

Tony Ianucci is picking me up in an hour and he wanted to come in and say hello to you.

Oh does that mean he is going to be my future son in law?

Ma…..no. Well most likely no….but…ya never know.

Tate?

Mom I am kidding it's like a first date.

You kissed Tony Ianucci on my front porch Tate… it is **more** than a first date Tate. My Mother barks condescending at me..

Mom I can tell him that you're not feeling good.

No, no I would love to see Tony. I will get up.

Moms now don't go crazy and talk his ear off or start with 100 question. We are going into the city so it's just a quick hello.

What are you going to the City for?

We are having dinner and then seeing a show?

What **show?** My Mother inquires.

Wicked Mom (As I say it I have a flashback to crazy Darlene fleeing the Marriot Marquis and going to see Wicked.)

Wicked? Of course you take your boyfriend to see Wicked but not your **own** Mother. I wanted to see Wicked.

Mom he is taking me....

A-ha - gotcha so you **are** the woman in the relationships. I **knew it!**

Mother we are going as friends. He bought the tickets to the show and I am buying dinner.

Fine

Mom and I am **not** the woman.

Sure Tate you keep telling yourself that. There is no heavenly way possible that Tony Ianucci is the woman. Go get ready! You better look good because Tony Ianucci is one good looker and he can do much better than you Tate.

Oooooh Mother!

I walk back to my room and I am trying to figure out what to wear. Thank God I over packed because this weekend is definitely not the wardrobe I thought I would be wearing. I did remember a black sports jacket because I thought I would be seeing a show with my Mother. Never in a million years did I think I would be seeing one with Tony Ianucci though.

Well of course my insecure ass had to do 250 pushups before I got into the shower. After all Tony was like a 9.8 and stunning. Me on the other hand was maybe a 7.2 and starting to look pasty. It has after all been 4 days since I last tanned. I won't shave, that will help.... a little.

So I shower and I don't shave which my Mother will not like. I put on a pair of jeans which my Mother will hate but they make my butt look good. I put on a tight white T shirt and my black sport jacket to finish off the ensemble. I fix my hair, brush my teeth and it actually all comes together really nice. As

I am putting my shoes on, I hear the doorbell ring. I look down at my watch. Fuck! It's 450 and he is right on time. A little early actually but I think he allotted 10 minutes for my Mother. Good boy Tony, know your limits with my Mother!

Tate Tony is here! Oh shit it is Kelly and I can just imagine what is going to come out of her blabber mouth next.

Coming!!!

I go and take one last look in the mirror and as my last second of primping I hear.

Tony it is so **nice** to see you again. Would you like anything to drink? I think Tate has drank **all** the wine in the house but how about a beer?

No thanks Mrs. Connors how are you?

As I reach the top of the stairs and look down there is Tony in a full on suit. He looks gorgeous! His hair is slicked back; he has on a black suit with a royal blue tie that just makes his blue eyes pop. As he looks up at me he flashes that million dollar smile and my legs get weak in the knees. I cannot walk down the flight of stairs. I am frozen in my tracks. I do not think that in my entire life someone has made me weak in the knees and frozen still.

Tony says "Hey Handsome get down here."

With all of my body and strength I start to walk down the stairs without falling. I am praying that I don't just buckle over.

I hear my Mother say to my sister – In all my years I never thought I would hear Tony Ianucci calling my baby, handsome. I feel like I am in a really bad dream Kelly Marie.

Mom it is cute Kelly says.

You look amazing Tony I say. (It is awkward now because do we kiss, hug, shake hands? And in front of my Mother and sister)

We sort of embrace but we are both uncomfortable. Let me clarify we are uncomfortable with the environment and company because if I was alone with this amazing specimen of a man, it would have been an entirely **different** hello. We quite possibly would have missed the whole show if I was alone and could have my way..

You look great Tate. Wow your chest is so defined.

Kelly looks at me up and down and says Tate when did Miami Vice come back in style? I didn't get the memo....

Ha Ha (bitch)

He looks great! Tony says and out comes that million dollar smile.

Well apparently he couldn't fit his entire suit in his luggage my Mom says disappointedly. Well at least he is not wearing sneakers...

You look really nice Tate Kelly says

Thanks Kelly

You know Ron has some nice suits up there Tatey. He wouldn't mind loaning you one of his suits. You are supposed to wear a suit to the theater.

No thanks Mom.

Ok well "Suit" yourself… she says after she makes sure she takes a long pause after saying the word suit to me as sarcastic as ever..

Good Night Mom!

Good Night Kelly. Have fun on your date Kel!

Thanks Tate Have Fun. Bye Tony…now don't keep my Big Bro out too late.

Good Night Mom. I say as I give her a kiss goodnight and all while she is still looking disapproving on my outfit.

Nice seeing you Mrs. Connors. Tony politely says to my Mom. See you at Dagostino's soon.

Just as I thought we were out of there my Mother has one more thing to say:

So Tony if you fall in love with my son are you going to abandon your Mother too and move to Los Angeles?

Good night Mom. I say as I push Tony through the front door.

As we get outside. Tony gives me a kiss.

I have been waiting to do that all day.

(OK Ton don't be corny, shut up and let me just **look** at you…you know I am saying this to myself right?)

I hear chirp chirp and it is a car sound.

What do you think? I just got it.

Well it is a new black on black Chevy Camaro, with the shiny tricked out rims, the tinted windows, the Italian flag detailed to the side of the car and let's not forget the Catholic cross hanging from the rear view mirror.

It's um….Brooklyn!

It's great huh? Tony says beaming with pride, I just got it 2 months ago to celebrate the divorce being finalized. Get in!

We don't really talk that much as we drive to Manhattan because KTU has started there Saturday night Dance Marathon. I am thinking to myself there is no other place in the world besides New York City that would start a dance marathon at 5pm. Gotta love it though….right?

$24 dollars for parking? I hear Tony say.

I will get it Tony you drove.

Nah it's cool. I wanted to drive. I pay.

So after we got the car all settled into the parking structure we began to walk towards 8th Ave.

Let's remember where the car is Ton. It's on 50th between 7th and 8th.

We walk down 8ᵗʰ Ave and stop and read a few menus at various restaurants but we settle on an Italian restaurant (imagine that) and go right in.

It is only 545pm so the restaurant is completely empty. We get to choose where we want to sit and I choose a very secluded table. You could tell the hostess already picked up the vibe that we were gay and on a date of sorts..

Would you like to see a wine list?

I look at Tony and he nods.

We pick a bottle of Chianti off the wine list. We were in an Italian restaurant after all. We both than immediately looked at our menus and I could tell that this is where the evening was going to get awkward. We agreed on anti-pasta and some calamari to start with. Tony picks a very hearty pasta dish as his entrée and I choose the fish of the day. After we order I turn to Tony and I ask him a question that has been in my head:

Are you nervous?

Nah why?

Is this your first date with a guy?

No Tate…it is just… my first date… with a guy….that I actually do like…

Aww

Well that broke the ice. Tony and I talked about everything from our childhood, to his divorce and of course my coming out. We talked about our families and how hard it was for him to come out because he was an only child. He got married because he wanted to give his parents a grandchild.

The conversation flowed through the appetizers and dinner so fast. I cannot tell you if I have ever been on a date with somebody that the conversation flowed so easily. We had similar interests but we also had certain things that we didn't agree on. Tony was perfectly content with status quo whereas in I, there was always something else I wanted to try. He didn't have the passion for travel but was very interested in the places that I have been. A summer vacation to Disney in Orlando Florida was just about the furthest vacation he had been on. Tony was very simple with his life; whereas I am anything but simple. He was perfectly content working in the grocery store and living in Brooklyn Heights. Whereas I rebelled against Brooklyn, Tony embraced it and loved it. You would think this was a match made in hell but it was actually working really well, so far. I was starting to realize that I was connecting with someone, who would let me be the center of attention and not have a problem with it. Tony was so comfortable in his own skin that it actually scared me a little. He was not obnoxious about being comfortable. He was very charming, witty, sarcastic and very funny. I felt like I was in a dream and I kept wanting to pinch myself to be sure I wasn't in a dream. Why was this amazing guy on a date with a douche bag like me? I kept saying to myself just have a great time and stop over analyzing.

Holy crap as I look at my watch. It is 7:25 pm. I turn to the waiter and ask. Can we please have the check please!

The waiter brings the check immediately. I guess he is used to people seeing Broadway shows. I pay the check and we hurry off to the theater.

Where is the fire Tate? Tony teases

What?

We have a half an hour till the show starts. It is a beautiful night. Walk with me; let's not make this a race. I want to remember this.

OK but I just wanted to get…..

Tate please just walk with me. Relax…..After all these years and you still want to race to everything.

Relax! Tony says.

Ok I say but my head is out of control. I want to get to the theater, read the Playbill, make sure I do not have to pee and settle into my seat. I love Broadway plays and it is the one thing I miss from New York more than anything else. Los Angeles has the Ahmanson and The Pantages but it is nothing like New York Theater.

Thank you Tate !

I am also coming to learn that Tony has a real calming effect on me. I don't know what it is but I honestly trust him. Maybe because I am going back to LA on Monday, is the reason why I am not worried that he is going to shred my heart. I guess I know that this relationship has the shelf life of possibly 2 more days. Plus he is just coming out and he has to kiss a lot more frogs or shall we say fairies before he is ready to settle down. I forgot how **good** of a person Tony is. He is such a catch who probably doesn't **catch**. Yup….my mind is back in the gutter again and I was thinking about sex. Sorry I can't help it. If you actually saw what this guy honestly looked like, you would be thinking about sex too. Now I have to go watch two witches sing….

Tony and I arrive at the theater quickly and we receive our tickets from the will call line extremely fast. The theater is amazing and very old Broadway. I breath, in the New York Theater experience and do a weird intake of air. I was happy Tony was not paying attention because I am sure I looked like an idiot. We settle into our seats. They are great seats. I pretend I know a little about the play as I read the Playbill but honestly I don't. The play starts promptly at 8 o clock and as the lights dim Tony takes my hand and holds it. Well for the next two hours everything is kind of fuzzy to me because I am planning my wedding to Tony Ianucci. I am visualizing that we are a Hollywood power "gays" and I have the top rated sitcom in America. We have a beautiful house in the beautiful Hollywood Hills with 2 dogs named Molly and Pepper. They are Labradors Retrievers of course! We travel all over the world in private jets to exotic locations. Everyone wants to take our pictures and wants us to sign autographs...We are in all of the tabloids every week but only for jet setting around of the words and also for all of my charity work with the Trevor Project.

I come out of my dream just long enough to glance over at Tony who is **so** into the music. I try and start watching the show and after a few minutes I say to myself. Hey no wonder why my Mother wants to see this- it is like the Wizard of Oz, but on a stage! I try and try to concentrate on the show but I keep going back to my fabulous life with Tony Ianucci in Los Angeles. Of course I than start to think about the sex, the mind blowing sex, the everyday sex I am going to have with Tony. We just can't go more than a few hours without having sex. In our bed, on the beach, in the office, on set and every other possible location known to man, Tony and I have sex.

All of a sudden the lights go up and it is intermission time. I am not sure if I watched the first act or I just fantasized about having sex with Tony but I do have a raging hard on, that I need to hide effective immediately!

Let's grab a drink Tony says.

I am thinking to myself that would be great but I have a raging hard on in my pants and I cannot go anywhere. What am I going to do?

Um.....umm...Ok so I started to think about my sister naked and having sex with Kyle and Poof hard on gone...OK

Tony grabs my hand and starts to lead me up to the bar. Holy shit I am thinking is he really holding my hand...in public? I have been out a hell of a lot longer than he has and I probably wouldn't be holding someone's hand. Once we get to the bar, I pull my hand away. Sorry but I still have problems with public displays of affection.

What is the matter? Tony asks as I pull my hand away from him like I was just stung by a raging bumble bee.

Nothing I stammer.

OK what do you want to drink Tate?

A Red Bull with vodka in it. I tell Tony

Really? He asks

Yes I say and I mock my head up and down

What do you think of the show? Tony asks as I take the first sip of my drink.

It is great Tony and good job with the tickets. This is awesome and you can see everything from our seats. Good job Mr. Ianucci.

Don't call me Mr. Ianucci. That is what my employees at Dagostino's call me.

OK....sorry it was supposed to be endearing.

Drink up show is starting Tony chimes in.

We have our drink quickly and then head back down to our amazing seats. The conversation is very sparse and simple, mainly because I am still in shock that Tony held my hand in public. We settle back into our seats quickly.

Well with the second act I actually forced myself to watch because during the intermission Tony was asking me what I thought about certain songs and I think my answers were kind of odd to him. Plus I did not need to get another hard on thinking about having sex because I don't think I would have been able to control myself. He immediately grabbed my hand again as the second act began. I actually really enjoyed the second act of the show and I could tell Tony was mesmerized by the amazing music. Darlene told me on the plane but it was not the same as experiencing it first-hand. He felt the music as well and I really enjoyed watching him enjoy the music, just as much as watching the production itself. As the music would boom, Tony would squeeze my hand tighter and tighter. By the time the show ended I had goose bumps from both the production of Wicked and my date Tony Ianucci. When the show was over and the cast was doing their encores, we stood up and clapped and clapped and clapped.

As we were leaving the theater, I was on cloud nine and genuinely happy, that was until I remembered Antonio. I had an extreme flashback to this afternoon, the conversation and how excited Antonio was to meet Tony.

I need to use the bathroom Tony.

Ok I will meet you outside (Tony utilized the bathroom at the restaurant and during intermission. I don't want you to think he has a ball sack as big as China or something)

I race down to the bathroom and luckily get a bathroom stall right away and I am debating what to say to Antonio.

I turn on my phone and I immediately get a text from Antonio. I was so excited to meet you guys that I got to the Marriot Marquis really early. Text me when the show is out and I will order you guys a drink. When you get here the drinks should be waiting but the service is very slow. This place is packed by the way and I am **glad** I got here early.

I just couldn't risk it. This night has been perfect so far. I know I am being really selfish but I just cannot let Tony meet Antonio. I know I live in LA but I want him all to myself. He is mine and I will not risk him falling for Antonio. Antonio is **so** much better looking than I am and I couldn't even come close in the suave department. Maybe it was the fact that Tony held my hand so endearingly, or that I was planning my life with him throughout the show, but every single insecurity I ever had, had just come out. So I texted Antonio:

Tony is really sick and I have to take him home. I think he got food poisoning in the restaurant. I am so sorry! Maybe next time I am here in NYC we can all get together. I would have texted you sooner but it didn't start till after the second act. We are in a cab right now and if he doesn't feel good by the time we get back to Brooklyn I am going to take him to the hospital. Again sorry.

I send the text and I head upstairs to meet Tony. I washed my hands first for authenticity though...

I see Tony standing outside of the theater and he has his gorgeous head in the Playbill so I walk up and say:

Where to handsome?

Anywhere you want to go handsome? He smiles back

You know where I want to go as I look at Tony like a dog that hasn't been fed in an entire week and his owners have just returned from vacation not knowing I have not been fed.

Tony leans up against me and whispers in my ear.(My heart starts to pound in the brisk air and I feel a hard on building.)

Tate?

Yes?

I like you….

I like you too Tony.

I like you….you have been on my mind every second of this day but I am not going to sleep with you tonight.

Why? (insecurities have flushed right back in. Am I not cute enough? Is my body not perfect? Did I do or say something to turn him off?)

Because I really like you Tate and I do not want to mess this up.

I don't know if it was the way he said it or what but I just looked at him right into his beautiful blue eyes and said….

Fucking prude! (defense mechanisms have been turned on in full effect)

He laughed and then I laughed but honestly I would have had sex with him right then and there if I could have.

Ok let's go get a drink Tate.

Yeah you have a drink. I need a cold shower.

So you like me Tate? Tony asks me with this adorable look on his face

Yeah I **like** you Tony.

Wow Tate Connors likes me. Wait till **my** freakin Mother finds out about this! She has never fully forgiven you for getting her only son arrested and carted off to jail

(I just look at him and say to myself…dickhead are you trying to ruin the night but I ignore him) Come on let's get a drink Tony!

Where do you want to go Tate?

Anywhere but please not the Marriot Marquis Tony…anywhere but there.

We started to walk up 8th Avenue in the heart of Hell's Kitchen and we found a local gay bar and went inside. The bar was a little crowded but not that bad. We sat at a cute table next to the bar and ordered Martini's.

I have never had a Martini. Tony confessed.

Really I love Martini's but only one for you Mister, because you are driving.

Ok Mother

We of course we began bantering back and forth and just teasing each other. Our Martini's come quickly and we did a cheese ball cheers to our amazing date! We didn't realize that we had gathered an audience. At first we didn't understand why but then we started to realize that the average age of the men in this bar was about 60 years old.

All the men in this bar are really old Tate! Tony whispers.

So what...they are usually much nicer when they get to this age...or mean come to think of it. I have had experiences with both young and old.

Sexual? Tony interjects

No no no Tony I mean I have met some of the sweetest older gay men in the world. They have told me stories about the 70's and the pre AIDS days. I have learned about Stonewall and how much harder it was for them to be gay, than it is today. They talk about friends they lost to AIDS and they are always preaching safe sex. I might get around Tony but I am always safe. Sex isn't going to cut my life short or make me live a life of taking pills and live with the fear of dying. I look up to older gay man as the trail blazers, that helped make it a little easier to be a gay man today, than say 20 years ago. I think age is an accomplishment.

Tony don't get me wrong there are bitchy queens at all ages but the worst are the over 50 bottoms who just can't get laid without paying for sex.

Tony has a weird look on his face and then says: Paying for it I am confused. What do you mean? What the hell are you talking about? You still talk so fast and you change the subject faster than a race car driver.

I try and explain slowly to Tony: It's like in the straight world. They have male hookers and prostitutes but they are called escorts now. It is basically the same thing but you won't find them on the streets anymore. They are either in the gay rags or on the internet.

What is a gay rag? Tony innocently asks me.

It is a magazine for gay men. It is not like The Advocate, Instinct or Out Magazine but more like a localized gay publication. In New York City they have HX and out in LA they have Frontiers. You will find the magazine/gay rags in front of the bars and clubs. They are spread over the gay ghettos like Chelsea or West Hollywood all the way to the Castro in San Francisco to Halsted Street in Chicago. They have ads for local restaurants, events, parties and bars, as well as an escort directory towards the back. They vary from city to city but almost every city in the United States and Canada has a gay rag for their gay community.

I thought gay people generally live in nice and upscale neighborhoods Tate?

They do Tony.

Then why do they call it the gay ghetto?

I have no idea Tony. I guess maybe as long as you put the word gay in front of the word ghetto it makes it sound better.

Why do they…

Tony please give it a rest…please I am not here to give you Gay 101.(I look at his hurt face and I say). I am sorry I can be a bitch sometimes. What were you about to ask me?

Honey I will give you anything you want. You just name it baby as this older queen gets up and puts one hand on his hips and sashays over to our table.….. What do you **need** baby?

I am good Tony says and you can tell that he is nervous and doesn't know what to do or say to this older gentleman, who is trying to flirt with him.

I am sure you are baby um hmmm the older gentleman says.

They like you Ton I say with a smirk. I think that they have started a fan club for you already. I expect that you will be getting a free drink or two coming your way.

Thanks!

Can I ask you just one more question Tate?

Sure Tony! Bring it on!

So what happens now?

What do you mean? We finish our drink and go home I guess Ton.

No I mean with us. What happens now, do we have a future together Tate?

I am not following you Tony.

I mean are we dating? Are we Boyfriends? Or are we just friends?

Tony it has been less than 48 hours since we connected, please slow down. Who the hell knows where this is going. I go back to LA on Monday so what were you expecting to happen?

I...I...I don't know Tony musters.

Do you want to have another drink or head back to Brooklyn? I ask directly looking into Tony's beautiful eyes.

No I think we should head back to Brooklyn. Let's go! As Tony's demeanor has changed entirely in the last few minutes.

Let me get the check Ton.

I already paid at the bar Tate are you **ready to go?**

Ok are **you** Ok Tony?

I'm fine. Tony snaps at me.

Are you sure you are fine? What just happened?

Yes come on it is cold out here and I am tired. Tony quips.

Ok I say as I think back to a couple of hours ago when I was racing for the theater and Tony wanted to stroll and enjoy this beautiful night. As we are briskly walking back towards the car I notice Tony's face has a frown on it and he is pouting. Plus we are rapidly walking in silence.

What's the matter Tony? (as I look at him and he is clearly trying to tell me he is upset with me, without saying a word.)

Nothing as his head is looking at the sidewalk and he is shaking his head back and forth. Nothing at all is wrong... nope nothing.

As he is doing this I have a childhood flashback to every time Tony didn't get his way and guess what? It looked a hell of a lot similar to what is going on here on the sidewalk of 8th Ave. walking towards the car. He is on the verge of a temper tantrum because he didn't get the answer he wanted. He is mumbling under his breath as well. I cannot **stand** when someone mumbles under their breath so I turn to Tony and say :

Cat got your tongue Tony?

No he hisses.

Than what is it? I asked not hiding the fact that he is beginning to piss me off.

You know you haven't changed a bit since we were kids; you are still selfish old Tate Connors.

Really? Hmm….Ok any more compliments to end the night Tony?(I cannot believe he is doing this right on 8th Ave after an amazing night.)

You will **never** change, it always has to be about you, you, you Tate.(He is pointing his finger in my face and I cannot stand that)

What is **that** supposed to mean Tony? (Now I am officially pissed)

Figure it out Tate since you seem to know **everything** about **everything!**

I am not going to do this with you Anthony (yup I did just call him Anthony) I had a wonderful time with you tonight and I honestly don't know what I said or didn't say to piss you off or upset you. I am not going to sit here at 1230 at night and play a jig saw puzzle with you on 8th Avenue. I am not going to do it. I refuse to fight with you… so you have a safe drive home….Good night.

Where are you going Tate?

To the subway…**Anthony!** Good night….

I turn and I start to walk further down 8th Ave past where his car is parked. I am still holding onto my Playbill, but I am so confused and hurt as to what just happened, that I want to just chuck the Playbill onto the street and cry.

How did this night go from so special and amazing to downright awful? It was like from 0 to 60 seconds and I don't know what happened. What did he want from me? To commit my life to someone, I have only reconnected with a mere 24 hours ago. I am not a lesbian after all. Let me just chalk up the night to reconnecting with an old friend. I go back to LA in about 30 hours. Maybe I shouldn't have cancelled Antonio after all. The two of them could be holding hands on a horse and buggy in Central Park by now. That is what I get for being selfish asshole. Tony is right I guess I am selfish. Oh well I hope Kelly's date is going better than mine...

Tate, Tate, Tate, **W**ait I hear Tony yell!

I turn around and he is running towards me as I continue to keep walking. (I know this is starting to sound like a cheesy rom-com but can you give me this one? Please)

Tate I am sorry....W**ait!!!**

What do you want Tony? Did you just run down the block to throw more compliments my way? I am so desperate for more of your oh so special compliments...**Tony!**

Tate.....I'm sorry....you see.....I...I....

What Tony? What is it? How did this amazing and beautiful night just turn into this awful Lifetime Movie of the Week?

Tony gasping for breath says: I was really looking forward to this night and we had an amazing time but I didn't want it to end.

(I look at him with disdain for a second and then say;) Well you have a really funny way of showing it Tony I snarl (yup I snarl too)

Well Tate you see I had such an amazing time with you tonight, probably the best time I have had in years. When I am around you I can just be me. I don't have to butch it up and pretend to be straight. I can act goofy and I can do or say anything I want, without having to second guess myself, or worry about being judged. I don't have to rehearse things in my head before I say them out loud for fear they will come out wrong. You have made the past 24 hours so awesome. You make being gay acceptable and you are unapologetic for it. You are who you are and you beat to your own drum. I just started to get excited about the future and then I remember you are going back to LA on Monday. Me on the other hand I am stuck here, living in Brooklyn in a dead end job. I feel like I have to apologize to my Mother every single day for breaking her heart.

So what do **you** want from **me** Tony?

I don't know…I don't know Tate but when I asked you at the tavern what happens now you just brushed it off with no thought..

Tony what did you want me to say? Oh Tony let me run into your arms and stay with you forever? Tony I will give up my dreams and just be your boyfriend. I will move in with you and your Mother in Brooklyn or better yet, you and I can move in with my Mother and live happily ever after. Is that what you want? Because it is **never** going to happen Tony….**never!** It has taken me a long time to get to where I am and I am not going to back pedal Tony.

No…that is not what I am saying Tate but you could have said something like we will stay in touch, we can email and Facebook, we can talk on the phone and you can even possibly visit me in LA Tony…but no, you say **nothing** Tate and just blow me off.

I cannot promise you anything Anthony…Ok I just can't.

Ok and what is with this calling me Anthony...Tate?

Ha I remember when you used to piss off your Dad, he would call you Anthony. I don't know why I remembered that when I did but it just came to me. You used to get so mad when he would call you Anthony.

I know! (And now we are both laughing)

I am sorry Tate (a very long pause as Tony has his head down and looking at the sidewalk. He looks up at me and looks me directly in the eyes)

Can I be honest with you Tate and it won't scare you away? (I say yes but remember I am still a liar.)

Sure Tony what?

I am lonely Tate. I don't have any friends. The wife got those in the divorce as well. My Mother looks at me in disgust, people whisper about me as I walk down the street. Even the kids who work for me in the supermarket draw pictures of me, on the bathroom stalls of me giving guys blowjobs. I am way to awkward and nervous to go to gay bars in The City, so I go to The Ale House almost every night to drink my pain away. The alcohol helps me mask the pain, especially when my Mother just looks at me and wants to cry. You will never know how it feels to be this isolated and alone. When it gets unbearable I do cruise the promenade and pick up guys for sex. We have sex in parks, under the bridge or even in my car. Afterwards I feel so disgusting and dirty. I start to believe what everyone else is saying and I go numb.

(He wants me to host his pity party and I am not going to do it.)Then **do** something about it Tony. Move, start your life over and don't let your Mother guilt you. My Mother tries all the time to guilt me but you would be surprised on how resilient they are, once you force them to be independent. You can do anything you want to do. You have so much going for you. OK I am going to be shallow here but you are fucking hot as hell and can have almost any guy you ever wanted…including me. Why is it that the better looking the guy is, the more fucked up and insecure they are?

(Tony just shrugs and has tears swelling up in his eyes)

Tony do not stand here and throw yourself a pity party because I am not hosting it. Seriously you can do whatever you want. I was really digging you until you got all moody on me.

So you really think I can do whatever I want? Tony somberly asks

Yup.

And you really do think I am hot?

Yup

Well the next thing I know Tony comes toward me and pulls my body into his and we are full on making out, leaning against a building on 47th and 8th Ave and nobody seems to care. People are walking by minding their own business for a good 10 to 15 minutes. As soon as someone yells "Get a Room" nervous Tony jumps off me and says we got to get the car.

I was going to take the subway Tony remember?

Tate? Please?

I am kidding let's go get the Gumba Machine.

What? Tony looks at me confused.

Never mind. It is getting cold, let's walk fast. I am not going to miss this New York Winter that is for damn sure!

We get to the car and start heading back to Brooklyn. We keep the conversation light because it got heavy there for a minute. I started to think about how hard it would have been to come out in Brooklyn Heights. There is the fact that Tony married a girl and then got divorced because he was gay. Hey wait I thought he said he and his ex-wife are friends now? Not going to go there. I get it. I just wonder if he likes me because I am gay or that he truly wants to tear off my clothes and get it on. We all knew I would have sex with him in a minute. As we are crossing the Brooklyn Bridge I wondered what it would be like to be in Tony's shoes. Living with my Mother and working in Brooklyn just makes me cringe. On the one hand my Mother is crazy but she loves me and is not a bitch like Tony's Mother is. On the other hand, **wait** who am I kidding, this scenario would never happen to me and there is no other hand.

Tony pulls up to my Mother's house and turns off the car. We kiss for a few minutes and then Tony says to me:

Can I see you before you leave?

I have to go to my brother's tomorrow to see the kids but you are welcome to join.

Well Tony has the fear of God on his face and he looks at me and says:

Can I think about it tonight?

I just laugh and say sure! Call me in the morning but not too early.

OK and he then kisses me again.

As I am walking up to the front door, I am all tingly inside. What have I done? I cannot break this guy's heart? Maybe he will break mine? Why do I always end up in impossible situations? Why couldn't I bump into a guy like Tony in the Beverly Center, as I was shopping at Bloomingdales for a new pair of jeans? That would be too easy.

I turn around and wave as I open the door to the house.

Kelly? Kelly is that you?

No Mom it is Tate. What is the matter?

OMG Tate, Kelly is not home yet from her date! It is now 215am and she has been gone since 820pm. Something is wrong. I am about to call the police.

Mom calm down, Kelly is a grown ass woman. She probably went out for a night cap or something. Stop worrying and go to bed!

Tate if the conversation is stimulating and that is a big **if** dinner would be a maximum of two hours, two and a half the most! That would make it 11pm. If they went out for a night cap, that would be an extra hour. So she should have been home by 12:30 **tops!!** Something has happened I just know it.

I am thinking to myself, yea Mom… what has happened is Kelly is probably on her second orgasm by now or spooning Kyle. Girls love to "spoon."

Mom I met Kyle and he seems like a really nice guy. He wouldn't let anything happen to her. Did you call her cell?

Yes

Did you leave her a message that you were worried about her and to call her Mother?

I was going to but her mailbox is full. My Mother is in full on Academy Award winning performance of frantic Mother who thinks her daughter has been raped or murdered.

Her mailbox is full? That is odd….

As I look over at my Mother she is now looking like a dog that just took a shit in the middle of the living room.

Mom how many messages did you leave her?

I don't remember…

Mom? About how many?

I don't know 9 or 14 or so….

Mom?

Mom she is probably pissed off at you now.

Tate ladies are **not** supposed to stay out all night. I am so worried that she has been raped or murdered. It is 2:30 am in the morning. Nothing good happens after midnight.

Mom I didn't get home till after 2 am and I am fine. You didn't leave any crazy ass messages on my cell phone.

That's different Tate don't be a smart ass.

Why is that different Ma?

Because you are a boy….and people do not rape boys. Plus you have smart street skills.

Mom I will text her and find out if she is Ok.

You cannot the mail box is full….

Her voicemail is full not her text.

So how do I text her Tate???????

Mom I will text her I don't think you can text her from your dinosaur of a cell phone. (Plus there was no way in hell I was teaching my hysterical Mom how to text my sister at 245am)

So I text Kelly:

Hey whore bag Mom is out of her skin worrying about you. She thinks you are getting gang raped in a gutter somewhere. Are you? **Ha.** Text me back that you are OK so I can drug this crazy woman and put a valium in her herbal tea. How does it feel to be the slut of the family for once? Did you have a great right?

What did you say to her Tate? My Mom quizzes.

That we are both so, so, so worried about her and to please just let us know that she is **a-ok!**

You know Tate I love you and I miss you but I honestly have to say I cannot wait for you to go back to LA - your sarcasm is exhausting!

Arrr thanks Mom!

Chirp chirp my cell phone goes

Tate we are fine just tell Mom we fell asleep watching a movie.

Mom, Kelly just texted back that she fell asleep watching a movie and will be home in the morning.

Oh thank God I am going to bed **thank you** Tate.

So I text Kelly back:

Mom is cool. And Kell the only movie you would be watching right now, is if you guys were videotaping each other. Actually you could be watching Kelly does Kyle. Slut X, R

What an exhausting night I am going to bed. As I am washing my face and brushing my teeth I start to think about this trip. Between my dear old Mother, my newly slutty sister and my new/old gay pal Tony, I am started to get dizzy. Phew thank God only 1 more day left here in glorious Brooklyn because I am fucking exhausted. What am I going to do about Tony Ianucci? I have never wanted to have sex with anyone more. Hold up there Tate what about Mark Consuelo or Eddie Cibrian?

They are straight Tate...Tony Ianucci is gay and you actually do have the possibility of having sex with him. I wonder if his wife taught him to kiss. Phew he is amazing...

I didn't even feel my head hit the pillow. I didn't over analyze what dreams I was going to have tonight or complain about the extreme heat in this house. Nope... I just closed my eyes and went to fast sleep...**happy**. Yup happy!

Chapter 19

Last exit um... I mean day in Brooklyn

Knock, Knock Tate, Tate, honey?

Yes Mom!

Are you going to go to church with me? Your sister promised to go with me but she just called and said she over slept the alarm clock.

My Mother hasn't opened the door to my room and is talking through the door. The sun is blazing into the room and it is probably 50 degrees outside but my heart has just turned to ice.

Which church Mom the old people church?

No Tate...........um St. Anthony's

St. Anthony's Mom...really? The same St. Anthony's that says I am going to hell because I am a homosexual?

Um.....yes? As if she just answered me with a question.

Mom I love you but you will never get me inside a Catholic Church ever again.

Yeah I know ......as she sighs

Tate?

Yes?

(I can tell by the tone of her voice she has one more trick up her sleeve.)

Tony Ianucci brings **his** Mother to church every Sunday. And now since he is a homosexual **now** why does he still go?

Mom, Tony Ianucci is afraid of his Mother. He is afraid that if he doesn't obey every single command that witch says, she will lock him in the basement and chain him to the furnace.

Oh and you don't think I would do that to you Tate? You're not afraid of your Mother.

Mom we don't have a basement.

Drat!!!!!!!

Hey Mom I am going to invite Tony to Chris's today.

Hmmmm Well then....if you don't come to church with me I am going to invite Mrs. Ianucci over to Chris's house as well.

You wouldn't dare Mom!

Hurry up Tate we are going to be late. There is no time to shower. I hope you don't smell like a brewery this morning as well.

I do smell like a brewery Mom!

Well I guess we can be 5 minutes late to church. You have 3 minutes to get ready and I will turn the hot water off in exactly 3 minutes.

I am wearing jeans Mother!

That is fine dear.

I couldn't keep my **big** mouth shut...damnit now I have to go to fucking church! The church will probably burn down as I enter it anyway.

In 4 minutes and 30 seconds exactly I was dressed and ready to go to church. God help us now! God Save the Queen more like it!

(We rapidly walk down Montague Street towards St. Anthony's and I am dreading the next hour because it has been years since I set foot inside a church.

Of course we walked up the church stairs at the exact same time as Tony and his Mom did. There was no possible way to avoid them. As they made eye contact with us Tony turned white and Mrs. Ianucci turned redder than an apple.

Hello Denise and hello Tony my Mother said

Hello Jackie, Mrs. Ianucci said as she glared at me for corrupting her son.

Yup she still hates me. I was so tempted to grab Tony and start French kissing him in the middle of the vestibule of the church. It probably wouldn't have killed Mrs. Ianucci because evil doesn't die, but it sure as hell would make for some good gossip at the church's next bake sale.

Hey Tony Long time? How are you buddy? It's been what 10 years?

(I know I am sick but I love to watch him squirm)

Um…..um…..yeah

Let's go get seats Anthony as Mrs. Ianucci launches into the church dragging Tony. He turns around to look at me and I just mouth A_**n_t_h_o_n_y!!!**

The look of fear in Tony's eyes is so cute Mom.

Tate, Denise doesn't know that Tony is gay?

Oh she knows but could you imagine if she knew he was hanging out with me? And that we went out on a date last night?

Yeah and that you guys were making out on my front porch! My Mother snickers as we both giggle and head into the church.

Mom let's sit here.

Tate?

Come on Mom. **Go!**

Well guess where we were sitting? Yup….in the pew directly behind Tony and Mrs. Ianucci…..Wow church is going to be really **fun** today.

Mom what do you think the chances are that Mrs. Ianucci will shake my hand when it is peace onto you time?

Tate **stop** my Mom whispered (but I can tell she was enjoying this almost as much as me)

Nope no one could be enjoying this as much as me. As I so wanted to whisper in Tony's ear "Hey you want to go play altar boy and priest in the penance room??" Do you want to molest me? We could grab the blood of Christ and have a party? For you non Catholics the blood of Christ is red wine…

Happy Sunday Folks and the first week of Advent.…father Flynn says to the congregation

Well throughout the mass I knew that Tony was uncomfortable and sorry but I fucking **loved it**. Was it wrong? Of course it was wrong but since the Catholic Church is already telling me that I am going to hell, so what do I have to lose? I could see the hairs on Tony's back standing up and I knew I was going to catch hell for this later. I didn't really care because I knew he was planning out in his head, every possible scenario that could possibly happen in the next 30 minutes. Well now it is time to kneel. Wow when did they change the kneelers in church? These are comfortable. Or is it I just became more comfortable kneeling. See even in church I think about sex.

Here come the past baskets for our donations. My Mother actually gets weekly envelopes mailed to her. I think they do it because if you miss a week you still have to pay. I am sorry but organized religion is just another way to make money in this world. The Catholic Church is a multibillion dollar operation after all! As I look around at people putting money in the basket, I say to myself, are people giving money so it ensures that they are going to go to heaven? Is it to pay for their sins or indiscretions? Is it like buying your way into heaven? **Yuck**

Well it is Peace be with you time.…

Here comes the fun! So the priest says peace be with you and we say and also with you. It is now time to give peace onto our fellow Catholics. I turn to Mother and give her a kiss and then we turn around and shake the hands of the people behind us. Neither Tony nor his Mother even bothered to turn around to shake our hands. Wow that was rude. His Mother is a bitch even in church. I know Tony would have turned around and at least shook my Moms hand if that wicked witch wasn't with him. Why is it that Italian men cannot stand up to their Mothers? Maybe their Mothers put something in the spaghetti sauce. I don't get it. I am a little pissed off at Tony but I will get even with him later. It depends whether or not he hurt my Mothers feeling by not shaking her hand. I am sure she will tell me after mass. He may be out but he definitely has closet boy syndrome and it is not something I want to relive again.

Well now it is communion time and I have not received communion in years. Communion is supposed to be the body of Jesus but it is actually unleavened bread cut into round wafer, that are blessed by a priest. Row by row people go up and get a piece of this as it is placed in your mouth or hands. I will not participate in this part of the mass and when it comes to my pews time, I sit back and let everyone else go. My Mother looks at me like "Are you coming?" and I just nod no and she seems to understand and gets online. Well soon enough it is time for the next row and Tony actually gets up and follows his Mother to the line.

I cannot believe what a fucking hypocrite he is! He had his tongue down my throat less than 12 hours ago and now he is about to eat the "Body of Jesus" with that same tongue. How could he receive communion? Didn't he get a divorce? Isn't **that** a sin? I am repulsed by the thought of Tony receiving communion. I think I am going to be sick. Any attraction that I had for Tony is gone. I will **not** be attracted to a pussy whipped Momma's boy that cowers to his Mother. I can understand having to go to church with his Mother, I can respect his decision **not** to turn around and shake our hands but to go up there and receive communion from a repressed homosexual …..um I mean priest is unforgiveable. Does he even know the amount of horrible things the pope and the Catholic Church have done and said against homosexuals? The way they misinterpret the bible is appalling. I cannot sit here one more minute. If I do I swear I am going to go all Norma Rae and instead of yelling Union I would yell:

h-y_p_o_c_r_i_t_e_s_!!!!!!!!!!!!!

As my Mother comes back to the pew, I say to her: I don't feel well and I will meet her outside. She nods Ok because she knows I have had enough. Plus if I see Tony I would probably vomit on him. I cannot stand people that don't stand up for who they are. Now I am not saying that you have to scream from every roof top that you are gay but come on. Did Tony really just receive Holy Communion from a man that was probably fantasizing about sucking his dick? I do not need a closet case or a guy just coming out of the closet in my life. No soiree me Bob! I am done. If you cannot have a true identity of who you are and what you expect from people then there is no room in my life for you.

I have left the building. I have so many issues with the Catholic Church that I cannot even begin to tell you. I even have some self-esteem issues that were caused by the Catholic Church. Ya see I was an altar boy….who was **never** molested by a priest. What? Was I not cute enough to be molested or something? I would have rather enjoyed it actually and I **could** keep a secret! There was one priest that was hot as hell!

I waited on the street for mass to end. Well mass has ended and people are filing out of the church. I see many faces from elementary school but I could care less. I just want to find my Mother and get the hell out of here.

Tate Connors **wow** it has been years how are you? You look **great!**

Yuck it's Tina Caputo….thanks Tina can't talk right now; I am looking for my Mom.

It's been a long time Tate. I heard a rumor that you were a homo. I am glad that you found your way back to the Catholic Church Tate. You don't want to go to hell.

Found my way?

Yes Tate as Tina looks at me pitiful.

Well I see you still haven't found your way I snap.

Yes I have. Tina announces.

No I see you still haven't found your way to a plastic surgeon office you ugly bitch. You face still looks like a horse. Why don't you go find your way to a nose job Woody Woodpecker?

I just kept walking away from Tina. I know that I was just mean and she probably didn't deserve that but I am fucking sick of everybody judging me. Maybe I will find her on Facebook and apologize. I just need to get the fuck out of there. Everywhere I look I see an old teacher, a classmate or even my elementary school nuns and principal. They are all staring at me like who let the fag out? Finally I spot my Mom and I bee line right over to her.

Moms, are you ready to go?

We don't get that many nice Sundays in December Tate what is the rush? It is a gorgeous day! This is my friend Adelaide.

Nice to meet you Adelaide I say as I shake her hand.

You went to school with Adelaide's daughter Gretchen...Gretchen O'Leary my Mom tells me

She lives in San Francisco with her girlfriend Molly. They are both veterinarians' Mrs. O'Leary states proudly.

That is great! Tell her I said hello!

In my head I am thinking that if I said more than 20 words to Gretchen O'Leary in 8 years of elementary school that was a lot. I always knew she would end up a carpet muncher though...

I have to pack Mom and I still need to go into the city and get some things from the NYU book store.

Is it open on Sunday?

Yes I checked and it is open till 3pm.

I didn't know you went to NYU Tate? Adelaide looks inquisitively

My Mother can tell by the look on my face that I do not want to small talk with Gretchen O'Leary's Mother at this time.

Ok let's go.

No Mom you can stay. I just didn't want you worrying about me and looking for me all afternoon.

Go then... but be back by 3pm. If we are late to dinner Samantha's going to have my head.

Mom you have got to start standing up to your son's wife. Chris needs to tell her it is not Ok to talk to you the way she does. If she is rude to you today, I swear I am going to open up the library and start reading her Mother.

Library? What library? I thought you said you were going to the book store?

Never Mind Mom I love you. Nice to see you again Mrs. O'Leary and tell Adelaide that I said hello.

Take care dear.

Bye and I kiss my Mom on the cheek.

They grow up so fast I can hear Adelaide's Mom say to my Mom as I am walking away.

As I turn around I see Tony in the corner of my eye. So I just blink and turn the other way. Sorry man but that communion thing just soured me, possibly for good.

I walk extremely fast to the subway because possibly after the NYU bookstore I could stroll around the West Village for an hour or so, before I have to come back to Brooklyn. I am glad I bought this metro card because I hear the train coming....

Yipee I got on the **right** train going in the **right** direction.....this time!

In 11 quick minutes I was in Washington Square Park and nothing has changed. People playing guitars, people selling and smoking pot, friends meeting, dogs playing and every walk of life to boot. You had your clean cut people, hippies, musicians, drug dealer and homeless people. Washington

Square Park was like a melting pot to every walk of life known to man. I love it here but I gotta get some stuff done.

I get to the NYU store and it is kind of quiet. I bet the students are still home with their families or traveling back today from the Thanksgiving holiday. I peruse the sweatshirts and other things that are on my list to buy. Oh a license plate that says NYU alumni I **have** to have that! I actually got in and out of the bookstore rather quickly! I got a new sweatshirt, a T shirt, a key chain and let's not forget my NYU alumni license plate. I look down at my watch and it is 1pm. Good I have an hour to walk around Greenwich Village.

As I am walking around the village I cannot believe my eyes. Wow the men are out in droves. I cannot believe how many good looking men there are in New York City. They are not like the pretty boys of LA at all. Definitely not the Weho Boys! The men are naturally good-looking. There are so many ruggedly handsome men in this city. The one thing I do have to say about New York City is that I never did have a problem getting laid in this city. In LA they want to see your head shot and resume before they will go down on you. Who am I kidding, before they would actually even talk to you, they need to see credentials. That is if the entire Weho group that they are hanging with approves of you. In LA it is almost like your friends get a vote to see if you can date someone or not.

Yummy look at that Puerto Rican boy go by. God he is fucking gorgeous. In case you don't know, I tend to go for the Latinos and Dark skinned men. Actually to be honest if you blind folded me and put me in a room with 49 white guys and 1 Hispanic guy, I would be standing next to the Hispanic guy. Almost all the guys I have ever dated or slept with have of some sort of Latin descent. I did date a White Guy once but to be fair he had a really **big** dick.

I find Christopher Street and start strolling down the street. I am walking and walking and before I know it I am in Chelsea. I am going in and out of shops and buying a T shirt here and a pair of shoes there. I just can't help staring at all the beautiful men. All these beautiful masculine men for as far as my eyes can see. I think I said that a few seconds ago. Why did I move to LA again? Ha! Damn I am horny and I so need to get laid. I don't think I have ever gone a week without sex. Fuck it is 2:15 pm and I have to head back to my Moms house. I hope my Mother still keeps her Playgirl magazines in the same place. I so need to beat off....I cannot believe I have been here 5 days in New York and haven't gotten laid. This has **never** happened before! I blame Tony Ianucci...

I spot a tanning salon and I just **must, must** get a tan. I go in and fill out the paperwork and buy some lotion. The guy at the counter makes me lift my shirt to check out my tan line to decide which bed is best for me and for how long I should go for.

Wow you have a nice base the cute guy behind the counter says to me.

Thanks I live in LA and I go back tomorrow but I want to look cute tonight.

You look cute right now bud.

Aww thanks Man!

You're welcome. Why don't you do the standup for 8 minutes and that should be perfect?

So I lather on the lotion and hop right into the booth. Shit I forgot sunglasses.

I hop out in my underwear and go get glasses.

Yummy boy what do you need? The guy behind the counter asks.

I forgot glasses I say.

Here you go and he hands them to me, I grab them and run back to the booth. After all I have already lost a minute.

I think about how **much** fun I am going to have tonight with Kevin because it is never a dull moment with Knuckles. Knuckles is the name that I gave him because Kevin can stand for Knuck and he always is making me laugh. Kevin should be a matchmaker because whenever I go out with Kevin I meet tons of guys and always get laid. That is… when I want to get laid, which is usually all the time.

I finish up and get dressed quickly. The cute guy tries to flirt some more but he has a customer and I cannot wait to talk to him.

Take care man I say as I start to walk to the door.

Where are you going tonight handsome? He asks

I think Therapy

Maybe I will see you there.

Usually I would stay and flirt back especially when someone calls me handsome but….

I blame Tony…he made me like him! Damn him. Yes I will blame him for everything that goes wrong today. Damn that pussy whipped Momma's boy without liking pussy- asshole. I am going to call him when I get back to Brooklyn and see what he has to say for himself. I think I need therapy because the things I do for **even** the possibility of having sex are so **not** right.

Back on the subway and I am going "back back back to Brooklyn."

Mom I am home and with plenty of time to spare before we have to leave for Chris and Samantha's house..

I am in the kitchen Tate, she yells.

I walk into the kitchen and Kelly and my Mother are chatting and drinking wine.

Is that **wine?** I say with my eyes ready to bulge out of my head!

Yes Tate I hid a couple of bottles from you when you bought that case of wine on Thanksgiving Day.

Why Mom?

Because you would have drank it all Tate.

No Mom why are you drinking wine during the day? You have given me so much shit about drinking wine during the day.

Give me a break Tate I have had you two all week and now I have to go deal with your sister in law. She is a **Class A** Bitch!

Mom are you Ok? I have never heard you call someone a bitch especially not your daughter in law. How much wine has she had Kelly?

A couple of glasses Tate why?

Why Kelly? Have you **ever** heard our Mother call someone else a bitch? Especially calling her daughter in law one?

Mom why don't you go lay down for about a half hour. We will wake you Ok.

Ok but don't let me oversleep because when her food comes out horrible, which it will anyway, she cannot blame me because I was late.

I promise I won't Mom and she starts climbing the stairs.

We need to talk to Chris about the way Sam treats Mom Tate and Kelly has Ms. Concern face on.

Later ---first we gotta talk about the pussy pounding you got last night. How was it?

You are disgusting Tate.

Did he lick you?

Tate

I am not telling you that!

OK did you see it?

See what?

(I am playing with my crouch right now to give her a hint.)

You are wrong on so many levels Big Brother but yes I did see it.

Did you touch it? I ask like a greedy little kid wanted more candy.

Yes!

Did you **taste** it?

I did Tate!

Did you feel it?

Yes Tate we had sex and it was amazing. Everything was perfect....well everything but my cell phone going off every 2 minutes but...I should have turned it off.

How many times did ya...ya know fuck?

Tate we had sex and made love.

uh-oh

How many times?

Including today Kelly smiles and says er.....6 times.

Did you...you know Org

Everytime.... Tate everytime!

Good girl Kelly ! I knew there was an inner slut in you **somewhere!** I knew the tramp in you just needed to be let loose. I am so glad I was able to help.

So now you are going to take credit for me having sex?

Just a little....... (We are both laughing now)

What about you?

Kissed and made out but neither of us had a place to go. He wouldn't get a hotel first of all and secondly he said he wouldn't sleep with me because he liked me. What kind of bull shit is that right? I mean I like to get the sex out of the way right away. It will piss me off if I was to keep dating him and then I finally get him into bed and he is a fucking Princess Lay there. I would be soooo pissed. I would have wasted all my time "dating him" and then find out he is horrible in bed. No thank you! This is why I sleep with men on the first date. I mean if the sex is good then date, but if it is not then I say see ya.

Well maybe you would meet some good friends while dating. Kelly extremely innocently says to me.

Fuck that Kelly I have enough good friends and what I don't have enough of, is good orgasms. Speaking of that I hope Mom keeps her Playgirl magazines in the same place I need to go wank.

Gross! Thanks Tate I really needed it to know that…

Ring Ring (My cell phone is ringing)

Kelly answer my phone I yell as I am at the top of the stairs and if it is Tony, tell him that I am doing what he should have been doing to me last night.

I will answer it Tate but I am not telling him you are beating off Tate. You are a vial disgusting pig you know that right?.

No I am just honest Kelly I yell from upstairs.

Hello? I can still hear though….

Kelly?

Yes.

Hi it is Tony. Is your brother around?

He is in the bathroom!

Oh well this is his cell phone right?

Can you go knock on the door and tell him it is me.

No! Kelly gasps!

Why?

I cannot do that Tony…

Please??? Tony pleads I think I fucked up today with him at church.

Wait did you say church? Kelly is oddly confused

Yes.

Tate went to church?

Yes

As In Catholic Church? as in St. Anthony's?

Yes.

Wow!!

Can you go tell him it is me on the phone?

Can you call back in like 10 minutes? Kelly pleads.

Why?

Because he should be done by then.

Done with what?

His business.

I don't mind if he talks to me while he is taking a dump. I do it all the time Kelly.

You guys are disgusting. He is not taking a dump but **he** is on the toilet and that is all I will say. I will have him call you when he finishes.

Finishes? Tony is confused now.

Finishes yes…..

Click….Kelly has hung up on Tony.

After I finish my wank I come back downstairs and inform Kelly I finished.

Was it enjoyable for you Tate? You are a disgusting little perv.

Not really Kelly…Did you know that none of the naked guys in Playgirl have hard ons? All limp dicks. It was difficult to bring it home so I just thought of Tony. It worked.

Thanks for sharing Kelly says in disgust

Was that Tony on the phone before?

Yes of course it was Tate as Kelly glares at me

What did you tell him?

I told him you were in the bathroom, that you were **not** taking a dump but were sitting on the toilet and that you would call him back when you… um… finished your business.

Ha Great Kelly. You know a couple of more weeks with me Kel and I could actually make you a really cool sis!

A couple of more weeks with you Tate and I would finally have enough dirt on you, to finally have you committed…you psychopath. Call him I want to see what he says.

Psychopath huh…you know that is a compliment to me right? Go wake up Mom and start to get ready to go.

I am ready she snaps

Really you might want to look again. **Go!**

Ok ok geez

So I press last call number on my cell phone and Tony picks up after the second ring.

Hello?

You called Tony?

Yeah I was calling to see what you are doing tonight?

I told you. I am going to my brothers for dinner.

What about after that?

I am not sure. I am probably just hanging out with my Mom and sister before I go out. My best friend Kevin is supposed to meet me at Therapy around 10pm tonight.

Can I come with you? I want to see you today.

You did see me today.

I know, I know but

But what Tony? I guess I did want to pick a fight after all with him

You know my Mom Tate. She hates you after what happened with the police and all.

Tony it was 11 fucking years ago. You couldn't even shake my fucking hand in church? Or my Mother's hand? 8 hours earlier you had your tongue down my throat and you were shaking more than my hand buddy!

(I hear a whisper—this is getting good. It is my Mother and Sister eves dropping from the kitchen but I don't give a shit about that right about now)

Tate come on, I was nervous and I just froze today. I didn't expect **you** at church. You know my feelings for you Tate and I love your Mom.

You have feelings for me but you couldn't shake mine or my Mother's hand? What did Mommy forbid you Tony?

(How did you ever get Tate to go to church with you Ma? Kelly whispers)

(Blackmail Kel)

Tony is stammering: What no I just didn't want a confrontation in church Tate. You know here you come for a week to stir up all this shit, make a mess and then you get to leave.

Stir up shit…what shit Tony? Please tell me I implore you to. For the record you were the one looking for me at The Ale House.

You just **had** to sit right behind us didn't you? You made my Mother so uncomfortable throughout the whole mass Tate.

Are you sure it wasn't you who was uncomfortable there Ton? Think about it. Your Mother hates me for something I did as a teenager. You were worried she would find out that after all the shame you brought to the "Family". **Imagine** if she found out that you went out on a date with Tate Psychopath Connors. The boy that got her precious boy arrested. The boy who took a picture that was mailed to her son, of a girl sucking a dick and then that boy posted it **all** over the neighborhood. The boy who also happens to be gay, who definitely was the single person corrupting her son into being gay. Tony she would still continue to hate me but what would she then think about her precious little Tony. Were ya worried she would forbid ya again Tony? Is that what it is?

(He is good Kelly, I still think he should have been a lawyer) My Mother whispers loudly to Kelly

(Mom don't worry he will probably play one on TV one day) Kelly laughs back

496

(I would be convinced my Mother say, who is still trying to whisper)

Tony I am past all this in my life. I am not going backwards and I have dealt with all of my Mommy issues. My Mother and my sister are eves dropping in the dining room right now. Shall I get them? Would you like to ask them yourself? I do not have any issues with my family in regards to my sexuality. My Father doesn't understand it or respect it so guess what? He is not in my life.

Tate stop…. Please?

No…..I gotta go, it is 3 o clock and I am going to be late to my brother's. I am really looking forward to seeing my little nieces.

Can I call you later?

You can call but whether I pick up is another thing.

Tate I am sorry. I really am. Can I come with you tonight?

No I want to go out and just have fun with my best friend Kevin.

Can I stop by and say goodbye before you go out tonight….please? Who knows when I will see you again? Are you coming back for Christmas?

Are you fucking kidding me? I would rather hammer nails in my eyes than come back to Brooklyn next month.

Hey that's not nice Tate! As my Mother and Kelly yell in unison.

I know you two birds have been there the whole time. You might as well come on out of the dining room anyway. We should start walking to Christopher's; we are going to be late.

Tony I gotta go.

Wait Can I come see you before you go meet your friend in the city?

Oh alright but you cannot come with me. No matter how many times you ask and if you follow me, I am telling your Mother you are stalking me and want to adopt African babies with me!

Ha! Cool I promise! Will you be back by 9?

Fuck yea! I love my nieces but after about 3 hours I am done with them. I still want to go to the gym when I get back from my brothers house as well.

You do??? As the hens that are my Sister and Mother squawk at me.

Yes I want to go to the gym. Can I finish this call guys?

(They both laugh)

That's cool come by around 9.

OK and Tate again I am sorry…

Bye Tony.

Bye….

(I walk into the dining room where my Mother and sister are sitting)

You have totally forgiven him haven't you Tate my sister asks.

Yup completely, I know his Mother is a complete bitch.

Then why won't you let him go into the City with you Tate? My Mom asks sounding very confused.

Because Kevin will hit on him Mom and I want Tony all to myself. Trust me Mom he will hit on him and it will only get worse with the more Bacardi and Diet Cokes he has.

But doesn't Kevin have a boyfriend Tate? My Mom inquires.

Yes but that has never stopped him before. Plus I think they are on a break again. You never know with those two..

The gay's take breaks too? My sister asks.

Apparently so Kel! I haven't had a relationship last long enough to go on a break so I don't really know how it works and all.

It will take a lifetime for me to understand "The Gays" I swear my Mom says to my sister. Every time I think I have a grasp on his life, he comes out with another lingo-ism. You baffle me Tate but it can be extremely entertaining from time to time as my Mom teases me. It is seriously never ever a dull moment with you.

You should write a book Tate you know that? It would be hysterical. My sister says as we turn onto my brother's block.

You guys would hate me Kelly if I wrote a book.

No we wouldn't son, my new cheerleader of a Mom says I would be so proud.

Me too Tate. I would be the first one on line to buy the book my sister adds.

I am going to hold you both to that. You hear me?

Yes they say in unison.

My Mother says you could call it **Lost in your own Chaos**.

Or Just plain Chaos…Kelly adds

Ok we are here. Let's go in.

Ding Dong Ding Dong!

There here Mommy! Uncle Tate and Aunt Kelly are here!!!!!! (I hear my two very excited nieces through the front door of my brother's house.)

I need a nap already.

Well the door opens and my nieces Natalie and Breana just bum rush us! They are hugging us and want to be picked up. They are so cute and I just love them so much. Natalie is 6 and Breana is 3 and they are the two of the cutest little girls in the world.

We miss you Uncle Tate Natalie proclaims Can't you move back?

Arr you melt my heart. I just smother her with kisses. My work is in California so no sweetie, I cannot move back to New York. At least not for a while that is.

Can we come visit you in California Uncle Tate?

Sure talk to your Dad!(as I glance over at Chris)

Hey bro thank you because now every day for the rest of her life she will be asking me when we are going to see Uncle Tate in California.(Good)

Natalie is my God daughter and she is very much like me. Has to be the center of attention and not because she is jealous of her sister or anything but it is just who she is. The energy this kid has is amazing and I wish I could bottle it and take back to LA with me.

Breana is actually the younger quieter one. Actually she is like her God mother Kelly to be honest. Hmm never thought about it like that before. Quiet and very reserved but desperate to get out of her sisters shadow and into the spotlight. Sounds like two other people I know...

Come in, Come in Chris says and Sam is in the kitchen.

OK please tell me you have wine.

Of course we do. We have wine for my favorite brother in law! As I hear Sam's voice coming out of the kitchen.

Big hug and kiss for all and the blah blah stuff. She even gave my Mother a peck on the cheek. Ok we are off to a good start! Just gotta keep it that way.

Where did you say the wine was Sam?

On top of the refrigerator my brother yells from the living room.

I look on top of the refrigerator and I don't see any bottles of wine someone must have moved it.

I don't see it Chris I yell back.

My brother gets his lazy ass off his chair to come half into the kitchen and points to the top of the refrigerator and goes:

Right there… are you fucking blind?

First of all that is a box and secondly do you always curse in front of your kids? I snap at Chris.

Well my brother of course comes back with the sarcastic response:

First of all Tate yup in fact it is a box and second of all….of wine.

Ugh No way!

A box of wine? Do you seriously expect **me** to drink wine out of a box?

Why not? I do it all the time plus it's cheaper…

I do **not** drink wine out of a box Chris.

Its good…try it first before you start bitching. What are you a fucking snob now Tate? Are you too good for my box of wine?

I glance over at my nieces and they are waiting for me to respond. I look at their beautiful faces and I wonder how a fucking douche bag as big as my brother produced such beautiful kids. I so want to say that I am too good for my brother's shitty box of wine but I know it will only start World War 3 and I have been here less than 20 minutes.

I will **try** it but stop yelling at me like I am your fucking wife!

I figured if he was cursing in the house so would I. The difference is I admit I would make an awful parent. I will be making my babies in a tissue for the rest of my life that is for sure. I opened the box of wine and I pour myself a very "healthy" goblet of wine.

Would anybody else want some wine?

My sister and Mom in unison say **yes**. I don't know if they really wanted any wine or were afraid of what my brothers reaction would be if they said no.

What are we having for dinner Sam?

Leftovers from Thanksgiving my brother chimes in.

What? You are kidding right? I ask.

No I am not kidding. Sam's Mom had a ton leftover from Thanksgiving and she didn't want them to go to waste. We are all turkey'd and Thanksgiving out so we just figured we would fed it to you guys. We didn't want it to go to waste.

I am thinking to myself yeah ya cheap fuck that is what it is. You cannot even give us a fucking meal? I wouldn't have cared if it was hamburgers and hot dogs but Thanksgiving leftovers? What a dick! Every year for Christmas we get lists of what the girls want for Christmas and every year they are always the most expensive things on their lists. I have bought them a digital camera, an X Box and a Wii game. I know the cheap fuck probably un-wraps the gifts and then rewraps them saying it is from him. I fucking hate cheap people. I am so pissed right now but again I am here to see my darling nieces and I am going to ignore douchebag Chris..

Do you have a fucking problem with that too Tate?

You know what Chris. I do have a problem with that. I really do but I am not going to get into that with you right now. I am going to visit with my nieces, drink this **fabulous** box wine and try and enjoy the rest of this afternoon.

My brother just glares at me for about 15 seconds but then whatever God forsaken football game that is blaring from the TV set gets his attention. Of course Chicken Little Mother and her sidekick Tweety Bird Kelly don't say a peep about the Thanksgiving leftovers. My sister in law sits there like a subservient little woman that must obey her master. This makes me sick and I gotta get out of there before things become worse. Things becoming worse are basically me getting into it with my douche bag brother yet again.

Hey Natalie and Breana let me see your room?

Ok as they both cheer in harmony!

Let's go girls!

Well I get to their room and I gotta say at least my brother is not a cheap bastard with them. They have a computer and a flat screen television. There are dolls all over the place. They are starting to get into Barbie's because I see a ton of different Barbie dolls all over the room. When I was a kid I knew all their names. I wasn't allowed to have any but it was basically the only time in my life that I would play nice with my sister. My nieces had teddy bears and dolls everywhere. There was an Easy Bake Oven, lots of Sponge Bob, Elmo's and Barney's too. They had twister which I found strange. Both twin beds had princess sheets on them. The room was pretty neat and I wondered if they were very neat or Mom cleaned it for company. If they took after their Father, I would go with the latter one. They had a little table with crayons and coloring books on it.

What do you guys like to play?

Barbie's Natalie sang

I like to color Uncle T Breana said

Ok then why don't we color first and then play Barbie's after.

I don't like to color Uncle T Natalie whined

I **hate** Barbie's Breana shot back.

Well for the next hour I bounced between colorings in a One Direction coloring book to playing Barbie's with Natalie. They both had very complete opposite personalities. Natalie was very girlie and liked girlie things. Breana I have a feeling will probably never get into Barbie's but I see her being a very creative person. I was really enjoying myself when Samantha came in and asked me if I wanted any leftovers:

Would you like any leftovers?

No thanks I too am over turkey and Thanksgiving food.

I am sorry Tate but money is really tight right now and Chris is stressed over money, with the new baby and all on the way.

It is fine, no worries I tell her. I am just going to hang out in here with the girls for a little while longer, I say trying to be cheerful.

You can stay Tate but they have to come and eat, Samantha tells me like I am a 3 year old who has just been scolded for shitting in my pants.

Ok so we all head back into the kitchen. Chris has got his nose in the game on TV, Kelly is reading a magazine and my Mother is knitting. **Wow** they all really must like each other….so, so much! My sister in law feeds the kids. Hey why are they getting spaghetti? I want some spaghetti but I just shut up. My sister in law fixes a plate for my brother and of course his way of thanking her is a grunt. She then proceeds to make herself a plate and sits down right next to my sister and starts to eat. Is she fucking kidding me? Does she know what it means to host? I feel so bad for these kids. They are going to grow up with no manners. Finally about 7 or 8 swallows my sister in law realizes that she does in fact have guests and goes:

Help yourselves guys there are plenty of leftovers from Thanksgiving to go around.

Ok dear as my Mom gets up and heads to the kitchen.

Kelly just looks at me like what the fuck? Did she really just say that? Well we were staring at each other for a tad bit too long when all of a sudden I hear:

Is there a problem? It is my brother Chris who has taken his eye off the game… Actually it must be a commercial break for him to give us his undivided attention now.

There is no problem Chris we just don't want leftovers, as Kelly finally speaks up.

Suit yourself guys….as Chris glares at the both of us.

No offense Chris, Kelly continues I actually have a date tonight and he is taking me to the River Café around 8 and I don't want to spoil my appetite..

Good for you I hope we are not holding you from more important social gatherings Kelly. My brother snides.

No not at all Chris I wanted to see the girls.

Really cause you haven't spent more than 5 minutes with them. (Pointing at me) At least homo over there has been playing with them for the last 2 hours. You have been reading a magazine. What you don't like my kids?

(I am staying out of this one but I did wonder why Kelly really hadn't spent time with the girls).

Chris I love your kids and we spent all day Tuesday together. I just wanted to give Tate some alone time with them, that's all.

Well he could have cared less again…the football game was back on or so I thought.

Have either of you called Dad? Chris inquires.

I left him a message Kelly said

Nope didn't call Chris but the phone works two ways Chris! I emailed him and told him I was coming but never heard back from him.

They are skiing in Vermont. Dad bought a condo on Killington Mountain. We are going up there with them for President Week. The kids are off from school so Dad and I thought it would be a great time to teach the girls how to ski.

So what did you ask Santa to bring you for Christmas Natalie?

(Yes I am changing the subject because I really do not want to talk about my Dad. My relationship with my Dad is horrendous now due to me coming out of the closet. It is not bad enough he is homophobic, but his bitch of a wife tells him, at every opportunity she can that I am going to hell. I have just taken myself out of the equation when it comes to my Dad. I respect my Dad and yes he did pay for my college education but if you ask me if I love him they answer is….I think so. I do hope that will change as the years go by though.

I asked Santa for a Barbie Townhouse Natalie blurts and I have been really good this year.

Yes you have Chris says and gently brushes his hands through Natalie's hair.

I had a Barbie Town House when I was your age Natalie, Kelly informs Natalie

Yeah and Tate played with it more than you did Kel, Chris teases.

True…Very true

That is how I knew you were gay Tate my Mom says as she walks back into the room with her plate of turkey leftovers..

What? How Mom? I ask.

Well one day you were playing in the Barbie Townhouse and I noticed that you had two Ken dolls together in bed. When I told you that you shouldn't have two Ken dolls in bed together you got very angry. You **insisted** that you wanted them that way. I would try and explain to you why but you just kept insisting. That is the day I knew you were gay.

How old was I Mom? I asked.

About 8 or 9 I guess.

What is gay? Natalie asks and we all just freeze and look at each other.

It means happy Natalie, I say.

It means Tate likes boys Natalie, my brother states.

We all just look at my brother and he says:

What I am not going to lie to her. My brother is gay. There is nothing I can do about it? I don't agree with it or understand it but I am not going to lie to my daughter about it.

I like boys Daddy does that mean I am gay Daddy? Natalie asks.

No it is when two boys like each other or even if two girls like each other.

Well I like Francesca, my best friend Daddy does that mean I am gay too?

No, Natalie it does not make you gay.

Hey Chris don't ya think my answer was better now? I ask my brother with a hint of sarcasm.

Natalie….Gay means happy, my brother proclaims to his sweet innocent daughter.

Natalie looks confused and Kelly is playing Uno with Breana now. Samantha is picking up plates, while Mom is pretending to be into the football game now and I am just watching all of the discomfort on everyone's face. I am so ready to go home. I look down at my watch and it is 635 pm and it is time to go!

Well I gotta run I am meeting a friend in the city.

Did you know Tony Ianucci is gay? My sister asks Chris.

Yeah I heard but why should it affect you Kelly? It is just another man that would reject you anyway? Why do you have to gossip so much? I can't stand that about you. Seriously you need to go too.

Fight back Kelly I say to myself. Don't let him talk to you that way. Don't be his door mat Kelly. I didn't even mind that she said it to Chris but I never know how he is going to treat her. It is almost always cruel but every once in a while he throws her a bone.

Bye Natalie and Breana as I hug my dear sweet nieces. Email me as much as you can and tell me what is going on. Ok?

OK Uncle T Breana says

I will Uncle Tate Natalie says and then begins to cry. I don't want you to go Uncle Tate. Stay here with me and play…please.

I wish I could but keep asking your Dad when you can come visit me in California. Ask him every day as many times as you want OK?

Well the tears stop immediately and she turns to Chris and says when can we go to California Daddy?

We will talk about it after the baby is born Nat.

When is that Daddy? She inquires.

Soon Natty.

How soon Daddy?

Thank bro…thanks he says as I hug him goodbye.

That's what ya get for making me drink box wine little bro I say into his ear.

Dick, he whispers right back into my ear. I will send you the Girls Christmas wish list next week.

I hug Samantha goodbye and say Talk to you soon.

Sorry for the leftovers Tate, she whispers in my ear.

It's fine, I am actually hankering for some New York Pizza before I go back to LA.

We both laugh…

Mom are you coming?

No I am going to stay here for a while and help with the dishes.

You **don't** have to Ma, Samantha snaps. Go with them. We will talk soon. **Go!**

Well after another 15 minutes of goodbyes we are all out of the house and back on the street. We are walking up Henry Street when I turn to my Mother and Sister:

Fucking Thanksgiving leftovers? Is that not a fuck you to us or what?

They are struggling Tate especially with another baby along the way my Mom says on the defense of Chris as usual.

Struggling Mom…have you seen the kid's room. It looks like a commercial for Toys R Us. Let's not mention that Chris has every single cable station known to man! Did you see the tacky jewelry that Samantha had one? It takes a whole hell of a lot of money to look that cheap Ma. That tacky shit she is wearing is all 14 k gold Mom. He couldn't spend $20 bucks on some hamburgers and hot dogs? Maybe a piece of fucking chicken? And of course on my way out he made sure to tell me that he would be sending the girls Christmas list next week.

Of course he did Kelly chimes in!

Tate he is a parent. He has 4 mouths to feed. Plus the girls want a dog. He works long hours Tate and it is his money to spend on how he sees fit. My Mother AKA Chris's Defense Attorney cross examines back at me..

Mom why does he always get a pass for bad behavior because he has kids… why?

Yeah Mom? Kelly chimes in again.

When and if (as she looks at me) you two ever have kids you will understand but until then mind your business. –I can tell my Mother is getting annoyed with us now so I need to change the subject.

So when did Chris and Dad get so chummy?

Yeah Mom Kelly chirps in.

Kelly shut up you are starting to sound like a parrot I snap at her, as we turn the corner back onto Columbia Heights.

I don't ask…he doesn't tell me…so I leave it at that. It is none of our business Tate. Plus you are 3000 miles away so why is it any of your concern anyway? My Mother laments.

I am just going to leave it alone Mom.

Good open the door it is freezing Tate.

I am going to take an hour nap Mom.

You nap a lot Tate you know that?

Yup Mom I do!

I will be up in an hour, see ya then.

No Tate I am going to play **Bingo** at the church at 8 so I will see you later.

Which Church? St. Anthony's or Nuts and Bolts Mom?

It is called Empty Nesters, ya smart ass and you told me you had a really good time there on Friday night Tate.

I did I was just wondering that is all. I wish you would bite off your daughter in laws head like the way you bark at me Ma. I was just curious, that's all..

I snap at you because I always end up being the punch line to every joke with you verses Samantha is just a bitch, and now a pregnant one.5 more months of Samantha pregnant is not going to be a day at Great Adventure for me. I am coming to visit you in February Tate.

You are?

Chapter 20

It is Party Time in NYC

Mom I am going out tonight and won't be back till late.

But both you and Kelly have early flights in the morning. We are leaving here at 6am Tate. You better not stay up too late.

Mom I will sleep on the plane don't worry. I will be ready at 6 am tomorrow morning…..**Trust me!**

Ok

I am going to nap also before my date with Kyle. Let's wake each other up Tate?

If you agree to use the bathroom down the hall I will.

Fine!! Kelly snaps.

Well I take a nap and as the alarm clock is going off I hear the shower running. That fucking bitch is using my shower but I am not going to get mad…I am going to get even. Kelly thinks she is slick using the damn shower before I get up.. I go to the door and turn the knob to the bathroom door. **A ha** aces she didn't lock the door. I sneak in and turn the cold water on the bathroom sink to full blast and run out the door. About halfway down the hall I hear screaming but it is not a woman's voice....**Fuck** it is Ron, my Mother's boyfriend...Shit so I tear back to the bathroom and he is dripping wet turning off the faucet.

Sorry Ron I thought you were Kelly....

(Well he is pissed):

You fucking fried me with hot water Tate. Look you burnt me asshole.(I have never seen him this mad)I cannot wait for you two to go home tomorrow. You know you just gave me second degree burns on my ass Tate.

It is not that bad Ron let me see?

I am not going to show you my ass Tate.

A little homophobic there Ron?

Just get out.

Seriously sorry Ron I thought you were Kelly.

She is sleeping in your Mothers bed. That's why I used this shower, not to wake her. Silly me huh?

Sorry Ron I am.

You fuckers are going to kill one another one of these days, Ron says with a laugh.

Ron if we haven't done it by now it probably won't happen. Plus we all live in separate cities now and only see each other once or twice a year.

I can hope right can't I? And now he is laughing so I don't really think that I have given him second degree burns on his ass..

Ron is actually a good guy. He is good to my Mother. He sometimes enables her a little too much but he genuinely loves her and that is all the matters.

Kelly wake up, I just fried Ron's ass.(As I am shaking Kelly to wake her up from my Mom's bed.) Why are you sleeping in Mom's bed?

What ? Kelly says as she rubs her eyes.

I am going to use this shower but I will be quick.

Ok wake me when you get out.

Ok

I take a quick shower mainly out of fear of retaliation from Ron because Brooklyn water can scald you or freeze you in a matter of seconds, especially when someone else turns on the water in the bathroom sink or flushes the toilet..

Kelly get up. the shower is all yours. I will go get ready in the other bathroom. I am sure the steam in that bathroom has cleared by now.

I saved my best shirt for the last night. Even though I didn't work out that much this week, this shirt always makes me look awesome. Plus it is only 915pm and I am not meeting Kevin till 1030pm. I start doing pushups with the music blasting to KTU. I love KTU and after I do about 300 pushups I hop back into the shower again. I lock the door just in case and do another quick rinse. As I am just about done putting on my clothes and perfecting my hair there is a bang on the door.

Tony Ianucci has been down stairs for like 40 minutes waiting on you and yup it is Kelly barking at me. I am leaving on my date with Kyle. What is taking you so long?

Shit I forgot…. tell him I will be right down.

I look in the mirror for one last look. I am soo glad I tanned today.

I run down the stairs and I apologize to Tony. I lost track of the time buddy… sorry.

It's cool he says and I don't want to keep you Tate.

No its cool I still have over a half hour before I have to leave to meet my friend in the City, what's up?

Well what would you think of me moving to LA?

Why would you moved to LA Tony? I ask

For a fresh start with my life, like you did, I desperately need a change and also to see where things can go with us. It would be a dream come true to live somewhere without my Mother or anybody else interfering in my life. Tony says this to me like he has been planning this for months.

What would you do? I inquire.

I would get a job Tony says almost asking.

Hmmm

What is it Tate?

Tony if you want to move to LA for a fresh start don't let me stop you. But you need to do it for you. I cannot be the only reason you move to LA. That wouldn't be fair to either one of us. You would need a purpose and a plan to move to LA. I mean we only reconnected like 48 hours ago and I gotta say, my friend it has been bumpy. You cannot move to LA just for me. You will resent me after a very short time and I could possibly resent you.

So you are telling me **not** to come to LA? Tony asks like someone just stole his puppy.

No that is not what I am saying. Figure out a plan that is all I am saying. What you want to do, where you are going to live, money etc etc. I can be a factor in you moving to LA but **not** the only factor. Do you get what I am saying? Plus what are you going to tell your Mother? If she is anything like mine was, when I told her I was moving to LA it is not going to be pleasant. Plus I didn't live with my Mother when I lived here either.

I...I...Don't know. Don't you want me to come?

Tony let me get back to LA and process all this. Let's talk on the phone, email and facebook each other. I cannot promise you anything right now. Do you think I am being an asshole?

No I get it. There is a lot more to think about. Maybe I will go back to college out there.

Good idea but makes sure you have money in the bank Tony if you do decide to move to LA. It is expensive to start over.

I am in good shape Tate. Remember I haven't had a life in almost a year and I live rent free with my Mother..

OK give me a kiss I have to head to the subway.

OK

(Well Tony tries to go in with the tongue but I am not really feeling it right now so I pull away).

Slow down my friend.

What time is your flight in the morning?

8 am Ton

Wow so this is it? Tony asks.

For now (and I felt bad) do you want to walk me to the subway.

Sure Tony says.

Ok hold on while I get my phone and wallet.

Ok

As I run upstairs I already have my phone and wallet but my insecure ass needs to do final touchups on my hair in the bathroom.

About 5 minutes late, I am ready to go.

Tony walks me to the subway and we small talk but nothing more about LA. When we reach the subway station Tony looks at me with those beautiful eyes and says:

Are you sure I cannot come with you to meet your friend in The City?

Tony I really need to spend this night with my best friend Kevin.

OK and Tony gives me a hug goodbye.

I wave and smile as I head down to the subway. I don't look back but I know he is watching me go down the stairs.

I enter the train station and I start to think about Tony. Here is a guy I haven't seen in like forever and is willing to move to LA after spending 2 days with me. I doubt he will follow through with it but just imagine if he did. You know what the topper of all of this is? We haven't even had sex yet...Now I know I am awesome in bed but what happens if he does move to LA and he sucks in bed...then what?

He is in love with me now and we haven't even had sex yet. Once we do I will **never** be able to get rid of him **Ha**....You better think long and hard on this one Tate....especially if he is long and hard...that is **hard** to come by, especially in West Hollywood!

Well 20 minutes on the subway and off to Therapy I go. I get to around 54th Street and I turn down the block and Therapy is right there. I go in and it pretty much looks the same. Therapy is a video bar and all the bartenders are Hot. They have videos playing all over the place. It is darker than it used to be but it is still crowded, which is good. I go downstairs and check my jacket in. I turn around and I hear.

Bitch what did you do become anorexic in LA? What did you shave half of your ass off? Are you on steroid/diet pill combo bitch?

Ahh Knuckhead so nice to see you – you look great! (My nickname for Kevin, is Knucklehead and it is just a fun, idiot nickname, because Kevin will do almost anything to have a good time)

I know…Kevin says without an ounce of self doubt.

You look good, actually too fucking good. Maybe I should move to LA, Kevin states.

Not another one of you people….I mumble under my breath.

What did you say Tate?

Never mind I will tell you later, about my Thanksgiving weekend drama later.

Let's get a drink.as Kevin points to the stairs.

Yes I so desperately need one Knuckles.

You know you are the **only** person I let call me Knuckles.

Yes I know you tell me a least once every time we see each other.

Whatever come on let's get you a drink.

Well we go upstairs and my favorite bartender Kenny is still bartending. Kenny is so hot and I have had a crush on him for years. Unfortunately for me he has a gorgeous Latin boyfriend who is also very sweet. I see Kenny and he sees me right away:

Tate you looking fantastically amazing! How is LA? We are planning to come out to Los Angeles soon. We are facebook friends right?

Yup we are!

Bud Light Kenny asks almost like he already knows what I am going to order.

No Ken, vodka and soda with a Therapy of cranberry juice. I don't drink beer anymore, it bloats me way too much..

Yeah you are definitely living in LA my friend as he winks, and smirks at me. Look who is here, I hear that sexy Latin accent and it is Enrique, Kenny's gorgeous boyfriend.

Wow Tate muy guapo and he leans in and gives me a kiss on my lips.

I would so love to have a 3 way with these two guys that is for sure. They are both just stunning and have amazing bodies. You see at Therapy all the bartenders have to have amazing bodies because they are shirtless bartenders and usually in speedos or tight, tight shorts so you can see um...everything.

Well Kevin has allowed me to have about 4.2 minutes of attention so his time limit is just about up by now.

What about me uhuh? Am I invisible? I need another Kevin Twist...

Coming Kevin...Kenny teases with Kevin

Well Kevin and I start talking about what has been going on with our lives. Now Kevin is very over the top and extremely funny. We have this banter that we do, that I have honestly never found in another single gay man walking the planet. We can finish each other sentences and we genuinely enjoy each other company. We have had some ups and downs but in the end, we are as thick as thieves. We make each other laugh and it is never a dull moment when we are together. Half way through a story of him telling me about a trick gone bad, this obnoxious guy named Tino comes by.

Now Tino is this obnoxious fat guy that Kevin cannot stand. He is not attractive, fat and usually has to buy men for sex. He is always trying to compete with Kevin. Kevin never competes with Tino and tries to avoid him as much as possible. He doesn't bother me as much as he bothers Kevin. I guess because he doesn't try to compete with me. Well he comes up and starts telling us another one of his farfetched tales of some gorgeous guy that wants him, or someone whom he is dating or some sex escapade he is about to embark on. I just tune him out but he really bugs Kevin. Now Kevin can be the sweetest guy in the world but he also can be a bitch. He usually just ignores Tino, so I was hoping Tino would go away rather quickly this one time. It is my last night in NYC and I want to have fun.

We try moving around the bar but he keeps on finding us. Well after our fourth location move Tino spots us again. He comes running up and says

" I feel like a princess….no wait Dorothy from the Wizard of Oz! This hot guy wants to take me to dinner!!! (Ok I am thinking here we go with the Wizard of Oz….**again.** What the hell is with **that** movie and people obsessed with it?)

Well Kevin whirls around to Tino and without missing a beat and says Yeah? Well why don't you tap 3 times and Go the Fuck Home?

Well Tino looks at him and is about to start a fight. I am laughing so hard because Kevin really meant it. I have to compose myself because this will get bad in about 2 seconds.

Fuck you Kevin! Why do you always have to be like that?

Guys **please** I am only here for one night before I have to go back to LA, can you just get along for my sake and then go back to killing each other tomorrow?

Fine they both say in unison.

Can I buy you guys a drink? Tino asks

Sure I will take a Kevin Twist and Tate will have a vodka and um soda? As he turns to me to make sure he has my new drink down bat.

I nod and I am thinking to myself that no matter how much Kevin hates someone, he **never** has a problem taking a free drink from them. Ha Kevin you bitch, I love you and I so miss you.

Well as the night chugs on we are meeting lots of people. Each drink we have the guys keep getting better looking than the last. I need to take a break and start drinking some water. It is only 1230 am for heaven's sake and I want to keep going for a while. I want to have a full on New York nightclub experience to take back with me to LA. You can say lots of great things about LA but the nightlife is no comparison to New York City. Just as things are starting to close in LA is when things heat up in New York City. As the water is starting to sober me up a little, I notice that some of my friends are starting to get messy.

As the night has progressed we have started to pick up an entourage of various friends or acquaintances. There is Kevin's coworker Albert who is a sweet guy but has a face only his Mother could possibly find attractive, Jeffrey a catty and feminine fashion queen who works for Dior and loves to tell anyone within earshot of how fabulous he is. Then there is Donald who is the ultimate mess and has spent many a month's living on my sofa after being evicted from **another** apartment. Donald portrays himself as this Tate trust fund kid who wears Prada and Polo and pretends to be an upper class **wasp** snob. In reality Donald is a waiter who stays at the YMCA if he made enough tips that night to pay for the room. I think he has a locker at Port Authority or something to keep his belongings in. His parents live up state and every few months Donald goes up there to dry out or hide from people he owes money to. Now don't get me wrong Donald is a fun guy but I wouldn't trust a fucking word out of his mouth. Especially when he is the most famous for saying something is wrong with his ATM card and can he borrow $20 bucks and pay me back later. So let's just say this is a real Motley Crew huh?

I have to go back to drinking alcohol because I am starting to get bitchy. As I am sobering up, everyone else is getting drunker. Albert is actually making out with a guy that is uglier than him. I didn't think that was possible. I know that is very mean spirited but I wish I could grab someone glasses and put them on Albert. I would say look Albert you could do better...seriously look at him. **Yuck**! You see I have to drink because if they all get drunker and I am sober, kitty will sharpen his claws even more. In case you are wondering... yes...I would be kitty.

Kenny can I have a shot of tequila with a vodka soda chaser?

You can have anything you want handsome, as Kenny winks at me and starts to pour my shot of tequila..

Anything I say to myself? I would love to have you naked in my bed for a month. The things I would do to that man. I start to fantasize about being on a gigantic bed secluded on a beach. We would be watching the sunset and just holding each other. We would have had sex 11 times that day and we are just embracing each other when I hear: **well are you going to drink that or what?**

It's Kevin of course.

I grab the tequila shot and just down it as fast as I can. I almost feel like I was just busted for watching porn by my Mother. I wonder if Kenny knows I was fantasizing about him and I having sex?

How much Kenny? As I look over to him.

It's on me handsome! Welcome home he smiles and turns to another customer.

Kevin If he calls me handsome one more time I swear I am going to jump over that bar and...

Relax Tate he calls **everyone** handsome including Albert. Kevin snaps.

I think I like Tino better than you Kevin…. you bitch. I say in a funny but yet sarcastic manner that can be taken several ways.

You miss me Tate I know you do and Kenny doesn't call everyone handsome… Just you. I can just be a jealous bitch sometimes and you look great Tate. I heard that Kenny and Enrique have been known to pick up a third from time to time. Enrique hasn't stopped eyeing you all night Tate and he even asked me how long you were here for. I told him just for the night and he seemed to really like that.

Thanks Knuckles….maybe he just wants to make sure I don't hit on Kenny. Not that I would have a chance in hell but one can only dream, right?

So what's with this childhood friend that came out to you? You started to tell me on the phone but then you said you would fill me in later. Is he cute? Bless Kevin heart because you would think he is being genuine but also wants to know because he know I am going back to LA in the morning.

He is very cute Knuckles but you cannot have him. There is plenty of guy's right here in Therapy for you to torture without going after my childhood crush.

So **now** he is a crush hmm? Kevin says mocking me.

Look Knuckles let's just have fun tonight. I don't need to hook up or meet a guy. I would just like to spend some quality time with my best friend. Is that cool Knuckles? I ask

Tate I love ya and I miss ya but sorry…Momma **needs** to get laid tonight. Let's find me a man! I am so horny I would even do bridge and tunnel.

I laugh and say gotta love your honesty Knuckles! Let's go find you Mr. Right Now…

Amen sista!!!! Kevin slurs

We do Cheers, clink our glasses and just canvas the bar. Albert is still going full on tonsil hockey with the ugly guy, Tino has his shirt down 4 buttons by now, Donald is sending some poor guy downstairs to the bathroom with a bottle of cologne because apparently he has bad body odor. I just know that Donald was not very nice about it either but what can I do? I am a tourist now and what do tourists do? Yup they Sightsee and that is what I am going to do at Therapy tonight. I am going to sight see and maybe even pick up a couple of souvenirs along the way! Souvenirs as in who do I want to make out with?

Kevin let's walk around. I whisper in his ear.

Let me just pay for another round I ordered as he smiles and gives me this sinister look like I am going to get you drunk tonight.

Another round....already? I am not even done with this one yet. I tell Kevin.

Well suck it down. The night is still young and so is we Tate! Loosen up and get that stick out of your ass. You used to be so much fun. Kevin said almost a little hurtful.

I am fun! I bark at Kevin as he is handing me another shot and a vodka chaser.

Prove it!

So I do the shot and down my last drink. Yup there is in fact gay peer pressure too!!Ok I am pretty buzzed by now. What can I do that is fun, I say to myself as we walk through the club. Then it hits me. I am going to make out with every cute guy I see from here to the dance floor.

Well first it was this Hot Puerto Rican man but I don't think his boyfriend was too happy with me when I started kissing him. I think his boyfriend called me a Puta Gringo but I really didn't care because after all, I was a tourist. I must have made out with 4 or 5 different people over the next hour or so. Kevin got in on it too. Soon we were the kissing whores of Therapy but I didn't care one bit. After all I was a tourist...

Well its 230am and I needed another drink. I looked around for Kevin and he was on stage proving to a drag queen that his ass was just as tight as an ATM Slot. He was showing his behind and trying to get the poor drag queen to swipe a credit card down his ass crack. The drag queen was surprisingly kind of into it.

OK Kevin is officially drunk...

I head back to the bar and I ask Kenny for another vodka and soda.

You have been a mighty busy boy tonight huh Tate? Kenny says in a very flirty tone but I am drunk so I am not sure.

Just having fun I guess. I am a tourist now, I laugh hoping I don't sound like a drunken idiot to Kenny.

Yeah well can I have a turn? Kenny asks and I don't think, I know that he is really flirting with me now..

What turn I ask Kenny?

Kenny uses his finger to bring me closer in like he is going to tell me a secret. The next thing I know Kenny has his tongue completely down my throat and it feels incredible. I instantly have a hard on but a reality check sets in about 15 seconds later and I pull away.

Kenny? You have a boyfriend!! I say almost trying to make myself seem pissed. For the record I am not pissed at all, I rather enjoyed it but I am confused.

What? You're a tourist! Kenny teases and heads back to the cash register.

He comes back with a drink for me and a pen and paper. Enrique and I are coming to LA soon. We should **all** get together. Write down your number handsome. I am done for the night and need to go cash out my drawer. I would say come keep me company but it's probably not a good idea especially with that.

With what? I ask

Kenny is pointing straight to my pants and yup….fuck…I still have a complete hard on due to what just happened.

I am sure I am red as an apple right now.

Hey Tate it was great seeing you. See you in LA soon. He kisses my cheek, Pants my head like a good dog and heads back to his cash register.

I am fucking mortified and why was Kenny playing a mind fuck on me. I hope he doesn't call me when he comes to LA. What who am I kidding? I would probably sit by the phone like a 16 year old waiting to be asked to the prom.

I look around and I am like where did everybody go? Tino is gone, as well as Albert and Jeffrey. None of them even said goodbye. Oh well but there is Donald still talking smack at the bar. I walk over and say hey what's up? He starts to tell me about his new restaurant job and blah blah blah. I think LA has taught me how to block out bullshit but I do hear can I buy you a drink?

I look down at my watch and it is 315am already so I say what the fuck what is one more.

Vodka soda Enrique Donald yells.

I look up in horror and I realize that Enrique has been on the other side of the bar the whole time Did he see Kenny and I kiss?.

Hey Tate Kenny says we are going to meet up with you, when we get to LA.... cool! As Enrique winks at me

I just nod and say cool back.

It is a little awkward but hopefully and probably the awkwardness is just me feeling stupid. I turn to Donald and say:

Where is Kevin?

He left with the drag queen, Donald says very informingly.

Really?

Yup he said he didn't want to interrupt you and Kenny.

Ugh He saw it too I say to myself.

I excuse myself to the bathroom and it is now 330 in the morning and it is pretty sketchy now. Lots of drunk people **everywhere**. Lots of looks of desperation with last call looming in 15 minutes that's for sure. I do my business in the bathroom and I go up to say goodbye to Donald.

Ok I am out of here. My flight is in less than 5 hours and I gotta go home and pack.

Kiss Kiss

Tell your Mom I said hello, Donald says as I start to walk towards the door.

I will Donald I say as I start to wave.

See you in LA Tate as I look and see Enrique smiling at me.

I just smile and wave. I wonder if he would be smiling if he knew I was making out with his boyfriend on the other side of the bar about an hour ago. Or maybe they have an open relationship and actually have 3 ways.

I am definitely taking a taxi back to Brooklyn because it is freezing outside now. The convenient thing is there are about 6 cabs right outside the door at Therapy and so I hop right into one.

Brooklyn Heights please.

The cab driver just smiles and starts the meter. As we start heading toward the Brooklyn Bridge I tell the cab driver Columbia Heights and Pineapple and he nods again.

As I am looking at the skyline, the building's, the Brooklyn Bridge I start to think about my week here in New York City. It has been a jammed packed 6 days that's for sure. I think I really did a lot with my time here in New York City. I spent a lot time with my Mother, sometimes wishing it was a little less. I got reacquainted with my sister and we might actually build a better relationship with each other after this trip. For the first time in a long time, I can see myself spending time with her and actually enjoying myself. I know....I am shocked too!!! My brother and my relationship is pretty much the same and probably always will be. I am Ok with that to be honest. There have been some feelings from my past that are going to need to be addressed, especially with Tony Ianucci.

As we enter the Brooklyn Bridge I look over to Brooklyn Heights. I cannot believe I grew up here and it does seem like it was a lifetime ago that I lived in Brooklyn. I think about my Mom now that all her kids are grown and the struggles she has faced. I am thankful I got to meet her new church I really am. The people really love my Mom at that church and that makes me feel good that people are looking after her. I do miss seeing my Mother more often but I definitely do not miss living with her. I don't know how I did it for 18 years to be honest. As we are leaving the Brooklyn Bridge I have a very calming affect running through my blood. Things are going to be Ok. My Mother will continue living her life and driving me crazy. I honestly wouldn't want it any other way. I am grateful for my life so far and I am looking forward to the next chapter in my life. After being back in New York City for this week I can honestly say that I made the right choice in moving to California. I am excited for all the possibilities that are ahead for me. I also very thankful that

I have New York City in my heart and will always have New York. I wouldn't have wanted to grow up in any other city in the world. New York City has helped define me as who the person I am today. I wouldn't have wanted any other family, friends or relationships than the ones I was given. Every single person that has been in my life, at various stages in my life has helped mold me into the person I am today. My Mother would like to take credit for a lot of it and to be honest she should. I am my Mother's son tried and true and she will be with me always.

As I look back and look at all the lights still looming from the New York City skyline I just smile. Tomorrow, next week, or next year this city will continue to beat with or without me. Everyone will go back to their daily lives, whether I lived here or not. People will get up, go to work, drink, eat or fight and just live. I am just one small little nugget, who had the honor of growing up in the best city in the world.

I am probably still drunk and getting maudlin but I really do love this city. I don't always show it but I actually really love my Family...well most of them... but not all. I still stand by that I don't have to love someone because I am related to them. I choose who I love and I honestly can say I love my life and I love everyone that I choose to be in my life with me.

As I pull up to my Mother's house every single light in the house is on. I quickly pay the cab driver and hop out. What now I say to myself as I open the front door.

Mom???

Tate Connors where the hell have you been? It is my Mother frantic.

I have been calling and calling you. I thought something happened to you Tate and my Mother is full on crying.

Why Mom? I ask Why did you think something happened to me?

It is 4:30 in the fucking morning Tate!!!

(Oh shit, she is mad because she never really curses)

Mom I told you that I would be home late…..stop crying.

1:30 am is late but 4:30 am is morning already. People start to get up for work Tate. It is Monday morning Tate.

Mom calm down I specifically stayed out late so I could sleep on the plane.

So why didn't you call then Tate?

Mom because I am a grown man who is old enough to make his own decisions. I know you don't want to believe it but in fact it is true. I am fine and I love you for worrying but I figured you would be sleeping.

I was till I was thirsty and wanted some water. When I looked at the clock and it was 330am and both you and your sister weren't home I panicked. Kelly left me a message saying she would be home by 530 am this morning that she was staying over a friend's house.

Friends house my ass, that slut I murmur to myself.

You just had to get one more in there Tate to scare the be-jesus out of your old Mother before you went back to Los Angeles..

Mom I am sorry but I feel like this entire trip I am apologizing to you for something or another. You have to let go Mom. I am a grown man and I am old enough to make my own decisions.

Tate you could be 60 years old and I will never let go. You are my son and I love you. From the second you got here on Tuesday, I have been dreading saying goodbye to you and now here it is. I don't want you to go but I know you have to grow. Watching you this week at times you were a fish out of water. I know I give you grief for living so far away, but I hope you know deep down that I am really proud of you. It has just been a long time since I have had you in this house and I don't know how to act any more. I look at you and you will always be that 7 year old kid that insisted on wearing those break dancing pants to church.

Mom??

I know I know I am getting emotional but I don't know when I am going to see you again.

Mom it is 5am and I gotta go shower and pack. Can we talk about this on the car ride to the airport?

Yes Tate and Tate you better take a good shower because nobody wants to sit next to a brewery. Where you smoking cigarettes?

No Mom (I lied again….will this lying **ever** end?)

I go upstairs and take a nice long shower. I am going to miss it here. My Mother is a trip sometimes but I love her. She is an original that is for sure. I am just about to get out of the shower when the scowling hot water hits my back. I scream like someone is stabbing me in the back. I literally jump out of the shower and it feels like I have just ran through a burning building. I grab a towel and look up and there is Ron standing there.

Merry Christmas Tate…Merry Christmas!

I am in too much pain to get mad so I just say Bravo Ron…Now get the fuck out of the bathroom before I kill you..

The pain doesn't last that long and I finish everything I need to do. I dress, get me together and pack. How did I end up with so much more crap than I came with? I am sure my Mother has put sweaters or something in my suitcase but before I could even check, I hear come on Tate we are going to be late. Yup it's my Mother yelling at me…..**again!**

Bye Ron I yell and I hear a Knuckle and a bye as I am carrying my stuff down the stairs.

Kelly is packed and all ready but she looks like she has been crying. I ask her What's wrong with you?

I am going to miss Kyle she wails.

It hasn't even been 4 days since you met him, give it a rest woman. I say plus I am starting to sober up by now and feel tired and grumpy.

You don't understand Tate we have a real connection. She snaps.

Well connect with him on the internet, Skype and phone and stop your crying Kelly…seriously 4 days.(As I shove my four fingers in her face.)

Let's go guys we are going to be late.

We all get into the car and Kelly is going on and on about Kyle and how much of a connection they had. He could be the guy she marries. Mom he could be the one she says over and over. My Mom is just smiling and nodding to her. My Mother would be thrilled if it worked out with Kyle and she moved back to New York but it will never happen. Kelly will smother this guy and he will run fast.

All I am thinking is Thank God there is no traffic and American Airlines terminal is before Delta. I cannot listen to this delusion chick in the front seat with my Mother. Did I really say she was cool and that I could hang with her? What the fuck was I thinking? It must have been either a nostalgic thing or a moment of weakness. I cannot wait to get away from her.

Ahh American Airlines Departures…

As we pull up my Mother parks the car and turns off the ignition.

Tate I have a question for you…or actually a favor my Mom states.

Here I thought I would just hop out, give a quick hug and kiss, say I love you and be on my way but **Noooooo!!**

What Mom?

The Mother is staring at me through her rear view mirror. Well your sister has already agreed to this so I am hoping you will too.

What Mom? I say because I am starting to get nervous on what she is going to ask me.

Tate……will you come home for Christmas if I buy you the ticket????

What????????

Are you kidding me Mother?

No Tate I am not.

You seriously want to do this again in **less** than a month??? Are you insane? Come back for Christmas? (I am in shock right now)

Yes.

Holy Shit Mom…I don't know. Can I let you know?

No I need to know now….will you come home for Christmas? I need you guys here for Christmas, I just do.

(I think I am going to throw up)

Mom I stammer…I gotta see what's up with work…..I thought we drove you crazy Mom and you and Ron couldn't wait for us to go home?

I hop out of the car as fast as I can and I grab my bags. I run around the car to give my Mom a kiss and she is crying.

Tate please will you come home for Christmas?

Mom I don't know I….I…I….Can I let you know tomorrow Mom? I have to get back to LA and see what my roommate situation is, as well as to see if I still have a job.

Tate please for me, will you come back to New York and spend Christmas with your Mother….it is really important to me.

Mom I need to see.

Tate I need you home for Christmas (and now she is crying again)

OK OK OK I will come for Christmas but I am **not** staying here for New Years!

My Mother has flung her hands around me and she is kissing my cheeks over and over all while she is still in the car..

Thank you Tate, Thank you! This is very important to me.

You're **not** dying Mother are you? I ask

Why do you keep asking me that Tate? And no I am not dying! Is it so wrong to love and miss my children? To want them home on Christmas?

No Mother it isn't. I will call you to figure out dates.

Promise me you will come home Tate?

Mom I love you, I gotta go and I will call you when I get in tonight Mom. I turn to my sister and say thanks for the warning Kelly! How long did you know she was going to do this?

Since Tuesday afternoon when we were grocery shopping for Thanksgiving she asked me Kelly states.

Gee thanks sis and why didn't you tell me? I ask.

Not sure I was going to get along with you this week so I wanted to wait but I gave Mom my full support and you coming back for Christmas. You are kinda fun and I like having you around. And hey I am coming back and staying through New Years!

You are coming back because you are getting laid Kelly!

I am coming back because I love my Mother and my family. It also does enhance the situation that Kyle is here also Tate.

Isn't Kyle going home to see **his** family for Christmas Kelly? I snap.

He is only going for the day and I might go with him Kelly states.

(I want to barf again)

Good for you Kelly...Good for you... Goodbye. Try not and stalk this one Kelly. Kyle is a cool guy and he seems into you.

Shut up Tate I never do that. Kelly snaps

(Yea right)

Ok Mom I seriously have to go! Plus you have been parked in this departure terminal for too long. They are going to give you a ticket. Again I love you. I had a really great time this week with you guys.

Tate promise me you will come home for Christmas my Mother asks almost pleading with me all over again..

Mom we will discuss Christmas when I get back to LA I say

Tate promise me (and the tears I swelling up in her eyes again)

(Well what was I going to do? I didn't want to come back for Christmas and it was going to be even colder. I didn't really have any plans for Christmas but I hadn't really thought about it either. It was pretty standard at the restaurant that if you took Thanksgiving off, you had to work Christmas. I wasn't going to debate back in forth with my Mother about this right now so I did what any good son would do at this moment for his sweet Mother. That's right…(I lied).

Mom I promise you that I will try and come home for Christmas, I said as sincerely and genuine as possible.

Say you will and not try Tate my Mother insists (**wow** she is quicker than I thought and she got the word **try**)

Mom I promise I will come home for Christmas….

Going home….to LA…did I really just say that?

Well after I finally leave my Mother and sister in the departure drop off area of American Airlines, I head to the ticket counter. The line is not bad for ticketing but it is also 625am. I am starting to feel the effects of staying up all night and drinking so I decide to head to Starbucks first and then get on the ticket line. I order a large black coffee and then continue to the ticket counter again. Once I reach the ticket counter I am greeted by a very friendly American Airlines employee.

Welcome to American Airlines where are you headed? She asks **very** cheerful for 630 in the morning.

Los Angeles I say as I hand her my driver's license

How many bags are you checking sir? She asks like sunshine is coming directly out of her voice to me.

Just one as I lift it up to the belt

Going on Vacation? She ask inquisitively

No I am going home but I am originally from New York. I was visiting my family for Thanksgiving. (Did she really care or did I give her some TMI? I can never tell these days).

Did you have a good time? She asks me with a smile.

Define good time? I ask her with a Knuckle

The ticket agent laughs and says: I know the feeling, I really do.

I laugh and tell her…. but yea my Mother wants me to come back for Christmas and **she** is buying the ticket. So this means I have to come.

Just think of it, for the free miles you are going to get… that you can use to go on a **fun** vacation later on! The ticket agent cheers

Good point… I like her…Don't know that many people that could be this cheerful at 630 in the morning though.

Thanks good point I laugh.

She hands me my seat assignment, points me in the direction of the gate, tells me to have a safe flight and then sends me on my way. As I am leaving I hear the ticket agent being just as sweet to the person behind me…Ahh it is not me… she is sweet to everyone…good for her. I wonder what drugs she is taking. Should I ask? Nah….

I make it to airport security in less than 2 minutes and it is pretty empty still. As I ponder as to which line I should attempt to get on, I get this overwhelming feeling that no matter what line I get on they are going to search my carry on. My mind starts racing that there is something in it that shouldn't be. I keep reenacting in my head what is in the bag but everything seems normal, so I head directly down Line # 2. I take off my watch, shoes and I empty my pockets. I look down at my belongings and wonder why I have a condom in my pocket? I am too exhausted to even think about where it came from. All I can think about is Thank God my Mother didn't wash the dang condom. I could just imagine the disaster and the following conversation. Tate why do you have a condom in your pocket? Do you always carry condoms with you? How often do you use them? Ugh Mother get out of my head already!

I make it through security without a hitch…well except that I forgot my belt on my pants, but the cool TSA agent let me put it on the belt and didn't make such a big deal about it. After I have made it through security, I start to walk to my gate. I look down at my watch and it is almost 40 minutes until we board the plane. I don't want to sit down because if I do I would probably fall fast asleep and miss my flight. It wouldn't be the first time on this trip that I would have missed my flight and I am sure American Airlines would be none to please with me. Who knows they would probably put me in cargo or something. I decide I am going to just walk around and kill time. I head over to the Hudson News shop in the terminal by Gate 28 and start to browse through the various tabloid magazines. I last about 10 minutes reading US Weekly's various stories about the Kardasian's men or who or what Twilight star is sleeping with whom. I lose interest with the magazine really quickly and I ponder what I can do next to kill the next half hour. I wonder if there is a place to get a drink. Hmm a nice cold beer would be great or EVEN a Bloody Mary! I walk around and look for an open bar but to no avail…everything is closed. I am the only lush in this entire airport who would want an alcoholic drink at 705 in the morning… on a Monday!

I start to people watch and read various advertisements on the walls. This becomes the longest 20 minutes of my life I swear. All I want to do is climb into my plane seat and pass out. Who is the dumbass that thought it would be a good idea to stay up, drink all night and then go directly to the airport?

Oh wait….that would be me… I soon hear some of the most magical words that I have been longing to here for the past 45 minutes.

Flight 182 from JFK to LAX is ready to begin boarding…Hallelujah, Hallelujah, Hallelujah.

Finally the announcer say's Group 2 can now board the plane and off I go like a lightning bolt. I hand the ticket agent my ticket, he scans it and gives me the Ok to board the plane. I board the plane and start immediately looking for 24 E. As I am walking through first class I think I see Drew Barrymore but I am too exhausted to even look back to see if it is her or be star struck. I find my seat, put my carry on in the bin above me and take my seat. Thank Heavens it is the window seat! I put on my seat belt right away and I close my eyes. I cannot wait to get home, I cannot wait to get home, I cannot wait…..

ZZZZZZZZZZZZZZZZZZZZZZZZZZZZZZZZZZZZZZZZ

Chapter 21

Welcomes home ...gulp

Folks Welcome to Los Angeles International Airport where the time is now 1055 am and the temperature is 74 degrees....

What? How the hell can we be in LA? I just sat down in my seat like 3 minutes ago? I turn and I look at the person sitting next to me and I say we are in LA already?

Yup he says

Wow I must have slept the whole flight man because the last thing I remember was sitting in my seat in New York and now poof here I am in LA!

Yup you slept the **whole** flight.....and **snored** the whole flight as well.

Shit really?

Yeah but it was fine. I just put my headphones on so no big deal, as he leans in to tell me. Some of the other passengers weren't that happy though but it didn't bother me. We nicknamed you Snorzilla though....

Well I am mortified now I tell him

Yeah who cares you are well rested though huh? He asks me with a laugh.

I guess so as I start to add up in my mind how long I have been sleeping. I count almost 7 hours in my head....not bad. It is actually a cool way to fly I guess.

We depart the plane rather quickly and I do see some dirty looks coming my way but to be honest...I don't **really** care right now. I know what other people are thinking of me right now but I don't care because I am well rested and home!!! Well there is a first time for everything and honestly at this very second I don't care....

As I head to the baggage claim and big smile comes across my face. I am home and home is LA. This is the first time since I have been living in LA that I am actually calling LA home. It feels good, actually really fucking good! I cannot wait to get home to my apartment, My room, my cat and My life here in Los Angeles. I cannot believe **how** excited I am to be....home!

I wait about 10 minutes for my bag to arrive and then I hop on the taxi line. I don't mind waiting on the taxi line because the weather is warm and beautiful. The sun is out and it feels so amazing against my face. It feels like the sun is softly stroking my face and saying Welcome Home Tate! Well in less than 5 minutes I am in a cab and headed to the apartment. I am embracing the ride home and watching all the beautiful Palm Trees just lightly sway back and forth with the wind. Just the sight of the Palm Trees makes me all warm and fuzzy.

Well about 25 minutes later we pull up to my apartment and I cannot wait to see my cat Spencer. I think this is the longest I have ever been away from him since I got him as a kitten. I pay the cab driver, grab my bags and head into the building. The apartment building has the same familiar smell it had before I left. I don't know how to describe the smell but it was just…home. I grab the elevator up and as I exit the elevator I get a tingle of excitement.

I am home and the possibilities are endless. I feel a sense of safety and calmness in the air. I feel the energy and light in my core and it is all heading in the right direction for me. I am exactly where I am supposed to be…or so I thought.

I unlock my apartment door and as I open the door I am floored upon what I see. Besides this smell of just utter filth, the apartment is completely trashed. There are alcohol and beer bottles everywhere. Pizza boxes, cigarette boxes and garbage everywhere. I look over to the kitchen and there is garbage **everywhere!** The screen to the balcony is open and there are flies everywhere. The carpets are stained and soiled. There is what looks like feces on the walls as well. What the fuck has happened here I say to myself? Thomas better be dead and where is Spencer?

Thomas???? Where the fuck are you Thomas?

Thomas???

I don't fucking believe this!!

I look in Thomas's room and everything is gone. His bed, his dresser and all of his clothes are gone. All of a sudden I have this extreme panic attack and yell

Spencer??? Stevie??

I run into my room which has also been trashed screaming Spencer and Stevie's names over and over. All of a sudden this little emaciated head comes popping out from under my bed and does a barely recognizable Meow! I run to him and I immediately take him to the kitchen. I open the cabinet where the cat food is kept. Every single can that I left for Tommy to feed Spencer and Stevie is still there. How could someone do this to poor defenseless cats? How? I immediately open up a can and place the food in their bowls. Spencer immediately goes for it and I begin to cry. Stevie runs out at the sound of the wet cat food can opening. How could someone do this? They have destroyed everything. My room is trashed, the apartment is trashed and I can only imagine what is going to happen once the landlord find out.

I call 911 and the police are on their way. I figure I might as well go get the Manager and let her know what has happened before the police arrive. I go down to the Manager's office and before I even open the glass door to her office she is on her feet. As I open the door she says to me:

You have problems.

I know! What happened I ask?

The last 3 rent checks have bounced and we told your roommate he had to vacate the unit by Friday. We gave him 2 weeks to vacate and last Thursday night we received several complaints from neighbors about loud noise coming from the unit. We figured it was you in the unit since your roommate moved his belongings out that morning.

It wasn't me. I just arrived back from New York less than an hour ago. I have called the police and they are on their way. Did you know he left my cats in there all week and didn't feed him???

I had no idea but the damages are extensive. The lease is in both of your names and if you want to continue to live here there is a lot that needs to be worked out. I hope you have some money or a family member that can help you. This is bad …really bad.

I was in New York for Thanksgiving with my family. I just got back an hour ago.

I have been sitting here all morning and I didn't see you come through that door.(As she is pointing to the front door).

You gotta be kidding me right?

I never kid about this stuff. I think there are the cops you called. You have a lot of explaining to do. I have been right about you two all along. Both of you are no good…How could you trash an apartment like that? How?

I didn't do it lady!(Now I am getting pissed.).

Let's let the police handle this….

Before I can even walk over to let the police officers into the building the Apartment Manager has buzzed them in. As soon as she takes her finger off the buzzer she runs to them screaming:

He trashed my apartment **He trashed my apartment. Help!!!!**

I am standing there like are you fucking serious lady. You have no idea who you are fucking with. I just look at the police officer with this look like she is crazy as he walks up to me. I am trying to introduce myself to Officer Gonzalez but all you can hear is this woman wailing that I wrecked her apartment unit. Officer Gonzalez takes me to the side and asks me what is going on:

What is she hysterical about? The officer asks me like I am about to take a surprise pop quiz or something.

I came home about 20 minutes ago from the airport to find my apartment trashed and my roommate had moved out.

Liar!!!!!!!!(I wonder who told her? Did my Mother call?)

Lady what the fuck are you talking about as I turn and yell at this psycho bitch I **just** got back to Los Angeles an hour ago and I have my fucking plane ticket upstairs.

Calm down sir Officer # 2 says (I haven't caught his name yet)

I am sorry Officer but since the day I have moved in here she has hated me. I try and say as sympathetic as possible, I have an emaciated cat upstairs and an apartment that is trashed including all of my personal belongings. Can I show you my plane ticket and how my ex roommate is the one who trashed the unit?

I will go up to the unit and evaluate the circumstances Officer Gonzalez says to Officer # 2.

Can I come with you sir?

Yes Officer Gonzalez sternly says to me.

As we are waiting for the elevator, the ride up the elevator and the walk down the hall, I am trying to tell the police officer what happened. I tell him that I went to New York last Tuesday and everything was fine. I tell him that he told me, as I was walking out the door that my roommate was having a friend stay over I tell the officer that he didn't even feed the cats once while I was away.

Are the cats ok? Officer Gonzalez asks me.

I don't know sir I put a can down for them before I went downstairs to find the Manager and wait for you guys.

Who would **starve a cat? I should lock him up for that alone.** (you could now tell Officer Gonzalez was a cat lover because he was angry)

Apparently my asshole of an ex roommate I say.

As I open the door the smell is just unbearable. I see that Spencer and Stevie have each finished their entire cans of cat food, so I head to the kitchen and open up another can for them. He immediately digs right in.

Poor cat Officer Gonzalez says. This place is disgusting. I haven't seen a place trashed this badly since possibly Rodney King riots and I was 7 years old!

I reach for my bag and I hand Officer Gonzalez my boarding pass from my flight I was just on. He looks down at it and then asks to see my ID. I immediately pull out my driver's license and hand it to him. He compares my license to the ticket and hands me back my driver's license.

Can I show you what he has done to my room Officer?

Yes please Officer Gonzalez says as he is still looking around bewildered.

I bring him into my room and I show him that my desk is upside down, my clothes are ripped and thrown everywhere, every drawer on the dresser has been busted and my computer monitor is smashed. On top of all of that and although I cannot officially prove it, someone has peed all over the room including my bed.

Officer Gonzalez gets on his walkie talkie and says Joe come on up here this kid didn't do this.

On my way up, should I bring the Manager? Officer Joe asks.

Officer Gonzalez looks at me for an answer.

I don't care as long as she stops screaming at me.

Bring her up Officer Gonzalez speaks into the speaker of his walkie.

What am I going to do Officer? I don't have the money to pay to fix all of this.

Could you ask your folks for help?

Possibly but if my Mother ever found out about this she would fly to LA and make me move back home in a freakin minute. I am so dead.

Holy Shit this place is trashed Officer Joe says loudly as he walks through the door.

The Apartment Manager just starts to cry. She then starts calling me every name in the book in Spanish. Puta, pendejo, maricon and Officer Gonzalez who apparently speaks Spanish as well and says directly to her…Silencio!! No Mas! Officer Gonzalez than shows Officer Joe my plane ticket and boarding pass. Officer Joe than shows the Apartment Manager the plane ticket…

That's not him that is the one who moved out on Friday. The one that moved out on Friday he paid his rent on time every month. That is a why I let him move out with his things! You a liar! (She is back pointing her finger at me)

I am just standing there stunned.

Officer Gonzalez turns to the Apartment Manager and says Ma'am I checked his ID and he is Tate Connors as the officer is pointing directly at me.

He is a liar. He is Tommy Joseph the Apartment Manager says. He bounced all his checks for 3 months.

Can I show her my ID sir I ask Officer Gonzalez

Show it to me Officer Joe says.

I pull back out my driver's license and hand it to Officer Joe. Officer Joe looks at it and then again at my plane ticket. He picks his head up and turns to the Apartment Manager and says:

I think you owe this man an apology. He is Tate Connors.

No he is Thomas Joseph she **yells.**

Mira!!! Officer Joe says angrily as he shows the crazy Apartment Manager my ID.

The Apartment Manager looks at my ID and then looks up at me in horror. You are Tate?

Yes I am Tate

But…but the other boy told me **he** was Tate.

He lied to you ma'am Officer Gonzalez says. The man that actually is Thomas Joseph, is probably the one that did this to the apartment because this plane itinerary clearly shows Mr. Connors was in New York for the past 6 days. It looks like you let the other gentleman remove all his belongings from the unit and then he came back here and destroyed it. I think the first thing you need to do is give Mr. Connors an apology.

The Apartment Manager is stunned and says I need to go call the owner of the building. (And still no apology from the Apartment Manager though).

Officer Joe turns to the Apartment Manager and says let's all go down to your office and figure this out. The smell in here is unbearable and I cannot stand here and smell this for another second.

Grab your suitcases son there is no way you can stay in this apartment tonight Officer Joe says.

Ok but I need to grab my cats.

There is a cat in here? Officer Joe asks.

Yeah and the roommate didn't feed them for the whole week. He is lucky the cat didn't die Officer Gonzalez says first turning to Officer Joe and then to me.

Yes Grab the cats.

I will put all of this stuff in my car for now and meet you in the Manager's office. Can I look and see if there is anything salvageable in the apartment?

Later we are going to want to finger print in here first Officer Joe says.

Ok I say as I pick up my luggage, knap sack and Spencer. Normally Spencer doesn't like to be picked up but after what has happened he will gladly go anywhere with me now. We all head down the hall towards the elevator now. Of course by now every neighbor is out and wondering what is going on. I am getting tons of dirty looks because most of them haven't forgiven me about Sparkle Bottoms and the I am Beautiful fiasco. I stop dead in my tracks.... I yell

Stevie I forgot Stevie!

Who is Stevie? Officer Gonzalez says almost annoyed

The other cat we just rescued.

Oh shit I yell Please don't be dead!!

I hand Spencer to Officer Gonzalez and I race back to the apartment.

Stevie????? Stevie??? I am desperately listening for a little meet-meet from her.

Finally I hear meet-meet and she is hiding under the sink and you can tell she has been traumatized. I pick her up and I grab a couple of cans of cat food I found her I yell.

I walk outside holding her and everybody is just beside themselves on what is going on. I am saying to myself. Is this really happening? What did I do to deserve this? What am I going to do?

We get down to the Manager's office and I drop my luggage. I then feed Stevie and Spencer another can of wet food. I want Spencer and Stevie to split it because I am afraid they will get sick.

I ask the police if I can go check on my car and they say yes. I walk right out into the parking garage that is next to the Manager office. As I open the door to the garage and look for my car the pit in my stomach just explodes ....the car is gone...

I calmly walk back into the Manager's office and I don't know if it was written on my face or not but Officer Gonzalez just looks at me and says:

The car is gone too right?

Yup it is (and I cannot hold back any longer) as I start to cry.

Relax buddy it is not the end of the world Officer Joe says

Do you have insurance on the vehicle Tate?

Yes but not theft but it was a piece of crap anyway…..What am I going to do? I just look at everyone

Do you have any place to go? A friend's house maybe? Officer Gonzalez asks.

Not with 2 cats and no car sir…

We will figure something out Tate as the Apartment Manager for the first time looks at me with care in her eyes.

There is a vacant apartment on the 2nd floor. You can stay there until we sort out this mess.

Now she is being compassionate well there is a little small thanks for that I guess. She has called the owner and left a message about the situation. We all start to fill out the various police forms for the report.

How long did you know Mr. Joseph for? Officer Joe asks me

We lived together for a little over 6 months but we knew each other through mutual friends in New York.

Do you know any of his family members or friends? Officer Gonzalez asks me.

No…not really…we were roommates but not really friends.

Both police officers look at each other and shake their heads at one another.

What? I say as the tears are swelling up in my face

It happens all the time here in LA. You kids move in with strangers and they rob you blind. You all come to LA with stars in your eyes and end up being taken advantage of, Officer Gonzalez says as he is writing in his clip board.

I say to myself shut up….I am from Brooklyn and not some pow town in the middle of Kansas. I fucking knew this guy and while I knew he was an asshole, I never thought he was an evil spirited, cat abusing car thief? How could I? I keep thinking as I am looking at Officer Gonzalez with a scowl of disgust on my face – I thought you were actually a nice police officer. I even found you kind of cute but now…basically calling me stupid….I don't like him so much.

Ring ring

Oh shit as I look down at my phone….Yup it is my Mother calling to make sure I got home alright….Not now Mother, you are so going to voicemail – **Click**

Everyone is looking at me now as to who it was calling me…

It was my Mother and…I….just cannot tell her what is going on right now.

Ring ring

Guess who? Yup you are right…It's my Mother.

I answer the phone:

Mom I got in safely, let me call you back a little later, I am dealing with some apartment stuff right now. Give me an hour.

So how was the flight?

It was great Mom. Let me call you back?

Did you sleep? My Mother asks almost like my sentence never existed.

Yes Mom I did but I need to call **you** back!

Kelly's flight was delayed due to bad weather in Chicago.

Mom I have to call you back please?

You are not trying to avoid coming back home for Christmas, now are you Tate?

Mom no I gotta go. Love ya and I will talk to you later I promise.

Click.

I look up at the police officers and the Apartment Manager and they are all staring at me.

You didn't want to upset your Mom huh? Officer Gonzalez asks

No not until I have to. She has not been my biggest champion on moving to LA and will take any excuse to get me back to New York.

The Apartment Manager looks at me and saysm I just got off the phone with the owner of the building. He said you can stay in Unit 204 while we bring in a team to clean up the apartment. He is asking that you pay for half of the cleaning bill for now and we can evaluate the damages after the cleanup has been completed. We will continue the lease solely in your name. The owner is hoping that Tommy's security deposit will cover all the damages that were made to the unit. After that time you will have 30 days to find a new roommate to cover the other half of the rent. If you do not find a roommate at that time you will either have to pay the full rent for the unit and repay the difference of the security deposit that was used to fix the unit. You will also have the option to break the lease and move out at that time with no loss to your security deposit.

I am thinking in my head when did her English become perfect?

Tate I told him that you were a good kid. I told him how you rescued the cat from that crazy person living next door and I also told them Tommy has stolen your car as well. We are not heartless people but this is a business and we need to protect ourselves.

Is this fair to you Tate?

(I have an audience of two police man, an Apartment Manager and many fucking noisy neighbors looking on now)

It is very fair, **thank you.**

The police officers ask me a few more questions like do I have any idea where Tommy would go? Why he would do this? Is he on drugs? Did he have a history of violence? Has he stolen before?

Do you know what my answer was to every single question they asked me was?

It was…I don't know.

How pitiful is that? I have lived with the guy for 6 months and I knew nothing about him. I mean I knew his name and that he was from New York but I barely new anything else about him. It baffles my mind how stupid this sounds. He could have been a serial killer for all I know…I don't even know his Mother's name….I am just such a lame ass sometimes….sometimes … try all the time.

Well all of a sudden a light bulb goes off in my head. I turn to the Apartment Manager and ask:

Wouldn't there be information on his credit check for the apartment.

Good idea Officer Joe says

Let me check the file the Apartment Manager says

And what about his mail I ask the Manager as well.

Can I check the mail?

I have all the mail since Tuesday she says.

Oh Ok because maybe he has a credit card statement or something that the cops can you use to track him down.

Hey Tate do you want to become a cop? Officer Gonzalez asks me with a funny tone to his voice.

No but I would **love** to play one on TV, I joke back.

Well after about 5 minutes we have gathered where he is from, his references, family information, a copy of his driver's license, banking information and there was a credit card statement in the mail pile the Manager had been collecting. The police make copies of everything and tell me that if he tries to contact me to let them know ASAP. They give me the speech that I shouldn't go play "cop" and all. Let them do their job blah blah blah. They tell me that they will be in touch in the next few days.

On the way out Officer Gonzalez turns to me and says:

You seem like a good guy. Do yourself a favor and screen you roommates a little better.

I know officer, I am a schmuck...

Hey I have seen stuff like this happen to Harvard grads so don't be so hard on you. Just protect yourself. Also if I was you I would check all your banking and personal information because it sounds like this guy may be on drugs and desperate for money.

I will Officer thank you.

I shake hands with both Officers and I stand there and watch them leave. Officer Gonzalez is cute. I wonder if he is gay. His butt looks so good in those tight pants. Hmm this will need further investigation.

I turn back to the Apartment Manager and I ask her what is next. She hands me the keys to Apartment 204 and tells me she will let me know the cost of the clean up as soon as possible. She tells me she is going to try and get someone in there as early as this evening.

I will let you know the cost to clean the unit by morning Tate. And Tate I am sorry again for what has happened to you. I wish I could do more. I am really sorry I jumped to the wrong conclusion about you earlier today.

Thanks and it is not your fault or mine that Tommy is a psychopath. I should get these cats up to the apartment before they pee on something down here. We both laugh and look down at the cats and they are just chillin, watching people go by. They don't have a care in the world. They have been fed and I am with them now. I think Spencer is actually purring.

Can I have my mail as well?

Sure Tate she says and she starts dividing mine and Tommy's mail into two piles.

I notice that there is an envelope from my commercial agency and I pray to God it is a residual check.

Do you mind if I take my luggage and one of the cats up to the apartment?

Sure go ahead she says and it's a good thing we didn't turn the electric off in the unit huh?

Thanks again.

We will get through this Tate she says and looks at me motherly.

So I pick up my luggage and then I pick up Spencer and head to the elevator. I am not even out of the office for a mere second when I hear:

What happened?

Yup it is the Noisy Neighbor Police just waiting and dying to know what had happened. Inside I wanted to tell the noisy bitches to fuck off and mind her own damn business but I figured it would just add flame to the massive fire of the day.

My roommate went crazy and trashed the apartment while I was in New York for the Thanksgiving weekend..

There is **always** drama with you guys another woman snaps.

I whirl around and say Lady I just got back from visiting my family in New York to find out my apartment has been trashed, all of my belongings destroyed and both of my cats starving to death and that is what you have to say to me.....always drama?.

She looks down to the floor and doesn't say a word.

Nothing to say now huh?

(Silence)

Well go fuck yourself, you stupid bitch. He stole my car too. I cannot fucking wait to get the fuck out of this building.

There is no need to curse and swear dude, this guy yells as he is trying to do some bullshit chivalry or something.

Dude? Are you fucking kidding me? Somebody has either just destroyed or stolen everything I own and you are telling me not to curse. I then have this snotty bitch tell me that there is always drama...

I am about to throw down with this guy but just as I am on the verge Spencer just looks at me and **meows**. It had a calming effect on me and I take a deep breath.

Listen I am sorry it has been a long day, so say whatever the hell you want to…I don't care I say as I walk into the elevator.

I cannot believe how horrible the people around here are. The option of me just walking away from this apartment is what I am going to do. Let me just get my life back in order. It is after all 330pm and I have been back a whole 3 hours after all.

I open the door and drop my luggage in the new apartment. It still smells like fresh paint but it definitely smells a hell of a lot better than our place. The apartment is nice. It is a one bedroom and it looks out onto the pool as well. It has a balcony and the kitchen is almost the exact same style as my unit. Same carpets and a decent size living room but I am not going to get comfortable because I am **not** going to stay here, that's for sure. I turn to leave to go back down and get Stevie when I have a flash back to the first time I left Spencer in a new apartment so I turn around to him and say now don't pee till I get you the litter box….yeah like that will ever work.

I go back down and get Stevie and the Apartment Manager says that a cleaning crew will be in my unit in about 20 minutes. I turn and I ask her

Do you mind if I go into the unit and try and salvage some things like my pictures, books and possibly part of my computer?

Of course Tate. I got you a roll of quarters so you can to try and wash some of the things like your sheets and things. I have laundry detergent if you need some also.

I am not sure what I have till I get in my apartment but first I gotta get a litter box going, I say as I scoop up Stevie.

Well let me know if you need anything Tate. By the way I am having the locks changed first thing in the morning as well. The Manager reassures me.

Thanks.

Well I bring Stevie up to the unit, drop her off and I immediately head back up to hell or otherwise known as my trashed apartment. I find the litter box which is filled with cat shit but it is not overflowing. It is probably not overflowing because they hadn't been fed in 6 days. I dump out the litter box on the floor and grab the Johnny Cat kitty litter I had under the sink. I know I shouldn't have dumped the litter on the floor but the place is trashed anyway and I am paying to have it cleaned up anyway.

I pick up the cat bowls, some of their food and a can opener. Why the can opener when the cat food just pulls open? I don't know, I just need to salvage something. Hey it's a can opener I know but at least it is something right?

I get back to 204 and am shocked to find that neither one of the cats have pissed anywhere. I immediately make their litter box and put it in the bathroom. I then give the cats water and each of them another can of cat food. This time I actually put the food in their bowls instead of just giving them the can like I did earlier today. Once they are settled I head back up to my apartment and try and salvage what of my life is left.

I start with my closet and my pictures. The closet isn't that bad and not everything is destroyed. I basically take all of my memories first. Things like pictures, photo albums, year book and watches. I find a garbage bags under the sink in the kitchen and I just start to load them up. I take the sheets and blanket off the pee soaked bed and I head down to the laundry room.

Both washers are free so I put the sheets and pillows in one machine and the blankets in the other. I actually had a full bottle of detergent, almost like I was expecting to come home and have to wash my entire life. As I am walking back down the hall, my neighbor comes out of her apartment.

Would you like some help? She asks me in a very sympathetic tone.

I just look at her like... help? What kind of help?

I heard what happened to you and I think it is awful that someone would do something like this to **anybody.** How are the cats?

The......cats are Ok...thank you

I am very leery of anyone in this building being nice to me so I was caught a little off guard. It seems by now that the news spread like wild fire on what had happen to me and the trashed apartment.

It smells really bad in there I say as I kinda joke with her.

That is Ok I am a big girl. I am Melissa by the way as she extends her hand to me.

Nice to meet you Melissa I am Tate.

Nice to meet you so can I help? Melissa asks

Are you sure? It is really bad in there.

I told you I am a big girl and I can take it Melissa says with a cheerleading tone to her voice.

Yes thank you! I can use all the help I can get!

As I open the door and let her in she goes:

Phe-you – you weren't kidding. **Wow** this place is severely trashed man. Your old roommate must have really hated you huh? Did you do something to piss him off?

And I answer Melissa with today's million dollar answer....I don't know. I just don't know…

Well let's get cracking on this.

Melissa and I are trying to sort out my clothes when the cleaning crew shows up with the Apartment Manager. The Manager lets them in and starts explaining to them in Spanish what they need to do. She goes from room to room explaining everything and I just hear a lot of Si's.

After the Manager is done explaining she turns to me and says:

How is it going? Are you able to salvage a lot?

Well my pictures and memories I will and about half of my clothes I guess. Most of my shoes are Ok but the computer; printer and the bed are trashed. The TV and DVD player are gone but most of my books will be Ok. I am washing some of the sheets and things plus it looks like my extra towels and sheets weren't touched. I am going to try and do the glass is half full routine on this one. Even with all of my CD's being crushed and beer poured into my stereo I am going to look at this in a somewhat positive way. The stereo was old and most of the CD's were lame anyway. One day I will be able to buy a new one anyway.

Well again Tate if you need anything let me know as she looks up and sees that all the blinds have been torn apart. The Apartment Manager just shakes her head and then turns to Melissa and says:

You didn't hear anything this weekend Melissa?

I waitress Thursday through Sunday night and I don't get home till almost 3 in the morning if I am lucky. I asked my roommate and she said it just sounded like a couple of guys getting rowdy and having a good time.

I look around the room and say Ohh they had a good time alright!

The Manager leaves and Melissa and I continue to salvage what is left of my life.

Did he really have to go through all of my dresser draws including my underwear draw? As I start to cry again.

Hey hey come on we will get through this don't cry, Melissa urges me as she rubs my back.

I do what I always do when I am upset or vulnerable.

Well it is a good thing I packed like 15 pairs of underwear and socks to go home for 6 days.

It's a good thing Tate!! Melissa laughs.

Well Melissa spent the next 3 hours helping me salvage what was left of my bedroom, bathroom and the rest of the apartment. She even helped me lug all of my things down to apartment 204.

We only have the kitchen left to salvage Tate!! Melissa say's cheeringly

Great! I say but I am exhausted and have a headache.

Ring ring

OH shit I forgot to call my Mother back I say out loud!

Hello Mom sorry I haven't called you back Mom.

Well it is a good thing my life doesn't hang on you promptly calling me back Tate. Why haven't you called me back? Are you trying to avoid the conversation about Christmas? You promised me Tate Connors. You promised me also that you weren't going to lie to me anymore Tate. Did you lie to me this morning Tate? You know I will be so hurt if you did Tate.

Mom no…

Then why haven't you called me back?

(Melissa is watching this whole conversation as she is stacking plates and glasses in a box for me)

I thought to myself should I lie to her about what has happened? If I tell her the truth will she freak out? She is going to eventually ask me about Tommy anyway. I don't want to lie to my Mother and say that the asshole is good or moved or something so I decide to tell her a lie. I visualized how the conversation would go if I told her the truth.

Mom

My Mother cuts me right off

Tate why is your home phone disconnected? Did you boys forget to pay the bill? Don't you need that for your computer to connect to the Facebook?

This is how it would go:

Mom I am going to tell you something but you have got to promise me that you will **not** freak out.

What's wrong Tate?? Is something wrong with you?

Mom I told you I need you to calm down. Are you calm?

Yes…..um…I….amm….calm. What is wrong?

I look over at Melissa as she has just opened the freezer and found a full bottle of vodka in the freezer.

Score she yells and waves the bottle in the air.

I smile and give her a cheesy Fonzie thumbs up.

Who is there Tate? Is that Tommy?

No Mother it is not Tommy, it is my neighbor

Who is it?

My neighbor Melissa Mom?

Have I met her? My Mom asks me with the full intention of me giving her a straight answer.

Mom how could you have met her you have never been here?

I don't know Tate but you never know.

You don't know her Mom.

Well tell her I said hello.

I will Mom.

So what am I not supposed to freak out about Tate? You told me to calm down and now I am calm and you are changing the subject.

OK Mom here goes.

You are coming home for Christmas Right Tate

Yes. Mom will you please listen to me now?

Go ahead and there is no need to bite my head off Geesh. I am just a concerned Mother who wants to make sure her son got home safely.

Sorry Mom. Well when I got home and went to my apartment it was completely trashed.

Tommy forgot to throw out the trash? My Mother inquires.

No Mom he moved all of his personal stuff out of the apartment and then destroyed what was left of all of my stuff..

What do you mean Tate? My Mother asks a little nervously.

He destroyed the apartment, ruined half of my belongings. He stole my TV and DVD player. Poured beer in my stereo; broke all of my CD's; he urinated in my bed; broke all the blinds and Mom…he didn't feed that cats for 6 days!!!

Oh dear Lord….why Tate? Why would he do that? What did you do to him before you left for Thanksgiving? Are the cats OK?

The cats are OK Mom but I honestly have no idea what I did, but the Apartment Manager said he had bounced the last 3 months in rent checks.

That is illegal Tate my Mother informs to like she is teaching me something.

Really Mom? I **know** it is and he was posing as me to the Apartment Manager.

Why would he do that Tate? Not **everyone** wants to be Tate Connors my Mother says with utter sarcasm.

Mom I know that please let me call you tomorrow. I have to finish up here.

Well why was he posing as you? I don't understand.

Mom because my checks weren't bouncing. Even the Apartment Manager thought I was Tommy.

You don't look alike Tate. I have seen pictures of him.

Mom can I call you tomorrow.

What is this Apartment Manager do? I never heard of an Apartment Manager Tate.

I stop and think for a second and I then go. Mom it is like a landlady but who doesn't own the building.

Well why would she be the landlady if she doesn't own the apartment?

Mom she gets paid to watch the building.

Well the landlady gets paid also it is called rent Tate. What is her phone number? I want to talk to this Apartment Manager.

Mom I will call you tomorrow. Everything will be Ok. I love you.

Tate maybe Tommy will come back and clean up. Maybe he was drunk or something.

Mom he is not coming back plus he stole my car.

What????

Mom calm down it was a piece of crap anyway but I reported it all to the police.

Police??? Tate you need to come home right now. This is ridiculous; you cannot be living out there with all those crazies. Come home right now, live with me rent free and you will never have to worry about any crazy roommates again.

Yeah Mom all I would have to worry about is which is the most effective way to kill myself if I lived with you.

That is not **very** nice Tate and now my Mother is pissed.

I will call you tomorrow Mom. I love you. **click**

Would you like a drink?

(Melissa has cleaned 2 glasses and poured vodka over ice into 2 glasses)

Yes thank you!!!

I have a Mother too who is just like that. I am from Rhode Island, Melissa tells me.

Born and raised in Brooklyn here.

I couldn't tell if it was Brooklyn or Boston Melissa tells me

I am from Brooklyn but I am educated, so it sounds Bostonian.

(We both laugh and down our vodka)

Well I think this is about it as I look down at the remaining items to take downstairs.

Let's do it Melissa yells.

I ask one of the cleaning guys to help. He pushed my computer chair that is stacked with dishes, plates, cups, silverware etc etc. We make about 3 trips just for the kitchen but altogether over 75 trips in the past 5 hours.

All in all I salvaged a lot of my clothes and personal stuff. I salvaged a couple of chairs, a coffee table and some lamps. Some random furniture here and there and an oversized chair from the living room set is the only thing not destroyed. I will probably be sleeping on that tonight.

After we drag that back to Unit 204 I turn to Melissa and say can I take you to dinner somewhere tonight. I want to thank you for all of your hard work tonight.

Look I am exhausted can we just grab a pizza and go on our "date" another night?

Um sure but by date what do you mean? I ask confused.

Our date plus I want to get all pretty and sexy for you Tate.

Um Melissa I gotta tell you something. I stammer…

What is it Tate?

I am gay.

You are gay!!! O-h- M-y-Gg-o-d like I couldn't have figured that out with the amount of shoes you have or the entire broken Madonna CD's collection that your roommate busted? No straight guy has that many shoes and or **that** many Madonna CD's.

You're teasing me now huh?

Yup I am. Let's go grab a pizza.

I think I made a friend for life! Finally!!!!!

Yeah because I am a stalker Melissa teases….

Thank you so much for today Melissa.

I was bored. I needed a charity project anyway......as Melissa winks at me and puts her arm over my shoulder. Come on Charity Case lets go get us some pizza! I wonder if you are tax deductible. Ha!

We walk up the street to Bossa Nova and grab a table. Bossa Nova is this amazing Brazilian restaurant with great food and the waiters are **caliente!!** The service can be hit or miss but there is plenty of eye candy, so that makes up for everything else, well at least in my eyes. Plus it is walking distance from my apartment and they have a great bottle of red wine.

Melissa and I sit down at a table near the kitchen and almost immediately this Adonis of a waiter comes over and greets us.

Hello welcome to Bossa Nova can I take a drink order?

(I am melting because besides being drop dead gorgeous he has that sexy Brazilian accent that I swoon for)

Wine ? Melissa looks at me like um yes we are having wine.

Sure do you guys still have that bottle of Chianti from like 2 weeks ago?

We do!!! The Brazilian waiter says

Ok we will have that and a Margarita Pizza? as I am asking both the waiter and Melissa

Sounds good Melissa says

Ok I am Mauricio if you need anything else, the hot waiter tells us. I will bring your wine right away.

Thanks both Melissa and I say in unison.

That is exactly my type, I say to Melissa as the waiter walks away.

I think he is everybody's type Melissa teases me.

Yeah I know but I have enough man troubles right now as it is. I sigh to Melissa

I know seriously dude what happened with your roommate?

Melissa I honestly don't know what I did to deserve what he did to me. It seemed like everything was fine before I left. I mean we had some issues with my Mother calling too early in the morning, because she keeps forgetting the time difference but never anything major. We barely spoke to each other but we were cool and respected one another. I mean we were never friends who hung out or anything. I don't even think we ever even went to a movie together. He paid his rent and I paid mine or so I thought. We would watch TV together and have small talk but besides that…nothing. To be honest Melissa I never connected with him and I really didn't like him. I never planned on living with him that much longer as it is. I just don't know what made him do what he did to me.

Maybe he was bipolar or something? Melissa asks.

Nope I think he is just a straight up Paula Abdul style asshole!!

Ha funny

I just want to get past this and move on as I say with the strength of **Rocky** and the fear of a mouse trapped by a cat.

Are you going to move Melissa asks?

Before I can answer Mauricio is back with our wine.

Here you go guys as he shows me the bottle.

Cool thanks I say.

Would you like to try the wine? Mauricio asks me.

Sure I say.

Mauricio pours a little wine into my glass and looks at me with those gorgeous cocoa brown Brazilian eyes.

I try it and it is damn good!!!

Yes it is great I say and Mauricio pours two healthy glasses for me and my new friend Melissa.

We do cheers "To new friends" clink clink

Yes!

Clink -clink of the glasses

That's good Melissa says!!

Good and again thank you so much for helping me today. I don't know what I would have done without your help. I would definitely still be up there packing if it wasn't for you.

Stop thanking me already Melissa chastises me. I heard about what happened and I thought it was really shitty that someone would do something like that, so I decided to help. So do you think you are going to stay or move?

Well I haven't really made any friends in the building. There was the whole Sparkles Bottoms incident/disaster. Then there was the suicidal cat that I now have. I was busted hitting on my hot new neighbor, by his boyfriend. By the reception I got from the people in the lobby, I am guessing everyone thinks I am trouble and rude. The Apartment Manager only became nice after she realized I was not some crazy non paying rent lunatic. Maybe I will get some sympathy from people in the building now but I think that even after the apartment is cleaned I still won't feel safe. It will be a constant reminder of what happened but for now it looks like I will have to stay in the building. I have about $900.00 in the bank right now with no roommate or car. The owner is being really nice with me so far, so we will see what happens.

Do you think they will find him? Melissa asks:

Who knows but I know he became very disillusioned with the whole acting thing months ago and I don't know why he stayed in LA. He barely even left the apartment building..

What about you? Melissa asks – have you had any success since you have been here?

Some…I have a commercial agent now and I did a national Chevy Silverado commercial at the end of September.

That's **great** money! Melissa exclaims.

Well I have made about $1,200.00 so far but they say I will get another check soon. Actually in all the madness I think I saw a check in the mail from my agency this afternoon.

Great Melissa champions that could be the end of your financial problems because car commercials pay really well!

Enough about me tell me about you? I ask Melissa.

Pizza is here Mauricio sings to us as he arrives at the table with the pizza.

Thanks we both cheer.

Another bottle of wine Mauricio asks.

Of course I say with a laugh and Melissa raises her glass and says Amen to that!

As we start to eat our pizza I begin to look at Melissa and she is actually really pretty. Not model pretty but natural and wholesome pretty. I can tell that she has to be an actress because she is very expressive with her facial expressions. She is the type of girl that you know what they are thinking by the look on their face. I am very curious about her so I ask:

So tell me about yourself? Are you an actress? Musician? When did you move here? What are you looking to do with your life?

She looks at me and smiles and says:

OK Diane Sawyer

Hey!! That's not nice!!

Well I have been here in LA for almost 3 years and I am trying to do the actress thing. I get very distracted and don't always focus too much though. I am kind of a free spirit and I can get very wrapped up in boys. There is a part of me that wants to be a successful actress but there are times I would rather just be a wife and mom. I am 27 now so I am kinda rethinking what I want to do with the rest of my life. I have been waiting tables for over 10 years and I just don't know how much longer I can do it. I don't really get along with my roommate either but we tolerate each other.

Maybe you could move in with me? I ask.

Slow down Single white Homo we just met, Melissa teases me and I get this look of pure horror on her face.

OH no she is going to think I am just so pitiful. I say to myself.

Melissa just looks at me and says:

I am sorry I hope I didn't offend you with the homo word?

No not at all I say as cool as possible. It takes a lot to offend me chica.

Good!

Ring ring

Hey it's not mine for once. I especially know it is not mine because my crazy Mother would already be in bed.

Melissa rummages through her purse and finds her cell phone

Hello she goes. Hey just having some pizza with my neighbor. He had a bad day with his old roommate and I helped him out for a while.

Silence as I can hear that it is a man on the other side of Melissa's phone.

He is gay, don't worry is the next thing I hear as she is now looking at me and miming the words I am sorry.

I hear a bunch of Ok's and then a see you soon. Melissa clicks off the phone, smiles at me and then says:

I gotta go. I am meeting my boyfriend and some of his friends at the Trocadero on Sunset.

I smile and say: Cool, go ahead don't let me keep you.

Do you want to come? Melissa asks

Thanks but no I have had a long day and I need to get my life back together tomorrow. Even though I would probably love the distraction I gotta go home and make some semblance to my life. I think I am going to walk to Ralphs and get some boxes because as you know, I have things all over the place in the apartment downstairs. Thanks for everything today you have no idea how much I appreciate all the help.

Stop thanking me Tate. Call me tomorrow. If you need a ride somewhere, just let me know. I don't work till Thursday. Melissa says as she is getting up and giving me a hug. It is all going to work out Tate and maybe they have caught the jack ass by now.

Ha I say and then Melissa is out the door.

Mauricio comes over and asks if everything is Ok. I tell him everything is fine and can I have the check.

Is your girlfriend coming back? Mauricio asks

No…she went to go meet her boyfriend.

Oh and now Mauricio is looking at me like poor, pitiful guy who has just been dumped by his girlfriend!.

She is just my neighbor that helped me today.

Oh Ok Mauricio says as he hands me the bill. I look at Mauricio and of course I wonder if he is gay. Honestly I don't have the energy to even flirt with him.

I pay the bill, walk over and pick up some boxes at the grocery store (Ralphs) and then head home. While I am at Ralphs I also picked up 2 bottles of Merlot because I am going to need it tonight.

As I am walking back to the apartment I start to think about the past week and I start to think maybe I am better off moving back to New York. I mean I have no family here in LA and I have very few friends as well. I just feel so violated with what has happened to me today. It is almost like getting mugged in the subway or worse someone breaking into your house. The only difference is that I knew this guy and I gave him my trust. I am told all the time how I am judgmental to strangers and I should give people a break. In hindsight that when I was being judgmental to complete strangers, I should have been looking at what was going on in my own apartment.

I start thinking that Tommy never really worked the whole time we were living together. He would sleep late but then again he would stay up late. Maybe I should have asked him what he did for a living or questioned some of his actions. He did sell his car a few months back but I just figured he got rid of it because he didn't need it.

Was maybe Tommy a frustrated actor who just gave up? Maybe he saw my Chevy commercial running and it just triggered his animosity towards me? I guess I can sit here and beat myself up over why he did what he did. I could feel sorry for myself and wallow in a why me state. Or I could just pick myself up, learn from this and move on. I am a hard worker and I believe in myself. I am not a religious person but I think that God is testing me. A higher power is testing me to see how badly or how much I want this. I want to be a working actor living in Los Angeles and I want it badly. Maybe something like this is actually going to make me stronger. I hope it does something for me besides make me bitter and jaded.

I am going to believe in people. I will probably always be an equal opportunity offender. I can't help it, it is who I am. Maybe Tommy destroyed all of my things as payback to all the mean things I have said to people over the years? I can say a lot of maybes and I might never know the real reason why Tommy, did this but I do know that I will not give up.

I cannot believe that I am going to say this but even if I have to take the bus I am not going to give up. Did I really just say take the bus? Maybe I will buy a bike instead…..Guys on motorcycles are hot! I can totally picture myself on a motorcycle but that would probably do my Mother in…..

As I reach the building I can hear the vacuum cleaners going in my unit. I am sure there are a lot of neighbors pissed off at the noise but what could I do? I am going to stop worry about what other people think of me….well at least for right now. I open the building door and head straight for the elevator.

As I am heading to the elevator, I am trying to keep my head down. Who knows what daggers will be thrown at me now? I think to myself

Sorry to hear about what happened to you, I hear someone say and it is a familiar voice. I turn around and it is Antonio my new extraordinarily handsome neighbor.

Thank you I say and smile but I am just trying to safely make it to the elevator without any more neighbors ready to lynch me.

I am sorry because we heard a ton of noise coming from your apartment and we didn't do anything about it. We just thought it was a wild party and we didn't want to become "those" Neighbors that complain all the time about noise. Antonio says apologetically.

It's Ok how would you have known? I say did you smell the filth?

A little bit but we figured it was a sewer or something Antonio says.

Or something…. I say with a laugh

Are you Ok? Antonio asks

Thanks for asking I will be OK. They have me in Unit 204 until it's all cleaned up. I have to pay for half of the cleaning but it could have been much worse I guess. The owner is being really nice to me.

Well if you need something let me know. Antonio says with a smile.

(As I am looking at him and those beautiful lips I say to myself…if you only knew what I needed right now was just a hug.)

As I get into the elevator it suddenly hits me….Tommy has stolen all of my porn too….Ok now I officially hate him!!!! Son of a bitch you wreck my apartment, you starve my cats, you steal my car **and** you take **all** of my porn???? I hope you go to hell man. I am still in shock when I get to the apartment door. As I am opening the unit I am still saying to myself. He stole my fucking porn....

I open the door and both cats are sitting there staring at me. I instantly forget about the porn and I am just grateful that the two of them are Ok. Screw the porn what do I care, I have pussy......pussy cats that is.

I look around the room at the mess but right now all I want to do is open a bottle of Merlot I just bought. After I open the bottle and grab a glass from the floor I pour myself another healthy glass of wine. I start to peruse the room from one giant pile to another. This is what is left of my life and I say well at least he didn't burn it all. As I look around the kitchen I notice the pile of mail. I immediately pick it up and it is mostly advertisements and my credit card bill. The last envelope is from my commercial talent agency and it looks like a check. I put my glass of wine down and open the envelope. I freeze in shock as I look at the check that is enclosed.

I cannot believe my eyes. I am holding a check with my name on it for more money than I have ever seen at one time on a check written to me. I am staring at a check for $17,912.47. This has got to be a mistake! I am examining the pay stub and I keep refocusing my eyes at the amount of this check. I sit down on the floor in the kitchen and just stare for seemed like a second but in turn it was for an hour. When I came out of the trance I realized I had a cat on either side of me and still had a check for $17,912.47 in my hand. Holy shit!

I guess from staring at the check for so long plus my exhaustion from the day made me pass out. Please don't say it was the wine but I am sure it had something to do with it as well. When I finally reopened my eyes it was 1015 am and I immediately jumped up. I ripped open the suitcase that I had brought with me to New York and grabbed some clean underwear and socks. Yes...I knew my Mother would have done all my laundry before I came back to LA.

Chapter 22

I need some wheels

I took a quick shower, got dressed, fed the cats and was getting ready to run right to the bank to deposit this check. I went and found clean clothes also in my suitcase and was about to run out the door when panic struck.

Maybe this check was a mistake? What would I do then? This check could change my life. A million things run through my brain. Calmness comes over me eventually and I think Tate call your agent to find out about this check. I immediately dial her number and the receptionist tells me she just walked in the door.

Tate how was New York??? Welcome Back!

New York was great Nancy but I have a quick question for you.

What is it doll? She asks

I gotta a check for Chevy in the mail.

Pretty fucking amazing huh? Nancy asks.

So this is right Nan? I ask

Yup $25,000 and you will probably be getting another one. They just paid the holding fee. Nancy says proudly like good job kid!

OMG Nancy this couldn't have come at a better time. My roommate trashed my apartment and stole my car, while I was in New York.

What hon? Did you call the police? Are you Ok? You have a place to stay and all right? Are you Ok sweetie?

I am fine. It was a very traumatic day yesterday but they gave me another apartment until they can access the damages.

Well don't tell them about the check. Nancy says all motherly.

Ok but can I buy a car? My ex roommate stole mine. It was a piece of shit but it did get me to work and auditions.

Use some of the money as a down payment but don't blow it all sweetie. The commercial business is feast or famine, so you will need to save some when it is a famine. I will keep you booked out for today but try and get a car this week because in about 3 weeks this town becomes dead till well, after the New Year.

OK thanks Nancy I say.

Let me know if you need anything love she says

I will.

After I hang up the phone with my agent I grab my wallet, the check and a jacket and head off to the bank. As I am getting off the elevator I see the apartment Manager in her office and she immediately smiles at me.

HI Tate how are you today?

Better than yesterday I say.

Well good news….the apartment was just very dirty and not much damage. We cleaned the carpets as well and by what we can tell it looks like only a few of the blinds need to be replaced. We removed the cut up sofas' as well as your bed. There are a few things left that I think you might want to keep so we didn't throw them away. You can move back in as soon as Thursday. We want to repaint the dining room and living room also. The whole thing will cost less than $500.00 and we will take that all out of Tommy's security deposit. We will file with the police in regards to the three bounced checks as well.

That is **great**! I say **Thank you!!**

Can I ask you a question?

Sure Tate what is it?

How much would it be for the one bedroom I am in now? I don't know if I could go back to having another roommate after what has just happened to me. I think that after what happened to me, I want to live alone and not worry about finding a roommate.

I see she says. Well that apartment is in fact still available now. It goes for $1,215.00 per month. Would you be able to afford that Tate?

Yes I could I squeal.

You would have to give me the difference of the security as well.

I know.

The apartment Manager starts adding on her adding machine, what it would entail money wise, for me to have the one bedroom apartment.

After a few moments she looks up from her adding machine and says. You were paying $800.00 a month before and have a security deposit in the amount of $800.00. I would need an additional $415.00 plus the first month's rent of $1,215.00 by Thursday. Can you do that Tate?

Yes!!! Please let me have the unit, I love it! I beg and plead.

I will strongly suggest it to the owner Tate. He might ask for a pet deposit in the amount of $100.00 per cat. Is that Ok Tate?

Yes yes yes!!!

Ok I will call you later, Let me have your cell phone number again?

310-776-0370.

I walk out of the manager's office, out of the apartment building and I am headed straight to Wells Fargo and nothing is going to stop me now.

Things might work out after all huh? I say to myself as I enter the bank branch. Got there in 8 minutes....I do not think I have ever walked that fast in my entire life. I fill out my deposit slip and I sign the back of the check. I am still nervous thinking something is going to go wrong when I try to deposit the check. My stomach is in knots and I approach the bank teller's window. Please let something go right for me God! I hand my deposit slip and the check to the teller.

The teller smiles and says hold on and takes the check and walks away. The teller comes back with what looks like the bank Manager and I think I am about to throw up. Something has to be wrong with the check right?

Hi Mr. Connors, I need you to fill out this form and she hands me a form with various lines on it.

What is this I ask?

It is just a form for the government that you are depositing a check that is over $10,000 the bank Manager informs me. We do not see one on file for you right now.

I laugh

Yeah it is my first one for **that** amount I say!

Congratulation's Mr. Connors I hope that there are many more to come she smiles at me.

The form is pretty standard with name, address, social security number, date of birth etc etc on it. I fill it out and hand it back to the teller.

Would you like any cash back? The teller asks me.

Doesn't the check have to clear? I ask

The check is drawn from a Wells Fargo account, so the funds are immediately available for you sir, the teller informs me.

Wow immediately!!! I say.

Yes sir the teller smiles.

Um no just deposit it for now. I need to go buy a car.

Ok sir and the teller deposit's the check and hands me my receipt.

Have a great day the teller says.

You too!!!!!

I have so much excitement that I am ready to burst. I get outside and I start looking for a cab driver. I am going to buy a car today. I know I am being overzealous but I deserve this. I really do. I know exactly what car I am going to buy!

Taxi!

A taxi comes by in what seemed like forever but I didn't care, I was going to buy myself a car. I hop into the cab and the driver says to me where to?

To the Mini Cooper dealership please.

The cab driver turns his head and looks at me with this look of bewilderment:

Where? He asks

Mini Cooper of Universal City I answer him back.

Sure but you do know that that is in the valley sir? The cab driver asks.

Yes I was assuming it was right near Universal Studios, am I wrong?

No sir you are correct. I was just making sure because there could be traffic on our way over the hill and people get upset.

I will not be upset. Today is a good day as I look out the cab window and we are right next to the Hollywood sign.

As we are on our way my cell phone goes off and it looks like a familiar number but I just cannot place it. I answer it anyway:

Hello?

Tate?

Hi it is Maria Santiago from 1425 how are you?

I am good…um I hope as I nervously laugh (it's the apartment Manager from my apartment)

The apartment is yours Congratulations! The owner would just like you to sign a new 1 year lease agreement. We will transfer the existing security deposit over from your unit, to unit 204. I will need a cashier's check for the difference by Friday. Will that work for you?

I can probably get one to you by first thing tomorrow morning. I inform her

Great she says and Congratulations on the apartment again.

As I hang up we are just pulling up to Mini of Universal City on Lankershim Blvd.

Here we are the cab driver goes. That will be $18.50.

I hand him $25 dollars, tell him to keep the change and get out of the cab. As I get out of the cab I look onto the lot and there are about 25 different Mini Coopers. The colors are vast. There are blue ones, yellow ones, gold ones as well as an orange convertible with a blue roof. I walk directly to the orange Mini Cooper convertible that has caught my eye. As I look inside the car I am very impressed. Wow even the seats and the dashboard match the color of the outside paint. The dashboard looks like a space ship with these clock like looking speedometers. This car is so cool! It is also a lot bigger than I thought it would be. I hear someone approaching me and the car but I am still fascinated, with the whole package of the Mini Cooper.

Can I help you with a Mini Cooper today? I hear

I turn around and say **definitely!**

This older gentleman probably around 50 extends his hand to me and says hello my name is Dale Brinker.

I shake his hand and say nice to meet you. I am Tate and can I test drive this really cool car today? I ask.

Sure I just need a valid driver's license and I am already a step ahead of him and have it in my hand. Here you go sir.

I will be right back with the keys he says, as he is walking backwards towards the dealership.

Cool

Within like 2 minutes Dale is back with the keys to the Mini Cooper convertible and he ushers me into the driver seat of the car. The second I turn the ignition on I am in love with this car. The dashboard is so **cool!** It purrs like a kitten. It is not as small inside as I thought it would be. As I am driving down Lankershim Blvd, I take a deep breath and just breathe. The car hugs the road like a passionate love affair and after not even 3 blocks of driving the Mini Cooper, I knew I wanted it so badly. I turn to Dale and say:

Let's find out if I can afford this car Dale!

How is your credit? Dale asks.

Pretty good I say.

That is **great** because we have a bunch of great lease incentives and amazing buying offers going on right now.

Would you be prepared to take the car home with you today if we were able to make a deal with you? Dale asks.

Um….well….yes but I would have to go to the bank and get money right? For the down payment on the car I ask.

Do you have a check card linked to your bank or a credit card? Dale asks.

Yes I have **both** – I didn't even think about that I say.

Well as we drive back to the dealership Dale is telling me the history of the Mini Cooper. How it started in London in the 1960's and became an iconic car of the era. He started talking about why they were made for parking but I really was not paying that much attention to him anymore. I kept thinking about how cute I must look in this car. This car is definitely a fun car and it is sure to be a huge man magnet for me. I visualize myself cruising at Will Rogers Beach; I see a hot guy and ask him if he wants to take a drive in my

Mini Cooper convertible down the coast of Malibu. Of course he agrees and he hops right in.

I pull back into the Mini Copper lot, park the car right up front and I follow Dale into the showroom. In my head I am still driving down the coast of Malibu. As we get back to his office Dale puts a credit application in my hand and he asks me to fill it out. The application asks me the same old same old. Things like my name, address, social security number and date of birth. It took me less than 5 minutes to fill it out and I nervously hand it back to Dale.

Dale looks it over and tells me: I will be right back I have to go give this application to my Credit Manager to run your credit report.

Ok I say and I start to pace back and forth in Dales office.. I have never bought a new car before. I got a new car for high school graduation but my Dad bought that car. He probably bought me the car out of guilt for cheating on my Mom, come to think of it. That is an entirely **different** book though…. my Dad that is. Let's get back to my car story huh? I see Dale walking back towards me and he has a booming smile on his face.

You got good credit there kid, Dale says to me let's talk about your lease options.

Um Ok I say

(Now I don't really know that much about this stuff but I do need a car and I want that Mini Cooper so badly).

We can do $0 down and $359 dollars a month for three years. It would cost you about $800.00 to drive off with the car this afternoon.

$800.00 and the car is mine I ask him very excitedly?

Yup Dale smiles as he looks at me.

Let us do it! I say

Great let me get the paperwork ready and I am going to have them start prepping and detailing the Mini Cooper for you. Congratulations Tate!

Thanks I say as Dale is walking away to get the paperwork.

This guy Dale is your typical car salesman and just wants to sell cars. I completely understand that but I just wish he would let me finish a fucking sentence before he moves on to the next step in getting me out the door.

He goes and gets a stack of paperwork from the printer and then waves for me to come to him. The lazy guy cannot even walk over 10 feet to tell me to come over. I am surprised he didn't just rise up a biscuit or something and say come and fetch. I know I am trying to find fault in him now because I am starting to get nervous about the car purchase. $349 dollars a month isn't bad but then there is insurance and gas plus I just moved into a one bedroom apartment on my own. Holy shit that $17,000 is not going to last forever Tate are you sure about this?.

I still need to buy a new TV and a bed and a living room set and a kitchen set and a stereo…..I am in full on panic mode now. I am gulping really hard and I am beginning to sweat.

Dale ushers me to a table and before I can even sit down Dale is saying sign here, here and here.

Hold on Dale, I know you do this every day but just hold on a second before I sign my entire life away for this car.

What are the terms of the lease? I ask Dale.

All of that will be explained by my Manager I just need for you to sign about the down payment and then my Manager will go through the rest step by step Dale informs me and I could tell I was starting to annoy him.

Ok I say…and I am starting to feel like a wimp who is being backed into a corner by a bully and I don't like it Dale.

I am sorry Tate my Manager will be much more helpful with all of this stuff and will answer any questions you have. I am still new here.

Great I am about to sign my life away to a guy who is still "new" at the Mini Cooper dealership, I say to myself…**Great!.**

After I sign in the 3 places Dale tells me to sign, he then pulls the paper away faster than a police chase. Can I have your credit card to pay for the down payment?

What wait I thought the Manager was going to discuss terms with me?

He is,.,., but I need your credit card first Dale informs me.

(I don't know whether it was the emotions from yesterday coming out of me or just how much this guy was pissing me off, but poor Dale was about to get an explosion, that he had never even prepared to evacuate from.)

You are not getting my fucking credit card until I know what the fuck is going on. You are throwing papers in my face, mumbling shit to me, as you move on to get me out the door. This is not a race to me – do you understand that Dale? This is **huge** for me. This is the first new car **I have ever** leased and I need to know everything. I want to know what the hell I am getting into before I sign my life away. I know you said you were new but you need more freakin training on how to treat people!!!

(I am pissed now, if you haven't already guessed)

It is just the steps that I need to take sir. Dale says to me

Steps? What steps?

By this point the Mini Cooper Manager has seen and heard that I am not happy and he comes running over.

Sir, sir is everything Ok?

Do you **think** everything is Ok? Do people that are Ok act like I am acting at this very moment? What is your definition of Ok?

How can I help you sir? The Manager says

Look I don't mean to be an asshole, I really don't but this guy (pointing to Dale) is shoving papers in my face and asking me to sign this and that. I have no idea what I am signing and every single time I ask a question, he says that it will be explained by his Manager. Well **now** he is asking me for my credit card….I am not giving my credit card until I know what the hell I am getting myself into.

(Can you tell I am still pissed?)

I am sorry sir I will take it from here Dale. Come with me Mr. Connors as the Manager ushers me into his office.

Would you like something to drink he asks?

I would love some water, I say.

I will be right back the Manager says and he heads out to get me some water. He arrives back with a cold bottle of Evian and hands it to me. Here you go:

Thanks I say and I also say: I apologize for yelling but I am nervous, this is my first new car purchase and Dale wouldn't answer any of my questions. All he would say is just sign here and sign there. I hate to be ignored especially because this is a lot of money for me.

Well Dale is a **fucking idiot** the manager says.

Startled a little by the Managers blunt reaction I say **Thank you!!** I thought it was just me being an idiot.

The Manager continues: No he is just new but Dale doesn't seem to get it. He has been selling cars probably since before you were born, but he just is very old school I guess. Where are you from I detect an accent?

Born and raised in Brooklyn I say

Ahh cool man I am from Yonker's on the Bronx border the Manager says proudly. But I have been here for over a decade.

Cool another New Yorker, I feel better already I say.

Ok shall we get down to business about the car now? My name is Matt Lazlo by the way as he shakes my hand. I am the General Manager of Universal City Mini Cooper. I have been here for 4 years, so you can ask me anything about these cars. Would you like me to go over everything with you now?

Yes please I say.

It's a great car huh?

It is… I say but I am still a little standoff-ish and I am waiting to be scammed or the other shoe to drop. The guy says he is from **Yonkers** but I am detecting a different accent.

Well with your great credit score we were able to offer you $0 down payment. With the car's license and registration, plus last month's lease payment, and it comes in a little over $800.00. Are we cool so far Matt asks me?

Yes so far as I nod.

It is for 36 months and you will have the option to buy the car at that time or anytime throughout the lease. The cars warranty is bumper to bumper and includes all maintenance and scheduled repairs. So that means everything and I mean **everything is** covered, with the exception of tires. We have the best warranty program in the business.

Matt continues to go on and on about the car but I become distracted because they pull my new car into the show room and it looks magnificent. After that car came into the showroom and knowing that it was mine, he could have told me there was a dead body in the trunk and I wouldn't have cared. I was mesmerized by it. I couldn't wait for it to be mine. Ok I gotta admit I am back in Malibu cruising with the hot guy.

Matt went through everything with me and I signed and initialed everywhere he asked me to. I gave him my credit card with ease and I breathed a sigh of release. They weren't trying to screw me at all but after what happened to me yesterday, I think the world is out to screw me right now. I am not going to bother to explain to the Mini Cooper Manager, why I was so defensive, because honestly he probably wouldn't give a shit either. He was just better at hiding that he didn't give a shit better than Dale could. It was all about getting me in that car and out the door.

About 5 minutes later Matt came back with all my paperwork and the copies for my car. He explained the temporary registration in the window and that I would get the license plates in the mail in about six to eight weeks..

Mail???? Shit I just put everything to my old address **fuck**! I am about to be done do I really need to explain about the apartment change? I think for a second and I decide…Nah they will find me. It is the same building after all.

Do you mind if Dale shows you how everything works with your new Mini Cooper convertable? Matt asks me.

No I don't mind at all. I kinda owe him an apology for freaking out on him, I say to Matt

Don't apologize to him because maybe next time he will follow through, with the next customer and not be a fucking dumb ass. I am trying to teach the guy how to give good customer satisfaction and he fight me all the way. Matt informs me

Ok I say as Matt walks me to my car. Wow that felt good saying my car. **My car** ahhh….

Hey Dale – Tate is ready for you to show him how his new car works, Matt says. Explain to him everything he needs to love his new Mini!

Dale turns around and he looks like a wounded dog, that has just gotten his ass kicked by a pack of wolves. He smiles and ushers me into the driver seat. Dale starts to show me how everything works from starting the car, to the radio, the seats, lights and the amazing convertible top. I come to realize that Dale knows a lot about the actual car itself and how it operates. How to **sell** the car not so much, but how it works he gets an A plus. After he is done showing me everything possible about my Mini Cooper convertible he asks me:

Is there anything else you have a question about? He asks me in a fun way kinda like saying he is sorry for before.

I don't care what Matt says at this point. I just look at Dale and I say:

I am sorry Dale. I am sorry I freaked out on you. I was just really nervous and confused. You didn't deserve to be cursed at either.

Dale just smiled and shook my hand and said:

No worries kid. I am an old man that forgets how to explain things sometimes. Enjoy your car. Get in the car and let us take a picture of you with your brand new Mini Cooper convertible!.

Picture? I am **not** ready for a picture. Look at me. Nobody told me that I needed to have my picture taken to buy the car.

Dale just laughs at me and says Get in the car and let me take your damn picture.....

Fair enough Dale I say and I get in the car and let Dale take my picture.

Say **Mini** the sales team yells as they have all gathered to cheer me out of the dealership.

Mini I yell.

Hey Tate you picked a good day to buy a convertible. It is going to be in the 70's all week long Dale says. Do you want me to back it out of the showroom for you? He asks.

Nope I got it and I put it in reverse. Full on Butterfly's in my stomach right now and it feels so fucking good! I get out of the dealership with ease and I am not even a block from the dealership and my phone rings.

Ring ring

Hello

It's Nancy I have 2 auditions and a direct callback for you tomorrow. What are you going to do about a car?

I just bought one Nan!! I say with enough exuberance to almost fly!

What did you buy? She screams with excitement.

A Mini Cooper Convertible, I inform her calmly

What color?? I love those cars she is still screaming by the way!. She actually is sounding like she just bought the car herself.

It is actually called Hot Orange I say

Just like the driver she says….**hot, hot, hot** still screaming by the way. Ok I will email you but…by the way you have an audition for Pepsi in the morning, McDonalds in the early afternoon and a direct callback to casting for Hershey's at 4pm tomorrow.

Great, I will be at all of them. I have to pay for this car plus I moved into the one bedroom apartment in the building. Send me in for anything you think I will be right for Nancy. I am here to work, work, work!

Don't worry sweetie everything is going to work out just fine. Enjoy your Mini Cooper. I want to see it soon. Be safe and careful in that convertible. You better go buy some sunscreen, especially with the top down.

Ok Mother.

Yeah I will kick your ass if you get sunburn in that convertable and we need you to be skiing down a mountain for Hershey's during the winter. Tate remember it is winter in most of the country, you do know that right?

Yes I know Ha!

Be safe Bye!

Bye.

I gotta call my Mother and tell her but I am going to enjoy the car for a little while, before she gets all negative **Mother** on me. I just want to enjoy the car a little longer before we have to talk about the apartment, Tommy, plane tickets and Christmas.

Chapter 23

Cruising LA with the top down

Well I am cruising back towards Hollywood but I decide to take a longer route I decide that I will take Coldwater Canyon over the hill into Beverly Hills and come back home through West Hollywood. I just **love** how this car drives. It is amazing and it is mine. I am sure that while I am driving my new car around, with the top down I have the most ridiculous smile on my face. I don't really care though because I am happy. It was a whole other story just 24 hours ago though.

Isn't life funny? One day you are down in the gutter and the next day you have a new apartment and are driving around in a brand new car. I cannot believe the whirlwind of the past 48 hours. If you asked me yesterday at this time if things would turn out like this, I would have said are you nuts? 24 hours ago I thought I might have to move back to New York and live with my Mother. **One** simple residual check from my commercial and it has changed everything for me. I know things happen for a reason but I might not fully ever understand what Tommy did to me, but I will move on and learn from it.

LA is my home now. I have a job, money in the bank, a new apartment and this amazing new car. I earned every single one of these things, without compromising who I am. I am not always the easiest person in the world to get along with. I guess you could say I am an acquired taste. I think if you have gotten this far in the book you know that by now.

As I approach Coldwater Canyon I get into the left hand turning lane. It amazes me that the only time you are able to turn left in LA is not until after the light turns red. I really dislike making left hand turns in LA. I actually met someone that only makes right turns when she drives. I can only imagine how long it takes for her to get places huh? Finally after about 3 full traffic lights, I get to make my left hand turn from Ventura to Coldwater Canyon. I am still a little nervous; this is after all a brand spanking new car and I don't want to crash..

As I turn onto Coldwater, I start to think about my life over the past 6 months since moving to LA. There have been plenty of highs and a fair amount of lows. I have opened my mouth when I shouldn't have and closed my mouth, when I should have been saying something. I guess life is a journey and we learn something every day. I guess we learn something from every goodbye. Was Tommy a goodbye? Well I guess so but did I **learn** from him? Hmmmm, Well for starters the first thing I learned from that goodbye is to never have another roommate again **ever!!!** Or is it maybe I should have gotten to know him a little better.

You know what? Fuck that prick. I am aloud to hate him after what he did to me and I don't feel an ounce of guilt. You know what? I will never utter his name again because what I learned from Tommy is that he is a psychopath but not everyone is like that. Ok I have closed that chapter of my life and so my lesson from that goodbye is that I have to live solo.

Wow Coldwater Canyon is soo windy but it is beautiful up here. This car has amazing handling and I do not have one ounce of buyer remorse from this purchase. Not one bit. I think I was a dick to Dale but I am sure he made a good commission off of me, but that is still not an excuse to be a dick. One thing I have learned in the past 6 months, is that I need to control myself and my temper a little bit better. Every time I think I have it under control **Bam** it just escapes right back out. Speaking of tempers, I wonder what has happened to Jake. His Latin tempers were explosive and epic but I have to say he was amazing in bed. It was some of the best sex of my entire life. I miss him a little but we are not meant to be together. I actually miss his wife more.

Well I have reached Mulholland Drive, so now I start driving down the canyon. As I start to drive down Coldwater I start to notice all these beautiful homes. They are amazing but some really scare me. Some scare me because they are on the edge of a cliff and with just one earthquake they are a goner. I need my house to be on somewhat of a flat service or ground. I mean if you gave me one I wouldn't turn it down, let's not be ridiculous now. Just looking at these houses and the fancy cars that are driving by me I say to myself, there is **a lot** of money in this town. The further I drive down the hill the better the houses are now and yup, I am in Beverly Hills baby.

Beverly Hills is an interesting place because it is mostly residential. You probably have a 10 street radius of "city" between Santa Monica Blvd and Olympic and that is where all the fancy salons, boutiques and restaurants are. I actually hate driving there because it is so congested, with cars and tons of pedestrians, so I will be making a left on Sunset Blvd. One of these days maybe I will live in Beverly Hills but for the time being, I am happy in my one bedroom apartment in Hollywood. As I am making a left onto Sunset Blvd my cell phone rings:

Ring ring

Hello?

Tate it is Mom, is everything Ok?

Everything is great now Mom, I say with so much exuberance! I moved into a one bedroom apartment in my building, so you do not have to worry about Tommy anymore.

Why did you move apartments Tate? Isn't it going to be more expensive without having a roommate? My Mother asks eerily.

A little Mom but it is so worth it to, have my own space I explain

What about Thomas?

He is gone. He moved Mom and that is it.

(I didn't dare tell her what actually had happened because she would worry night and day about me, even **more** than she does now)

What did you do to him Tate?

Mom what? Why do you always think the worst of me?

I know you Tate Connors. I have known you for over 27 years so I know **how** you can be to people sometimes. What you think is funny, other people think is cruel. What other people believe to be true, you think is false. If everyone wants to go right then you automatically want to go left. You are not easy to live with. Ron and I are still recovering from your last visit. You didn't tell me you burnt Ron's ass in the shower Tate.

Mom he burnt me too. What a snitch he is!

He did not tell me I saw the burn marks on his ass and I asked him what happened. Ron doesn't lie so he told me you thought your sister was in the shower so you turned on the cold water to burn her. Is that about right Tate?

Kinda….Mom! It's funny!

So tell me the truth Tate, why did Tommy move out? I want the real and honest reason why Tommy moved out. What did you do?

Mom…..no I did nothing, I swear.(I pause now to decide what to actually tell her) Tommy couldn't pay the rent anymore so he moved out. He moved out while I was in New York, Mom.

He didn't tell you he was moving out? My Mother asks.

No Mom, I had no idea.

Well that wasn't very nice of him. He should have given you at least a 30 days' notice. That is the proper thing to do. Did you have to pay his share of the rent Tate?

No Mom that is why I moved into the one bedroom apartment. It is in the exact same building, two floors down from my old one.

Oh so you couldn't **find anybody** else to move in with you? My Mom asks. Why am I not surprised about that?

I didn't want to find another roommate Mother, plus Tommy didn't leave the apartment in a very…um…um (choose your words **very** wisely Tate, I say to myself) clean manner to say the very least.

He left you a mess Tate?

You could say that Mom but it is over with and I have a fresh start. I don't want to think or talk about Thomas ever again..

Where are you Tate? My Mother inquires

I am driving through Beverly Hills and I am almost to West Hollywood Mom.

Why is it so loud? Do you have the windows open?

Mom I have another bit of news for you as well.

OK....my Mom sounds a little worried and nervous. What other "bit" of news do you have for me? Should I sit down?

I **bought** a new car today Mom

You did? What was wrong with your other car? Did it break down or something?

(Ok how do I get out of this one, without telling her Tommy stole my car???)

Mom it was old and it was not very reliable. It was definitely time for me to buy a new car. I need a reliable car to get to jobs and auditions.

What did you buy? My Mom asks

Actually I leased a car Ma.

Ok Tate what did you lease?

A brand new Mini Cooper Convertible I say as proudly as one could possibly say it.

A brand new one!!! My Mother shrieks

Yup a brand new Mini Mom! It had 14 miles on it when I drove it off the lot today! I love it!

Where on earth did you get the money for that Tate? Tell me you didn't do something stupid. You didn't sell your seamen to a sperm bank now did you?

Mom!!!!!!

What? I heard that is the entire craze out there in LA. I heard it pays a lot of money because then the lesbians can have babies.

Mom I didn't do anything stupid or donate my **swimmers,** to any lesbians and I only had to come up with about $800.00 to put as a down payment on the car. I am going to pay about $369 dollars a month for the car lease.

What swimmers? Do you know swimmers?

Never mind Mother!

What about insurance Tate?

It's about $125.00 a month Mom.

Hmm so let me get this straight. You have been back in LA for less than 2 days and you already have a new apartment and a brand new car? How did you manage all of that? Also how can you afford all of this when you are just a waiter?

Mom I am not **just** a waiter, I am an actor.

One commercial doesn't make you an actor Tate. You actually got more work in less time when you lived in New York Tate. My Mother says angrily

Mom that is not fair and you **know** that one commercial you just mentioned?

Yeah………. she says like Oh no what is he going to say now? What is going to come out of that **mouth** now???

When I got back home yesterday, there was a check for almost $18,000 dollars in my mailbox, from the Chevy commercial I did Mother.

$18,000 dollars??? My mother says in disbelief

Yup almost $18,000 Mom.

That is impossible Tate!

Mom before you say it, I am not lying to you. It is called residuals. Look it up if you don't believe what I am saying. I make money every time they play my commercial and it has played **a lot** of times all over the country..

I believe you…..I think.

So you get a big check like that and you immediately go out and get a new apartment and buy a brand new car? Did you at least shop around?

Mom I leased the car and I knew what I wanted. Why are you making me feel like I am 9 years old and just spent all of my allowance, in the candy shop? Why can't you just be happy for me? Maybe…I don't know …you can say Congratulations Tate or Good Job? Is it possible for you to ever be happy for me? God Mom really?

Look at who is being all over dramatic now, my Mother states like she has the definition on lock down of what over-dramatic means.

Mom?

Ok Ok Tate Congratulations. I just hope that you put some of that residual money away for a rainy day.

Moms haven't you heard? —It never rains in Southern California and yes I am singing it.

Ha **Ha** Tate! Can we talk Christmas now?

Mom I go back to the restaurant tomorrow night. I cannot get fired, I have a new car and apartment to pay for now. Can we talk about it on Friday?

I guess so Tate but quit stalling, I have to buy the tickets soon. You promised me you were coming home for Christmas.

Mom I have to go into work and see if I can get it off. Usually if you take Thanksgiving week off, you have to work Christmas week.

So you are telling me you might not be coming home for Christmas after you promised me you would Tate? My Mother snaps

Mom I didn't say that. Let me talk to you about this on Friday after I talk to my boss. Let me see what I can do.

Fine...Enjoy the car.....**Click!**

Ok she is pissed and just hung up on me. What else is new? She wonders where I get some of my bad habits from!

(I just yell into the phone):

I get them from you Mother– you crazy crazy woman!!!

Of course I do know she is no longer there on the phone but I still needed to get it out. Look I **"good lied"** to her and didn't tell her what actually happened to me yesterday. Did I do it so that she would not crazy worry about me? Possibly….Did I do it so that she wouldn't give me grief almost every day about bad people living in Los Angeles? More likely….Did I just want to get her off the phone and enjoy my new car? Absolutely, no doubt about it!

Oh look there is a Wells Fargo, I say to myself as I am driving down Sunset. Let me get the cashier's check for the rent and security deposit, for the apartment while I am here. I find a spot right up front and I pull my brand new Mini Cooper convertible right in and go into the bank. I get the 2 cashier's checks. One is for the security deposit and the other is for Decembers rent. I think I could have given her a regular check for the rent but with the situation from yesterday I would rather be safe. The whole process took less than 10 minutes and I was back driving my Mini.

I have spent less than $2,500 and I already have a new car and an apartment. I cannot live without a bed or a television. The TV is for research for the roles that I audition for and the bed is for sleep and what is usually on my mind 24/7….. Sex!!!

Chapter 24

Thank fully

As I get back in the car that I have had for 24 hours now. I feel really good right now. My queen size bed will be delivered tomorrow. I got a flat screen TV and the cable will also be installed tomorrow. I ordered a sofa from Ashley Furniture and I just booked a Hershey's commercial. I need to say: Thank you Dad, for teaching me how to ski and taking me skiing every year. I booked this job because of it and I am going to Big Bear for two days next week to shoot. My boss in the restaurant has given me December 23rd through the 27th off, mainly because I had him listen to the 5 hysterical messages, my Mother left on my voicemail in the past 24 hours. I also promised him, I wouldn't take another weekend off from the restaurant unless it was for a job **ever!**

As I start to drive home from my audition I look around the car. This is **really** my brand new car! I have so much excitement for what the future holds. I think back on all I have achieved in the past 6 months. I remember the first day that I was in LA. Actually within the first hour of living in LA, I was in a car accident with the Asian Lady on the 405 who didn't speak a lick of English. What a lesson that was. I had to learn to be a defensive driver here in LA. I had to learn to always think the worst of every driver on the road especially Asian women. Actually about a month ago an Asian guy seriously walked into my car as I was driving in the parking lot of the gym. I learned that they walk like they drive....Hmm lesson learned!

One of the biggest things I am thankful for is that in LA they sell liquor in the grocery stores. I don't buy 3 bottles of vodka anymore at one time and I have a car now too. I can still remember trying to lug all that vodka back to the apartment but only one bottle surviving the walk. I have to laugh because it really annoyed me in New York, that I had to go to a separate liquor store to buy alcohol and wine. The convenience of one stop shopping makes it all worth it. I think I have a great answer to my Mothers LA question. She must ask me on a weekly basis what is so great about LA! My new answer is…. because they sell vodka in the supermarket!

I can see why the Apartment Manager didn't like me after all. Between being really late to pick up the keys to the apartment, on my first day to seeing me traipse through the lobby with **no** shirt on and smelling like vodka. My Mother would call me a brewery but the look that Apartment Manager gave me…ugh… I guess I would have been pissed too but I did talk to her in Spanish though!

As I am approaching La Cienega and Sunset a bus cuts right in front of me and I have to slam on my brakes. Fucking buses I hate them. I still haven't gotten over my last bus ride almost 6 months ago. I wonder if the "Umbrella Man" has gotten out of the hospital. I can still see him bleeding on the bus floor. I am happy to say that I have not been back to Inglewood since that adventure. I wonder if they ever caught the guy who stabbed him?

As I am passing the Mondrian and the infamous Sky Bar, I remember my illustrious night out with Amanda. I was so excited to go to the Skybar and in hind sight it was just another LA pretentious spot. I cannot believe all the pink Mary Kay ladies that night, there was more pink there than on a West Hollywood Pride Parade float. What were those 2 girl's names that were yammering in my ear from the valley? I cannot tell you how many times Colonel Sanders has helped me out of a bind over the years. Choking Chickens for the Colonel!

As I continue to drive I see Myagi's which is closed and replaced with another Pink Taco now and a minute later there is Crunch. I think I was kinda an asshole to a few people that last time I was there. I was really nervous about going home for the first time. I shouldn't really make excuses for my douche bag ways. I should just accept them, embrace them and try to control them I guess. I have gotten better with the gym and my insecurities have decreased immensely. I feel like I am a part of the gym. If you asked me 6 months ago, why people attach themselves or identify themselves to a certain gym, I would have told you because they are superficial idiots, but now I get it. If you asked me to explain why I had such a strong opinion about the gym, I probably couldn't give you a definitive answer but I get the gym thing today. I go to the gym often but I don't let it control my life or become obsessed with it. The only thing I wish I could control is when and where I fart at the gym, to be honest. I still will try to blame others when I pass gas as much as possible, but I need to work on controlling it better.

See I am still a work in progress. **Ha!**

As I get older, I need to stop blaming things I do on my childhood. I had good parents that loved me. They just didn't love each other enough to stay together. I love my siblings or I hope I do, but do I regret any of the things I did to them growing up? **Not in the least bit** actually. I am a menace and I do like to tease and torture. It is in my blood. It is true that my siblings would embarrass me or get me into trouble. I would always find ways to get even with them or find ways not to be around them. I used to wish I had some of the families that were on TV but you know what....I am OK with the one I have. I am Ok with it because it is mine...whether I like it or not. Do I still wish I was an orphan with a trust fund? To be honest... it depends on the day!!! Some days I plot their demise while other days I embrace my family whole heartedly. I still do watch Law and Order reruns and take notes, on ways to get away with murder, but not as often as I used to.

Look there is El Compadre and I immediately think of Jake. Jake will always be known as my first boyfriend in Los Angeles. Things didn't work out and to be honest, I miss Sofia more than Jake. I wish I could stop in for a drink and say hello to Sofia but the fear of running into Jake, keeps me driving. I should take that back because I am not fearful of anything, I have just learned to avoid drama as much as I possibly can avoid it.

I am still headed down Sunset when I spot an interesting woman in a full on gown, waiting at the traffic light. Wait that is not a woman, it is a drag queen. Now we all know I do not have the best track record with drag queens and I can never listen to Christina Aguilera the same way again. I now know who is a drag queen and who is just an ugly woman. A little piece of advice for you – don't tell either one you think they are ugly.

So I have learned a bunch of non-useful traits, that you probably wouldn't be able to utilize in any other city in the world. I also have a sharp tongue and I am still very quick with the smart ass remark or comeback. I guess I am like a fine wine that keeps getting better with age. Many would probably say that that bottle of fine wine, has a crack in the cork and is spoiled but I will keep on believing I am that fine bottle of wine.

I am narcissistic, vain and shallow. I don't apologize for it but I do recognize it though. I care what other people think of me and I can be very insecure with my body, looks and appearances. I secretly want to be desired by everyone but I settle for the few that can actually stand me. I am a smart ass and I use that as a defense mechanism so I do not get hurt. I don't believe in degradation of any sort and it drives me crazy when somebody has to make fun of someone else to get a laugh. I like to make fun of myself as much as possible, but then again who am I kidding, I make fun of almost every walk of life. I guess you could say I am an equal opportunity offender. You cannot call me racist or prejudice because I just talk….That is right, I just talk a good game. Sometimes I win and other times I lose miserably. I try and be honest…..well except with my

Mother but I am sure by now you know…**I have to lie to her**!! She is bona fide crazy right?

Am I mean to my Mother? Sometimes I guess. Do I do it on purpose? Sometime I do…I guess a lot of things I say to people could be considered mean. It is who I am. Am I perfect? Absolutely fucking no way in hell I am. I did learn something recently though about myself. I can be mean to whomever I want to but if you are mean, rude or hurtful to someone I love; you better watch the fuck out because I will rip your head off. Don't even try and be an asshole to my Mother…I can be one, and have done so many times, but if you even dare to – game fucking on.

I think I have learned how to do well in bad situations. In emergencies or disasters I have learned to stay calm. I certainly didn't learn that from my McDonalds experience or Tony Ianucci's slut ex-girlfriend's picture days. I think I learned from those situations, as well and will continue to grow from what I learn in the future.

I just love driving this car **BTW.** I just passed my apartment building on Sunset I was thinking and spewing all of my worldly bullshit nonsense and I missed my street. I will make a right on La Brea and head back up to my apartment via Fountain. I love driving on Fountain because there aren't that many cars and it moves rather quickly. I was told that years ago Fountain was the biggest secret until a 2 year construction plan on Santa Monica Blvd happen and people discovered Fountain Ave. I think Bette Davis has very famous quote about Fauntain

I turn onto Fountain and I am cruising along. All of a sudden this fat queen walks out from behind a parked truck into the middle of my lane…..

Holy shit I am going to hit him!!

I slam on my breaks as hard as I can. I can hear the screeching noise of my tires. Please God make the car stop. The car is brand new and he is **really really fat**! I don't want a dent in my not even one day old car. Please car **stop!!!** Well within a centimeter of hitting this fat guy my car stops.

Phew and I look at him now standing in the middle of my lane with his hands on his hips and boy is he glaring at me. I wonder if he is the same guy from the plane that the poor Asian lady almost had to sit next to on my way back to New York.

Next thing I hears is:

You need to watch where the fuck you are going asshole! He screams at me.

I am thinking **to myself** what the fuck?

All of a sudden his girlfriend comes out from behind the truck and yells "Yeah asshole this isn't the Indy 500, slow the fuck down. "We are pedestrian's and we have the right of way."

I am in shock that these two are talking to me like this. So of course I have to yell back:

Pedestrians??? What the fuck are you talking about? You came out of nowhere dude!! Do you have a death sentence? I say with my full on Brooklyn accent now.

Well the fat guy is still yelling at me that he can cross the street where ever he God damn please and blah blah blah

As he is spewing his bullshit at me, I look up and there is a traffic light seriously less than 200 feet away from him.

This fat guy is still spewing bullshit at me, while the nasty girl he is with, is still glaring at me.

(There is traffic light about 200 feet away from where this is all going down).

I cannot take any more of this so I say:

Why don't you walk to the traffic light ya Fat fuck....you might lose a pound or two??

In unison they both yell **Asshole** as they now run across the street.

I look back up at the traffic light; I shake my head, give my obligatory **Fuck** you back to them and start driving again.

Well do you know what the moral to this story is?

No, I will tell ya. Let me tell you this first though. I am not a role model and please do not try and be me. There is only one of me and that is enough. You can ask my Mother if you want to, but she will agree that one Tate Connors is enough for this world. This book was written to entertain you and for me to make a lot of money. Do not attempt to do, say or try anything that I have done in this book. I promise you that it will have a completely different experience and outcome for you if you do.

So what is the moral to the story?

You can take the boy out of Brooklyn but you can **never** take Brooklyn out of the boy.....no matter how hard you try.

I hope you enjoyed reading the trials, tribulations, ups, downs and the obnoxious utter chaos, that my life gets lost in.

Tate Connors

Ring ring

Hello?

Tate it is Tony Ianucci! How are you?

I am great! Things in LA are really working out for me. It was great seeing you and reconnecting during the Thanksgiving Holiday. I am coming back for Christmas, so hopefully I can see you, but it is a very short visit again.

Tate that is great and I am already looking forward to you coming back in a few weeks but I have amazing news for you as well!

That is great Tony! Do you want to tell me **now** or do you want to wait until I come back to Brooklyn in a few weeks?

When are you coming back for the Holidays? What are the dates you are here? I can definitely pick you up at the airport.

My Mother usually likes to pick me up at the airport but I will ask her. Actually maybe she doesn't **like** to pick me up, so I will ask her. I get in at 630 in the morning on the 23rd. I am taking the red eye out of Los Angeles on the 22nd. I come back to LA on the 27th because I have to work New Year's Eve at the restaurant I work in. I can hardly hear you Tony. Where are you?

I am at work now so I cannot talk long plus, I do not want anyone over hearing my conversation. Well hopefully we get to spend a lot of time together when you are here. You have been on my mind all week long and I cannot wait to tell you my news.

News? What news? I saw you less than a week ago Tony. How much could have possibly changed in less than a week? (Yes I know I am a big hypocrite... only I could have lots of news within a 24 hour time gap)

I told my Mother all about you. I told her **everything** and she was really supportive. I told my Mother that I am moving to LA!

What?????????

Gulp...

Tate they are calling me to the cashier lines, so I have to go. We can discuss and plan all of this later tonight or when you come to visit. Can I stay with you a few days in LA, while I look for an apartment?

Um....sure but... I told you that jobs are hard to find out here in Los Angeles.

I already have one lined up at Pavilions in West Hollywood. I applied online and they **hired** me. I start January 10th. I am so excited about my new life. Tate, thank you I would never have had the courage to do this if it was not for you. I gotta go, they are calling me again, to the cashier lines and it sounds really serious. Talk soon. I love you!

Click

I am stunned. Not because he told his Mother about me. Not because he is moving to LA and got a job at Pavilions. I am stunned because I **think** he just told me he loved me. I have never heard the words I love you from a male voice in my entire life....

Tony Ianucci you better be fucking **amazing** in bed!

Printed in the United States
By Bookmasters